D1432108

Dark Mists of Ansalar
Blood of Dragons

Visit www.booksurge.com to order additional copies.

T. R. CHOWDHURY

DARK MISTS OF ANSALAR
BLOOD OF DRAGONS

2009

Dark Mists of Ansalar
Blood of Dragons

PROLOGUE

CY380 Pre-Cycle

The lounge was dark. Upon each table was a small lantern, and one could see only the persons seated nearby. Every once in a while, one could catch a glimpse of someone seated at a nearby table, their profile briefly illuminated by the light. It was only momentary, and just enough to make one wonder . . . It wasn't every day that a man encountered a woman with beauty such as hers.

Then Shire was seating himself at her table. He made certain to place himself next to her, and then to glance over at the table at which Tallachienan was seated with Trebexal. TC felt the anger rise within him as he noticed the self-satisfied expression cross Shire's face. Damn, he would never have thought something like this would ever happen . . . to become at odds with one's closest friend over a woman. TC realized the fault was just as easily his as it was Shire's, but the knowledge didn't make the situation any easier. Tallachienan still wanted the woman, and Shire knew it. The fact didn't stop the other man from pursuing her, and that was the crux of the problem. It seemed that Shire had chosen Tholana over his friendship with TC, and the reality of that fact hurt more than he could ever have imagined.

Tallachienan drummed his fingertips over the table-top. Trebexal placed his hand over that of his friend and applied pressure. "Don't let it get to you, Tallachienan. It's not worth it. You have known her but only a fortnight. Let Shire be the one to make a fool of himself over her."

TC shook his head. "I feel as though we are broken already. I can't believe that our friendship is so tenuous as to be unraveled so easily by a beautiful woman."

Trebexal shrugged noncommittally. "You are allowing it to be that way. Just let it go, and you will find there is nothing left over which to be rivals."

TC shook his head. Trebexal was his good friend, and his thoughts were valued. Yet, the other man didn't really understand the intricacies of what was taking place between he and Shire. As one born of dragon-kind, Trebexal could only *imagine* what was happening and then offer his advice. He meant it to be for the best, so TC did not mind listening to his friend when he stated his thoughts. But he couldn't completely take them into consideration in light of the species gap.

Tallachienan had known Shire for as long as he could remember. As boys, the two had been inseparable, and they grew up together as the best of friends. Once entering that stage between child and manhood, the boundaries of society began to weigh mercilessly upon them. It was then that they came into contact with a dragon pair. They were young and impetuous, and Trebexal and Khaan seemed to suffer the same societal malady.

So the foursome set off to explore the world together. Only their enemies knew that the two cimmereans traveled in the company of a rezwithrys and a helzethryn. They were a conundrum in of themselves, for normally no rezwithrys would be known to form a company with a helzethryn and no cimmerean mage would find himself in kinship with one of a separate class and alignment. But such as it was with them. Right from the start they had their internal conflicts, but it never got in the way of their camaraderie. At the end of every day, they were still together. Until now . . .

Tallachienan kept his gaze riveted to the the table at which she sat. The priestess Tholana was the most exquisite woman he had ever met. Not only that, but she was humorously witty, calmly seductive, and his intellectual equal. Tallachienan could ask for nothing more. Yet, there was something about her, something that bade him stay away. He fought against the instinctual reaction, shaking his head at the absurdity. He had yet to see anything from her that might give him cause to be suspicious. And of course, he had competition . . .

Just barely a fortnight ago, Tallachienan and his comrades had come across four cimmerean women. It was quite out of the ordinary, for one did not see many of the cimmerean race mingling with people in the above world. Known as 'dark faelin' cimmereans were largely distrusted, condemned for the actions of their ancestors, and driven to live within the bowels of the *Underdark*.

It wasn't long before Tallachienan, Trebexal, Shire, and Khaan learned that Tholana, her sister, and her two maternal cousins were at odds with another cimmerean family. It was a matter of honor, for the rivaling family had brought shame upon Tholana's own family name. TC's heart went out to the women for he knew how it felt to be dishonored. TC's father had left his mother when he was only but a babe within her womb. The man had never bothered to come back to her, never thought to find the means to take care of his son and the woman who had borne him. It had taken Seida many years to find a man who would take her as his wife. She had developed a negative reputation . . . brought shame to herself by bearing a child out of wedlock. To many she was nothing but a whore. Only to Vanyar was she something more.

Tallachienan looked away from the neighboring table only when the serving wench came to clear the one at which he and Trebexal sat. He nodded

CHAPTER 1

24 Brinaren CY631

The heat was oppressive in the rocky mountain pass. Aeris stumbled for the third time and cursed to herself in hinterlic. She narrowed her eyes at Lorak, who chuckled as he walked beside her. The dusty larian she was leading snorted through her nose, and Aeris rolled her eyes as she felt the wetness from the spray begin to roll down her arm. Lorak chuckled even more, and only when he caught her glaring at him did he bother to hide his laughter behind the arm he raised in front of his face.

"Just think, Aeris. It could be worse. It could be *raining*," chuckled the ranger.

Aeris pursed her lips but said nothing. She wasn't feeling very well, and not for the first time she wished that they had a cleric in their midst. Such a person would know what types of herbs they could use to reduce the effects of illness, and perhaps she wouldn't have to suffer needlessly.

Raissa fell into step beside her, leading her own mount. "We can stop if you want, Aeris. It won't hurt to rest for a few hours longer this night. Besides, you need it."

Aeris shook her head. "No. I want to make it out of this pass before tomorrow evening. If we stop early today, then we will be stuck here for another night."

Raissa shook her head. "It isn't all that bad. We have met very little trouble so far."

"But that doesn't mean that we won't. This pass holds too much significance in my family history. The sooner we are out, the better," said Aeris adamantly.

Raissa was quiet after Aeris' declaration. She was well aware of Aeris' dislike of their location and why. It was within the Ratik Pass that Aeris' mother had met her grandfather, Thane Darnesse, and killed him before he laid waste to her and the rest of the group who followed her. The Wildrunners had won the battle, but the negative aura surrounding the pass remained. Aeris and her brothers grew up hearing the stories: how their mother had made Thane a mortal once again, and that Adrianna's sister had struck the final blow that would finally put him to rest forever.

For the rest of the day the small group progressed through the Ratik Mountain Pass. Upon leaving Elvandahar a few months ago, Lorak, Doran, and Mavik had been asked to accompany Aeris and Raissa to Andahye. The three young rangers had agreed to the task, and once the women reached the city, they went to the Vanderlinde Academy and took the required tests that would place them within the ranks of other journeyman spell-casters.

For two weeks they were in Andahye. Aeris and Raissa passed their tests and the group then journeyed to the city of Celuna, located within the realm of Monaf on the eastern side of the Ratik Mountain range. It hadn't been part of the original plan, but the women had a way of getting what they wanted. Besides, the rangers weren't against an adventure themselves, and they required very little persuading. They spent a few days there, and then headed back west towards Elvandahar.

Finally the group stopped for the evening. Aeris started the fire and began to prepare the tea while Raissa set out the tents and bedrolls. Meanwhile, Lorak saw to the larian and Mavik and Doran hunted for their evening meal. Aeris was glad to finally be out of the pass and thought perhaps they could make another detour to the city of Sangrilak before finally heading home. She wouldn't mind seeing Volstagg again, and then stopping to make a visit to Tianna and Triath Solanar, parents of her brother's closest friend, Tigerius. The man was a scoundrel, and his mother and father deserved to know that he was up to no good. Aeris had received the 'pleasure' of seeing Tigerius while they were in Celuna, and his activities were focused around the more unsavory variety. He was a trouble-maker, and Aeris hoped that perhaps she would be doing him a favor if his parents knew of his, rather reprehensible, activities.

Aeris sniffed disdainfully at the pathetic fire. Under different circumstances, she could have done much better. But as it was, she hardly felt up to the task and thought that she might fall asleep right there at the spot. But the tea was beginning to boil, and the men would soon be back with something for the stew pot. Aeris was no cook, but the group relied on her to make the meat at least somewhat edible. She lamented her inadequacies, as well as those of everyone else in their group. Could not at least one of the rangers her father chose to accompany her known how to prepare a simple meal?

Raissa and Lorak completed their own activities just as Mavik and Doran returned with some ptarmigan for the stew pot. Aeris took the birds from Doran, and Mavik winked at her before accepting his mug of tea. She swore that he was sweet on her, but had yet to make any overtures. Not that she would have responded to them if he had. Aeris wasn't interested in anything the young man might offer her, which was, most likely, only a frolic in the bed-furs. She wanted something a bit more tangible from a man, a solid foundation for a future more promising than simply the wife of a ranger.

Aeris shook her head. No, that wasn't quite it. Her mother was the wife of a ranger. Yet, Adrianna was also much, much more. She was one of the founders of the academy that she and Dinim had constructed when the Wildrunners returned to Elvandahar after their battle with Lord Aasarak.

It was at the Medubrokan Academy that Aeris herself had been trained in the art of dimensional magic, and Dinim had been her master for as long as she could remember being there. She was early to exhibit her Talent, just out of childhood at a mere fifteen years of age. Her mother had decided that it would be best for her co-founder to train her daughter, feeling that perhaps she had too much vested within Aeris to make a proper teacher. Aeris had no complaints. Dinim was an excellent master. He had taught her well enough for her to pass her tests at the Vanderlinde Academy with flying colors. The masters there had congratulated her upon her skills, and she had given credit where the credit was due.

Aeris handed one of the ptarmigan off to Raissa and the two women made quick work of removing the feathers and gutting the birds before roasting them over the spit. Soon after, the meat was added to the stew pot, and while the rangers sparred with their staves, the meal cooked slowly over the fire. Aeris leaned back on a rock, one of the many that were strewn around the pass. It was then that she began to hear the strange trilling sound.

Aeris frowned as she listened. Oddly, it sounded as though the noise was coming from beneath them. Within moments the sparring had stopped, and all five of them were focused upon the sound that seemed to be coming from right below the encampment. The sound became louder, and suddenly there was an eruption.

From out of the ground in the middle of the encampment emerged a huge creature. The worm reared above the group, most of its long brownish body concealed below the ground from which it had come. It appeared to have no eyes. It's mandibles were huge, and it was from the strange nodule at the top of its head that the trilling sound was generated. Aeris had only heard of creatures such as this . . . behiraz that burst from the ground, devouring all that was within its range.

Aeris jumped up from her position near the fire. Raissa had done the same, and the three young rangers eyed the worm from the other side of the encampment. Aeris considered running from the threat that the worm presented, but she had heard that the behiraz were fast, much too fast for her to escape. And then what of her comrades? She couldn't very well leave them behind.

As Aeris began to concentrate upon her first spell, Raissa did the same. The rangers waited for the behiraz to attack, and possibly didn't even know what they faced. The only reason Aeris knew was because she had seen it once in one of the many manuals she had been bade to read whilst in training at the academy. It was a creature that was rarely seen, commonly making their existence within the temperate hills and mountains.

Aeris cast her spell just as the worm made its first attack. The lightening arced from her fingertips as the behiraz lunged for Doran. Within the sharp mandibles of the worm, Doran screamed as he was brought before the yawning maw. Then he was gone. Aeris' *Lightening* spell struck the behiraz just before Raissa's *Flamesphere*. The creature emitted an eerie wail from atop its head, and Aeris found herself cringing from the sound.

The worm fully emerged from the ground. It was long, so long that it coiled its body against itself. At the tip of its tail was something that appeared to be a sharp stinger. It dripped with fluid, and Aeris could only imagine that it was some type of poison. Mavik and Lorak attacked the creature with their swords, an attempt to penetrate the thick hide. But it was to no avail. The tail end of the creature descended. It missed Lorak by only a hairsbreadth, and when it swung around to grab Mavik with its mandibles, it was an unexpected move. Mavik had disappeared within the maw of the worm just before her second spell was cast. Aeris watched as her *Lightening* struck the creature yet again, this time leaving a scorched mark on its thick hide. The worm shrieked again, and Aeris had to struggle not to put her hands over-top her ears.

Raissa completed her incantation, and another *Flamesphere* hit the worm. In response to the flame, the creature coiled more tightly around itself. Deep scores of flesh fell from its body and Aeris could almost sense its hesitation . . . perhaps the cost wasn't worth continuing the meal it had chosen for itself.

But then the worm struck again. Aeris felt her heart almost stop in her chest as she saw the stinger descend upon her. She was quick to move, but she wasn't quite fast enough. Aeris fell as the thick body of the worm moved into her line of vision, blocking her escape route. The stinger embedded itself into her thigh and pinned her to the ground. She immediately felt the poison begin to work its way through her body as she saw Raissa get picked up by the worm. The woman was torn in two before she reached the creature's mouth.

Aeris suddenly felt herself gasping for breath. The poison was doing something to her, stopping her from being able to breathe. She saw Lorak fighting the worm, piercing it with his sword, the glow of it permeating the darkness that had begun to descend. *His blade must be enchanted . . .* But then Aeris lost the thought as she succumbed to the darkness.

***

Aeris slowly awoke to the feeling of silk beneath her fingertips. She slid her hand over the smooth fabric and knew herself to be in bed. She shifted her body and was about to begin a stretch, when the pain invaded her consciousness.

Aeris' eyes snapped open, and she groaned deeply. What in the Nine Hells had happened? Her gaze took in her surroundings, most of which were hidden to her due to the gauzy dark green canopy that enveloped the large bed in which she lay. Aeris struggled to sit upright, despite the terrible pain in her leg, and once she was able, she moved aside the veil nearest her.

Aeris found herself to be within a large chamber. The stone floors were covered by expansive rugs. The furnitures appeared to be made of the finest wood. They were embellished with engravings and then stained a rich chestnut. Upon the walls were hung lush tapestries and ornate wall scones that held torches. The dancing flames cast shadows among the depictions of exotic landscapes, great battles, and mystical beasts.

By the gods, what am I doing here? Where is 'here'? Her leg ached abominably . . . and where were her clothes? Aeris unconsciously brought the cover up to her chest, which was covered only by a thin camisole. *Where are Raissa and the rangers?*

Suddenly it all came rushing back to her. She remembered the Ratik Pass and how much she hated being there. She remembered the behiraz and the deaths of her comrades. Then there was the excruciating sting of the barbed tail as it entered her leg. But after that there was nothing. She recalled aught of her escape from the monstrous worm, not to mention how she came to be in this chamber. But at least now she knew why she was in so much pain.

With tears in her eyes and a cry in her throat, Aeris jerked the blankets free of her body. She gazed down at her leg, which was wrapped neatly in clean cloths. She felt a mixture of anger and sadness well up inside of her, and she struggled to retain her calm. Her best friend was gone. Aeris would never see Raissa's smiling face or hear her sweet voice ever again. And then there were the others, the three men with whom she had shared her childhood as well. All of them were gone.

Aeris fought the urge to claw the bandages off of her leg. She battled with the realization that she should be back in that Pass with her dead comrades, not here within this chamber, sitting on a bed made for a queen. She tried to resist her need to scream, to call out to the gods in her agony and tell them of how unjust they had been to allow the others to perish while she received the chance to live another day.

But Aeris was not quite so successful with that fight. She screamed as loud as she could, her voice reaching every crevasse within the chamber. Hot tears streamed down her face, and she screamed until she had no breath left. She gasped, and when her chest was full, she screamed again.

Aeris wasn't aware that someone had entered the room until he was standing beside the bed. Her breaths came in ragged gasps, but somehow she was able to form the words she wished to speak. "Where in the Hells am I?" she asked with a hoarse voice.

The man leaned over her and despite the anxious look on his face, he replied in a soothing voice. "Please, calm down. You are going to be just fine. The Master has been taking care of you . . ."

Aeris grabbed the front of the man's tunic and jerked him closer to her, bringing his face so close that she could feel his breath on her nose. "Get me the Hells out of here, right now!"

The man's eyes widened, and only then did Aeris realize how uncommon they were. They were colored a deep gold, and she vaguely thought that they were familiar. But that did not deter her. Aeris pushed back on the man, releasing his tunic. She then scrambled to swing her legs over the sides of the bed.

"Please stop. I will tell you everything if you would just . . ."

Aeris penetrated him with her eyes. "Where are my clothes? By the gods, what have you done with my clothes?" She could sense the increase in the pitch of her voice, but she couldn't seem to control it, nor did she really want to. Her friends were dead, she was lying in a strange bed without her clothes on, and a man with flaming red hair and gold eyes was telling her to remain calm.

Aeris stood up from the bed, having forgotten her injury. She suddenly found herself falling, and then barely being caught before her body hit the floor. She struggled against the hands that held her, raking them with her fingernails. She cried out and realized that the tears continued to fall. She felt the rawness in her throat as she cursed at the man who held her, and she was pleased when she saw the blood that streaked the tops of his hands.

"Pylar, leave her."

Aeris startled when she heard the voice. It was loud as it filled the room, and it exuded power. Aeris was suddenly left to tumble to the floor as the man left her side. She looked in the direction that the voice had come, and when she saw the person who stood at the entry of the chamber, her breath almost caught in her chest. She knew the man because he had been the one to train her mother in the art of Dimensionalism. She had met him only twice in her life, but Aeris would know him anywhere. It was Tallachienan Chroalthone.

Aeris watched in silence as the sorcerer slowly crossed the room. His lavender gaze was critical as it assessed her where she sat on the floor. Aeris suddenly was very aware of her state of undress, but she refused to feel intimidated, and she made no move to try to cover herself. When TC finally stood over her, Aeris just stared up at him. He stood there for a moment, watching her, but his expression had softened.

TC slowly extended his hand out to her, bridging the gap between them. Aeris hesitated only a moment before taking the hand. Then she was being pulled up, caught about the waist, and then guided back onto the side of the bed. She hissed as she seated herself again, and then remained quiet with her head lowered.

Tallachienan looked down at the young woman. Hells, she looked even more like her mother when she was awake than she did when she was sleeping. Her slightly canted eyes were the same dark brown, and her face the same oval shape. The only real differences lay with complexion and hair color. Where Adrianna's skin tone had been a pale gold, her daughter's was deeper. Aeris' hair was a golden red, while Adrianna's had been so pale, it often seemed to be the color of Shandahar's largest moon, Steralion.

It had been many years since TC had seen Damaeris last. At the time, she had been merely a child. But now it was fully apparent that she was a woman. He was made even more aware of that fact by her state of undress; all she wore was a camisole and her small-clothes. She had her mother's small frame with all of her shapely curves in all of the right places. And aside from her injury, she was in good physical fitness.

Several days ago, one of his journeymen had contacted him via the Travel Notebook. Torres explained that he had killed a behiraz, but not before the creature succeeded in bringing down a small group of young people that had been traveling through the Ratik Mountain Pass. Torres bade TC to come for him, hoping that TC would be able to save the life of the only survivor of the attack. TC had come immediately, and when he saw who that survivor was, he was desperate to get her back to the citadel and into the hands of Hermod.

Aeris should not have lived. The poison had already paralyzed her lungs, and her breaths had stopped. Torres breathed for her until TC came, and that had probably kept her alive long enough for him to get her back through the portal and into the citadel. TC continued what Torres started while he awaited Master Healer Hermod. Then the god had worked his magic. Aeris would not be well for quite some time, but at least she would live.

Aeris finally lifted her head to look up at him. The rims of her eyes were red and puffy and her hair an unruly mass around her shoulders. Her lower lip trembled before she mustered up the will to speak, her voice naught but a whispered croak. "Tell me that I am dreaming."

TC felt his chest constrict with emotion. Her eyes were haunted, and she had become only a glowing ember that remained of the flaming anger and defiance that met him upon his entry to her chamber. Aeris felt the loss of her companions keenly, and TC could not blame her for the outcry. He wished that he could tell her what she wanted to hear, but to do so would be an injustice.

All TC had to do was shake his head. As Aeris' shoulders slumped and she began to cry, TC sighed and seated himself next to her on the bed. He took her in his arms and held her tightly against him. The young woman clutched at the front of his robes, and she sobbed piteously onto the wall of his chest. TC just sat there and stared solemnly into the space before him.

The breeze was cool and brisk, a herald to the end of the youth and vibrancy of the warm season. As all good things come to an end, so must also the joy of summer. The tinkle of her sweet laughter drifted to him in the winds and he reveled in it, opened himself to the simple delight of her presence. He turned as she emerged from around the bend, her once youthful body now bent and creased with age. The jauntiness was gone from her step, and silver had overtaken the locks of her dark hair. Over one arm hung a basket of flowers, those last remaining valicas and lirylacs of the season. They were her favorite ones, all shades of fuchsia, indigo, and azure. Her blue eyes shone with happiness and Tallachienan felt his heart melt at the sight of his sister, still the epitome of beauty despite her advanced age.

Briyana slowed as she neared him, her lips pursing slightly as she turned her face to look up at him. "Don't look at me like that Talli. I know what you are thinking."

TC shook his head. "I will bet you have no idea." He crossed his arms at his chest and struggled for an expression of nonchalance. It had become difficult for him over the past few years. As TC remained young and strong, he was forced to watch as his little sister began to wrinkle and shrink into the tiny woman before him. The years simply did not ravage him as they did other people, and he had come to the conclusion that it must be something about his paternal parentage that gave him that attribute. While TC was the son of some mysterious man whose identity his mother had never truly divulged to him, Briyana had been sired by a 'normal' man whom TC had met on several occasions. And incidentally, she would age as any other 'normal' woman.

Yet, Tallachienan had not stayed idle. Over the years, as he grew in strength and power, he developed the means to prolong mortal life. The concoction was not perfect and would have to be imbibed every so often to maintain its effect. However, it would serve to keep Briyana with him for as long as she wished it.

But therein lay the problem. Briyana did not want to partake of TC's potion.

His sister's eyes narrowed mischievously and the corner of her pursed lips turned up. TC felt his stoic demeanor crumble. He had never been good at keeping the truth from his Briyana. She had a way of breaking him down like none else could. Yet she was his anchor, his guiding light. She had been there during his most brilliant accomplishments and a shoulder to lean upon after his most dismal failures. It devastated him to know that he would soon be forced to go on without her.

Tallachienan gently took Briyana's shoulders in his hands. "Briya . . . please let me give you the elixir." He smiled tremulously. "We can stand here in the garden this time next year. Your flowers will still be blooming here for you."

Mischief faded into sadness as Briyana brought a frail hand to TC's face. "Brother, I am not like you. I was not made to live so long. Do you really think I want to keep on this way . . . old and withered? I am hardly able to walk without stumbling. You have to help me every morning and every evening to dress myself. You prepare all of my meals . . ."

"But I don't mind doing those things, Briyana. I would do those things forever if it meant having you here beside me." TC paused and then continued, "I don't want to lose you."

Briyana's lower lip trembled minutely. "But Talli . . . I don't want to be old forever. Your elixir can only lengthen my life. It can't make me young again. Every day is a struggle, and age has brought me pain. Besides, you have Trebexal to keep you company. You don't need an old woman holding you back."

A shimmering tear ran down her cheek. TC cupped his hands around her face, wiping the wetness away with his thumbs. He hated to see her cry and now he wished he had never brought up the subject of the potion. He felt selfish and undeserving of her . . . she who had always given him so much.

Briyana was right. His elixir could not give her the youth and vitality she needed for her to have a wholesome life. It was wrong of him to want her to stay by him when all she wanted was to rest . . . to be free of the fetters of old age. He swept her up in his arms and he had the pleasure of hearing her laugh once more. It was a song to his soul . . . all he needed until the end.

TC stared solemnly into the darkness of the chamber. Briyana had died centuries ago before the cataclysm that brought about the Cycling of the world. But he remembered that day like it was yesterday, remembered holding her in his arms as she took her final breaths. At first it had seemed like a dream. But the passing of Time made it real and he mourned. He had mourned the way Adrianna's daughter now mourned for her lost comrades. He wished he could tell the young woman that it was a dream and when she awakened her friends would still be there at her side. But not even Master Tallachienan Chroalthone was that powerful.

***

From the corner of her eye, Aeris glanced at the man who walked beside her and smiled to herself. It was late, and TC was escorting her back to her chamber. After dinner, they had played Shockwave, a complex game in which one was at the mercy of the bones that were cast and the cards that were dealt. She wasn't that good at it yet, but with some more practice with Pylar during the day, she hoped that she would soon be a worthy opponent for the Master.

Aeris' chambers were not far from Tallachienan's, and it was not much longer before they reached their destination. Aeris paused before opening the door, and then turned to face TC. He regarded her intently and once more she marveled at his youthfulness. His thick black hair was pulled back and tied at the nape of his neck with a velvet cord. Black brows winged over lavender eyes and his mouth delicately sculpted beneath a noble nose.

She couldn't help looking at him. He was quite possibly the finest man she had ever seen. She knew that her perceptions were jaded, for he was a god, and she only a mortal woman. And yet, Master TC was so . . . old. Her mother had told her the stories of her life in the citadel whilst she trained to become a dimensionalist. That was almost forty years ago. Gods only knew how many years he had lived before that.

"Thank you for another fine evening, my Lord. We must do it again sometime soon." Her eyes twinkled as she spoke, for she already knew his response.

TC let his gaze linger on her full lips for a moment before he replied. "You know that will be tomorrow evening, Lady." TC felt the corner of his mouth twitch upwards as he tried to keep himself from smiling at her silliness.

Aeris nodded and opened the door to her chamber. She then slipped inside, smiled, and then closed the door gently behind her. TC stood there for a moment, staring at the closed door. He then turned and walked back down the hall to his own chambers.

It had been two weeks since Aeris first awakened from her poison-induced sleep. Since then, she had healed nicely. Soon she would be strong enough to return home. But Tallachienan wasn't ready to think about that just yet. It was a pleasure to have her within the citadel, and he knew that Pylar felt the same way. For his bond-mate, it was like having a little bit of Adrianna back again . . . and for TC it was much more. Granted, Aeris was like her mother in many ways; but there were many other things that made her so different.

TC would have greatly enjoyed having Aeris as his apprentice. She was intelligent and always quick to catch on to what he was teaching her. In that way, she was much like Adrianna. She was proficient in her skills and abilities, and TC felt proud to know that it was Dinim who had molded her into such a fine spell-caster.

However, it was more than just pride and admiration that TC felt for Adrianna's daughter. He felt drawn to her. He found himself thinking about her all day whilst he was instructing his students, waiting for the evening to draw near. Then, when the time finally came, he was relieved to be in her presence and reveled in the happiness her mere presence brought him.

How these feelings had come about, TC was not certain. He delved into his inner mind, exploring the possibilities. Was it because she reminded him so much of Adrianna? If he had the daughter, would he somehow have the mother again? Or was it simpler than that . . . merely that he found her attractive and wanted to have her because of that fact alone? Mayhap it was more complex. He was aware of the origins of their ancient bloodline. Somehow did that blood call out to him in an inexplicable way?

Did it matter?

TC fought the urge to get up and pace the floors. Who would ever have thought that this could happen to him? He felt torn; he knew that he should keep his distance from her because he knew of the effects he had on mortal women. He didn't want her to feel an attraction that would otherwise not be there. But at the same time, he wanted to submit to his desires. He wanted to go to that chamber and claim Aeris as his own.

Finally TC made his decision. He would choose the middle ground. He would neither keep his distance nor stake a claim on her. He would leave well enough alone for now and wait to see what would happen. Yet, in the meantime, he would go to see her in the morning before he met his apprentices in seminar. Perhaps he would invite her to sit in on the discussion and see if she had anything to offer to it.

Aeris slipped beneath the blankets and then pulled them over her shoulders. Her mind was full of Tallachienan and what he had come to mean to her these past two weeks as she recovered from her battle with the behiraz. In both body and mind Aeris had found healing. When she was finally able, she explored the citadel. She spent much of her time in the huge libraries, but even more in the gardens and courtyards. Aeris remembered her mother describing the darkness of the citadel, but Aeris felt none of that oppressiveness. She even liked the stone walls that surrounded her, and preferred it to the treetop daladins of Elvandahar.

On a few occasions, Aeris came into contact with TC's apprentices and journeymen. TC must have told them that she was a visitor, for they nodded to her as they happened by in the corridors. Other than that, they paid her little mind. Most of them seemed preoccupied, and she remembered her own days of intense study. Master Dinim had often been hard on her, but in the end the work paid off. Her training ended a full year before that of her other classmates, and she was free to take her tests in Andahye.

There were a couple of days when TC was able to see her during the day. He put her through her paces, and even taught her a thing or two. His methods were not too different from those of Master Dinim or her mother, and she found the familiarity to be comforting. She also found herself feeling that she was part of something that encompassed much more than the academy she left behind in Elvandahar. And then there was the Master himself.

Aeris sighed softly in the darkness. She knew that she was a fool. She shouldn't be thinking about Master TC in such a way, but she couldn't help it. In his presence she knew contentment like she had never known before, and all she could think was that she wanted him to pull her into his arms and never let her go. His lavender gaze seemed to penetrate her very soul, peeling aside the layers of her innermost self to expose the love beginning to blossom from within.

Aeris felt the tears that began to burn beneath her closed eyelids. Yes, she knew that she loved Tallachienan. She realized the futility of her situation: he was a god and she a mortal. Yet, it didn't matter much to the heart that seemed to beat just for him. Despite never having felt it before, Aeris knew that it was love. Her soul cried out for him, and when he was near, her skin tingled in anticipation of his touch.

But Aeris knew how he must see her. To him, she was still but a child, the daughter of one who had once been his student. TC had seen the Cycles change, had watched the history of the world unfurl countless times. He was quite probably the most powerful sorcerer that walked Shandahar. There would be no reason for him to view her as anything more than a fledgling spell-caster, nothing about her that would make him want her . . . need her the way she knew she would soon come to need him.

Aeris knew what she needed to do. She was almost completely healed of the wound she suffered from the behiraz. Realistically, she need not remain in the citadel any longer. By staying, she only delayed the inevitable; the confrontation she knew awaited her back home. She also made it more difficult for herself. The longer she stayed, the more her feelings would grow for Tallachienan.

Aeris resolutely turned on her side, took the closest pillow, and wrapped her arms around it. She would awaken early, prepare her belongings, and then tell Tallachienan that she wished to go home. It was that simple, and he would not refute her. Most likely, he would feel relieved that he would not have to entertain her in the evenings anymore. Aeris would go home, and she would forget that she ever met Master Tallachienan Chroalthone.

CHAPTER 2

The fortress was vast. Built entirely beneath the surface of the world, it was situated atop an even larger city that sprawled hundreds of zacrol and sustained a population of thousands. It was the largest cimmerean stronghold upon Shandahar and the home of Queen Tholana.

She slowly walked the battlements of her dark citadel. Spires rose all around her, the tallest almost touching the stone of the grotto ceiling. The cave system was massive, the perfect place for her fortress, and easily sustained by the catacombs that formed a maze around and beneath. Her people lived there . . . her most devout and powerful priestesses and their families. It was a theocracy ruled none other by the goddess herself.

But despite her fortress, her city, and her followers, there was something missing. Tholana had no living children, but it wasn't lack of these that made her introspective. She hated her weakness, and was able to divert her attention away from it most of the time. But not this day. For some damnable reason, she was unable to keep Tallachienan Chroalthone from her thoughts.

Tholana clenched her hands into fists. For centuries she had sought to bring the dimensionalist master to her bed, and for just as long she had failed. And yet, a puny apprentice was able to have him. Like a fool, the girl had cast him from her. Adrianna Darnesse . . . stupid whore. She chose a mere woodland ranger over a master and a god. Adrianna had no idea what she had given up the day she bid Tallachienan stay away.

Tholana smiled malevolently. Of course, it only served to be to her own benefit. Tallachienan still had no mistress. And Tholana had exacted her revenge upon the imprudent Adrianna; many of her precious Wildrunners were now dead. But why was she pondering Tallachienan so hard right now? What was happening to make her think of him so heavily?

Tholana stopped. It would be easy for her to spy upon her nemesis. She should have thought of it before. It seemed that she fought so hard to keep TC from her thoughts that she seemed to lose all rationality. She would ease her mind and then get back to more pressing concerns. One of them happened to be Razlul Daemon-keeper. Since securing a place for himself with the Daemundai more than three decades before, he had become much more powerful. His work was testimony to that fact, for she had begun to hear of more daemonic infiltrations than ever before. Perhaps it would be advantageous for Tholana to re-initiate her acquaintance with the Daemon Prince. After all, if he were to happen to become one of the new power-players in Shandahar, it would behoove her to ally with him. That is, if the notion suited her.

**

Aeris packed the rest of her clothes into her travel sack, on top of which she placed her cloak. It was summer and she knew that she would not be in need of it. Her spell book and extra components were at the bottom, followed by the clothes she had worn prior to her arrival at the citadel. They were clean, and she had thought about putting them on. Yet, she so much preferred the sleeveless robe and matching trousers she found in the closet several days ago. She hoped TC wouldn't mind if she took those with her.

Aeris slung the pack over her shoulder. She took another long look around the room to be sure she wasn't leaving anything. At that moment, second thoughts began to race through her mind. She really didn't have to depart this very moment. She could spend one last evening with Tallachienan and leave tomorrow instead. Besides, she hadn't had the chance to say good-bye to Pylar, who would most likely feel betrayed by her leaving without doing so.

Aeris adjusted the sash around her waist. From it hung her pouches of spell-components and the sword her mother bequeathed to her before she left for Andahye. "It is enchanted," Adrianna had said. "I don't know the spell, or who placed it upon the weapon, but it saved me the day I met Aasarak. Perhaps one day it will save you too."

Aeris caressed the polished hilt. Thoughts of her mother brought tears to her eyes. No. She should not stay here. She needed to go home, needed the strength that only her mother could give. Although, Aeris had to concede that TC had done rather well on that front.

Aeris suddenly felt her heart ache with thoughts of the Master. Gods, she would miss him. She felt herself tremble minutely as she walked to the door. It was time for her to go to him, tell him that she needed to leave. *Damnation. I wish that this could be easier. But I know it won't be . . .*

Aeris opened the door and suddenly stopped at the threshold. She slowly looked up into the eyes of Tallachienan. Her heart lodged itself in her throat, and for a moment she couldn't breathe. He looked so handsome standing there at her doorway, so self-assured and confident.

Aeris unconsciously stepped back and TC entered the room. He took in her attire: the pack slung over her shoulder and the sword at her hip. She saw the question in his eyes but he refrained from asking it. "I came to see how you were this morning," he said.

Aeris hesitated a moment before she spoke. She had spent half of her night tossing and turning, her mind filled only with thoughts of him. And when she finally slept, her dreams were the same. But dreams were often not what one expected them to be. She remembered the feel of his arms around her, the touch of his lips on her skin . . .

Aeris felt her cheeks begin to flush and not for the first time she silently prayed that TC was not a mind-reader. "I am well, thank-you."

If her voice sounded a little bit husky, she hoped that he wouldn't notice. If her eyes were a little too wide and her face flushed, she hoped that he wouldn't notice that either. She felt her heart begin to hammer against her chest as she watched his gaze focus upon her face, first settling onto her mouth and then back up to her eyes. His expression had changed, and Aeris couldn't help but feel that, indeed, TC had noticed.

Suddenly feeling nervous, Aeris cleared her throat and spoke again. She tended to do that sometimes when she felt anxious. "Actually, I was just coming to look for you." She hoped that her voice wasn't as wobbly as it sounded like it might be, and she was putting a lot of effort into making it sound less husky.

TC's eyes slowly began to darken, and they burned with intensity. Very slowly he began to step towards her. She felt a tension in the air, an expectancy that had begun to build. "What do you need me for? I'm here now."

His voice was deep, more so than usual. Every word he spoke seemed punctuated, drawing her attention to his lips. Aeris felt her belly clench, felt the blood rushing through her veins. Her first impulse was to step back as he advanced towards her, but then she thought better of it. She held her ground and nodded in response. Yes, he was here now. She could feel the incredible strength of his aura, feel the intensity rolling off of him in waves. Finally TC stood before her. He wasn't that much taller than she, but it was enough that he looked downward into her face. He just barely stood outside the boundaries of personal space. With him so close, Aeris ached to bridge the gap that separated them, but dared not.

"Don't tell me that you were planning on leaving." The voice was suddenly low, although just as deep. His gaze became hooded as he searched her face. "I feel that I am not quite ready for you to do that just yet."

Aeris could only stare at him for a moment, mesmerized. By the gods, he was asking her to stay. Her heart leaped within her chest, but it was tempered by the reality that continued to weigh upon her. "Master Tallachienan, I . . ."

TC raised his hand to her face, placing two fingertips to her lips. "Shhhh. You need not say anything." It was then that she realized that he had stepped into her space, and that hardly anything separated them. She felt herself breathing deeply, inhaling the rich, masculine scent of him. "You will not be needing this." She suddenly felt his hand at her shoulder lifting the travel pack and sliding it down her arm.

"No," she agreed in a soft voice. Aeris heard the gentle thud of the pack as it dropped to the floor near their feet. Her eyes remained locked to his, their lavender depths seeming to pull her within.

They stood before one another, saying nothing. The air was thick with suppressed emotion. It pushed at Aeris and she could hear the sound of her own breathing. It would be nothing to simply reach out to him . . .

Aeris pulled her eyes away from his and she tentatively raised a hand and placed it at the neckline of his tunic. The fabric was soft beneath her fingertips. She began to caress the pulse at his neck when his hand reached up to capture hers. Time seemed to slow down, and she was suddenly aware of his breath disturbing the wisps of hair that curled at her forehead. She felt like she was in a dream and she never wanted it to end.

TC threaded his fingers through hers, holding her hand at his chest. Hesitantly she looked back up at him. He regarded her with an intensity she finally began to recognize as passion. With his other hand, he gently brushed a tendril of her hair back from her face. "Tell me that I am dreaming," she whispered. They were the first words she had spoken to him two weeks ago. Then, she had most certainly hoped that she was. But now . . .

"This is no dream." He spoke the words just under his breath. He watched her from half-lidded eyes, his fingers caressing the side of her face. She took her hand from his grip and then moved it up to his jaw, smoothing over the lines around his mouth. Tallachienan closed his eyes, moved his face so close to hers that his breath washed over her lips. And then Aeris finally brought her body in closer, bridging that small space that remained between them.

Tallachienan brushed his lips softly against hers. A lick of fire raced through her body and down to her pelvis, settling there deep within her belly. Aeris returned the kiss and he deepened it, putting his hands at her hips and back, pulling her into him. She swept her hands over his chest, felt his body's response to her nearness. Her mind whirled away within a vortex of emotion. She couldn't believe what was happening; it was so much like her dream the night before, only better.

Aeris opened her eyes and it was only then that she realized she had closed them. Tallachienan watched her from eyes that were barely open as he continued to take her with his mouth. She felt a thrill sweep through her, finding his interest in her response to him highly intoxicating. Beneath her palms, she felt each beat of his heart . . . each breath that he took. At that moment, both seemed to be just for her. Then he was suddenly pulling away from her. He continued to hold her in his arms, but he separated them enough so that he could see her. Her passion cooled as he regarded her, his emotions hidden once more. She began to wonder what it was that she thought she was doing, giving in to whims and flights of fancy. Again she reminded herself that he was a god, and she merely a mortal. There could be nothing between them; they lived worlds apart.

Aeris felt a pregnant pause . . . the moment that TC seemed to make his final decision. Once again he was vulnerable to her, his emotions plain for her to see. His hand came up to caress the side of her face, and his expression swiftly became one of desire. He wanted her, and his body was testimony to that fact.

Aeris melted into his embrace. She felt him lift her from the floor and carry her to the canopied bed. He laid her gently on the blankets and then followed her down. Passion's fire swept through them, searing them with its heat. But Aeris was not afraid. She wanted this, wanted him so much that it hurt. She knew that tomorrow things might be different. But at least she had this day, and the man who would have her love him.

***

TC stood in front of the well. He stared down into the dark depths, remembering when he had first created it. He had been younger then, and not yet the fully accomplished mage that he would become. Yet, even then he held great power. He had created the entire portal system that currently existed throughout Shandahar, open to all who knew of its existence. That tended to be those who were the most powerful and trustworthy. Yet, he knew that many undesirables knew of it and sought to use it for their own personal gain. Such was the way of many things of the arcane variety.

Tallachienan pressed his lips into a thin line. He knew that he needed to send her home, knew that he could not continue to keep her there indefinitely. Gods only knew that he wanted her to stay, but it just wasn't right. He felt guilty for taking advantage of her in her weakened state, and his decision to send her back to her homeland was absolute.

Almost three weeks had passed since he first made love to Aeris Timberlyn. In her he had seemed to find a soul-mate, that person who could make him happy in life. But he could not forget his station, or the fact that she was very young. She hadn't even reached her prime, having so many years left to discover the power that he could feel lying deep within her. It was not right to keep her here behind his stone walls. If she was anything like her mother, Aeris would soon begin to crave the wide open spaces and the fresh air needed for her to be happy and whole.

TC turned when Aeris entered the room. Just as he requested, she had brought her travel pack and attired herself appropriately for a journey. He had bid Pylar give her the message for he knew that he would not be able to go to her himself. Inasmuch, he had not the heart to tell her that he was sending her home.

17

Slowly Aeris walked towards him. Her gaze was questioning, and he saw her brows draw together in the beginning of a frown as she took in his solemn countenance. He gestured her over to him, and she obeyed, finally coming to stand before him. TC gestured to the well. "Do you know what this is?"

Aeris regarded him oddly. "It's a well. One obtains water from it."

TC shook his head. "Not this well. I created it to be the mechanism that can teleport one to anywhere on Shandahar one wishes to be."

Aeris nodded, saying nothing. She was confused as to the reason why she was there. Pylar had been unable to answer any of her questions, telling her only that TC wanted her to prepare for travel. She was to bring everything that she would take as though she were to be going on a long journey.

TC took one of her hands and held it within his own. "Aeris, it has been five weeks since you first came here. You are completely healed, and have been ready to return home for several days now. I have brought you here today so that you may do so."

Aeris' frown deepened and she knew that her hurt shone through her eyes. "Are you telling me that I am no longer welcome here?"

TC pitched his voice into a soothing tone. "Your parents are probably worried about you by now. They have heard nothing from you now in almost . . ."

Aeris shut herself away from his words. He was telling her to leave. She couldn't believe what she was hearing. Up until now he had said nothing of her leaving, and had even seemed happy to have her there. She was such a fool. She had given herself to him, and now that he was tired of her, he thought that he would send her back home.

Aeris removed her hand from his grip. She stared into the empty space before her, her gaze unfocused. "I can't believe this. I can't believe you are telling me to leave." Yet, she could believe it. He was a god, and she only a mortal. She should have expected it.

TC saw the desolation in her eyes, the self-censure, and the feelings of betrayal. But she had it all wrong. He didn't want to keep her away from him forever. He wanted her to live her life and fulfill her destiny, whatever it may be. Then, when the prime of her life had passed, he wanted her to come back to him to spend the rest of her days at the citadel.

"Aeris, you are taking this the wrong way." He spoke with a mild rebuke in his voice. "But I am right when I tell you that you don't belong here. You have your entire life ahead of you. One day, I would have you return to me. When you wish it, I will come for you."

Aeris shook her head and refocused her eyes. She penetrated him with her dark gaze, and when she spoke her voice was caustic. "Come for me . . . you make it sound like you will come to find me like I am a thing that you had once lost." Her voice began to rise in pitch, her anger fueling her to continue. "Oh yes. I remember the wemic pup I once had. I must go and find her now, bring her back to be my pet again."

TC stiffened in shock. He wasn't prepared for the attack. But before he could form a reply, Aeris spoke again.

"Oh yes. When you remember, please come for me. It will be no problem for me to wait a few hundred years for you to decide that enough time has passed and that I have lived my life to its fullest."

"Damaeris stop." His voice rang throughout the chamber. "It won't be like that. You could never be an afterthought to me." He put his hands on her shoulders for emphasis. "I *will* come for you."

Aeris shook her head, her eyes bright with unshed tears. She inhaled deeply, seeking to take control of her emotions. "I don't believe you."

She whispered those words, and they were like a bucket of cold water falling over him. His body tensed and he felt something akin to a searing poker enter his chest to pierce his heart. TC had broken her trust in him.

Aeris turned away in an effort to hide her emotions. He put his hand beneath her chin and moved her head to face him once more. She kept her eyes averted, refusing to look at him. But TC would not be deterred. He pulled her into his arms, hoping to show her that he did not intend to hurt her, and that he deeply cared for her.

Tallachienan lowered his head to kiss her. Understanding his intent, Aeris pushed him away and pulled herself from him. "No. You no longer have that right. You are not my husband, and I owe you nothing." Aeris paused and then continued. "You are right. It is time for me to go home. I am ready." Aeris seated herself upon the lip of the well.

TC heard the sorrow in her voice and she would not allow herself to meet his gaze. He knew he couldn't allow it to end this way, but he didn't know what to do or what to say to change the course of events that were unfolding before him. Shaking his head, TC knelt beside her. He took her hand and slid a ring over her middle finger. Aeris pulled her hand free, and when she saw the ring, she only gave him a small smile.

Before she could say anything, TC spoke. "I promise I will come for you, Aeris. Never take the ring from your finger. It will protect you and help me find you wherever you might be."

Finally Aeris looked up at him. The desolation in her gaze was almost intolerable. "I should have left that morning three weeks ago. I should never have stayed. Yet, I trusted you, believed in what I felt happening between us. I never thought that you would betray that. I was such a fool. Please return me home, Tallachienan."

Aeris turned away from him once more, and he felt his chest ache. He would not allow her to have the last say. Not only was it against his nature, but she was wrong to believe that he betrayed her and the feelings they shared for one another. TC grabbed her around the waist with one arm and took her jaw in his other hand. Then he kissed her.

Aeris felt her body tremble when his lips descended to hers. He always had that effect on her, but she refused to be disarmed by him. None too gently he kissed her, his teeth bruising her lips until she almost groaned. She could sense that he wanted her to submit, but before he could truly hurt her, he released her mouth. He regarded her intently, his gaze dark and turbulent. He continued to keep her close as he began to speak. At first it was only a mumble, but in the end she could just barely make out what he was saying. "This promise I have made to you, I swear to keep until it has been fulfilled."

Aeris only vaguely understood what was happening. Strangely, it sounded like the words one would speak in conjunction with a spell. His voice was full of suppressed emotion, and she could feel the trembling of his arms as they held her. "All you have to do is think of where you want to go. The well will take you there," he said.

Aeris felt the familiar burning ache in her throat as she fought to contain her emotions. She closed her eyes, and in her mind she saw the silver forest that was her home. Elvandahar. Once more, TC tilted her face up to his. She cracked her eyelids to find herself looking into dark pools of lavender. Then he was kissing her again, his lips softly claiming hers in a sweet caress. "I love you." She heard the words as she began to fall, words she had never heard him speak before. Then her mind was whirling away into nothingness.

***

Aeris walked deeper into the Silverwood. The air was cool, and the rays of the newly risen sun were just beginning to break over the horizon. The silver leaves on the great oak trees of her homeland glistened brightly with early morning dew. Soon it would dazzle her eyes and she would begin to squint through the cacophony of prismatic light. But until then, she could enjoy the sheer glory of it.

Aeris shrugged her travel pack more firmly up onto her shoulder. Despite the beauty that surrounded her, Aeris was unable to find much joy in it. In the darkness of predawn she had awakened to find herself lying on the ground. Almost immediately she knew where she was, but how she got there was an enigma to her. She remembered the deaths of her comrades, but not how she had been able to escape the behiraz. She did not know how her wound had become healed, or how she came to be wearing a set of clothes that were not her own. And even more mystifying was the ring that circled the middle finger of her left hand. The opalescent stone at the center swirled with pale blue and green color and she knew that it must be worth a fortune.

Aeris traveled west through Elvandahar. It wasn't long before she realized how close she was to Sefranim, her father's village. The closer she came, the harder her heart pounded in her chest. Any moment now her father's rangers would materialize out of the trees around her. They would escort her to Sirion, asking questions about her journey. They would want to know about Raissa, Lorak, Doran and Mavik. Once reaching the village, she would be forced to make a public statement concerning the deaths of the four young people. Many would wonder the same thing she did herself. How did she escape when no one else was able? Why did the others die and only Damaeris Timberlyn be alive to tell the tale?

Aeris stumbled over an exposed tree root, but was able to catch herself against one of the massive oaks before she fell. She laid her forehead against the tree and dug her fingernails into the rich bark. She took a deep breath, inhaling the scents all around her. The calm she sought was elusive, and before she knew it, the tears were flowing. Her body trembled and she began to doubt her sanity. She didn't feel ill, but she knew that somehow she must be. Otherwise, how could she have forgotten the past several weeks of her life?

Aeris pushed away from the tree and started to move again. Half-blinded by tears, she weaved around trees and shrubbery. She almost fell a couple more times before she finally stopped before a rumo bush and vomited. She waited a few moments for her stomach to settle, and then moved on again. She didn't realize that she was surrounded until she heard a voice speak to her.

"Princess Aeris, is it you?"

Aeris looked up to find that an entourage of rangers had formed a semi-circle before her. The men should have had their bows drawn and arrows ready, but they must have known it was she. The bows remained slung over their shoulders, and the daggers at their hips. The men regarded her expectantly, and with more than a little concern. None of them stepped towards her, and she quickly realized the reason why when another man walked out from behind them.

It was her father. Aeris felt an ache start in her chest that slowly made its way up to form a lump in her throat. His beloved face started her tears anew, and her body began to tremble. With a muttered curse, Sirion dropped his long-bow and ran to her. Before she could fall, Aeris found herself caught up in his embrace. She inhaled the familiar scent of him as he crooned soothingly to her in hinterlic, and then swung her up in arms that used to toss her up in the air as a small child. Pitching his voice away from her ear, Sirion shouted at his rangers go and tell her mother that their daughter was home. Aeris clutched at his vest and she started to cry great heaving sobs that left her breathless. Her father held her close and told her that everything would be all right. She knew that it wouldn't be, but they were just the words she wanted to hear.

***

Aeris stared up at the ceiling of the alcove. What little light entered the room through the curtains that lead out onto the balcony swayed and shifted with the material that hung there. But she had neither interest in the light, nor the fresh air. She heard the sounds of everyday living going on in the village outside the daladin, but she cared not for that either. She knew that her mother and father worried about her, but she would not be moved to ease them of their concern. All she wanted to do was lie there and forget the world as she knew it.

Three days had passed since her return to Elvandahar. The only reason she knew was because her mother made it a point to tell her at the break of every dawn that a new day had come. Just that morning, Aeris had watched Adrianna while she placed a tray of food on the desk, pulled aside the curtain, and put fresh water in the washbasin. Her mother's pale curling hair was pulled back from her face with a pin, and then allowed to fall haphazardly down her back. As a child, Aeris remembered thinking that her Ama was the most beautiful mother in the world. Aeris still believed it to be so.

Aeris had watched her mother perform tasks that were customarily set aside for others to complete. Aeris knew that she did them because she wanted to be there for her daughter, to show Aeris that she loved her and wanted to share her company. Aeris knew that Adrianna should be at the academy, but instead chose to be at the daladin. Finally feeling the weight of Aeris' gaze, Adrianna turned around and smiled. Then she came to sit on the edge of the bed. Aeris was silent as her mother brushed the hair back from her face, and then pressed her cool lips to her brow. Aeris noticed the unshed tears in Adrianna's eyes when she left the alcove, but Aeris made no move to stop her mother.

After Adrianna left, Aeris got up and closed the curtains. Then she went back to bed, lay on her side, and pulled the covers over herself. She didn't really need them, for it was warm enough. But she somehow felt more protected with them covering her, and they were there if she were to need to hide beneath them. Aeris closed her eyes and dozed. Despite the dreams, she did a lot of that now. She knew that she was tormenting herself, but she couldn't bring herself to truly care. The deaths of her friends played over and over again in her mind, and were reiterated in her dreams. It was penance, she thought, for being alive when she should really be dead.

Aeris awoke when she felt a presence behind her. She opened her eyes and looked over her shoulder to see Asgenar sitting in a chair beside her bed. She cursed to herself, rolled her eyes, and turned away from him. Asgenar was one of the last people she wished to see. Before leaving for Andahye, they had fought bitterly, and she had not the patience for him.

Asgenar was her eldest brother; at least ten years her senior. And despite that fact, he was quite possibly the most beautiful man she had ever seen. Like their mother, he had hair the color of palest gold and eyes a deep brown. In almost every way he was Adrianna's child, even in temperament. However, he was also his own person. Even in childhood, Aeris remembered him as always being the dictatorial older brother, and he never seemed to tire of telling her what to do and how to go about doing it. As it turned out, those qualities were good for him, for he was the heir to the realm of Elvandahar.

When Asgenar came of age, he was sent to the Sherkari Fortress to take his place as the Prince of Elvandahar. Rigorous training ensued as he began to learn the ways of ruling a kingdom. He visited home often, and it seemed that each time he did so, the more authoritative he became. Aeris and Alasdair, her second eldest brother, often found themselves at odds with Asgenar, and a rift appeared amongst them. Moreover, as Asgenar began to spend lengthier times away from home, they became ever more distant from one another.

However, one thing had started to appear in favor of her commanding older brother. In the past couple of years, he had begun to change. He had begun to curtail some of his dictatorial habits, and had even begun to show some measure of respect for their opinions. But old ways are difficult to alter, and on the eve of her leave-taking Aeris and Asgenar had a disagreement. It was the same old story, Asgenar attempting to enforce his will upon her. Aeris had become a grown woman, and independent in many ways. His stubbornness battered at her resolve to see him in a more favorable light. She left Elvandahar angry with him, and now her reaction to his presence in her alcove was testimony to the fact she had not yet forgiven him the harsh words he spoke to her on the eve of her first foray away from home without the company of her elders.

Asgenar must have noticed her reaction to him, but he said nothing of it. "Ama and Babu have a hard time keeping things from me. I came as soon as I found out you were home." His voice was as beautiful as his face, and Aeris found herself grimacing to herself. She said nothing in reply, and silence reigned between them for several moments before he spoke again.

"Aeris, I am sorry about Raissa, Doran, Lorak and Mavik. I know what they meant to you."

Keeping her back to him, Aeris gave an exaggerated sigh. "What are you doing here, Asgenar? Don't you have anything better to do with your time?"

"Right now, nothing matters more to me than your well-being, Aeris." She was pleased to hear the note of annoyance in his voice. She had gotten to him already and he was barely several minutes into their reunion.

She said nothing, despite all of the possible retorts that ran through her mind. What was the point? Another battle would be waged between them. And for what? A simple few moments of glory when she had made Asgenar so angry that she felt she had won the fight? She found that she just didn't care anymore. Or maybe she had simply grown up a bit since she saw her bothersome brother last.

Once more the alcove rang with silence. He had said that he knew what her friends meant to her. That was wrong. He knew nothing of them and even less of their relationship with her. Aeris hated it when people said things that they imagined were the right things to say, even if it wasn't the truth.

Finally she heard him sigh, a soft sound that made her think that he had intended to keep it to himself. "I know that things aren't right between us, but I want you to know that I am here for you. I am not returning to the fortress until I know you are well."

Aeris considered saying nothing, but then she said, "Asgenar, don't stay here because of me. I have gotten this far in life without you and I am sure that I will continue to live many more years the same way. Go back to your fortress. I don't need you."

Aeris cringed when she heard the tone of her voice, but she hadn't been able to stop it from sounding the way it did. It was sorrowful, with a tinge of despair. She hated that, and hated even more that Asgenar had heard it. He was nothing if not perceptive.

At first her brother said nothing. But she could feel that he pondered her words. She knew not what he was thinking, and refused to turn around to look at his face. Finally he cleared his throat and rose from the chair. "You think that you do not need me. That is fine. But I will be here anyway." His tone was devoid of emotion, and somehow she knew that he schooled it to be that way. She was sure it was one of the things that he learned in order to be a king one day. Aeris heard him walk across the floor to the door. Then he was gone. The room was silent. For a long time she lay there, and then she fell asleep once again.

***

Aeris heard a pounding at the door, and then it swung open. She stared at the figure standing at the threshold with sleep-bleary eyes. It was man. He strode purposefully towards the bed, and when he was standing before it, he reached down with both hands and tore the covers from her.

Aeris shrieked with indignation and scrambled for the blankets that Alasdair wadded into a mass and threw across the room. It landed in a pitiful heap in the far corner. From the middle of the bed, she looked up at her brother, the one person she loved more than anyone else in her life. Just as Asgenar was the image of their mother, Alasdair looked like their father. His hair was copper red, and his eyes the color of molten amber. He stood over her with his hands at his hips. It was a stance so much like Sirion's that, if she had been anyone else, she would have thought that it was the older man who stood there.

"By the gods, Aeris. What in the Hells are you doing holed up in here?"

"Get out, Alasdair," Aeris spat. "I told Ama and Babu I didn't want to see anyone."

Alasdair's brows pulled together into a frown. "That doesn't include your family, especially me. Besides, I know that Asgenar has been to see you already."

"Our parents are weak. He said something and they told him I was here."

Alasdair's frown deepened. "Our parents are *worried* about you, and they shouldn't have kept this particular information from us."

"Oh, so you are on *his* side now."

"No. I am on your side, but that happens to be Asgenar's side as well." Alasdair paused. "This time at least."

Aeris rolled her eyes. "Whatever. Give me back my blanket." She pointed to the far corner.

"No. Get up and get it yourself."

"Effin calotebas," she growled. "Just get out." She stood up from the bed and made towards the blanket.

"No. I can't believe that Ama and Babu let you stay in here this long. Life is going on outside this alcove, Aeris, and it's time you rejoined it."

Aeris stopped before she reached the blanket. "Haven't they told you? There is something wrong with me. I can't remember anything after they died."

Alasdair spread his arms. "Aeris, we can get through this together. I will help you to remember."

She shook her head, picked up the blanket and moved back towards the bed.

"Talemar and Cedric have been beside themselves," continued Alasdair. "Ama and Babu have been keeping visitors away. When I found out that it was at your request, I just had to come up here to find out what was going on with you."

Aeris slumped back into the bed and began to pull the blanket back over her. "Besides memory loss, nothing is going on with me. I just want to be left alone."

Alasdair grabbed the blanket again and kept her from covering herself completely. "Left alone to die?"

The words rang through the alcove, words that she had thought but never said. Alasdair knew her so well, too well. Finally she looked up at him, locked her gaze onto his. "Let go, Alasdair."

"No. I won't let you do this to yourself."

Aeris felt her lips begin to tremble. She despaired that she had become so weak and pathetic. She couldn't even keep herself from crying anymore. She knew that she should somehow find it within her to be thankful that someone had found her after the ordeal and healed her wounds. But she just couldn't do it. "I hate you," she said.

Alasdair swallowed convulsively for a moment, almost as though it took a great effort for him to control his emotions. "I love you too," he said softly.

Aeris could see the pain in his eyes, pain that she was causing him. She looked away from his face, and instead focused upon the sun-darkened hand that continued to hold the blanket. "I just don't think I can do this." Her voice cracked and she knew the tears were soon to come. The hand moved out of her range of sight and she felt her brother settle himself next to her on the bed.

"We are going to do this together. I will be right here with you every moment of the journey."

Aeris shook her head. "I should be lying in that pass. I shouldn't be here, alive, while they are all dead." Said out loud, the words sounded so harsh. She felt her brother's body stiffen, heard the rush of his breath as he expelled it all at once. She felt the tears begin to fall, the first ones after her breakdown almost four days ago when their father found her struggling through the forest.

Suddenly, Aeris found herself in his arms. Alasdair rocked her back and forth as she cried. He said nothing, merely holding her until the sobbing subsided. Then he continued to cradle her as she fell into sleep. With his arms around her, there were no dreams. With his arms around her, she thought that, maybe, just maybe, she would find the strength to go on.

CHAPTER 3

1 Tiseren CY632

Tallachienan sat silently within the confines of the massive oak chair. It was his favorite one, the one he always sought when he was broody. It had been his companion throughout the centuries, and the faded velvet upholstery was testament to that fact. He could scarcely remember when he had acquired the chair, or why he had chosen it in the first place. Perhaps because it was so deep, he could become hidden within it if he so chose. Or maybe it was the quality of the workmanship that shaped the fine wood, carefully polished with a chestnut sheen. It had been so long ago, and the chair had served him for so long, he had forgotten. TC could only wish that other, more disagreeable memories would meet the same fate . . . to simply be forgotten.

TC steepled his hands before him, his fingers meeting just beneath his nose. He couldn't stop thinking about her . . . the way she moved in the shadows of all his dreams, her perfumed scent like the sweetest of desert blossoms at midnight, and the way her smile lit up those darkest corners of his soul. She would be here with him still . . . if only he had not sent her away.

TC exhaled slowly, closing his eyes with the sudden pain that arced through him. He had tried to tell himself that it was for the best . . . that she deserved more than he could give her there at the citadel. He had tried to tell himself that he didn't really need her, that it was only the fact that she was Adrianna's daughter that drew him to her in the first place. Yet, he still could not shake the feeling that he was his own worst enemy and that she was the one . . .

TC lowered his hands and gripped the armrests. He fought the urge to go to her despite knowing that Aeris would not remember should she see him. He had cast a spell . . . one that would suppress her memories of her tenure at the citadel. He hated to do it, but at the time he saw no other way, and he didn't relish the thought of her possibly suffering through her life without him. Now he second-guessed himself . . . wishing that he had never cast the spell. He remembered the desolate expression in her eyes when she realized he wanted her to leave, followed by distrust. TC scoffed to himself. He had surely earned that lack of trust when he cast the *Memory Lapse* spell. He had taken away a portion of her free will . . . the ability to make the decision to remember him for herself. But by now, TC was accustomed to making decisions for others . . .

Unbidden, the memories resurfaced, memories of another time and another place. They were memories of a time long passed . . . of when he was young. Gods, that was centuries ago . . . centuries of Cycles ago. He had lived and become powerful within that first Cycle, a descendant of the gods themselves. He didn't even know the truth about his heritage until he began to notice strange things about himself, things that didn't happen to normal folk. Then there was the day his mother told him about the time she had been seduced by a god . . .

Since then, TC had lived hundreds of lives. His mortal half-sister had lived and died before that first Cycle, as had his own mother. With his newly emergent power, he was able to withstand the merge of the first Cycle into the second. It was a painful experience, both mentally and physically, one he would undergo four more times until Adrianna and the Wildrunners finally broke the curse in the fifth Cycle.

TC rubbed a hand over his face and then swept it back through his ebony hair. His power had only grown after that first Cycle. He went on a quest . . . a mission to discover the truth of his identity. He discovered that he was the son of Odion, one of the most ancient of the gods, and that it was his father who had cursed the world to repeat itself over and over again until the Balance could be shifted back into alignment once more.

It wasn't until the third Cycle that he met Adrianna Darnesse for the first time. Right from the start he was intrigued by her strength, determination, and pride. He had made it his purpose in life to aid her in the struggle against Aasarak, another man who had matured in power since the first Cycle. TC had always thought how unfair it was that Aasarak was allowed to grow in power with each passing Cycle, to survive each one as did Tallachienan . . . when the one who was destined to defeat him was made to be reborn with each change. Yet, Adrianna had finally persevered despite the odds against her. TC liked to think that he had a hand in her success, but he could never truly be sure. In that regard, he reveled in his ability to thwart his father, and he had to admit that he didn't even like Odion.

TC drew his hand away from his hair and looked at it in the flickering torchlight. He didn't look any different from any other cimmerean. However, he knew that there was a world of difference within him and that his exterior was merely a shell. He was not entirely faelin, nor was he wholly a being of Shandahar. He was a *god*, a being that was often called immortal. He knew that he was not, for he could be killed, and he knew that he would one day die of old age. Moreover, he had studied enough of the gods to know that they were not always what they appeared to be . . . appearing to people as simple humans and faelin when, in fact, they were something much, much more.

In part, TC had dared not explore that aspect of himself. Long ago, he had decided that he was happy with the form with which he had been given a birth. He never shifted it, nor did he find a reason to do so. Others of his station shifted form without thinking twice about it. Tholana was one of those, sometimes altering her shape into that of a huge spider with the head of a faelin woman. Trebexal was the same, shifting from dragon to faelin form with ease. There were many others . . . those of which he had little knowledge . . . those who would one day make themselves known. They were the children of the gods, and one day they would rule over Shandahar. At least, that is what Tallachienan used to think. But now . . . now things had changed. With the Pact of Bakharas broken, daemon-kind was free to roam Shandahar again. Once more, the future of the world was in a precarious balance. Where were the legendary Wildrunners now that they were needed again? He knew that many of them were dead and gone. All that remained were their children . . .

**

***

Aeris walked slowly down the corridor, deep in thought. Just that morning, Alasdair had announced that, within the next few weeks, he intended to go to the city of Sangrilak in order to obtain some supplies he had been unable to purchase anywhere in Elvandahar. Meanwhile, he would also make a visit to his good friend, Tigerius Solanar, whom he hadn't seen for a long while. Her brother immediately invited Aeris to accompany him. At first she declined, claiming that she had enough of traveling. However, he asked her to give it further consideration. He didn't need a response for another couple of weeks or so, plenty of time for her to think about his proposal.

Five months had passed since Aeris made it home from her ill-fated journey from Andahye. Much had happened since then, and Aeris felt that she was just getting accustomed to living a normal life again. She still had no memory of what had happened to her after her companions died in their battle against the behiraz, but she ceased to let it bother her so much. With the support of her family, Aeris finally came to realize that no one blamed her for the deaths of the others, and that she was blessed to have survived the attack at all. Contrary to her belief, no public statement by her had to be made, and all discussions of the deceased were had in private with the affected families.

Aeris would never forget the day she went to speak with Raissa's family. The girls had always been the best of friends, and Aeris knew Raissa's mother, father, and brother well. Of course, they knew of their daughter's demise before Aeris came to visit the daladin. However, by hearing her story of the struggle with the behiraz, it allowed the family to put their questions about Raissa's death to rest. Aeris paid her respects, and then bowed gracefully out. Her father had accompanied her, standing unobtrusively to the side while she spoke to the family. Sirion put his arm around her as they walked slowly back to the daladin, a solid bastion of support in her time of need.

It was only a few weeks later that Aeris heard talk that King Thalios had started to treat with the King of Karlisle. For decades the two realms had bickered over rights to the Denegal River, and only now had they finally begun negotiations. It wasn't long after that Asgenar was betrothed to be married to Elinora, the eldest daughter of King Zerxes. It was decided that an alliance such as this one would be good for both kingdoms. Aeris could only imagine how her brother felt about the turn of events, and she didn't envy him his station.

She turned down the next corridor when she heard a voice behind her. "Aeris, wait up." She turned to look back down the hall from which she had come to see Talemar hurrying towards her. She smiled when she saw him and waited for him to catch up. He grinned when he stopped in front of her, only slightly out of breath. He leaned into her, kissing her soundly on the mouth, and then walked beside her as she began to continue down the corridor.

"I didn't expect to see you here at the academy today."

Aeris shrugged. "I thought I would make a visit to the library. I need a new book to read."

Talemar grimaced. "Just like Master Adrianna, you are."

Aeris chuckled. "Who told you that?"

"My father. I know more about your mother than you think I do."

"And Master Dinim knows her so well, I suppose."

Talemar shrugged. "Perhaps."

Aeris cast him a sidelong glance. Talemar looked much like his father, with black hair and a pale skin tone. There was no doubt as to his parentage, for he even had the same white streak that started at the peak of his hairline and trailed down the left side. The only difference was that his eyes were a pale blue instead the typical cimmerean lavender, and his complexion not quite so pale. He was handsome, as cimmerean men were wont to be, and even from a young age, Aeris found herself to be quite attracted to him.

But at least Talemar felt the same way. She had been young when she lost her virginity, much younger than most other hinterlean females. It was something that just simply happened one day while she was in Talemar's company. She had just begun to come into her Talent, and Talemar had been assigned to help her along with her studies. What stared out as an innocent kiss ended up in mutual love-making. She never regretted what they had done, and she rather hoped he didn't either.

It had happened again only one other time after that, three or four years later. She was older then, and more able to understand the emotion that was behind the act. They agreed that they would not commit to one another, for Aeris felt that she wasn't ready for something like that, and she needed to keep her mind on her studies. The kiss they continued to share was customary . . . something that had become commonplace between them since they shared intimacy. Now, walking beside him, Aeris suddenly realized that nothing kept her from committing herself to Talemar. But the subject had not been broached, and she wondered if he even felt that way about her anymore. She thought that sometimes he did, but then there were other times that he was closed to her.

As Aeris and Talemar approached the library, her thoughts shifted to the mundane . . . like what type of book she wished to read this week. They entered the large room through the double doors constructed from the oak trees that made up the Silverwood. The library was large for a fledgling academy, many of the books having been donated by the man who had instructed all of the masters that taught there: Master Tallachienan.

Suddenly Aeris stopped. Thinking about Master TC made her pause, but for some reason, she didn't know why. There was something in her subconscious just beyond the reaches of her memory, some vague recollection she strove desperately to capture.

"Aeris, are you all right?"

She refocused her eyes to find Talemar standing before her, his hands on her arms and an expression of concern on his face. She smiled wanly. "Yes, I am fine."

Talemar grinned. "I didn't know where you were for a moment there. You looked so far away." He tapped the tip of her nose with an index finger.

Aeris swatted at his hand. "Pish, I just had a strange feeling, that's all."

Talemar nodded and released her arms. He had an unreadable expression on his face, and she found herself wishing that he was more accessible to her. She wondered if her interest was due to her recent revelation. She would have thought about it for a moment longer if Master Tridium had not entered the library. Aeris once more found her attention diverted, and thoughts of Talemar placed at the rear of her mind.

The cimmerean master smiled. "My dear Damaeris, It is good to see you." The woman embraced her warmly and then stepped back. "I hear you might accompany your brother to Entsy. I think it is a wonderful idea. It will be good for you go."

As always, Master Tridium spoke bluntly. Many apprentices found this quality to be a bit bothersome, but Aeris thought it rather refreshing. It was something that her mother had also appreciated from Tridium when the two studied together under Master Tallachienan.

Aeris felt Talemar's eyes on her as she nodded. He obviously had not heard about her leaving. "I will need you to get a few things for me while you are there. I will make a list and give it to you before you leave," said Master Tridium.

Aeris smiled inwardly. It was just like Tridium to assume people would do as she felt they should. Aeris had never let it bother her and found that the woman never seemed to hold it against her when Aeris didn't take her advice on things. As usual, Aeris didn't bother to correct her. It wasn't worth the disagreement that might ensue.

Master Tridium continued. "I need you to take something to your mother for me. It is from Myan. She will know what it is when you give it to her." The woman held a small blue leather pouch out to her. Aeris simply took the pouch and placed it within a larger one that hung from the sash around her waist. Master Myan had also studied with Adrianna during her apprenticeship with Master TC. The three of them were boon companions. As a girl, Aeris loved to hear the stories her mother had to tell. It was always so heartening to know that Adrianna had not been infallible . . . . capable of making the same type of silly mistakes that Aeris often found herself making.

A few years after their tenure with Tallachienan, the three friends one day found themselves once more within one another's company. Adrianna told them about the plans that she and Dinim had made to found their own school for the study of Dimensionalist magic. Tridium and Myan agreed to participate in the endeavor and before long they were naming it the Medubrokan Academy. King Thalios supplied the man-power and materials to build the school, and Master Tallachienan provided the fledgling masters with their first apprentices.

Aeris nodded. "I will give it to her when I see her this afternoon," she said. "And if not then . . ." She let her voice trail off when she felt a tremor beneath her feet. She had never felt anything like it before and her brows pulled into a frown. An expression of concern appeared on Master Tridium's face as they began to hear the rattling of the wall sconces and candelabras.

As the shake built in strength, Talemar took Aeris' arm to steady her. The three magic users knelt near the floor. Books could be heard falling from the shelves and Aeris winced when a loud crash resounded from somewhere else in the library. The freestanding bookcases stood solidly by, but Aeris couldn't help but glance at them fearfully. She imagined the wreckage that would ensue if they were to all begin to fall into one another, causing a cascading effect that would destroy many of the tomes and parchments. Not to mention, perhaps kill someone that might be taking refuge among them.

The shake continued. They could hear nothing of what could be going on outside the library. Then, just as Aeris began to wonder if it would ever end, the quaking stopped. The sudden silence was strange to behold. Slowly the three rose from the floor, and without speaking, began to make their way out of the library and out into the hallway. Others were also making their way into the corridors, and they began to congregate in small groups to discuss what had just occurred. Aeris was worried about things at the academy, but the most pressing concern was her family.

Almost as though she had read her mind, Master Tridium stopped Aeris with a hand on her shoulder. "You go home. I will see about everything here."

Aeris nodded as Talemar took her hand. Together they sprinted down the next corridor that would take them out of the school. She could only hope she would find that everyone was safe.

***

The man dreamed of a familiar place. The shadowed halls were made of stone, the rooms lavishly decorated, and the aura of the place tranquil. He heard voices whispering at the corners of his mind, speaking words that he could not quite capture. He felt the draw of the place . . . a massive citadel nestled within steep mountain crags. He could remember the feel of the cold wind on his face as he stood on the parapets of the highest tower, the smell of winter in his nostrils, and the sight of a barren landscape far below. The citadel was a place he could never forget. It was home . . .

The man felt a droplet of water on his brow, quickly followed by another. He cracked open his eyes, saw dark clouds moving overhead, and then heard a crack of thunder. He inhaled deeply and took in the scent of vegetation all around. Just as the rain started to become a downpour, the man sat upright. Cold, naked, and wet, he found himself in the middle of a field. Confused, he looked around himself and wondered, *Where the Hells am I?*

The man shivered as the cold water slicked his body and plastered the hair to his skull. He let out an explosive breath, the air escaping lips starting to become blue with the cold. He brought himself into a crouched position and then began to make his way slowly through the field. He poked his head above the tall vegetation only once, saw the house in the distance, and continued to move in that direction.

As the man neared the edge of the field, he slowed his movement and began to move with more caution. Before him was the house, a small one that a farmer would build for his family. Outside there were lines of clothing that had not been brought indoors before the rains came. Slowly making his way over to the lines, the man selected a shirt and trousers, pulled them from the line, and then readjusted the remaining clothing so that it appeared relatively undisturbed. He then made his way over to a small cart close by, settled himself behind it, and began to don the wet clothing. He struggled for a moment with the trousers, the wet fabric unwilling to slide up his legs, but he finally had both shirt and trousers in place.

The man huddled there behind the cart, his arms curved around him with his hands underneath. Puddles had begun to form upon the ground and he found himself staring into the one nearest him. The face that looked back at him was unfamiliar, the flesh so pale it seemed almost blue. The eyes were a deep shade of lavender and the hair was long and black. He smoothed a hand over the planes of his face, took in the angular jaw and the long nose. He then reached up to the tall pointed ear and fondled the engraved golden cusp that encircled the outer edge. He felt around the cusp, thinking to find the place where it could be detached. Finding none, he pulled at the object, hoping to remove it from his ear. Perhaps it would tell him something about himself, for he had begun to realize that he had no idea of his identity. Not only was his face unfamiliar, but he could not recall his own name. He neither knew where he was from, nor why he had awakened in the middle of a field with no clothes on.

The man pulled ineffectually at the cusp. He felt the area around it begin to object to the rough treatment, and after only a few moments longer, dropped his hand from the ear. *Damnation.* He felt the frustration rise within him. What had happened to him? Why couldn't he remember anything? Suddenly noticing that the rain was beginning to dissipate, he moved away from the cart. He would not approach the house for he was wary of people he did not know. Not only that, but he also did not know how the strangers would see him.

The man walked for what seemed to be a long time. He went through field after field, bypassing all of the houses. He had briefly considered approaching one, hoping to obtain some type of sustenance. His belly grumbled with hunger, and he could feel his energy waning. Yet, he could not bring himself to do so . . . some instinct within telling him he would find nothing but hardship.

However, the sun would soon begin its descent upon the horizon and a rumbling in the distance warned him of approaching rain. Darkness would fall and he would have no shelter. He cursed at himself as he strove to increase his pace. He should have gone to one of the houses he passed earlier . . . perhaps his fears were unfounded. At least then he would probably have a bit of bread to eat, and maybe even a slice of cheese.

Suddenly his foot caught upon something and he fell heavily to his knees. The man bit back a cry as a sharp rock pierced his left hand. As he pulled himself into a sitting position, he cradled the injured hand, sucking at the blood that flowed freely from the wound. He looked around for the thing that had tripped him, and his eyes finally settled onto an oddly shaped rock set into the ground. Crawling over to it, he saw that it was a grave marker, one that had been made for a baby. The boy child had died only a mere day after his birth, but his parents had given him a name: Magnus Larenchir.

The man felt his heart go out to the small boy who never had a chance at life. His parents must have loved him dearly to have had a grave stone made for him. Looking above the tall grasses, he saw no houses within his line of vision. The grave was alone out in the field. Crouching back down, he ran his fingers over the smooth face of the stone, marked only by the name carved into it. Magnus. Yes, it was a good name. He had no name of his own . . . at least none that he could recall. Perhaps he would take this one as his own in honor of the child who would have borne it had he lived past his first day.

Murmuring thanks to the spirit of the baby, Magnus stood and began to walk once more. He glanced at his hand and saw that the blood flow had ceased. More than anything else it was bruised, and it would heal in a couple of days' time. Again he heard the roar of thunder in the distance. It was closer this time, and the sky was beginning to darken. It was then that he saw a stone structure up ahead. It wasn't a house . . . it was much too large for one. Magnus hurried towards the shelter, and as he got closer he realized that it was a temple. As he approached, he looked around to see if anyone was there. He saw no one, and as he reached the temple, the first rains began to fall.

Magnus stood in the shelter of the wall for a few moments as he paused to consider his situation. He considered walking through the front doors of the establishment, but then rejected the idea. It would be better for him to continue to remain unknown. Slowly he began to walk around the periphery of the structure. It wasn't long before he found a set of doors in the ground. It was what he had been hoping for: a cellar. Wearily Magnus opened one of the doors. Stepping within, he began to walk down the stairs and closed the door behind him. He stopped to allow time for his eyes to acclimate to the darkness, and once they had done so, he walked deeper into the cellar. Against the walls there were crates of all shapes and sizes. The place was obviously used for storage. Along the far wall, he spied a door that he knew would lead into the temple proper. The cellar was small, but plenty large enough for him to find a spot to rest his tired body.

Magnus shuffled around in some of the crates, and finally finding what he was looking for, he took the worn, woolen blanket to a place he had noticed in between two large crates. He laid the blanket out on the floor and then settled himself onto it. He then wrapped the remainder of the fabric around his body. Despite the hunger gnawing at his belly, it wasn't long before he fell into sleep.

Magnus shuffled around in some of the crates. Finally finding what he was looking for, he took the worn, woolen blanket to a place he had noticed in between two large crates. He laid the blanket out on the floor and then settled himself onto it. He then wrapped the remainder of the fabric around his body. Despite the hunger gnawing at his belly, it wasn't long before he fell into sleep.

***

Pylarith wandered the dark halls of the citadel. They were empty . . . as empty as his soul since Tallachienan left. What had happened to his bond-mate, Pylar did not know. All he remembered was TC speaking incoherently . . . something about a mistake he had made and that his life was nothing except a chain of similar mistakes. He had then renounced his life, his lineage, and his power. When all was said and done, TC was gone in an intense flash of light. Pylar had suddenly felt his connection with the man severed and had been alone ever since. He knew that Tallachienan was not dead . . . despite the broken link, Pylar would have known it if he were. It was almost as though the link simply didn't exist, and he suddenly knew how Xebrinarth felt when Adrianna went back into her own time after meeting her bond-mate in the past.

Pylar's mind focused sluggishly. Adrianna. He hadn't seen her in such a long time. She had gone to meet her destiny, and instead of finding her demise like she had all of the Cycles before, Adrianna and her comrades persevered over the dread Deathmage, Aasarak. By the gods, that had been decades ago, and so much had happened since then. She had come to the citadel once or twice, but her visits were always brief. Pylar always figured that it had much to do with her family, for she had borne her husband a son not long after Aasrak's defeat.

Pylar smiled wryly to himself. Yes, Adrianna had birthed a son . . . but nothing had been more surprising to him than the discovery of another son sired by Dinim Coabra. Right from the start, there was no doubt as to the boy's parentage, for Talemar had the same streak of silver running through his hair. The boy had simply shown up at the doorstep one day, accompanied by a travel-weary priest. The priest informed Dinim that the boy's mother had died not long ago of an incurable malady, and that she had informed him of Talemar's parentage before her passing. The priest had been searching for Dinim for quite some time, and was glad to finally fulfill his last obligation to the mother.

Dinim knew that Talemar was his, but he had no recollection of the tryst that may have resulted in such a child. He asked the priest the identity of the mother, and when he heard Sharra's name, the memories had come rushing back. Dinim met the woman a few years ago just after leaving TC's citadel as a journeyman. They had been instantly attracted to one another and shared several nights together before Dinim left Sangrilak. Talemar was obviously the result of their union.

However, there was more to the story than just that. Upon learning Sharra's name, Adrianna and Sheridana conducted a search for their mother's sister who went by the same name. When they realized that it was the same woman, they were slightly taken aback. Not only did Dinim have a son of which he had no prior knowledge, but that son was related to them by blood.

It wasn't long after that Sirion left Elvandahar on a mission to discover the new power behind the Daemundai. With him went Sorn, Dartanyen,

Triath, and Adria's brother, Gareth. While he was gone, Adrianna and Dinim continued to build the school that they would later dedicate to dimensional magic. Tridium and Myan left the citadel in order to pursue the opportunity to teach other young Talents at the new academy. Pylar felt nothing but pride when they left, and he knew that TC secretly felt the same way.

Pylar sighed wearily. Now TC was gone, and he had no idea what he should do with himself. Coaxtl had already taken matters under his control at the citadel, delegating responsibilities to the other masters that resided there. The apprentices' studies were continuing in the absence of TC, and all was going smoothly. He told Pylar to go in search of his bond-mate, but Pylar had been unable to bring himself to leave just yet, harboring the hope that TC would return.

Two days went by and Pylar had begun to realize that his hopes would not become a reality. Until now, he had wondered where he should go first in his search for TC, and he berated himself for not thinking of her right away. Adrianna would surely be able to find his bond-mate. And if she couldn't do it, there was little hope that anyone could.

***

Magnus awoke to the sound of voices. His eyes shot open, and he quickly looked around himself in order to get his bearings. Then he remembered where he was . . . in an old cellar beneath a temple. He rose from his place on the floor, taking note that the door he had noticed the night before was slightly ajar. Cautiously he made his way over to the stairs and then up to the door. Just as he was about to put out a hand to touch it, the door swung open.

Magnus stumbled back away from the door as he heard a curse issued from the human man who stood on the other side. He was clothed in nondescript brown robes and his silvering brown hair was cropped short against his head. With a hand to his chest, the man considered Magnus standing in the stairwell for a moment before he spoke. "By the gods man . . . have you no care for an old priest? You almost startled the life right out of me."

Magnus regarded the man solemnly. He had noticed the guarded expression in the man's eyes before he spoke, belying the lighthearted tone he gave his voice. But he had made a decision, a quick one made simply upon first impression alone. The man had sensed nothing threatening from Magnus and had chosen affability over enmity. Magnus didn't understand why the man had been compelled to make such a decision in the first place, but he accepted it. "My dear sir, I deeply apologize. I had no idea you approached on the other side of the door."

The priest raised a dark eyebrow. "Son, what may I ask are you doing in the cellar?"

Magnus shrugged nonchalantly. "I had no place to go, and the cellar looked as good as any."

"Why didn't you approach through the front door? We would have admitted you for the night."

Magnus gave the priest a piercing glance. "Would you?"

The question was loaded and the priest knew it. However, hesitating for only a moment the other man replied. "I have no doubt."

Magnus nodded. For some reason, he trusted this man. There was a goodness that emanated from him, and Magnus began to foster the hope that perhaps this priest could help him.

The priest stood aside and beckoned into the corridor that stretched behind him. "Please, come up from there. We have a bath to offer, as well as a proper bed."

Magnus nodded once again, and he took the last few stairs through the door. The priest began to lead him down the corridor, talking amiably as he walked. "My name is Cassius . . . Brother Cassius. What may I call you, son?"

Magnus hesitated for only a moment. "Magnus. You can call me Magnus."

The priest nodded. "That is a good name . . . strong and distinctive."

Magnus concurred. "I think so."

The priest stopped at a door and opened it. "Here, you can have this room for a day or two. I will have a bath brought, as well as a hot meal. Then perhaps we can talk for a while."

Magnus inclined his head. "I thank you for your kindness. I didn't expect it."

The man smiled warmly. "I am pleased to have been able to surprise you."

Magnus continued. "I would like to attend any worship services you have planned for today so that I may offer my thanks to your god as well."

A stricken expression passed over Brother Cassius' face. Then he shook his head. "I am afraid it would do no good."

"What do you mean?" asked Magnus.

"Our high priests have bidden us not to speak of it, but you might as well know what is happening." Brother Cassius paused for a moment before he continued. "It seems that our gods have deserted us. It isn't just one or two . . . but all of them. Priests and clerics all over Shandahar have lost their power."

Magnus silently digested the information, instantly realizing the ramifications of an event such as this. Priests and clerics obtained their power through blessings given by their god or goddess of worship. The more experienced, skilled, and faithful the priest or cleric, the more power was bestowed upon them. Without their power, priests would not be able to perform one of their most important tasks . . . healing the sick and critically wounded. People would be forced to rely only upon more mundane methods to tend to the ill, making intimate knowledge of herbal lore that much more important.

Magnus shook his head. "I am sorry to hear about that. I wish there was something I could do to help."

Brother Cassius shook his head. "Pray for us. With so many prayers, perhaps they will begin to listen again and once more bestow their blessings upon us."

Magnus inclined his head. "I will indeed pray and hope that it makes a difference."

The priest nodded his head. "Come, make yourself comfortable. After you have bathed and eaten we will talk more."

Magnus nodded and entered the room. Brother Cassius closed the door behind him. Magnus looked around and when his gaze settled onto the bed, his body went over to it upon its own accord. Truth be told, he had not slept well last night upon the hard stone floor. The bed was inviting, and when he laid his body upon it, he sighed deeply with contentment. When Cassius returned, he would speak with the priest about his dilemma. Perhaps the priest would be able to help him and if he could not, at least direct Magnus to someone who could. Magnus settled himself deep into the pallet. He then promptly fell asleep.

CHAPTER 4

4 Jicaren CY632

Damaeris rolled her eyes as she listened to Tigerius. It was obvious he thought much too highly of himself. He was a rake and a scoundrel, and Aeris pitied the women who fell to his nefarious charms. There had even been a time or two when he had directed those charms towards her, but she quickly put a halt to that, letting him know that there was no chance there could be anything but simple friendship between them.

Much to her dismay, Alasdair found it all quite amusing. He listened interestedly as Tigerius spoke of his exploits. He even seemed to enjoy the raunchy stories the other man told. Once again, Aeris rolled her eyes. It seemed that she was destined to constantly be in the company of men. There were her brothers of course, and then her cousin, Cedric, the son of her mother's sister. Here was Tigerius, the son of her parents' good friends, Triath and Tianna Solanar, and then there was Talemar, the son of Master Dinim. He had been raised almost as her brother, and she knew him just as well. But Tigerius . . . he was a man she almost didn't want to know at all. He was recondian, with brown hair and blue eyes. She supposed Tiger was handsome; he had many of his father's features, and Triath was quite an attractive man, even for a human of his years. However, it seemed that Triath didn't age as other humans. He was at least sixty-three, but didn't look a year past thirty. The same could be said for his wife, Tianna.

"So what do you think, Aeris?"

She turned her head to look at Alasdair. She hadn't realized that he was speaking to her until he asked her the question.

"Think about what?"

Alasdair frowned. "You know . . . about talking to the caravan master to be a guardsman."

Aeris shrugged and pretended she knew what her brother was talking about. "Sure. I suppose so."

"Most likely, it will put us back a couple of weeks. We won't be home until the middle of Decaren at the least."

Aeris shrugged again. "I think Ama and Babu will be able to live another few weeks without us."

Alasdair grinned. "It's good to have the old Aeris back again."

Aeris smiled back and nodded. She turned back to her own thoughts as the men began to make their plans. Alasdair saw only what was on the outside. She struggled to constantly put forth a brave front, when sometimes all she wanted to do was run away and hide. She was reticent to follow her brother about the countryside like this, but she knew that she couldn't stay home forever. In Elvandahar she was stagnating, and life seemed to have ceased carrying purpose for her there.

So she chose to accompany Alasdair to Entsy. The initial plan was to go to Sangrilak, but a few days before their journey, Alasdair had received a message from Tigerius telling them that he was in Entsy. So they went there instead, a much shorter journey than the one to Sangrilak. Despite his shortcomings, Aeris had enjoyed visiting their friend. Now that there was talk of a job, Alasdair was excited. He wanted to hone his skills. He had been offered a position as a ranger in Elvandahar, but like Aeris, Alasdair felt that he needed to branch away from his homeland. The wanderlust seemed to be in their blood, much as it had been for their father and mother in their earlier days, and it refused to be denied.

The threesome made it back to the Golden Griffon Inn. Aeris would stay there until the men had returned from their meeting with the caravan master. Then they would partake of the evening meal together. Aeris didn't mind staying at the inn. She had some books that she brought with her from the Medubrokan Academy, and she had yet to find the chance to read any of them.

Aeris settled down on the veranda outside of the inn. She reached up to finger the crystal that hung from a short golden chain around her neck. Sometimes she imagined that it felt warm against her skin. It was something Adrianna had given to her when she was yet but a child. She wore it often, for not only was it beautiful, but it reminded her of her mother. For a while she read one of the books she had brought with her from Elvandahar, but it wasn't long before she found herself watching the people who passed by in the street.

The population of Entsy was well diversified, much like Sangrilak. It was home to humans, faelin, and halfen alike. The highest percentage seemed to be made up of recondians. They were the prominent human race that tended to make up this part of the continent. Most of the faelin were of terralean heritage. Unlike hinterlean and savanlean faelin, they tended to be less particular about where they made their homes. They didn't seem to mind living in villages, towns, and cities that were built by humans. And the halfen . . . well, many of them tended to stay for only a portion of the year. They preferred to return to the hills or mountains of their birth during the winter months, and then returned in the spring with minerals and gems they had mined during the time they were gone. The only ones who stayed were those who owned smithies and had an income coming to them all year around.

Inconspicuously, Aeris watched the passerby. Most of the people seemed to be quite ordinary. But then she saw him . . . a cimmerean man. Outside of her sphere of influence, she didn't see many of those. They tended towards the dark arts, and more than once Master Dinim had warned her to stay away from them. When she was younger, she had thought that rather odd. Dinim was a cimmerean himself, and she could scarcely understand that he was different than most. But now, looking at this man, she thought that perhaps she need not be wary.

Aeris watched the man as he walked down the street. He wore simple tunic and trousers, and a nondescript belt circled his lean waist. Upon the belt was hung a variety of pouches and a dagger. She thought that, most likely, he was a spell-caster. Within the pouches, he would carry his spell components.

However, spell-casters continued to be relatively uncommon. Most people viewed them in a more unsavory light, unaccustomed to the Talent needed to be a good sorcerer. The more common term for a spell-caster was a warlock, or in the female sense, a witch. People tended to distrust that which was unfamiliar, and despite the rise in those who stepped forward to claim some degree of Talent, many people continued to view them unfavorably.

The cimmerean man looked up at the inn as he approached. He caught Aeris' gaze and their eyes locked. His gait seemed to slow as he neared the building, all of his attention now focused upon her. Only momentarily, Aeris thought about breaking eye contact. Mesmerized, she continued to watch him as he passed. He was handsome, very much so. His black hair swept back from his face and was held at the nape of his neck by a strip of leather. His face was finely chiseled, and his lips flawlessly sculpted. Beneath his clothing, she could only imagine that he was perfect in all of his masculinity.

The man turned his head as he passed. For only a moment longer their eyes remained locked, but then he finally looked away as he continued down the street. Aeris continued to stare at him as he moved farther away, wondering about him. What brought a cimmerean to the city of Entsy?

Aeris was still pondering the man as Alasdair and Tigerius returned from their meeting with the caravan master. They seemed happy, and she knew that the news must be favorable. Aeris gave them her full attention as they told her that they had both been hired to guard the caravan as it made its way towards a village at the northern tip of the Sheldomar Forest. Knowing her geography, Aeris realized that it must be the small village of Grunchin, located just outside of the forest before one reached the city of Andahye. Of course, not many knew of the location of that city, it being the seat of arcane knowledge in western Shandahar. However, Aeris considered herself one of the privileged few.

"The caravan is leaving the morning after tomorrow. Gharlas, the caravan master, gave his permission for you to travel with us. We will need to stock up on supplies before we leave."

Aeris nodded. "I will send a message to Ama and Babu tomorrow morning. Then we will get supplies for the larian."

Alasdair nodded. "We will leave the planning up to you." He paused before he continued. "Come on. Let's get something to eat. The evening meal is just starting to be served."

Aeris rose from her spot on the veranda, already having forgotten about the cimmerean man. She followed her brother into the inn behind Tigerius. She was nervous about the journey, but she trusted Alasdair. In his care, she knew that nothing could ever happen to her.

***

Adrianna walked out into the courtyard of the Medubrokan Academy. She smiled a greeting at Xebrinarth, who awaited her there in order to fly her home. Climbing upon the leg he offered, she settled herself upon the golden back of her dragon bond-mate. She fastened the harness about her upper thighs and the belt around her waist. It would aid in keeping her astride his broad back . . . keep her from slipping upon the smooth scales. The dragon knew when she was ready, and he was aloft within moments. As always, the scenery was beautiful. As they flew over the silvery treetops, she reveled in the experience and felt blessed to be able to share such moments with him.

Upon the back of a dragon, it took Adrianna only a fraction of the time it would ordinarily take to reach her home. On foot, it would take a seasoned ranger at least two days. With Xebrin, it took only an hour. She looked forward to seeing her husband after a long day spent with her apprentices. It would be even better if her children were there, but Asgenar had returned to the Sherkari Fortress, and Alasdair and Aeris were taking a trip to Sangrilak. It was Aeris' first foray from home after the ill-fated expedition that took the lives of her dearest friend and their escort. Despite her misgivings, Adria ultimately knew that her daughter was safe in the hands of her older brother. Hopefully they would be home well before the cold season.

Shifting her thoughts away from her own family, Adrianna decided to ask Xebrin about his own. He hadn't seen Saranath and Mordrexith for quite some time, and she wondered how everything fared amongst them. Sensing the questions in her mind, Xebrinarth answered before she could form them into words. *They are fine. I am in contact with them often.*

What of your son? How is he?

Adrianna heard a rumble of laughter. *As well as Mordrex's sons and daughters. My friend is a good father to my son.*

And Sara a good mother.

Indeed, a very good one. Xebrin replied.

Mordrexith and Saranath must be very happy together.

Adrianna felt the negative before she heard it. *Not as happy as I am with you.*

Yet they have children together and share a good life.

But they are not bond-mates. Neither will know the happiness that I possess until they have found their own. Xebrin paused and then continued. *They envy me of that.*

Yet, Mordrex cares for your son as though he was his own?

Mordrex is a wonderful friend. I couldn't ask for any better.

Adrianna paused before speaking what was on her mind. She withheld it from Xebrinarth, closing her thoughts to him. Through the years, she had realized that her mind need not be an open book, and she had learned to control the thoughts that were transmitted to him through their link.

You know that I would not mind it if you went to them. I would miss you abominably, but you have a responsibility to your offspring and the drenna who is his mother.

Adrianna felt Xebrinarth focus his full attention upon her. *I have told you before, Zahara . . . you are my primary responsibility. I am fortunate that I have Mordrexith to see to my son. However, I would not shirk my responsibility to you. Not to mention that I would be a wretched mess without you near.*

Adrianna grinned to herself. Of course, Xebrin knew that Sirion would protect her with his life. The two of them had actually formed quite a friendship over the past years. Then, sensing a sudden shift in Xebrinarth's demeanor, Adrianna attuned herself to the surrounding environment. He was suddenly on the alert, his senses searching the area ahead.

There is another dragon here.

Is it one we know?

Xebrinarth paused. *I am not sure. His signature seems familiar to me, but I do not know where I have encountered it before.*

Silence reigned as Xebrinarth carried her the rest of the way back to the home that Sirion had made for Adrianna and their children. It was far removed from many of the other daladins in the village of Safranim, for Xebrinarth needed to have his space. Even though the dragon did not take up residence there, he visited often enough that a sizable area around the daladin was needed in order to sustain his presence. And now there was another dragon there, one who had enough presence of mind to condense into his faelin form. Xebrinarth flew down through a break in the canopy and landed beside the daladin, kicking up only minimal leaf litter as his feet touched the ground. He stood upon his hind legs next to the daladin so Adrianna could step off onto the balcony that circled the premises. She alighted from Xebrinarth's back, using the foreleg that her bond-mate proffered for her. Through the link that she maintained with him, she could sense the strong presence of the other dragon. She walked across the balcony to the other side of the daladin, and when she turned the corner, she was met with a most unexpected guest. The dragon was Pylar.

Adrianna felt her eyes widen with surprise. Through their link, Adria could feel that Xebrin's surprise equaled her own. "Pylar, what are you doing here?" Even as she formed the question, her mind was jumping to conclusions. Yes, what would Pylar be doing at her doorstep? He would only be there if . . .

Sudden fear swept through her, and Adrianna drew her brows into a frown. "What has happened? Where is Master Tallachienan?"

"Adria . . . I didn't know where else to go."

Adrianna rushed to her friend and enveloped him in an embrace. Her heart beat a staccato rhythm in her chest, making her suddenly lightheaded. If something had happened to TC . . . "Pylar, tell me what has happened."

He pulled back and looked her in the eyes. "To be honest, I am not sure. Those last few weeks he wasn't himself. He was sullen and withdrawn . . . much worse than I had ever seen him before. He started to block me out, and the only time I could reach him was when he was in the deepest of sleep. Then one day it happened. There was a flash of brilliant light and I heard him scream. The sound of it reverberated through my mind, rendering me immobilized. I couldn't get to him in time. When the light was gone, so was Tallachienan."

Adrianna simply stared at the faelin man before her. His eyes were wide and his complexion paler than she always remembered it to be. His thick red hair made for a disheveled crown and had been haphazardly pulled back at the nape of his neck. A makeshift travel pack leaned against the wall of the daladin . . . at least Pylar had the presence of mind to bring one.

The dragon solemnly regarded the woman before him. He had not seen Adrianna in many years . . . more than he cared to count. She looked the same as he always remembered . . . dark brown eyes framed by a face of pristine beauty. Her long pale blonde hair curled upon her shoulders and down her back. Even her figure remained unchanged despite the three children, two sons and a daughter, which she had carried in her womb.

Pylar blinked back the vestiges of his grim reality. It was after Aeris' departure that TC ultimately began his decline. Almost immediately after sending her away, the sorcerer realized that he may have a made a grave mistake. He meant well when he erased her memories of her stay at the citadel; however, it was a serious breach of trust. Not only that, but he had recognized something her . . . that she wad the soul-mate whom he had been searching for all of his life. At one time, that woman may have been Adrianna. However, once meeting Aeris, TC realized that it had always been Adria's destiny to give life to his true partner.

Pylar sighed inwardly. That was a part of the story that he could not divulge to his old friend. He could only imagine the turmoil Adria would suffer if she knew that the Master who had once seduced her had also bedded her daughter. He hated to keep the information to himself, but he saw no other way. It would be even more difficult when he saw Aeris herself. They had become friends during her stay at the citadel and he would have to pretend that he did not know her.

Finally Adrianna spoke again. "When did this happen?"

Pylar frowned and shrugged. "I waited for a few days to see if TC would return. When he did not, Coaxtl decided that he would stay behind at the citadel while I came to see you."

Adrianna shook her head. "Why didn't you go to the academy? Dinim is there."

The frown eased away from Pylar's face and his features softened. "I wanted to see you first."

Adrianna felt her lower lip begin to tremble. "I have missed you, old friend."

Pylar gave her a crooked grin. "I know."

She embraced him again, her mind swirling with uncertainty. Yet, despite the circumstances of his arrival, she was happy to see Pylar again. Finally she pulled away and then bent down to pick up the travel sack. She put it over her arm and led him to the front of the daladin. "You must come inside. You look thin. After a good rest, you should go and hunt with Xebrin. Tomorrow we can go to see Dinim."

Pylar followed behind obediently. This is what he needed. Adrianna would take care of him and then help find Tallachienan. Strangely, Pylar still could not reach the man through the link they once shared. Even now, it was a though the connection had been severed. Never before had he heard the likes of it; however, there were very few dragons throughout history who had formed attachments with faelin. However, he had faith in Adrianna. The woman would not rest until TC was recovered.

***

Just that morning, the caravan left the city of Entsy, traveling north across the steppes. It was a beautiful day; the sun shining high overhead, and the breeze ample. At this time of year, the climate was neither too hot nor too cold, and it was perfect for travelers.

Aeris rode her larian amongst the wagons of the train. His color was a pale blond, the lightest she had ever seen. His spiked mane was white, as was the tuft of hair at the tip of his long, sinuous tail. The beast was young and spirited. He pranced with high steps despite her attempts to make him feel at ease.

It took Aeris a while to realize she was being watched. Once the larian was relatively quieted, she started glancing around. After a moment her gaze came to rest upon the nearest wagon. Inside, sitting with his legs hanging over the back, was the cimmerean man she had noticed the other evening from her spot upon the veranda of the Golden Griffon Inn. He was watching her handle the larian with avid interest. Their eyes met and locked, much as they had that evening a couple of nights before.

After a moment, Aeris spoke the first words that came to her mind. The silence was disquieting, and the larian beneath her beginning to react to the shift in her demeanor. "What? Haven't you ever seen a woman ride an untrained larian before?"

The man shook his head. "Not really."

Aeris furrowed her brows into a frown. "Is that a 'no' or don't you know?"

The man cleared his throat. "No. I mean . . . that is a no. I have never seen a woman train a young larian before." He looked away from her then, obviously embarrassed.

Aeris immediately felt badly about having put him on the spot. "My name is Aeris. My brother is one of the guardsmen for the caravan." She gestured towards the leading wagon. Alasdair was on scouting duty, and Tigerius was riding somewhere along the the train, leaving her to her own devices.

The man nodded. "I am Magnus." Then he paused before continuing. "I didn't mean to stare. I'm sorry."

Aeris shook her head. "No. You did nothing wrong. I'm just not used to . . ." She paused then, knowing what she was going to say, but suddenly thinking better of it. She didn't wish to make him feel more uncomfortable then he did already. "I'm just not used to an audience," she improvised.

Magnus nodded towards the larian. "You are good with him."

Aeris chuckled. "They told me that, with my abilities, I should be a druid." She shrugged her shoulders. "But, I'm not so sure the highly restrictive lifestyle of the Order is the right thing for me."

"Who is 'they'," he asked.

Aeris smiled. "Friends and family from home."

"And where might this home be?"

"The village of Sefranim in the realm of Elvandahar."

Magnus nodded and said nothing more. She wondered why he was so curious about her, but then quickly decided that it was simply because it was something to talk about. "And where are you from," she asked.

When Aeris saw the expression that passed over Magnus' face, she wished she hadn't inquired. After a few moments he answered her. "I don't know. Something happened to me, and I can't remember."

Immediately, Aeris felt sympathy for the man. He seemed to have suffered much the same way as did she. "I understand how you must feel. I have been through something similar to that myself."

Magnus shook his head. "I remember nothing from my life, including my own name. Magnus is just a name I thought of when I awoke up in the middle of nowhere."

Aeris swallowed heavily. It appeared that his situation was much more severe than her own. "You can't remember anything at all?"

Magnus shook his head. "All I know is that I have . . . abilities. They come to me when I least expect it."

Aeris knew to what abilities he referred. He was a spell-caster, and as such, had a certain amount of Talent. Despite his inability to remember, his subconscious was still able to draw on that Talent. However, she said nothing to him about it. He would reveal more information when he was ready. He probably wondered if he could trust her. Aeris grinned to herself. She was thinking the same thing about him.

Aeris felt the twitch in the larian's withers before he began to misbehave once again. She struggled for a moment to bring him back in line, the iridescent scales beneath his pale fur shimmering in the sun. Finally, she had him well in hand. Aeris turned back to find Magnus grinning at her. Feeling herself suddenly captivated, she felt a rush of familiarity. It tugged at the fringes of her consciousness for a moment, but then it was gone.

"When you are ready for a break, you are more than welcome to share the space next to me on the back of this wagon," he said.

Aeris nodded and returned his smile. "I'll keep that in mind." She then nudged the fractious larian forward. The animal wanted to move faster, burn some of the energy trapped within him. She could sense it simmering deep within him, ready to spew forth. She would give the young larian what he wanted, and then return to the friend she hoped she had found in the handsome cimmerean man.

***

Aeris cast a sidelong glance at her brother. She knew that something was amiss with him, but didn't know what. She thought that it must have something to do with her, for he had been rather short with her as of late. She thought about an attempt to pry the information from him, but then thought better of that idea. She knew what would happen if she tried to get Alasdair to talk before he was ready. His temper usually got the better of him, and he didn't need a display of that, especially now when he wanted to impress the caravan master.

For three days they had slowly made their way across the steppes. On the morrow, they would reach the city of Driscol, the caravan master having decided to make a stop there before going to Grunchin. Another day or so after that, they would reach the outskirts of the Sheldomar Forest. They would then travel the eastern periphery of the woodland. The caravan was too large to simply pass straight through, not to mention that the inhabitants would be none too happy about the intrusion. Another two or three days later, they would finally reach their destination. From there, Magnus would continue to Andahye. He had told her of his desire to reclaim his memory, and how the priests in Sangrilak suggested he go there. They had noticed his propensity for magic. Their hope was that one of the masters in Andahye would recognize him and help him to regain what had been lost.

Aeris stood from her spot near the evening fire. There was still some light, but the night was fast approaching. She would go sit with Magnus for a while before she went to bed. Just as she was about to move away, Alasdair stepped in front of her. "Where are you going?"

Aeris frowned. "Not far." She gestured in the direction of Magnus' campfire. "Just a few campfires away."

Alasdair leaned in close to her, pitching his voice to a low growl. "What the Hells do you think you're doing?"

Aeris' frown deepened. "Making a friend. I enjoy his companionship. I get lonely during the day, and he keeps me company."

Alasdair swept his arm to encompass the entire caravan. "Are there not plenty of other people here with whom you could have chosen to make friendship?"

Aeris planted her hands on her hips. "Magnus is just fine. I don't need any other friends."

Alasdair scowled. "What is it with you and cimmerean men?"

Aeris raised an eyebrow. "What do you mean by that?"

"You know very well what I mean."

"That's not fair. I told you the relationship between Talemar and I in the strictest of confidence. You can't throw that in my face."

"Aeris, you have a history. Talemar is a good man, but this Magnus guy . . . I don't know him."

Aeris waved her hand in the direction of Magnus' fire. "So, go and meet him then," she said with an irritated tone.

Alasdair shook his head. "It doesn't matter. I still think you should stay away from him. Cimmereans are trouble."

Aeris sighed heavily. "That's not fair. You could give him the benefit of the doubt."

"Alasdair's voice was steady. "No. He is a cimmerean, and I don't want you near him. Do you understand?"

Aeris ground her teeth, felt the anger building inside her. "You are not my keeper. I will see whomever I choose."

"You are my responsibility, and you will do as I say. Get in the wagon." Alasdair pointed commandingly.

Aeris pressed her lips into a thin line. She whirled away from him and made towards the wagon. Next to it, her larian was tethered. Before Alasdair realized what she was doing, she had released the knot and was swinging up onto the animal's back.

"Aeris, where the Hells do you think you're going?" She heard Alasdair shout as she cantered past. "Aeris, stop."

She urged the larian into a gallop and rode away from the caravan, Alasdair's voice fading behind her. He was not half the rider she was, and would struggle with the tether before he freed his own larian in order to pursue her. Tigerius was the one who would have had any chance at catching her, but he had chosen to take his meal at another campfire.

Aeris rode about a zacrol away from the confines of the caravan. She relished the feel of the wind through her hair, the press of her legs around the power of the larian, and the scent of the prairie all around. Securing the ropes beneath her thighs, Aeris raised her hands to the sky. She felt free, suddenly realizing there was no where else on Shandahar that she would rather be. She had been a caged animal in Elvandahar, trapped by events that took the lives of her comrades, followed by the loss of her memory. Until this moment, she had been unable to reclaim herself. But now . . . *Here I am. This is me. There is nowhere else in the world I would rather be* . . . Perhaps this could be a new start for her and she could finally learn to forget.

Aeris once more took up the ropes, slowing her mount to a canter, and then a trot. She knew that she needed to turn around and head back, for the sun was quickly setting over the horizon. The first moon, Steralion, was already beginning her ascent. The pale orb would offer some semblance of light as the sky darkened to night. She turned the larian and started to head back to the caravan. As her anger cooled, she realized that Alasdair was merely looking out for her well-fare. He cared about her and didn't want to see her meet any misfortune. But Aeris was not a child anymore. Sometimes he just needed to have a little bit of faith and believe in her judgment. Magnus had passed all of her mental tests. He was not out to harm her. He was genuine and needed a friend just as much as did she.

Suddenly, Aeris heard a sound. She jerked her head around to see that she had been so wrapped up in her thoughts, she hadn't realized what was happening until it was too late. She was surrounded by caravan raiders, and it appeared that they had decided to accost her on their way to their final destination. They were recondian, and all rode lloryk, the larger cousins to the larian that faelin tended to ride. The one in the front aimed his cross-bow at her, the bolt ready to be cast. She immediately sat back on her larian, and he came to a halt. Despite the tension that had suddenly beset her body, the animal was calm beneath her.

Eleven raiders regarded her intently. They were all dressed in plain tunic and trousers, each man carrying a cross-bow over his shoulder. Aeris struggled to remain calm. She didn't want to alarm her larian; she had enough with which to contend without the added pressure of keeping him in control. Despite her earlier anger, she hoped that her brother had chosen to follow her. She was no fool . . . the chances of her escaping this encounter were slim to none.

As unobtrusively as possible, Aeris began to cast her spell. She hoped that they had very little knowledge of magic-users and that they would not know what she was about until it was too late. She was aware that she had very little time . . . knew that they meant to kill her before they proceeded to the caravan. Either that, or they would incapacitate her for their base pleasures at a later time. Regardless, she knew that she had to act.

However, the leader knew that she was up to something. He let his bolt fly, and it hit her in the chest near her right shoulder. Disrupting her spell, the force of the bolt took her off of the larian, and she fell to the ground with a soft thud. The animal reared on his hind legs and sprinted across the plains back to the caravan. Aeris could only hope that his appearance there without her would alarm her brother and bring him before she succumbed to the raiders.

Despite the pain, Aeris began to cast the first offensive spell that came to her mind. It was *Flamesphere,* the most destructive spell she had at her disposal that required the least amount of concentration. The crossbow bolt had gone straight through, and the tip protruded from her other side. She ached to tear it out of her chest, but she refrained from doing so, knowing that the blood loss would be all the greater.

Just as she completed the spell, the second bolt went flying past where she lay on the ground. Then there was a third. The fourth found its mark just above the first one. By the gods, she was relieved that none of the raiders were better marksmen, for she could easily be dead by now. The *Flamesphere* slammed into the raiders, and she heard the screams of the men and their lloryk within the brief conflagration. She slumped onto her side, knowing more than ever that her time was limited. The pain was excruciating, and she knew that she would not be able to muster the concentration required for another spell.

The flames subsided, and through the billowing smoke rode the leader of the raiders. His clothes were charred from the *Flamesphere*, as were his arms and the hair on his head. He cantered towards her, drawing his sword from the sheath across his back. He raised it high overhead, and a battle cry issued from between his lips. Aeris steeled herself for the blow that she was sure would come. Her labored breathing became loud in her ears until it was all that she could hear. The raider bore down upon her, and just as the lloryk's cloven hooves were close enough to trample her, another rider appeared.

The periphery of Aeris' vision began to go dark just as she saw Tigerius enter the scene. Following him were Alasdair and Magnus. In her mind, she felt some measure of relief. Yet, the darkness pressed in around her until her vision grayed into black. Then there were only the sounds of battle. She listened for only a moment until her mind slipped into oblivion . . .

***

Aeris awoke to the feeling of pain in her left side. She was cold, and despite the furs that covered her, she shivered with the air against whatever skin was exposed. She shifted uncomfortably and then felt the pain in her shoulder, excruciating pain that made her groan deep in her throat. She opened her eyes into slits and found herself in a wagon. Through the cracks in the drape that covered the back, Aeris could see that it was dark outside.

Suddenly there was someone there kneeling beside her. A hand imposed itself beneath her head, and it lifted her to meet the cup that she felt pressed at her lips. Aeris drank thirstily of the water, and when she was through, she was allowed to lay her head back down on the pillow.

The hand then moved from the back of her head to her brow. It swept away the hair that stuck there, and it was then that Aeris realized she was damp. She opened her eyes a bit wider and blurredly took in the shape of the person sitting beside her. It was none other than her brother, Alasdair. "Wha . . . what is wrong with me?"

"Shhh." Alasdair put a finger to his lips and leaned close to her. "Your fever is breaking. Thank the gods you will be all right. We thought that the infection would be the end of you. Now rest. Tomorrow we will talk."

Aeris nodded. Already her eyelids were heavy. She closed them and fell asleep to the feel of her brother's hand at her forehead, pulling his fingers gently through her long hair. He had remembered how she always liked that . . .

Aeris once more awoke. She could tell that it was daytime, the sunlight streaming through the sides of the thick fabric drape that shut her away from the outside. She shifted on the pallet upon which she lay, and again felt the horrible pain in her shoulder. But it was not as bad a before, and she slowly reached her hand up to touch it. Beneath her fingertips she felt only bandages.

Aeris sighed and returned the hand to her side. By the gods, how many more times would she become injured before people realized she was a liability and keep her home?

"Aeris, are you awake?"

She turned her head to the sound of the voice, immediately recognizing it as belonging to Magnus. She smiled when she saw him moving closer to her, a mug in his hands. "Here, drink this. It will give you the energy you need to heal."

With his hand behind her head, Aeris drank the milk, still warm from the body of the tobey from which it had come. Magnus then situated the pillows so that she could sit upright. He helped her, and despite the pain, she endured until she was in a semi-upright position.

Aeris shook her head. "What are you doing here?"

Magnus grinned. "Don't you know? You are in my wagon. Alasdair brought you here after the skirmish."

Aeris frowned. "What skirmish? I . . ." Then she remembered. Because of her foolishness, Alasdair had been forced to come after her. Magnus must have accompanied him, as well as Tigerius, for she remembered all three of them laying siege to her attackers as she lay helplessly on the ground.

Aeris turned away from him. "Oh. Now I remember. Alasdair must really hate me right now."

Magnus shook his head. "He is only happy that you are alive. The wound to your shoulder became infected. We thought we had lost you. Without a healer here to help, we could only wait until we reached Driscol before we could find someone up to the task. And even then nothing was definite. Priests and clerics all over Shandahar have lost their power, not just those in Sangrilak and Entsy. They had to rely on more mundane means to bring healing to you."

Aeris then tuned back to Magnus. "How did he . . . I mean . . . how did you . . ."

Magnus grinned. "When I saw that you were in trouble and that Alasdair meant to go after you alone, I called him a fool. I then followed him, accompanied by your friend, Tigerius. Together we defeated the raiders. A few of them escaped with their tails between their legs, but most were not so fortunate. Alasdair brought you to this wagon, for there were too many who shared the one in which you kept your travel supplies. It even seems that, over the past few days, he has come to trust me."

Aeris nodded. "Thank you. You needn't have gone through all of this trouble."

Magnus gave her a strange look. "What are you talking about? You are my friend. It is no trouble. Even if it was, I do not require your thanks. This is what friends are for."

Aeris felt herself becoming tired and she slumped sideways. Magnus helped her to settle back down into a supine position, and then pulled some blankets over her. "I am glad you're here," she said.

"It is my pleasure."

Aeris reached out and touched his face. "I don't care what you say. Thank you for helping my brother with me."

Magnus reached out and touched her face in return. He brushed his thumb across her lips. "I didn't do it for him," he whispered in reply.

Aeris closed her eyes. She felt content. With Magnus by her side, she felt just as safe as she would if it had been her brother. She wondered at that only momentarily before sleep claimed her.

Magnus continued to watch her as she slept. Her face was pale, but looked better than it had even just yesterday. He was relieved that she was recovering from her wounds. Priests and clerics had lost the power of their prayers, and he was finally beginning to realize the impact of that fact. He picked up Aeris' hand, and as he was holding it, he felt a cool band of metal against his palm.

Magnus moved his hand aside to reveal a magnificent ring that encircled her middle finger. He was instantly captivated by the pale blue and green swirls of color that moved lazily within the oval of the central stone. On either side of that, he vaguely recognized colorless crystal chips that would glitter beautifully in the light. Momentarily he wondered why he had not noticed it before, for she probably wore it at all times.

Magnus rubbed his thumb over the central stone. There was something about it, something that called to him. Yet, he resisted the slight pull. He knew that the ring should be significant to him somehow, but he didn't know why. He then placed Aeris' hand beside her on the furs. Not only was the woman an enigma to him, but he was very attracted to her. Even in her absence she was never far from his thoughts, and it was her face that he saw in his mind's eye before he fell into sleep at night.

Magnus drew his legs up in front of his chest, encircling them with his arms. Once their destination was reached they would part ways. He would go to Andahye, and she with her brother on whatever work he was able to secure next. Magnus had told her about his propensity for magic. She tried to act as though she hadn't known, but he knew better. Somehow, she had surmised that about him when they first met.

Magnus remembered Aeris as the woman sitting on the veranda of the Golden Griffon Inn two nights before the caravan departed Entsy. He had been unable to get her out of his mind since that night, and when he saw that she traveled with him on the same caravan, his heart leaped in his chest. He was determined to make her acquaintance, and when she took her fractious larian for a ride later that morning, it made it only that much easier for him.

Magnus allowed his gaze to rest on her yet again. She had been grievously ill. Many people died of wounds less than hers. However, the cleric in Driscol was very skilled, and even without the power of his prayers, he was able to save Aeris' life. Alasdair asked the caravan master for an advance in payment, and then gave the cleric all of his earnings in return for the attention he paid Aeris. Now Alasdair had no money. He would be forced to find more work. Magnus felt badly about the other man's situation, but knew he could do nothing to help. Magnus himself had no gold, and the only reason he was on this caravan was because Gharlas owed the priests at the Temple of Corellian in Entsy a favor. Transporting Magnus to the village near Andahye made that debt paid in full. Aeris told Magnus that she would show him the direct path to the mystical city. He looked forward to that, and had high hopes that the master spell-casters could give him what he needed.

CHAPTER 5

The caravan approached the small village of Grunchin. As they moved closer, there was a sudden flurry of activity as the villagers came to greet them, folk who were happy to receive whatever bounty was being delivered. The people followed as they moved to the center of the village. From her place beside Magnus, Aeris watched the goings-on, happy for the people who were so excited about the arrival of a mere caravan.

Aeris turned to Magnus to find him staring at her. His gaze was dark and unreadable. Nonetheless, she could see the tumult reflected there. Her heart did a curious little flip in her chest, and her throat became suddenly dry. She looked away from him, dropping her eyes to the ground and then back to the activity going on around the caravan. They had stopped and the merchants were unloading wares from their wagons. Happy children skipped amongst the men who labored beneath heavy crates and women who had begun to busy themselves setting up tents.

Aeris hopped down from the back of the wagon. Contrary to her brother's belief, she was well enough to help set up camp. So far, he had only given her the responsibility of preparing the evening meal, which rankled her to no end. Not only did she feel that the food was merely satisfactory, she hated to do it simply because of the memories that the activity invoked. Yet, she would never tell Alasdair. He would feel guilty, and that was the last thing she wanted. Inasmuch, she suffered the duty and only begged her brother every night to be allowed to pitch the tents in his stead.

Aeris was aware of Magnus following her as she sought out Alasdair. This new awareness of his proximity had begun to make her nervous as the days passed. She knew she was attracted to him; there was never any question of that. But now . . . now there was something more. She was developing feelings for him, feelings that were comforting and disturbing at the same time.

Despite the pleasure Aeris found in Magnus' company, she was afraid of the emotions she had begun to feel when they were together. At the opening of every new day, she looked forward to seeing him, and in the deep of the night, she yearned to have him there in the bed beside her. She had never felt this way before, not even for Talemar, and she thought that she should be happy. Yet, there was a pall over her, a feeling that she had felt this way before despite knowing that such as thing was not possible.

Aeris probed her mind, searching for answers to the questions that plagued her. Why couldn't she remember the time between the deaths of her comrades and her return to Elvandahar? And now, why did she feel that she had loved a man before when she could not consciously remember who that man could possibly have been? It was torture, pure and unadulterated. It made her feel that she should not, could not, feel emotion for the man who had recently become her good friend. She knew that it would be easy for her to love him. The reality of that fact made her afraid. Deep in her mind, she knew that she had loved before, despite her inability to remember it. Perhaps she should wait for this man to make himself known to her, or to come for her if he chose. Perhaps she should give at least another month so as to recall her lost memories.

Consequently, Aeris began to keep a distance between herself and Magnus. It was so hard, for all she wanted was to bask in his company. She could see that her behavior was confusing to him. However, she didn't know how to tell him that it was nothing that he had done to make her begin acting differently.

Despairingly, the more she resisted, the more tempting his presence became. And now, all Aeris could do was seek him out in spite of her better judgment. She continued to feel torn, but she tried not to let it interfere with the camaraderie she shared with Magnus. She refused to feel that she should be trapped by some subconscious memory her mind refused to bring into light.

Magnus followed Aeris as she began to make her way among the people that thronged about the caravan. As far as he could tell, the entire village had come for the event. It seemed that few caravans bothered to make the trip to Grunchin, and the people were ecstatic with the prospect of purchasing goods that came around only so often. He regarded Aeris' back as she deftly weaved through the crowd. Now that they were at the village, Magnus knew that his time with her was limited. He hated that reality, and disliked the situation even more because he had begun to notice the distance she endeavored to place between them.

Broodingly, Magnus allowed his thoughts to replay over the past few days. He had continued to stay with Aeris throughout her recovery. The only time he wasn't in her company her was at night. At the close of every day Alasdair came to take her back to his campfire and to share the evening meal with her. The next morning he would bring her back to Magnus' wagon. It was an arrangement they had made when Magnus offered to help Alasdair with the burden of caring for his critically ill sister, for he still needed to maintain his position with the caravan master. Alasdair was in debt to Gharlas, and it was in his best interest to work as promised.

As Aeris became stronger and more alert, she began to bring her travel pack with her when she came to Magnus' wagon. They spent much of their days pouring over the volumes she had brought with her from her mother's library in

Elvandahar. She told him of the academy that had been built there, dedicated to the art of Dimensional magic. She shared stories of her life whilst in training as an apprentice to one Master Dinim Coabra. He couldn't help but think that if the mages in Andahye were unable to help him, then perhaps the masters in Elvandahar would be the next ones to visit.

Magnus stopped when he saw Alasdair come into view. He watched as Aeris rushed towards him and put her arms around his neck in a sisterly embrace. She planted a kiss on her brother's cheek and laughed when he said something that, most likely, was the epitome of ridiculous. Magnus envied them their relationship and wished that he could remember something of his own past. Not only that, but he wished that he could also be the recipient of her affection, albeit in a different fashion.

As the days passed, Magnus began to develop feelings for Aeris. He was sure she had started to feel the same towards him, but suddenly her behaviors began to alter. He suddenly found that he wasn't so certain anymore. Yet, that didn't stop him from discreetly pursuing her. He thought that it seemed to be the appropriate action, opposed to a more obvious approach, for he was aware of her memory loss. He had discovered her secret when he asked her about the ring she wore. Hesitantly revealing that she did not remember how she obtained it, and that there was a chunk out of her life that was lost to her, Magnus felt he had found a boon companion.

It wasn't long before most of the crates were carried away and the encampment established. Word began to circulate that there would be a celebration this night, not only for the successful delivery of the medical supplies contained within the crates, but in honor of the season of rebirth and the goddess Beory. Magnus watched as everyone spent the rest of the day in preparation for the evening festivities. The men hunted while the women began to cook. When the hunters returned, braces of hares and burbana were quickly skinned and disemboweled. They were then placed upon spits and given over to the fires. Two leschera had also been brought down. Those took longer to prepare, but with the help of so many, the meat was soon joining the tubers and legumes in the stew-pots.

It wasn't long before the tantalizing aroma of marinating meat was drifting throughout the village. The children were excited, running from fire to fire, hoping that those who sat before them would offer a taste of the food within the pots and cauldrons that hung over the flames and then from the pits that had been dug nearby. Barrels of ale were breached, and casks of mead and wine opened. The festivities began before the food was finished cooking as the musicians brought out their instruments and began to play their music.

As the sun began to set over the horizon, Magnus watched the goings on from within the sanctuary of the wagon. Torches were lit and tied on top of poles set into the ground. Once the sun's light left them, the flames from tens of torches took its place. Meanwhile, Steralion's pale light shone down on them from above. As always, his mind was devoid of any memories the festivities may have invoked. Magnus envied the people their happiness, and he wished he had the capacity to join in their free-spirited carnival.

But then *she* was there. Aeris was the epitome of beauty, hanging on the arm of her brother. On her other side was Tigerius, who had his fingers laced through hers. Absorbing the light cast by the many fires, her red hair was like a bright curtain that hung alongside her face and down her back. From his place within the shadows of the wagon, Magnus saw her glancing from side to side every once in a while, almost as though in search of someone. From his vantage point, he could see the attention the other men of the caravan paid her, as well as that from men who made their residence in Grunchin. She had an almost ethereal quality, a magnetic personality and beauty that drew people to her.

Right from the beginning of their acquaintance, Magnus had noticed the charisma about her. He easily saw the attention the men of the caravan paid the sister of one of the newly hired guardsmen. But she paid them all no heed, and even seemed oblivious to their infatuation with her. Magnus heard the talk . . . they wondered why she sought out the lone cimmerean man when she could have her pick of any of them. Magnus couldn't help but smile at that fact. Yes, indeed, why would she seek him out above any of the other persons who traveled with the caravan?

Magnus downed the contents of his mug, felt the warmth of the ale suffuse him as he jumped down from the back of the wagon and began to make his way towards the trio he saw several feet away. He noted the fleeting disappointment on Aeris' face when she didn't find whomever it was she sought. Magnus wondered who it might as he moved closer. Tigerius handed her a fresh mug of mead, relieving her hand of the old one. Magnus snorted to himself. Perhaps the man thought he would get lucky this night.

The bards began to play a new song as Magnus stepped up to Aeris. He did the first thing that came to his mind and held out his hand to her in a silent invitation to dance. A smile lit Aeris' face, and she didn't hesitate as she took the proffered hand. As Magnus led her away from Alasdair and Tigerius, he hoped that he knew how to dance. He would look an utter fool if he did not, for he felt dozens of eyes watching. He took her hands within his and simply let his subconscious take over. The steps came easily to him as he followed the cadence of the music, and he quickly discovered that Aeris was as good a dancer as he.

Aeris smiled at the man who held her loosely within his arms. Magnus had come for her, much like she hoped he would. She had been searching for him, and had begun to fear that he had retired for the night without bothering to join in the festivities. But now, here he was. It felt right to have his arms around her, and she was equally as pleased to find that he knew how to take the complex steps of the dance the bards and musicians played. At first he seemed hesitant, but soon he started to take the lead. He began to grip her more tightly around the waist in preparation for the movements that were to come, and when they were executed, Aeris knew that they were without flaw. Despite his inability to remember the past, Magnus was somehow able to call upon his unnamed skills. Someone had once trained him in the art of dance, and for him to perform as well as he did, she knew that he had learned from an excellent instructor.

After a short while, the dance ended and another one began. This one was slower, and did not require the complex movements of the previous one. Aeris was ready to step away if Magnus chose to release her, but when she saw that he would not, she moved closer to him for the duration of the dance. She could smell the slightly musky scent of the bath oils he used and allowed herself to be drawn into the rhythm of the music. With his arms around her, and the effects of the mead rushing through her body, she gave into the power of the moment and allowed herself to be swept away.

For the first time since the deaths of her friends, Aeris set herself free. She moved to the sound of the music, let it carry her away upon wings of sound. She followed Magnus' lead, relied upon his skill to support her as she executed the more creative and intricate movements of the dances in her repertoire. Only vaguely did she recall that her brother and Tigerius would be watching . . . and somehow it had ceased to matter. Let him see . . . it was just another aspect of her that Alasdair would learn to tolerate.

Magnus continued his dance with the woman in his arms. He knew that she was intoxicated, but despite that fact, she was very skilled. She let the music dictate her movements and he followed suit, taking the lead when she relinquished it to him. The bards kept the music going until one song melted into the next. They simply adjusted their dance to fit the rhythm. He could feel several pairs of eyes watching their every step, but it didn't seem to matter. All he cared about was the woman in his arms, and the way she felt as she moved against him.

Suddenly the musicians began to play a different kind of music . . . music that originated from the western deserts. They played a denedrian song, something that would be heard among the gypsies. Those people were renowned for their beautifully provocative music, and Magnus hesitated for a moment. He thought that Aeris might decide to pull away at this point, refrain from dancing to the cadence of the gypsy music. But when he realized she had no intention of stopping, he quickly stepped into the beat of the music and allowed the melody to take over.

Aeris was aware of the shift on tone, slipping into the movements with ease. Her mother had taught her most of what she knew about the art of dance. Adrianna had developed a propensity for it, and passed the skill down to her daughter. Many of Aeris' favorite memories were of Adrianna teaching her the steps of one dance or another. Many of those dances happened to originate from the western deserts. Inasmuch, Adrianna had also taught her daughter how to move to the rhythm of gypsy music. In Aeris' opinion, it was the best part of her instruction, for they had fun with the wanton movements. Yet, there was also much more to it than that. The songs taught Aeris that such freedom of movement was an expression of passion and desire. Never before had she danced like this with anyone. And now, to have Magnus holding her so close, it was almost like making love . . .

With an abandon she had never known before, Aeris danced. She felt his hands at her hips and waist, a technique he used to garner her next move. With his skill, Magnus could tell by the tension of her muscles how she would move next. He would reciprocate, shifting the lead from himself to her. He spun her about with ease, pulled her into him, and then bowed over her. The long curling tresses of her hair pooled onto the ground as she arched back. Just as it seemed that they paused for too long, they pulled up, and Aeris began to execute the complex movements that were the heart of the dance. Without knowing how he knew, Magnus partnered Aeris through, his body singing with its proximity to her, responding to her nearness whether he wished it or no.

Then the music stopped. Magnus held Aeris close, felt her heart beating where his hand rested at the center of her back. He felt her breath on his face, felt her breasts pressing into his chest as she inhaled. Almost without thinking, he laced his fingers through hers as he held her hand. He looked down at her, and he realized that she was so close he could kiss her. She opened her eyes, their dark brown depths beckoning him within. She regarded him intently for a moment before she began to smile. Her face lit up and her eyes shimmered with merriment. He had never seen her so suffused with happiness, and he felt honored to have been the one who could have contributed to that.

As the bards rose to take a break from their music, Magnus and Aeris moved towards the closest refreshment. She found herself buzzed with some newfound energy, feeling a contentedness she had not experienced in a very long time. Alasdair and Tigerius met them at the refreshment. By the look in his eyes, Aeris could tell that her brother was dumbfounded by her knowledge and skill with dance, and perhaps gypsy dance in particular. Tigerius was equally as stupefied, although perhaps for a different reason.

Alasdair took her gently by the arm as Aeris took a drink from her mug of mead. "My dear sister, what other secrets do you hide behind your sorceress' robes?"

Aeris knew that a part of him was teasing her. However, there was that other part of him that was serious. There was no way that he could know that she had learned all that she knew from their own mother unless she had told him so. And as of yet, she had not.

"Surprised that there are things about me that you still don't know?" Aeris countered. "While you were off training with our father to be a ranger, our mother took me aside to teach me other things besides dimensionalism."

Alasdair shook his head. "You never yet ceased to amaze me, and I never knew that our mother was so . . ." Alasdair paused, not knowing the words to use.

"She would surprise you with the things she knows. Perhaps you should endeavor to spend more time with her."

Alasdair nodded. "The next time I am home, perhaps I will."

Aeris drank again from her mug. Once more, she felt the effects of the mead sweeping through her. She bowed to her brother and took Magnus' arm, allowing him to pull her away towards the nearest fire so that she could sit and rest. Aeris watched as Alasdair studied Magnus intently for a moment before he seemed to come to a decision. He then turned away to focus upon his own activity.

Aeris seated herself at the fire next to Magnus. For several moments, she simply stared into the flames until she realized that she was being watched. She turned to her companion to find him staring at her. Magnus sat with his elbow propped against his raised knee, a hand resting at his chin. He wore an expression of bemusement on his handsome face.

Aeris raised a questioning eyebrow.

Magnus shook his head. "It seems that your brother has the inclination to keep you a child as long as he can. He has a difficult time seeing you as the woman you have become."

Aeris grinned and nodded, casting her gaze back top the fire. "It does appear to be that way." Then she looked back up at him. "Despite knowing me so well, in many ways he has yet to discover the real me."

Magnus smiled knowingly. "Ah, but you keep that so well hidden."

Aeris drew her brows together and nibbled at her lower lip. "Perhaps." In the background she could hear the bards beginning to play once more. The haunting melody of the *Ballad of Shinshinasa* drifted through the air, and Aeris was immediately caught up in the romantic quality to the music. She became suddenly aware of the proximity of the man sitting next to her, remembered the feel of his arms around her, saw the intensity of his gaze upon her.

"Sometimes I fell that I need to protect him . . .them . . . my family." Aeris blurted the words without really knowing why. "I am afraid that they will not like what they see."

Keeping his eyes locked onto hers, Magnus leaned forward and reached out to the mug Aeris held in her hand. His fingers brushed hers as he took it and raised it to his lips. He drank and then slowly lowered it. "I can't possibly understand why they wouldn't."

Aeris shook her head. "I am not the person they all think me to be."

The corner of his mouth pulled up into a smile. "And what type of person is that?"

Aeris frowned. "Now you are making fun of me. I shouldn't have told you anything." She shook her head and felt a lump began to form in her throat. What was she thinking, divulging her secrets to a man she had only known for barely two fortnights? She made as though to rise, but suddenly Magnus' hand was at her arm, staying her.

"No. You have it all wrong." He paused for a moment and then continued. "I only want to see more of what I saw tonight."

Aeris shook her head. Only vaguely could she still hear the beautiful music of the ballad. His face was so close; Aeris could almost feel the warmth emanating from his body. His lavender gaze was intense as he regarded her. She could smell the mead on his breath, and it whispered past her lips as he spoke. "And what did you see?" she asked.

Magnus cupped her jaw in his hand and caressed the side of her face. "I saw the most beautiful woman in the world," he said softly.

Aeris looked deep into his eyes and saw the sincerity reflected there. She struggled to breathe past the lump that remained in her throat, fought to control the intensity of the emotions that suddenly swept through her. Magnus leaned towards her and she met him halfway.

Their lips touched . . . a slight brush that only hinted at what was to come. Then his lips pressed into hers and she returned the kiss. It was slow and passionate, just like she imagined it would be. His kiss was none like she remembered experiencing before, even from Talemar. For several moments she allowed herself to be swept away in the moment, luxuriating in the feel of his mouth on hers. One hand swept into her hair while he pulled her nearer to him with the other one.

All of a sudden, Aeris had a moment of clarity. Her memories told her that she had never felt this way with a man before, but she somehow knew that she had. She broke the contact, resisting the urge to continue. She felt torn, just as she had the past several days since she recognized her feelings for what they were. She was falling in love with Magnus, and she just didn't know if that was something that she could deal with right now.

"I had better go." Aeris saw his confusion as she pulled away from him and stood. She glanced back only once as she hurried away from the fire, wanting so much to go back to him but knowing that she could not. There was a man from her dreams that she could not remember. She wanted him more than life itself. How could she have a relationship, and begin to have feelings for Magnus, when she knew that the other was somewhere out there waiting for her?

Tears burned behind Aeris' eyes as she approached her brother's wagon. She climbed inside and sought out her bedroll in the darkness. She then lay there and began to cry softly. On the morrow she would show Magnus the way to Andahye. Then she would leave him to seek out the answers to his identity. A part of her was afraid that she would never see him again. The other part knew that it was for the best.

***

Adrianna sighed heavily in frustration. All of her efforts had been in vain, and she was no closer to discovering the whereabouts of Master Tallachienan than she was several days ago when Pylar first arrived at her doorstep. Beside her, she could feel the same frustration simmering within Dinim. They had exhausted all of the scrying techniques they had at their disposal to no avail. Something was keeping TC's whereabouts hidden from them . . . something powerful. Adrianna could only wonder what it was.

Adrianna turned to her friend. Dinim regarded her solemnly from deep lavender eyes. He was tired . . . exuding fatigue in waves. She knew that he felt the same from her, for they had not rested since Pylar came to them with news that TC was gone. Dinim shook his head and turned away from her. She knew what needed to be done now . . . tell Pylar that his bond-mate could not be found despite the magnitude of their power and skill.

Adrianna followed Dinim from the chamber, losing herself in her thoughts. What had happened that made TC withdraw from Pylar? How could the Master have simply disappeared in the fashion that Pylar described? There was so much that Adrianna did not know, and now that they were at an impasse, she would have to ask Pylar to elaborate on a few of the details.

It wasn't difficult to find Pylar, as he spent most of his time in the company of Xebrinarth. Contacting her bond-mate, Adria asked him to bring Pylar and to meet her and Dinim in the academy courtyard. They had not long to wait before the two golden dragons were winging into sight, their effervescent scales reflecting the rays of the late-day sun. Effortlessly they landed in the massive courtyard . . . one that had been designed to accommodate several dragons at once. Upon touching her mind, Xebrinarth knew that Adrianna's news for Pylar was not good. Yet, he refrained from letting his friend in on the information, knowing that it was up to Adrianna and Dinim to tell the other dragon what they needed to say.

As the dragons approached, Adrianna felt the query in her mind, sensed the hopefulness behind it. She hated to let him down, but she would not not speak untruths to her friend. She opened her mind to Pylar, let him see that they had made several efforts to no avail. There was something that was concealing Tallachienan's location, and more than once Adria had wondered about the use of some type of anti-scrying device. Yet, Pylar's rendition of the events that took place did not leave much room for that type of probability. Pylar made it seem as though TCs departure had been of the precipitous sort, and mayhap even a bit forceful. She doubted that the Master would have thought to have anything of real arcane value upon him.

Yet, she asked the question anyway. Pylar hesitated only a moment before replying in the negative. She didn't doubt the authenticity of his response, yet she got the distinct impression that there was something he was not divulging to her. Adrianna kept the thought to herself. She hoped that Pylar would tell her in a day or two. Perhaps he just needed some time to work things out in his mind. At that point, she hoped to make more headway with their search for the Master, if indeed the information Pylar concealed had any relevance to the investigation. Adria hoped wholeheartedly that it did.

***

Tholana hissed in irritation, and with a well-aimed kick, sent the priest sprawling to the floor. She then knelt beside him, taking a fistful of his black hair in her hands. He disgusted her, as most men were certain to do. Much of the time, she didn't even recall why she bothered to tolerate them within her dark citadel. But then she remembered that they were necessary . . . almost as indispensable as the air they breathed. Without men, the cimmerean race could not be perpetuated.

Tholana regarded the face of the priest. He sniveled piteously, begging her to spare him. Actually, he had done very little to irritate her himself, but she was perturbed about other things. Unfortunately for the priest, he was now the outlet for that frustration. With another hiss, Tholana savagely released the man's hair and rose. She then kicked him again. The crack of his skull against her long boot-heel reverberated throughout the chamber. She watched as blood began to pool around his head, the circumference of the area widening with each passing moment. Without remorse she watched, her thoughts turning inwards to ponder the events that had taken place over the last few fortnights.

Tholana was a master scryer. It had been easy for her spy upon her nemesis, even as he resided within the confines of his unnatural citadel. She had always thought it a strange place within which Tallachienan made his home, a place that shifted and changed continuously, a place that seemed to have a mind of its own. She hated his residence actually, recalled the discomfort she had felt the few times she visited there. Very little in life could intimidate her . . . but

TC's citadel could do what most other things could not. She avoided the place like the plague.

Within her mirror, Tholana spied. She saw the object of her disturbance . . . the daughter of none other than that bitch sorceress, Adrianna Darnesse Timberlyn. And what was most disturbing was that Tallachienan was all over the girl.

Tholana went into a rage. Her anger could see no bounds, but there was little she could do. History seemed to be repeating itself, and her hatred of Adrianna and her family grew. What was this cruel twist of fate that had brought Aeris Timberlyn into the arms of the only man Tholana had ever truly wanted? Sure, she had desired many men in her countless years. Yet, they had been nothing but tools, simple animals to satisfy her sexual cravings.

Tholana frenzied over the union of Tallachienan and Damaeris, but it wasn't long before other events began to spiral out of control. It was something she would never forget, something she had never experienced in all of her lifetimes. It was a tremor that shook the world of Shandahar and the entirety of the universe beyond. And when the dust settled, the gods found that they had fallen.

It was the pain Tholana would always remember the most. Everything suddenly went dark, and her body became wracked with agony. She felt the essence of her power torn away, removed from every fiber that made up her being. Then she felt the sensation of falling. She thought that she must be dying . . . how could she feel such torment and not be in the throes of death? Yet, when she finally opened her eyes and found herself lying upon the cold ground, devoid of her divine power, Tholana almost wished that death had indeed claimed her.

It didn't take long for Tholana to take stock of her situation. She found that much of her power remained intact, yet the power that gave her god-like status had somehow become unattainable. Many powers were easy for her to employ, while others were difficult to access. She could no longer transcend over the world and go to that place where only the gods go. But at least she still had her dark citadel and her followers. Tholana refocused her gaze to the dead priest. Well, at least most of them.

Turning on her heel, Tholana gestured towards the swath of curtains encompassing the entire far wall of the room. A young priestess stepped out from behind it. "Find someone to get rid of this mess. Then have something brought to me. I find that I am famished."

The girl bowed out of Tholana's presence and then scurried to do her mistress' bidding. Like all of the other novice priestesses, she would be a servant to Tholana and higher ranking priestesses until she reached sufficient rank of her own. With extraordinary skill and treachery, she would work her way to the top. Once she was there, she would reap rewards she would otherwise only dream.

Tholana swept into the adjoining chamber. There she picked up a goblet of wine and immediately handed it off to the nearest priestess. The woman drank of the liquid. A few moments later, when Tholana saw no ill effects come upon the priestess, she took back the goblet and drank of it herself. Despite her magnificent power and station, Tholana knew she could trust very few. The poison would not kill her, but it had the potential to weaken her enough so that another attack could result in that undesired state. Especially now, when her powers were not at their strongest, she felt vulnerable. Tholana hated that.

The goddess sank into the softness of a pillowed divan, swirling the contents of the goblet thoughtfully. Soon she would be meeting with Razlul Daemon-keeper. With the lord of the Daemundai, she had secured a somewhat tenuous alliance. He had become quite powerful, his daemonic abilities strengthening over the years. He was a specimen of magnificent proportions, and despite the absurdity of her situation, Tholana found herself yearning for him. Tholana grinned widely. And he for her. She could feel his lust every moment he was in her presence.

Tholana ran a hand up over the top of her thigh, the curve of her hip, and across her belly to rest at her breast. She could imagine him even now: long hair so light it was almost white . . . cerulean blue eyes so intense they sent shudders down her spine . . . fingers so adept they only left her panting for more. Razlul was a splendid lover, and she had graced his bed more than once. The power he possessed was so unlike her own, and she felt herself drawn to it despite the depth of her own splendid ability.

Tholana slid the hand from her breast down to the juncture of her thighs, arching her lower back into the sensations her fingers elicited. Yes, Razlul had power . . . and plans. Already he had built himself a strong following, not only of the Daemundai, but a group of people whom he had begun to refer to as 'dragon-slayers'. What had begun as a pathetic band of simple cut-throats and mercenaries was turning into a strength to be reckoned with. Through training and discipline, they were becoming an elite force.

But there was more. Razlul had other plans . . . a campaign that did not involve the slaying of dragons. Tholana should not know so much of it either, but she was good at obtaining information that otherwise would be known only to cold stone walls. He was bent upon bringing something else to Shandahar . . . a menace that the world had never known before. It was from the most remote of the Hells, a monstrosity that would devour all within its path. She called it Leviathan.

CHAPTER 6

Magnus walked through the busy streets of the city of Xordrel. He had only been there for two days, but already knew that he was no closer to finding the answer to his dilemma. Master Tannin had been wrong, as had most of the other Masters in the distinguished city of Andahye. The old sage, Paxil, could tell him nothing, and spoke only in riddles. Magnus should have trusted his instincts and gone to Elvandahar instead. *Besides, then maybe he would have been able to see Aeris again.* Magnus struck the thought angrily from his mind. She had broken her word. She had shown him the way to Andahye, promising to see him in a few days when he returned to Grunchin. But when he arrived back at the village, he discovered that she had left two days before with her brother and the caravan that brought them there.

Magnus shook his head. He had yet to be able to get the young woman out of his mind. Thoughts of Aeris dominated his every waking moment and his dreams were filled with moments spent with her . . . real and imagined. He was hurt to find that she had gone, and she hadn't even bothered to leave a message. For many months after he allowed his anger to carry him along, and even now he felt it simmering there, just below the surface. However, despite her broken promises, he could not escape the fact that he still loved her. Such a reality was a great motivational factor that should have taken him to Elvandahar. However, the masters in Andahye informed him of an old sage who resided within the port city of Xordrel. They speculated that Paxil would be able to help Magnus recall his past. He spent a little over fourteen months within the mystical city. He had unlocked many of the secrets of his Talent, but nothing more. He still didn't even know his real name.

So, Magnus made the long journey to the southern tip of the realm of Torimir. The journey had been relatively uneventful, and he was happy when he finally arrived there. But now, finding himself nowhere near discovering his true identity, he felt himself wondering what to do next.

As the sun began its descent, Magnus walked up the steps to the establishment in which he had chosen to stay. It was a nice place, with spacious bedrooms, a common room, and a tavern. The masters in Andahye had recommended it to him, and even gave him enough gold to stay there for several days. They had also provided enough gold to see him to Xordrel and back. However, Magnus had no intention of returning to Andahye. Yes, the masters there had been generous, but they were foolish and arrogant. They had ample opportunity to work with the academy that had been built in Elvandahar, but instead chose to impose restrictions upon the students who apprenticed under the masters there. The students were forced to journey to Andahye to take their final Tests, and Magnus felt it to be a waste of time and energy. The masters at both the Vanderlinde and the Medubrokan Academies would find it in their better interests to work together for the betterment of their students. Through his research, Magnus had found most of the fault to lie with the Vanderlinde masters. It was a shame that they sought only to discredit their peers. Yet, such was often the case in matters of politics and power.

Magnus entered the Silver Serpent Inn. Slowly he made his way up the stairs to his room. In the morning, he would go in search of anyone who was traveling north from the city. He vaguely recalled hearing about a caravan that would be leaving within the next couple of days. Once again, it would be a long trip. But at least there would be some measure of safety within the numbers afforded by the caravan. He would get as close as possible to Elvandahar and then hire someone who could lead him through the forest to get to the academy.

However, at this point, seeing Aeris again would only be a bonus. Magnus was intent upon discovering the secrets to his past, and had come to feel that the masters in Elvandahar might be able to help him. He had heard great things about them within the arcane circles he kept whilst in Andahye. One of the masters happened to be Aeris' mother, Adrianna Timberlyn. The other was a man called Dinim Coabra, a man he recalled Aeris telling him was her own master.

Once in his room, Magnus removed his clothing and then lowered himself into the bath that awaited him there. The water was still hot, and he luxuriated within the tub. He stayed there until the water started to become tepid. He then he got out of the tub, dried himself on the thick cloth that awaited him on the bed, and then donned fresh tunic and trousers. Magnus would go downstairs, procure himself a meal, and then bring it back to the room. He would sleep for a while, and when morning arrived, he would find the next caravan out of Xordrel.

***

Aeris, Talemar, Alasdair, Tigerius, and Cedric walked into the city, leading their respective larian and lloryk. Darkness was falling, and they had only a limited amount of time to find an inn. Alasdair knew that Aeris looked forward to it; he had promised her a nice one this time. He had the gold, for he had earned a good amount of it as a guard for the caravan master, Gharlas.

After leaving the village of Grunchin, Alasdair, Aeris, and Tigerius spent the remainder of the warm months traveling with Gharlas' caravan. The man thought highly of Alasdair and his abilities, and had wanted to keep him on as long as possible. However, the time came when Alasdair knew he had to return Aeris home. He wouldn't have minded staying away for a while longer, but he knew that Aeris had suffered recent hardship and still needed the comfort of her family. She would never admit it to him, but he knew better. Not only that, but she had been different since they parted ways with the young cimmerean man. Alasdair knew that they shared a connection, and he had even begun to think it bordered on something more when he saw her dance with Magnus the night of the festival. He had never seen that aspect of his sister before, and it made him realize that there were things about her he did not know despite their close relationship.

So, as the weather started to become colder, the companions returned to the forested realm of Elvandahar. They remained there for the coldest months, but when winter began to loosen its icy grip, Alasdair found himself yearning to be away again. He asked his sister to accompany him once more, but Aeris declined, claiming she had work to oversee at the academy. Two days later, he and Tigerius departed. Aeris was there to see them off. He could still remember the expression on her face, one telling him that she would much rather be going with him than staying at home.

Aeris' wishful expression remained with Alasdair for the next several weeks. Working for Gharlas, he had begun to garner a reputation, and it was easy for him to find work. However, when he finally found a lull in his activities, Alasdair returned home, determined to collect Aeris and have her accompany him as he worked for the rest of the warm season.

However, when he arrived back in Elvandahar, Alasdair discovered that Aeris and Talemar had been requested to make a journey to the distant city of Xordrel located at the southernmost tip of the realm of Torimir. It was in response to a correspondence concerning a young Talent that resided there. Adrianna and Dinim had been working to recruit new students for their program, individuals with a high level of Talent. When it came to his mother's attention that such a Talent resided within Xordrel, and that he might be willing to make the journey to Elvandahar, preparations were immediately made to collect the boy. Cedric and Alasdair were bid to accompany Talemar and Aeris. They would be invaluable in keeping the young journeymen safe. Tigerius decided to go only because he had little else to occupy his time. However, Alasdair was left to wonder if there may be some other underlying cause to his going, perhaps something to do with his sister.

Surprisingly, it took them only a few weeks to reach the city. Since travel had mainly comprised of the plains, they were able to ride fast. None of them had ever been this far south before. It was interesting to feel a warming of the air the father south they went. However, Alasdair knew that he had to be vigilant in keeping track of the time. Already it was the middle of Cisceren. In another month, the colder weather would begin to come. They may not feel it as intensely this far south, but as they traveled back north, they would most definitely notice the change in seasons.

Inasmuch, Alasdair told his sister and cousin that they needed to conduct their business quickly. He did not want to hit any weather-related problems on their way back home. However, he knew that everyone was tired, they having ridden hard to make it to Xordrel in such a short amount of time. Everyone deserved a rest, and Alasdair would not begrudge them that. But once everyone was rested, he wanted the journeymen to make haste in completing their business. Aeris and Talemar would first have to find the boy. Then they would meet with his parents. The people would have a big decision to make, for Elvandahar was a far-away place and they would not be seeing their son for quite a long time. Meanwhile, Alasdair, Cedric, and Talemar would stock up on supplies. Alasdair foresaw them being in Xordrel for at least two weeks. He only hoped it would not be any longer than that, and it would be great if it were less.

Alasdair turned off the main road and began to make his way down a side street. He had asked the men at the city gates the location of a good inn, and they directed him down this street. His companions followed behind, and when Alasdair reached the building, he stopped. Upon the sign was the name of the place to which the men made reference: The Silver Serpent Inn. Indeed the place appeared reputable. His sister should be happy here. He jumped down from his larian, and was about to lead the animal to the rear of the establishment, when a boy came rushing over to them.

"This way, my lord. Here, let me take him for you." The boy took Alasdair's larian and began to lead the beast away. Two more boys came to take the larian from his comrades. Alasdair's opinion of the inn increased . . . the stable hands were good. Yes, Aeris should be happy here.

***

Goldare and Vikhail walked down the street that led them to the construction site. It was a long road, narrow and winding. No one thought to maintain it, especially after what had happened at the end of that road nearly thirty years before. Goldare glanced at his companion, took in the solid build of the halfen man, the long brown hair tied back at the nape of his neck, and the beard that was drawn into four braids that hung down his broad chest. He wore simple tunic and trousers, as well as a bronze-handled battle-axe across his back. His boots were well-worn, as was the belt around his middle. A pouch hung near the front, but it swung easily about from the movement of his strides. It was easy to see that not much rested within.

Goldare turned back to the road. He didn't like it . . . not one bit. But they had promised Vardec that they would meet him there after he finished his work. It was close to the time that he would be setting aside his tools for the night, and the halfen man would be looking for them.

Goldare's thoughts turned to the history that surrounded the grounds to which they approached. It was a relatively secluded spot, making it easy for the Daemundai to take a foothold and build their temple. The general populace didn't realize the true nature of the place until a group by the name of *Thritean's Pride* entered the city. They went to the temple and destroyed it, along with most of the despicable priests who had made residence there. A member of the group, a man by the name of Gandor, had died in the conflict. He was honored by the King of Torimir for his valor, and a bust of Gandor's likeness was made and placed within the library. At the celebratory opening, the bust would be transferred to the academy currently being constructed atop the remains of the temple. It would be a place of learning and research, a project headed by Dugan Viplending and his lovely daughter, Esmerelda. Viplending had gold, too much gold to know what to do with; his daughter was testimony to that fact. She was arrogant and standoffish, but at least she wasn't unreasonable and callous like many others of her social station. She was smart and meticulous, and her father had named her the supervisor of the team that was hired to build the academy.

The ground had been leveled and the foundation prepared. Slowly the building rose from the ashes of what had been before. However, not enough time had passed for the people of Xordrel, and the site was avoided even by the most reprehensible of scoundrels. Only Esmerelda and her crew went there to work. Darkness was quickly approaching, and Steralion was rising. Now that the day had come to a close, the workers had left for the night.

Goldare and Vikhail stepped onto the grounds. Right away they saw Vardec, who was leaning against a wall that had been erected just that day. The mortar was still soft, and it would set for several more days until it became fixed and strong. He walked towards them, his pack slung over his shoulder. It was full of the tools he had brought with him that day. He dared not leave it at the site, for he could expect not to see them when he returned in the morning.

"What took ya so long?" he growled. "I was gonna leave without ya."

Vikhail frowned. "Fine. Nex' time we won't come. Walk yer own self home."

Vardec only shook his head. "Shut yer face, Vikhail. Yer just jealous 'cause I have a real job."

Vikhail's frown deepened. "Oh, so runnin' the smithy idn't a 'real job' now eh? What would support yer arse during the cold season? This?" Vikhail offhandedly indicated the construction site. "I think not."

"Like I said . . . yer jealous."

Goldare looked from one brother to the other. They looked much alike, down to the color of their eyes and the shape of their faces. Only Vardec wore his beard cut shorter than Vikhail's, and he separated the mass into only two braids.

Vikhail snorted disdainfully. "Ar father would hang yer arse out to dry if he heard ya talkin' like this."

Vardec gave his brother an apprehensive look. "Ya wouldn't dare . . ."

"Try me," replied Vikhail.

Vardec grinned. "Ya know I'm only joshin' ya. I love ta see the look on yer face."

Vikhail punched Vardec in the arm. "Effin calotebas dung."

Vardec put a hand to the offended spot and rubbed it. "Hey, careful wit de arm. It's been workin' hard all day . . ."

Vikhail applied his fist to Vardec's arm a second time.

"Yeowch!" cried Vardec. "I'm not takin' any more of . . ." Before Vardec could finish, they heard a scream.

The three men turned towards the partially constructed building. An expression of alarm passed over Vardec's face. "That sounded like da lady Esmerelda."

The men glanced at one another for barely a moment before they were rushing into the building. They heard another scream, and sensing it coming from below them, they flew down the partially constructed stairs into the cellar. Only Goldare had the presence of mind to grab one of the torches still lit from earlier in the day. Following the sounds of a struggle, they went deeper into the cellar. Moments later, they entered the next room and paused at a scene that would make even the strongest of men weak at the knees.

Near the far wall there were three creatures. They were tall and slender with skulls that swooped back from long faces. Their skin was entirely black and their eyes glowed eerily orange around horizontal oval pupils. Two of the creatures flanked the third, who had a woman pinned against the stone wall with two of his three legs. She moaned from between bruised lips, and blood flowed down her face from a laceration on the side of her head. The men were held immobilized by the sight, for the woman's skirt had been torn away from her body. Her blood-streaked legs were parted and the daemon was viciously driving himself into her with no apparent intention of ceasing his activity. Despite her battered condition, the woman's hips gyrated in response to the thrusts of the daemon. There was no doubt as to the origins of a beast such as this one . . . a creature that exuded the epitome of absolute evil.

Vikhail was the first to move. He released his battle-axe from its harness and let it fly. The weapon sped through the air with deadly accuracy, but just as it was about to reach its mark, the daemon stepped out of the line of trajectory. The axe embedded itself into the chest of the defiled woman, and she slumped lifelessly to the floor.

Shaking himself free of shock, Vardec reached for the dagger he had sheathed at his belt. The daemons rushed at them just as he had it in hand. He muttered a prayer to the god Forseti as combat ensued. Up close, the creatures were larger than he had first thought, bigger even than Goldare, who was quite tall for a human. Vardec lunged at the daemon that approached the closest, and the only thoughts that entered his mind were those of survival.

Talemar ran through the partially erected structure, dodging various building materials as he approached the stairway leading downward. Hearing the sounds of melee from within, he hurried down and then made his way deeper into the cellar. He paused before entering the room as he saw creatures borne of his worst nightmares. He then saw the human and two halfen men who were fighting them.

Earlier in the day, Talemar had parted company with Alasdair, Cedric, and Aeris. He had a few things he needed to buy, and he didn't see the point in dragging everyone else along with him. He knew that Cedric had gone to the smithy in order to repair a blemish on one of his swords, and Aeris had gone in search of the residence of a sage by the name of Paxil. It was the same man who had sent a message to Master Adrianna, telling her of the presence of a Talent in Xordrel.

After his errands were complete, Talemar decided to walk by the construction site, for he had heard much talk about it as he made his way around the city. As he walked down the street that led towards the site, he heard a woman's screams coming from up ahead. He didn't know what was going on, but it didn't sound good. And now, viewing the scene before him, Talemar could only wish that he had been more prepared. The three men were definitely in a fight for their lives, for the daemons were well-equipped with their own natural weapons. Talemar responded in the best way he knew how.

The spell sprung easily to his lips and the magic rallied with little effort. A burst of light erupted before him for a moment, and just as it disappeared, a stream of electrical energy leaped from his outstretched fingertips. It struck the closest daemon, the energy slamming into the creature to make it recoil from its prey. The halfen stepped back from the smitten daemon, his eyes wide with incredulity. However, Talemar was not impressed. As the creature shook his head and began to slowly walk back towards the halfen, Talemar realized that the spell was having very little effect upon the daemon.

"Damn. That was a good spell."

Talemar swung around to find himself face-to-face with a cimmerean man. He hadn't even heard the other approach, so engrossed upon the melee before him. He realized the seriousness of his error too late, for the dark faelin was close enough to sheath a dagger into his belly if he so chose. Talemar swallowed convulsively as he prepared himself for an attack.

"Perhaps fire will prove to be a better weapon." With that, the cimmerean began his incantation. It was only then that Talemar realized that the faelin was not allied with the daemons. He stood by as the man cast his spell, watched the small spheres of fire as they struck their target . . . the daemon who faced the other halfen warrior. The daemon seemed to absorb the fire, totally unaffected by the flames.

The two men turned to regard one another. The situation had suddenly become direr than they initially realized. "It's your turn," said the cimmerean solemnly.

Talemar turned back to the fight. Both halfen had taken note of his presence and as they retreated from before the enemy, they led the creatures closer. The men were hard pressed against the physical prowess of their opponents, who were not only much larger than they, but had wickedly sharp claws on their hands and opposable toes on their flexible feet.

Talemar began the words to his incantation and put a hand into the pouch that hung from his sash. He withdrew a pinch of lytham powder, sprinkled it into the air before him, and completed the spell. He shouted for the halfen to get back as a cloud of noxious vapor began to form in the space before him. Talemar stepped away from it and then began the incantation to another spell. It was a simple one . . . only a mere cantrip. A breeze wafted into the room, blowing onto the cloud and causing it to drift towards the two closest daemons.

The creatures didn't know what had happened until it was too late. As they inhaled of the poisonous vapors, their movements began to slow. Once the cloud began to dissipate, the halfen rushed their opponents. Within moments the battle was over. Wearily, Goldare stumbled towards his comrades. The daemon he had fought lay in a bloody heap on the floor not far away. Long gashes stretched along one arm where he had been scored by the enemy, but other than that, he had suffered no harm. The lacerations would need to be cleaned, but they were not deep enough to require stitching.

Together, the group silently went over to the woman who lay against the wall. She stared at them from sightless eyes; there was no doubt she was dead. Vikhail shook his head dejectedly. It was his fault she had died. He bent to retrieve the axe from her chest and winced at the sound it made as he pulled it free. He would never look at the weapon the same way ever again. It was the first innocent the axe had claimed, and he hoped that it would be the last.

***

Magnus followed the men into the Silver Serpent Inn. Goldare, Vikhail, and Vardec had led the way through the city streets. The two halfen were residents of Xordrel, and Goldare visited the city often enough that he very well could have been. They were pleased with the invitation to join Magnus and Talemar at their inn. They would share a meal and drink ale to honor the battle in which they had taken part. Most likely, they would stay up well into the night, telling tales of past exploits and adventures.

After leaving the construction site, Magnus had learned that he and his fellow spell-caster were staying at the same inn. Much like himself, Talemar was of cimmerean descent, although he did not appear to be of full blood. His eyes were blue instead of lavender, and his complexion not quite as pale. His hair was black, but starting from the top near his forehead was a streak of white. It ran down the entire length of his hair and into the strip of leather that tied it at the nape of his neck. Magnus was impressed with his casting abilities and hoped that perhaps the other man would share some of the spells in his repertoire.

The common room was still crowded at this time of the day. Many patrons had already partaken of the evening meal and subsequently gone to their rooms for the night. However, many more sat around the tables: eating, drinking, and talking. Vikhail and Vardec made their way over to a vacant table and Goldare, Talemar, and Magnus followed. The men seated themselves, and within moments, a serving girl approached. Everyone asked that she bring some stew and a couple tankards of ale.

Magnus watched the goings on as he ate his meal. The halfen seemed to be very well known, for almost a dozen of the tavern's patronage bid the brothers a good evening as they quit the establishment. There were brief exchanges of pleasantries as well as good-natured pats on the shoulders and back. Goldare spoke of the caravan with which he traveled, and the destination that was next on the agenda. It was the city of Yortec, located just a few days to the west. It too, was a port city, although not quite so large and influential as Xordrel.

Throughout the meal, Magnus saw that Talemar seemed to be a bit distracted. More than once, Magnus noticed the other man looking around the room, almost as though he searched for someone. It wasn't until they had finished their meal and began to drink in earnest that the tavern began to clear of many of its patrons. It was easier to see to the far side of the room, and Talemar finally caught sight of those whom he had been looking for.

Magnus watched Talemar rise from his seat, excusing himself from the table. Then, the other man made his way to the other side of the room in order to greet some people that sat at a table against the far wall. It was a faelin man and woman, and when Magnus suddenly realized who they were, his mind stuttered.

Magnus looked on as Aeris rose from her place next to Alasdair. She was the epitome of beauty, hardly changed from when he had seen her last. When Talemar reached the table, he stepped up to the young woman and they shared an embrace. Magnus felt his heart become still in his chest as he watched the man kiss her soundly on the mouth. When Talemar finally released her, he gestured in the direction of Magnus and the rest of their group.

It wasn't until Alasdair and Aeris had almost reached the table that she noticed him. Magnus had been waiting for this moment, dreaming of it every day since they parted company all of those months ago. He was taken aback when Talemar kissed her, claiming her for his own before those who were present. But Magnus did not allow it to affect him. He would think about it later, in the sanctuary of his room. He kept his gaze on Aeris, and when the young woman finally looked towards him, Magnus was ready.

Magnus watched as she realized that, indeed, it was he that sat at the other side of the table. Alasdair was the first to say something to him, and Magnus tore his gaze away from Aeris only long enough to greet her brother and shake his hand across the table.

"Magnus, my good man. It is a pleasure to see you again," said Alasdair.

Talemar looked back and forth between the two men questioningly.

"Likewise," Magnus replied with a smile.

"You two know each other?" asked Talemar.

Alasdair nodded. "We met at the advent of the last warm season on a caravan train to the village of Grunchin. It was my first employment opportunity with Gharlas."

Magnus swung his gaze back over to Aeris, and she nodded her greetings to him, seating herself in a chair that Talemar had brought. He was pleased to note her discomfiture. Talemar introduced Aeris and Alasdair to Vikhail, Vardec, and Goldare. All three of the men stood from their seats at the approach of the lovely lady, and when they were introduced, they each bowed courteously to her.

Alasdair ordered another tankard of ale, and when it was brought, the men settled to their drinking. Aeris was quiet, simply taking in the conversation going on all around her. The halfen were good storytellers, and already were offering a rendition of the events that took place earlier that eve. Noticing that Tigerius had entered the common room, Alasdair beckoned to him and another man. When the two men approached, another table was pulled over to join the first. Everyone spread out across the two tables, and chairs were brought for the newcomers. Magnus remembered Tigerius, and when he was introduced, learned that the other man was Aeris' cousin, Cedric.

Magnus surreptitiously watched Aeris from across the table. At first she seemed rather nonchalant, but when Vikhail began to describe their enemies from the battle, her gaze suddenly sharpened. From her expression, Magnus could tell that she was taking in every word of the halfen's story. The group knew that the creatures they fought had been of daemonic origin, but they dared not say the words aloud, even in whispers. They would take the risk of bringing attention to themselves, and that was something they did not want or need.

Aeris trained her gaze on the halfen brothers, both of whom were taking turns telling the events of the skirmish in which they had taken part prior to arriving at the inn. She knew that they knew that the enemy they fought had been from the Hells. The knowledge that daemon-kind was becoming ever more prevalent disturbed her. They were infiltrating the most influential cities, and wreaking havoc where they could. Master Tallachienan had warned her mother and Master Dinim that this would happen. When dragon-kind had given aid to the Wildrunners in their fight against Lord Aasarak, an ancient pact between dragon and daemon-kind had been broken. Since then, both dragons and daemons had begun to run amok throughout Shandahar. The rendition to which she now listened would become more and more prevalent as time went on. People would die, and the world would be thrust into chaos.

Aeris continued to ponder the tale long after the completion of its telling. The men went on to discuss other things, but she paid them little heed. From across the table, she could feel Magnus' eyes on her despite the appearance that he participated in the conversation. Judging by the way he greeted her, she knew that her precipitous departure from Grunchin was foremost in his mind. She hadn't even left him a message. She had only the lousiest of excuses for her lack of respect, and not for the first time, wished that she could take back the choices she had made all of those months ago.

When Aeris first laid eyes on him after so long, her heart had skipped a beat. She remembered her body's response to him, the old familiarity rushing back. She was surprised to find him in Talemar's company, but even more to find them both in the company of a gypsy man and two halfen. When she heard their story, their camaraderie was justified. Experiences less than that had joined others of even more diverse origin. Aeris remembered the story her mother told of how she had met Dartanyen, Zorgandar, Armond, and Bussimot. They were some of the people that made up the group of people that would, one day, be known as the Wildrunners.

Once more, Aeris glanced over at Magnus. This time he didn't even try to hide the fact that he was staring at her. Unwaveringly, she met his gaze. She refused to back down from him. His gaze was virtually unreadable, and after several moments, he finally looked away. Aeris lowered her eyes to her hands, which were tightly clasped beneath the table. Despite her yearning to be near him again, she wondered when he would be away from her. She hated the overpowering effect that he had on her, and the sooner she could escape it, the better.

It wasn't until quite some time later that Aeris finally excused herself from the table. On the morrow, she had work that needed to be done. The same applied to Talemar, but he was a man. Most likely, he would stay up as long as the others, despite the responsibilities that awaited him. As she slowly made way to her chamber, Aeris wondered about Magnus. Why was he in Xordrel? Did he now remember his past? She wished only the best for him, despite any animosity that now existed between them. Hopefully she would not see much of him whilst she conducted her work in Xordrel, but she knew that those chances were slim. She would simply have to deal with the upcoming situations as they arose.

***

The sound of hoof-beats thundered through the dusty street. People stared at the hinterlean riders as they passed. It was an unfamiliar sight, for such faelin rarely visited Xordrel. The men were garbed in fine chain-mail, and they wore the insignia of the king of Elvandahar. Most people didn't recognize it, but those who did widened their eyes in surprise. Never had the city been visited by hinterleans such as these.

The riders finally stopped at the front of the Silver Serpent Inn. All but two dismounted and made their way up the steps and onto the veranda. They swung open the door to the inn and strode quickly inside. The six men looked all around the common room, obviously searching for someone. When Alasdair saw them standing there, his heart almost leaped from his chest.

Alasdair stood from his seat and quickly moved towards the men. Aeris stayed where she was seated, almost afraid to move. By the gods, what was going on? Why would the King's men have followed them all the way to Xordrel? Had something happened to her mother or father?

Aeris sought to calm the erratic beating of her heart as Alasdair spoke to the king's men. She noted the paleness of her brother's complexion and quickly realized that something was seriously amiss. She felt a lump form in her throat, and tears begin to burn behind her eyes. She prayed that her mother and father were safe, as well as her brother, Asgenar, whom she loved in spite his shortcomings.

It seemed like forever before Alasdair returned to the table. He took in Aeris' countenance and immediately laid a hand on her shoulder. "Ama and Babu are fine."

Aeris breathed a sigh of relief. "What of Asgenar?"

"He too, is fine. Although, he may beg to differ."

Aeris frowned. "What do you mean?"

Alasdair sighed heavily and seated himself. "Princess Elinora of Karlisle has been taken captive."

Aeris felt her eyes widen with shock. Before she could even begin to contemplate the ramifications of that statement, Alasdair was speaking again.

"King Zerxes has requested the aid of Elvandahar in recovering his daughter. We are honor-bound to comply since our Prince is betrothed to the girl." Alasdair snorted. "I bet Asgenar is loving life just about now."

Aeris cast her gaze to the table. She felt sorry Asgenar, knew how trapped he must feel. Despite her tendency to stay away from most things political, Aeris was strongly aware of what was going on. Throughout history, Elvandahar had stayed out of business concerning their neighbors, especially their human ones. But now things were different. When Elvandahar started to make peaceful negotiations with Karlisle, they knew that changes would be made. When the two houses agreed to become joined in honor of their new treatise, the two realms agreed to stand by one another in good times and in bad. Now Elvandahar would be forced to participate in a fight in which it wanted no part.

Alasdair sighed heavily, and Aeris looked back up to find him regarding her intently. "King Thalios' men have come to escort Cedric and I back to Elvandahar. Zerxes is amassing a group of specialists to determine Elinora's whereabouts, and we have been 'asked' to accompany the expedition."

Aeris shook her head. "But we just got here. I haven't had a chance to conduct my business."

Alasdair spoke in a monotone. "They want to leave the day after tomorrow."

"That isn't enough time."

Alasdair nodded. "I know. But I don't have a choice."

Aeris placed her hands before her on the table and slumped back in her seat. Damnation. Why did everyone else's business always have to come before hers? What about the academy? The Talent that she and Talemar had been sent to collect was the strongest they had yet to find. They couldn't just turn back and leave without him, not when they were so close. Finally, she looked back up at her brother.

"You know that I am not going with you."

Alasdair's brows drew together into a frown. "The Hells you aren't. You are going to be riding by my side when we leave here the morning after next."

Aeris shook her head. "Just like you, I have a job to do. I can't be expected to abandon my efforts because you suddenly have your own work."

Alasdair's frown deepened. "I can't believe we are actually having this conversation. I am your guard. That is still my job. I intend to fulfill that obligation by returning you home before I proceed to Karlisle."

"Then you will simply have to wait for me."

"You know I can't do that."

"Then you will have to leave me."

Alasdair pressed his lips into a thin line. "No."

"I am a big girl now. I am sure that I can find another escort home."

Alasdair's expression remained resolute. "No."

Aeris rose from her chair. "You don't have a choice." She paused and then continued. "There are things I have to do today. I will see you for the evening meal." With that said, she turned and walked out of the room.

Aeris felt her brother's gaze boring into her back until she was out of his line of vision. She hated fighting with him, but she saw no other way. She began to walk up the stairs to Talemar's room. He should be almost ready to start the day. She would tell him about what was going on and hope that he did not spend too much time dawdling over it. She knew that her chances of getting anything done prior to the mid-day meal were small, but she would at least try.

***

Magnus glanced up as Aeris and Talemar walked into the common room. The two looked around the place, and when they saw Alasdair, Cedric, and Tigerius, they made their way over to the table. Aeris and Talemar nodded to Magnus as they sat down. He noticed the questioning expression on Aeris' face, but she said nothing. Truth be told, he had been surprised when Alasdair invited him to join in the evening meal. He realized that Alasdair must consider him a friend, and he felt heartened. However, he accepted more out of a desire to see Aeris than for companionship. He couldn't help it . . . she had been all he could think about since seeing her the evening before.

Magnus immediately sensed the tension that began to stretch across the table. He had heard about Alasdair's need to return home, and that he had every intention of taking Aeris with him. Likewise, he had heard of Aeris' refusal to leave Xordrel until her work there was complete. He didn't know what that work entailed, but it was obviously important to her. However, Alasdair did not have the luxury of time. He needed to leave right away. But Aeris would have none of it. Magnus knew that he was about to hear the next installment of their argument.

Aeris sat across the table from her brother. She knew it was only a matter of time before Alasdair brought up their conversation from this morning. He would begin with some pleasantries, followed by an inquiry about her day.

He would then make an off-hand comment about the journey they would be taking the morning after tomorrow, and he would wait with tense expectancy for her response. More than anyone, Aeris knew her beloved brother. He was predictable, and for that she was grateful. His stubbornness was already almost too much to bear, and unpredictability would have set him beyond the realm of tolerable.

However, much to her surprise, Alasdair remained silent throughout their meal. He said nothing but for a few snippets of conversation with Tigerius and Cedric. Magnus was an interesting addition to their table, but since she had not expressed her desire to stay away from Magnus to Alasdair, she couldn't blame her brother for inviting the man to join them.

When the remnants of their meal were cleared away, they sat over mugs of steaming chag. Aeris was especially partial to the beverage, which was brewed from the large, dark seeds of the chagatha plant that grew in this region of the continent. She would have to remind herself to purchase a few bags of the beans to take home, for the beverage was a rare commodity in Elvandahar.

"Aeris, I hope you have pondered the talk we had this morning," began Alasdair, "and that you realize the idiocy of your words to me before you left."

Aeris felt her eyes widen with surprise as she looked up at her brother. It was obvious he was angry with her, angry enough to have gone outside of his comfort zone to do the unexpected. Either he wanted to pick a fight with her, or he truly thought that she would recant and offer him an apology.

Aeris schooled her expression into one of disapproval. Her mother once told her that she would be a good master one day with the types of expressions she could muster in the blink of an eye. "Indeed, I have not. I must say, my day has been full of other activities besides entertaining thoughts about an unsavory conversation I had the misfortune of sharing with you."

Alasdair gave her a sardonic grin. "Why, pray tell us about your busy day, dear sister, so that we may all understand the strenuous work you conduct."

Aeris felt Talemar stiffen beside her in response to the underhanded jab at their profession. She put a hand on his arm to quiet him as she spoke. "Brother, so kind it is for you to ask about my day. I must say, for a moment there, I began to wonder about those manners our poor mother pounded into you for all of those years." Without a break in stride, Aeris continued. "Talemar and I spoke to our informant today. Sage Paxil was able to give us an idea of the boy's abilities, as well as the location of his home. However, as it took us most of the day to discover the location of the sage, we had to put off visiting the boy until the morrow."

Aeris finally stopped to regard Alasdair's thunderous expression. His brows were drawn together into a deep scowl, and his eyes glittered with anger. Cedric and Tigerius remained conspicuously silent, knowing better than to interrupt a family matter such as this one. Nothing either one had to say could have altered the situation anyway.

"Damn, what a shame. The future of your work seems even bleaker than before. You may get the chance to meet him just once before we will begin our journey home."

Aeris shook her head. "Like I said to you this morning, you will have to leave without me. I refuse to depart this city without my work having been completed."

Aeris felt Talemar shifting in his seat. It was obvious that he was uncomfortable. However, she had no sympathy for him. He had witnessed plenty of family arguments before. Why should this one be any different than the others?

"Stop this nonsense!" exclaimed Alasdair. "If I have to sedate you and tie you to your larian, I will do it. You are behaving like a child!"

Aeris' eyes glittered malevolently. "I dare you to try."

"Challenge accepted," Alasdair growled.

Magnus looked from one sibling to the next. Damnation. They were serious. Alasdair meant to take her, whether Aeris wanted it or not. Aeris was just as determined to stay. Magnus could understand both sides. Alasdair had to leave, but at the same time, Aeris was his responsibility. In his right mind, he could never allow her to stay in Xordrel without escort. On the other hand, Aeris wished to complete her responsibility to the academy. She refused to leave without making attempts to bring the young Talent with her. In her right mind, she could not just turn around and leave now . . . they were far too close.

Then the solution came to him. Alasdair would be able to leave, and Aeris able to complete her work in Xordrel. If Alasdair thought him a friend, maybe, just maybe, he would entrust his sister to his care. Magnus held up his hands. "Wait. Stop. Perhaps I can help."

Magnus suddenly found himself the focus of their undivided attention. He turned towards Alasdair. "I know you want to see Aeris home with you, but consider what she would be giving up. To come all of this way for nothing is difficult for anyone to bear. But for her, to be so close to completing the task, it would be ten times worse. Consider allowing me to escort Aeris back to Elvandahar. Goldare, Vardec, and Vikhail will accompany us. They are good fighters, and will protect Aeris with their lives."

Alasdair and Aeris only stared at him for a few moments. The table was quiet . . . even Cedric and Tigerius didn't move. Magnus could see Alasdair pondering Magnus' words, weighing them in his mind. He knew that it was unlikely Alasdair would agree, but it was worth putting forth the offer. Besides, Magnus wanted to go to Elvandahar anyways. It might make the trip better if

Aeris were to be a part of it, and he didn't mind waiting until she was finished with her work in Xordrel.

Several more moments went by before Alasdair finally answered. Magnus was surprised when he heard the response . . . more than surprised.

"Fine. I will allow you and your comrades to see Aeris home, just as long as you promise not stay here for too long. I will provide you with silver and gold for the trip, and I will contact King Thalios about the change in escort."

Alasdair's expression was unreadable as he rose from the table. "I have a long day ahead of me tomorrow, and the next morning I will be leaving. I am turning in for the night." Alasdair then nodded to everyone and left.

Aeris sat there, dumbfounded. She couldn't believe the events that had just unfolded before her. Alasdair had relinquished his responsibility for her to a man from which she only wanted to escape. How crazy was that? However, she was free to continue her work. Aeris turned to Talemar, who glanced at her for only a moment before rising from the table himself. His expression was solemn as he nodded to her and left. She knew that he went to speak to her brother, ask Alasdair if he was making the right decision about allowing Magnus to accompany her back to Elvandahar. But, if she knew her brother, nothing would be able to change his mind . . . unless she was to say something.

Aeris then focused upon Magnus. He turned when he noticed her attention on him. His gaze was shuttered, but she sensed that he was just as surprised as she about her brother's decision. Aeris abruptly rose from her own seat. She would go to her room to think about what would happen within the next few days, for she would say nothing to Alasdair about her reticence towards Magnus. If this was what she would have to endure in order to complete her task, then so be it. The journey would last only a few weeks, and then she would be home. Once again, Magnus would become merely a thing of her past, and she would be free to remember only what she thought she should . . . the man from her dreams who, somewhere in the world, awaited her.

CHAPTER 7

Aeris stood upon the veranda of the Silver Serpent Inn. Before her were eight hinterlean men, each standing by his larian. They were isterian, men from the palace who served to keep the place secure. Now they would be an escort to their prince, the man who would be next in line to the throne of Elvandahar should something happen to Asgenar.

Aeris turned when she caught sight of Alasdair leading his larian from the stable alongside the inn. Behind him was Talemar, leading his own animal. Aeris knew how difficult it was for him to make the decision to accompany Alasdair to Karlisle. Aeris could see that he would rather stay with her in Xordrel, but he knew that his true duty lay with Alasdair and Asgenar. If Aeris had been a man, the same would have applied to her. However, as a woman, she was not expected to go into battle, and her primary responsibilities lay with the academy.

Aeris stepped down from the veranda and approached the two men. She walked over to Talemar first, wanting to give herself the chance to collect herself before she faced her brother. Looking into Talemar's eyes, she could see the regret echoed there, as well as something more that she couldn't quite decipher. He was the first to reach out, and he pulled her close to him almost roughly. His grip was tight, but she returned the embrace in kind. He buried his face into her hair, and she could feel his breaths as he inhaled and then blew out. Finally he released her, but she could tell that he didn't really want to let her go. Before she knew what he was doing, he was pulling her into him again, kissing her with an intensity he had never used before. When he pulled away, she was breathless.

"Just say the words and I will stay," he said in a voice deep with emotion.

Aeris was silent for a moment before she responded. "You know I will not. I am very aware of your place. I would not ask you to step away from it."

Talemar put his lips alongside her face, close to her ear. "I will do it even if you do not say the words."

"I know. That is why I will tell you to go. I do not want you to stay. Besides, I have Tiger to keep me company," she whispered.

Talemar nodded and stepped back. As he had no immediate blood ties to Elvandahar, Tigerius was not bound to the king and thus not required to serve him. He was free to accompany Aeris on her return trip to Elvandahar. Despite her reservations about the man, she knew he was a friend and that she could trust him in this protective capacity. It would be good to have him at her side on the long journey home after she completed her work.

Aeris turned and made her way over to Alasdair. He stood silently by his larian, waiting for her to bid him farewell. Aeris felt the tears burning behind her eyes. She loved him so much. Not only was he her brother, he was her best friend. She regretted fighting with him, but ultimately knew that it was for the best. If she didn't fight for her place in the world, she knew that she would never have one. The people she loved most would keep her from it . . . not because they sought to do her a disservice, but simply because they loved her.

Aeris stopped when she stood before him. Just like always, he knew that she was about to cry. He wrapped his arms around her and drew her close. "You can still change your mind. We will wait for you to gather your things," he said quietly.

Aeris shook her head. "No. I need to do this, you realize that now."

Alasdair nodded. "Yes, I know. But I just wanted to be sure you knew that there is still a choice."

Aeris felt the emotion begin to swell inside of her. She knew that Alasdair would be placing himself at risk when he placed himself in service to the king of Karlisle. Throughout her life, it had been rare that she regretted the gender with which she had been born, but now was one of those times. As a man, she would have been expected to go to Karlisle with her brother. She would not lie to herself; she would much rather do that than to chase after a boy in an unfamiliar city far from home. Regardless, she had not the choice. If she was anything like her aunt Sheri, they may have given in to her simply because she was good at getting what she wanted. Not only that, she was damn good with the sword. But Aeris was neither good at getting what she wanted, nor was she particularly skilled with the sword. She was only a journeyman spell-caster . . . delegated to accompanying new recruits back to the academy of her training.

"I am afraid for you Alasdair," she whispered.

Her brother pulled back just enough so as to look into her face. "By the gods, why?"

Aeris sniffed and shook her head. "It's only that I wish to see you again, is all. Life would be incredibly boring without you."

Alasdair cupped her face in both of his hands. "Aeris, you worry too much. Nothing is going to happen to me. Besides, I would be afraid to find out what would happen to all of those people if it did." Alasdair grinned.

Aeris tapped him on the side of the face with the flat of her hand. "Bad man. You shouldn't pick fun with me. I am serious, you know."

Alasdair wiped the smile off his face. "I know. I love you, Aeris. I *will* be back for you."

Aeris grabbed the front of his leather vest and put her cheek to his studded leather, clutching him close to her. All the while she fought the feeling that she had heard those words spoken to her before, by someone else. Finally, she released him and stepped back. Alasdair reached out his hand to caress the side of her face before turning to his larian. Everyone else was already mounted and ready to depart. They began to make their way down the street as Alasdair mounted his own beast in one fluid motion. Once settling himself into the saddle, Alasdair raised his hand in farewell as he turned to follow the rest. When he reached them, they all kicked their larian into a gallop. The sound of receding hoof-beats echoed through the street. Aeris stood by until the sound was gone, staring in the direction in which Alasdair had ridden. She could only pray that no harm would come to him as he answered the call of duty.

Aeris turned back to the inn. She almost walked into Tigerius, who had been standing behind her. When she looked up at him and into his eyes, she saw the sorrow reflected there. He put a comforting arm around her shoulders and she allowed herself the luxury of leaning into the reassurance it offered. Perhaps Tiger wasn't the scoundrel she had always thought him to be.

***

Aeris was in the middle of plaiting her hair when she heard a knock on the door. She thought it must be Tigerius, coming to get her so they could enjoy their morning meal together. "Come in," she said, hastening her pace so that he wouldn't be forced to wait for her.

The door opened to admit Magnus, who stepped into the room and closed it behind him. Aeris ceased her activity to regard him for a moment, but when she realized what she was doing, she resumed. Gods only knew what he was doing there, not to mention she hadn't been expecting him. Of course, she should have realized that he would come to her at some point, for they had yet to really speak to one another since the morning she had shown him the way to Andahye.

"Good morning, Aeris."

She nodded in response, taking the thin piece of leather from the table and tying it at the end of the long plait that now lay across her shoulder. Magnus watched her as she completed the task. When she turned her full attention to him, he began to speak once more.

"I just thought that I would come to offer my services as you go to speak with Mateo's family today. I wouldn't want you to go alone, and I thought you could use the support."

"Thank you, but Tigerius said that he would be coming with me today."

Magnus nodded. "I know, but I spoke to him about it, and he agreed that I would be better suited to accompany you. He left earlier this morning to acquire some supplies for our trip back to Elvandahar. We have a lot of planning to do, especially since we will not be traveling with a caravan. Vikhail, Vardec, and Goldare have many preparations to make, and Tigerius said that he would be able to help."

Aeris nodded. Great . . . this was just great. Now she was stuck spending the whole of her day with a man she wanted to keep as far away from as possible. But she knew that was silly. They would be traveling together for quite some time. She supposed that she needed to get used to his company.

Aeris rose from the bed. She picked up her sash and began stringing her pouches and her dagger upon it. She then tied the silk around her waist, knotting it inconspicuously at her side. "You know," began Magnus, "if I had known that you were looking for Paxil, I could have told you his whereabouts. We have already become acquainted."

Aeris looked up at him questioningly. "Really? How is it that you have come to know the sage?"

Magnus shrugged. "The masters in Andahye sent me to him when they realized they couldn't help me."

Aeris took in this information. So, the masters had been unable to restore his memory. "Was Paxil able to help you?"

Magnus snorted. "Are you kidding? The man speaks only in riddles. Of course he couldn't help me."

Aeris sighed. Yes, Paxil did have that tendency. However, he had been very forthcoming about the location of the Talent she sought . . . Mateo, the boy for whom she had traveled so far. She only hoped that his family would see the benefits of having him return to Elvandahar with her.

"I am sorry to hear about that. I always hoped that the masters would find a way to help you," she said.

"Did you?"

Aeris turned to Magnus. He regarded her from piercing lavender eyes. "Of course," she replied with a frown.

Magnus only nodded.

"Come, we have much to accomplish today," she said.

Magnus simply nodded again and followed Aeris out of the room.

***

Having completed the last of his errands, Tigerius made his way back to the inn. He hoped that Aeris' day had been just as fruitful as his own, and that they would soon be leaving the city. It wasn't that he didn't like Xordrel; on the contrary . . . he enjoyed staying there very much. However, things had changed dramatically when Alasdair left. Tiger had suddenly become responsible for someone other than himself. He had never been in such a situation before, and

Tiger felt it more than a little disconcerting. He wouldn't rest easy until the girl was in her bed back in Elvandahar.

Reaching the steps, Tiger took them two at a time up to the veranda of the Silver Serpent Inn. Once entering the establishment, he took another set of stairs to the second story. He then entered the room he had been sharing with Alasdair and Cedric not more than two days ago. He missed his comrades already and wished that circumstances had not taken them away from their first mission to see Aeris home after conducting her business.

Tiger removed his belt and boots, and then fell onto the bed. He enjoyed the comfort it offered, very aware that he would be leaving it in the near future. Yet, he didn't mind sacrificing that luxury. He knew that it was more than just his desire to unload his responsibility. For the first time in his life, he had begun to miss his home. It had been a long while since he last saw Sangrilak, and he imagined his mother and father must be wondering about him . . . perhaps even *worried* about him. Somehow he had never had it in him to care before, and he didn't have the slightest idea of what had changed.

Tiger shifted from his back to his side, suddenly introspective. He never remembered a time that he didn't want to escape the city he had begun to know as his prison . . . not to mention those who were his prison-keepers. Somewhere deep within himself, Tiger knew he loved his parents, but his lust for freedom finally overrode anything else in his life. Since his leave-taking with Alasdair and Aeris at the end of Tiseren the year before, he had never returned to Sangrilak . . . not even to see his mother and father. Within the down-time between travels, Tigerius had stayed in Elvandahar, sending only the briefest of correspondences to let his parents know that he was alive and well. They had sent a response, telling him that they wished to see him home again, even if only for a short while. He hadn't bothered with a reply.

Now he wondered what had been wrong with him.

Tigerius shook his head. It couldn't have been his attraction for Aeris that kept him away from Sangrilak. Although, he did admit that it may have a played a part. For quite some while he nurtured romantic feelings towards her, but had never been able to tell her so. She always seemed to keep him at a distance, despite his attempts to make conversation. Only now did he realize that he may have been trying too hard, not to mention that his forays with other women were not topics about which she wished to have knowledge.

It wasn't long after that he came to realize that Talemar felt the same way towards Aeris, despite their familial relationship. And when he discovered what had transpired between the two of them, he couldn't help but feel some measure of jealousy. However, that didn't stop him from making attempts for her affections. How could he not? Then she was gone . . . having taken a trip to a city they called Andahye. She had almost perished on that journey. No one, including Aeris herself, knew who had saved her from certain death. Since her return, she had never been the same.

And now here he was, a companion to a woman whom he had known his entire life. In many ways, she was a stranger to him. Nevertheless, something connected them on a level with which he had no familiarity. Tigerius stared into the encroaching darkness beginning to pervade the room. It seemed he would have plenty of time to figure it out.

***

Magnus regarded Aeris, who rode before him on her larian. Just that morning, the group left the city of Xordrel in the company of the boy Talent Aeris had been sent to bring back to Elvandahar. He rode before her on his own larian, one that had been purchased for him with the gold that Alasdair had given her before he left. Magnus was surprised at how easy it was for the boy's parents to let their son go. Just three days before, they had met Mateo and his family for the first time. The mother and father seemed ill-at-ease during their visit, despite Aeris' attempts to make them comfortable with their presence. The fact remained that they were sorcerers . . . that rare breed of individuals about which many people spoke only in whispers. By the end of the visit, it was obvious that Mateo's parents were ashamed of their son, afraid of the emergent powers with which he had been endowed. The mother had pulled Aeris aside at the end of the visit, asking her what were chances that any of her other offspring would inherit the 'Talent' that Mateo now exhibited. Magnus only watched as Aeris shook her head, saying something to the woman he could not hear . . . did not care to hear.

Magnus watched Aeris' backside as it swayed with the movement of the larian. He loved watching her, and could hardly keep his eyes off of her. A couple of times already, Goldare had caught him staring at her. The other man simply raised an eyebrow inquiringly. Goldare never said anything, but Magnus thought the man must think him to be rather lecherous. Most likely, it was plain for Goldare to see that Magnus was infatuated with the woman and that he wanted her. It was easy for men to notice those types of things.

Magnus looked beyond Aeris to the boy. He had medium brown hair that tended to hang down into his vibrantly blue eyes. He was gangly and awkward, his body growing too fast for the rest of him to keep up. He had seen about fourteen or fifteen years and was going through the transition from boy to man. The day after their initial visit, Magnus and Aeris returned to the boy's home to find that his few possessions were already packed into an old travel sack. Looking at Aeris, he could see the disgruntled expression on her face before she concealed it from his family. The farewells were brief, and only a short time later, they were leading a downtrodden Mateo away from his home. Magnus knew that ignorance dictated the parents' actions, but he hated that two people could so easily turn away from their own son. Sure, he and Aeris had given them the nice speech . . . Mateo would learn to be all that he could be at the academy, they would take care of his needs, and he would be a member of a family. But Magnus rather thought that the decision should have been more difficult to make, for it was unlikely that these people would see their son for a very long time.

The group moved west towards the city of Yortec. They kept a rather good pace, for plains travel was relatively easy. Their only obstacle was the thick grass that swayed with the winds. Goldare, Vikhail, and Vardec kept the lead. Goldare rode a dark gray lloryk, while the two halfen sat upon creatures that were unfamiliar to Magnus. They were much the same height as a larian, but much stockier. The hooves were not cloven, and their diet purely vegetarian. There were no scales beneath the thick layer of coarse hair that covered their sturdy bodies. "'Tis a type of horse," said Vardec. "Haven't ya ever seen one before?"

Magnus could only shake his head. "The lloryk don' like the climate this far south," said Vikhail, "and we're a bit heavy fer the standard larian. These animals come from the eastern side of Ansalar."

Magnus could only nod his head in understanding. The animals were interesting to him, but not half so much as the men who rode them. He had never seen a halfen ride astride before. Heretofore, he had always known them as a people that preferred to keep their feet on the ground. But these two were different. Against their father's wishes, the brothers left their work at the smithy to accompany Magnus and Goldare to a location far to the north. Perhaps it was for the gold that had been offered to them, but Magnus rather thought that it had much to do with wanderlust. They were still young, and had a desire to see new places. This was the perfect opportunity to do so, especially since they were getting paid to do it.

That night, the group slept beneath a canopy of stars. After the evening meal, which Vikhail and Vardec had taken the honors of producing, Aeris spent most of her time with Mateo. Magnus did not interfere; he knew that this was the beginning of a long relationship for them. The boy would be returning to Aeris' home to be trained either by her mother or the man who trained her. Mateo needed to learn that Aeris was someone he could trust, someone who placed his needs as a priority. Despite the fact that he wanted to have her in his own company, Magnus refrained from giving in to his own selfish desires. Perhaps he would have plenty of time to spend with her later, after she had developed a rapport with Mateo.

However, Magnus was pretty sure that she didn't have the same inclination for his company. More often than not, it seemed that she sought to stay as far away from him as possible. This was so different from the Aeris he had known before when they traveled with Gharlas' caravan. Then, she couldn't seem to get enough of his company. And when he kissed her the night of the celebration in Grunchin, Magnus thought that she wanted him as much as he did her. As it turned out, such was not the case.

Magnus turned on his bedroll to look in her direction. On one side of her slept Mateo on his own bedroll. It too, had been purchased for him before they left Xordrel. On the other side was Tigerius. Magnus frowned. The man fancied himself her protector, hardly ever leaving her side. Magnus found himself slightly annoyed. He didn't remember Tigerius caring this much before. Perhaps it was because Alasdair was no longer there to fill the position that made Tigerius feel he should take the job in his place. It was just another obstacle Magnus felt he must somehow overcome.

***

The next day dawned pleasant and warm. The group got a head start after a quick breakfast, and they made good time until the mid-day meal. They ate of their travel rations, and then continued to move west and slightly north for the rest of the day. They decided to set up camp early in the later afternoon when they found a copse of trees that surrounded a small lake. Aeris, being a woman, was the first to reap the benefits. Magnus had to keep himself from staring in the direction of the lake when she went there to bathe. His imagination went wild the entire time she was there, and it was only when she was finally in their midst again that it calmed.

The halfen brothers were the next to go, using the evening meal as their excuse. "The earlier we clean up, the earlier we can begin to prepare our dinner," said Vardec. Vikhail only nodded in agreement. Magnus shook his head as he watched the brothers jauntily make their way towards the lake. He expected that they wouldn't be too long, but his assumption was erroneous. The sun was close to beginning its descent by the time they returned. Even Goldare, who was usually quite relaxed, was showing a hint of irritation.

While Vikhail and Vardec prepared the evening meal, Tigerius, Goldare, and Mateo took their turn at the lake. Aeris had prepared the fire and boiled some water before the brothers' return. When they began to make towards her, she quickly got up and left them to their work. Magnus watched her, saw how she kept herself distanced from everyone but for Tiger and Mateo. It was easy to see that she did not care for anyone else's company.

Magnus pressed his lips into a thin line. He could almost imagine that she looked upon her escort with disdain, and that she was above them. He hated the turn his thoughts had begun to take, for he did not want to believe that of her. He wondered if his mind was simply concocting the expression, or if it was real.

It wasn't long before the others returned from the lake. Magnus nodded as he passed them on his own way there. He could have bathed with the others, but found that he needed the time to be alone. Once reaching the water, he removed his tunic and laid it on a low-lying branch. His trousers soon followed it. The feel of the water on his body was wonderful, and he took his time reveling in it.

Magnus allowed his thoughts to wander, thoughts that concerned Aeris, and even more . . . himself. For the thousandth time since waking up in the middle of nowhere with no idea of his location or identity, Magnus wondered who he was, where he was from, and what had happened to him. Certain things seemed to tug at his memory, and he hated that he couldn't grasp the string that fluttered just beyond his reach.

When he was finished, Magnus walked out of the lake and reached for his tunic. It was then that he saw it. It was a magnificent spider, about the size of his thumb, and perfect in every detail. It somehow seemed familiar to him, but he couldn't quite remember ever seeing a spider colored quite like this one. Its legs were black, as was the marking in the shape of an arrow on its abdomen. The rest of its hairy body was a reddish brown. He found himself reaching out to the creature, and then picking it up and placing it in the palm of his hand.

The goddess Tholana watched Tallachienan from the eyes of her spider. He looked so young, much younger than she remembered him to be. But then again, he was mortal now, just like she was. She was pleased that she had finally found him. She had been following him and his companions since they left Xordrel, and had only been waiting for the perfect opportunity to catch him unawares. It was strange . . . despite her aptitude for scrying, she had been unable to detect her quarry, much less track him. Yet, she was able to follow the woman, Aeris Timberlyn.

Tholana licked her lips. She was giddy with suppressed excitement. Tallachienan seemed to have no idea of his true identity. He referred to himself as Magnus . . . what kind of a name was that? And he didn't even appear to be in possession of all of his powers. What was even more delicious was that, not only had TC lost all of his memories, but he was in the company of the daughter of her most hated enemy. Many years ago, Adrianna Darnesse had been Tallachienan's first choice for a mistress, and Tholana hated her for that. Now, Tholana would make Damaeris Timberlyn suffer for the transgressions of her mother . . . if it was within the scope of her limited power, of course.

As Tholana continued to watch TC, her followers began to strategically place themselves around the encampment. As of yet, no one had taken notice. They were fools, all of them. She remembered the prowess of the ranger, Sirion Timberlyn, and knew that she would not have been able to get this close if he had been there. He was a much older man now, and had sired the girl that would be the target of her attack this evening. Despite her desire to place her focus upon Tallachienan, Tholana would restrain herself. With the plan she had in mind, she would be able to influence him in ways she could only imagine.

It wasn't long before her priests were in place. TC had placed her spider in the palm of his hand and allowed it to creep about upon his arm. Tholana smiled. Her pet mesmerized him, and she felt gratified. The spider moved over the soft place behind the elbow and she quickly issued a command. "Bite him now!"

Magnus recoiled slightly when he felt the spider bite him. He frowned slightly, for it had been unprovoked. He then gently brushed the spider off of his arm, watched as it fell to the ground and crawled swiftly away. He looked at the wound it inflicted, saw the red marks it left in the crook of his arm. Damn, he would have to put something on that.

Once dressed, Magnus began to walk the short distance back to the encampment. The bite on his arm throbbed abominably, and he wished he hadn't been fool enough to pick up an unfamiliar spider. It was then he suddenly began to feel a strange sensation. It spread quickly, first numbing his chest and torso, and then moving to his arms and legs. Within only a few short moments, he was immobilized, the poison of the spider paralyzing him. Magnus slumped to the ground, and the only things he could move were his eyeballs. Lying on his side, he gazed upon the woods before him. Then, from out of the lengthening shadows walked a woman.

Magnus felt his eyes widen. For the second time, a sense of familiarity swept over him, but then it was gone. The woman was beautiful, with hair colored like the blackest of night and eyes a deep lavender. It was easy to see that she was a full-blooded cimmerean. Once reaching his side, the woman knelt beside him on the ground. Her eyes danced with laughter, and her red lips were pulled up into a grin. Her body was exquisitely made, her curves barely concealed beneath the thin fabric of her gossamer gown. She pulled him up, leaned him against the nearest tree, and then chuckled.

"Hello, my dear. It is so good to see you again after so long. I am pleased that you found my spider so fascinating. She packs a rather powerful bite, does she not? It would be fun to give you the details of your identity, but even more so to watch you discover it for yourself." She paused for a moment before continuing. "My name is Tholana. You don't remember me now, but one day soon you will. You will rue this day, mark my words." With that, she took his jaw in her hands pressed her lips forcibly against his.

A part of Magnus would have recoiled if it could, but another part of him responded in the way a man does to any beautiful woman . . . especially with a kiss such as this one. Her breasts brushed against his arm as she pressed close to him, but then she was pulling away. He was left to watch as she left his side. Yet, it was but a moment later that he saw Aeris enter his line of vision, flanked on either side by two dark-robed priests. It was only then that he took note of the sounds of battle coming from just beyond the line of trees behind him. *Damn . . . this was an ambush.*

Aeris was livid with indignation, disgusted with herself for being taken so easily. But the cimmereans had taken them by surprise, attacking with swiftness and efficiency. They melted out of the trees that surrounded the encampment, their spells and weapons ready. Five of them, a woman and four men, trained their focus immediately upon her, most likely because she was a spell-caster and able to do the most harm from a distance. They disrupted her spell, incapacited her with relative ease, and then bound her wrists before her with a sticky rope. Two of the men grabbed each of her upper arms and the woman led her away. Meanwhile, the two other men herded Mateo alongside.

Aeris looked down at the substance that bound her. It was made of several white strands all stuck together to form a rope. The priestess, who was able to handle the material without it adhering to her, held the other end of the rope. Aeris noticed that the woman's hands seemed glossy, and she realized that the priestess used some type of oil that made it possible.

Aeris then glanced from one man to the next. She attempted to give them a false sense of docility, tried to make them think that the blows the priestess had inflicted upon her had been enough. She tasted of the blood that flowed from her left nostril, finding the tickle of it most irritating.

Suddenly she acted. She dug her heels into the ground and then pulled back on the rope. The priestess was jerked backward with the force of Aeris' pull, almost falling onto the ground. Aeris applied her elbow to the gut of one of the priests while kicking out at the other one with a well-aimed foot. Both men grunted in surprise, but then they were quickly taking hold of her once again. The priestess quietly composed herself and then slowly approached. The malicious gleam in the woman's lavender eyes was warning enough to Aeris, and she braced herself against what retaliation was to come.

"You stupid little bitch," hissed the woman. Aeris tried to double over with the fist to her abdomen, but the men pulled her back up. The priestess than slapped her across the face, bringing instant tears to her eyes. The woman smiled with triumph and then reached her hand into the neckline of Aeris' tunic. She took a nipple between her thumb and forefinger, twisting it savagely until Aeris cried out. "Don't cross me again."

Aeris said nothing as the woman then walked away from her, once more pulling her along. Her nipple burned and throbbed from the rough treatment, and she seethed with humiliation. Only moments later they were approaching the lake. Within the shadows cast by the trees, another woman awaited them. "Here she is, my lady Tholana, just as you commanded," said the priestess.

The woman walked towards her and Aeris felt her heart still in her chest. No. This couldn't possibly be the same Tholana whom her mother had fought all of those years ago. Lavender eyes glittering, the woman smiled, and Aeris instantly knew that Tholana recognized her. She felt her pulse quicken as she made the realization that this woman was indeed Adrianna's nemesis.

"Well, well, well. I can hardly believe my good fortune," drawled Tholana in a mesmerizing voice.

Aeris swallowed nervously, yet held herself up with an air of dignity despite her bruises. She would not let this woman intimidate her.

"The daughter of the woman that I despise most in this world stands before me. My, has she grown. I haven't seen Adrianna Darnesse Timberlyn since before this one was even a seed in her mother's womb."

Aeris watched as the woman circled her and only then realized that the priests had left her side. The priestess stood a short distance away, intently watching the scene. Mateo continued to be held by the other two priests a few steps behind her. She couldn't help but think what would happen to them. So much good an escort had done her . . . and *where in the Hells was Magnus?*

Tholana narrowed her eyes. "I know something that you don't." She lowered the pitch of her voice, giving it a malevolent timbre. She paused for a moment, almost like she was waiting for something. "Don't you want to know what it is?" Her eyes glittered in the approaching darkness.

Aeris slowly shook her head. "No. I am sure it is something I do not wish to know."

Tholana brought her lips up into a mirthless smile. "I am sure you know who Tallachienan Chroalthone is, do you not?"

Aeris only nodded.

"He is your mother's Master, the man who taught her all about his infamous school of magic." Tholana's voice had become scathing. "But do you want to know what else he is?"

Aeris said nothing. She knew that Tholana would tell her whether she wanted her to or not.

"He is your mother's lover," she spat. "They fornicated together whilst your mother studied within the bowels of his citadel. Adrianna was *Promised* to be married to your father, but she couldn't resist the temptation to lie in the bed of a god."

Aeris reeled with disbelief. It was a lie . . . it had to be. Her mother loved her father dearly. She would never have done such a thing, no matter what the temptation.

Tholana stopped in front of Aeris, her lavender eyes wide with intensity. "You don't believe me. Tsk tsk. Now why would I fabricate something like this? Haven't you often wondered why she says so little about training with her Master? Haven't you wondered why your father becomes so irritable when Tallachienan's name is mentioned?"

Aeris' mind recoiled at the truth behind Tholana's words. Yes, she had noticed those things, but did it have to mean that her mother had been unfaithful to her father? She shook her head slowly. "Why are you telling me this?"

Tholana's smile widened. "Everyone thinks that Adrianna is the epitome of what is good and right . . . that she is so infallible. Everyone thinks that Tallachienan is so generous and that he is a hero for helping the Wildrunners save the world. I just wanted to set the record straight." Tholana brought her condescending voice down to a whisper and stepped close to Aeris, bringing her lips to her ear. "Adrianna was Tallachienan's whore. The Master took her as his mistress, and the only reason they are not together today is because of the duty Adrianna had to the prophecy."

Aeris shook her head and stepped back. "Yes, you are right. I don't believe you. You are sick with jealousy because you could not have Tallachienan for yourself. He rejected you and you can't accept that." Aeris knew that she was treading on treacherous ground, but she suddenly didn't care. "Now you tell me lies so as to turn me against my mother because you know she has become powerful enough that you can no longer hurt her. It has been centuries since Tallachienan turned you away. Is it not about time that you stopped following him around like a vixen in heat?"

Aeris suddenly recoiled at the hand that struck her across the face. Tholana wrapped her other hand around her neck and began to squeeze. "You don't know what you are talking about," she hissed at her ear, "and you will pay for your words." Aeris felt herself being whipped around. Once more the priests were there, holding her arms. It was dark, but with her faelin-sight, she could still see Tholana easily. The woman stood before her, placing her hand across Aeris' brow. "Yes, you will regret what you have said to me this night. I will make sure of it."

Aeris slowly began to feel a strange compression in her mind. Her breath caught in her throat, and within moments fear began to close over her. What was happening? She looked into Tholana's eyes, saw that the color had turned from lavender to a bright red. She vaguely sensed Mateo struggling behind her, felt his fear mingling with hers. The hand across her forehead became like a brand, and the pressure against her mind increased. Aeris closed her eyes, concentrating only upon fighting that which sought entry. Her heart pounded in her chest and her breaths exploded from her mouth. The pressure increased and pain arced through her head. Aeris felt her mental barriers crumble, and she screamed.

***

Magnus broodingly stared into the fire. The effects of the poison had finally worn off, and all that was left was a mild ache in his joints. Once more he glanced over at Aeris. She was unconscious . . . as was Mateo. Goldare, Vikhail, and Vardec had found them like that after the skirmish. The men brought the two back to the encampment and had been waiting for them to awaken. Magnus wasn't sure if he was ready for that . . . for he had seen the meeting between Aeris and Tholana. The scene played itself over and over again in his mind, and he felt betrayed to the very core of his being.

Within the gathering darkness, Magnus had seen Aeris being brought to Tholana. His body was stiff from the paralysis, and he had begun to hear a loud *whooshing* noise in his ears that drowned out every other sound. The effects of the poison thundered through him, and once more he cursed his stupidity. Anger coursed through his mind, for he could do nothing to help the men who fought at the site of the encampment. Neither could he help Aeris.

Magnus had watched as Tholana circled the young woman and began to speak. He struggled to hear what was being said over the sound filling his ears to no avail. Held just a few steps away from Aeris, there was Mateo. The boy's eyes were wide with fear. It was easy to see that all Mateo wanted to do was run. Magnus then began to squint his eyes. The poison was beginning to affect his sight and he strained to continue to see what was happening. Tholana had finally stopped and was standing in front of Aeris. The woman stepped closer to her, bringing her face close to Aeris'. Magnus' vision began to darken, and just as it went to black, he saw Tholana embrace her . . .

Magnus shook his head. It was hard to believe, but it was true. Aeris knew Tholana, and it was likely she had played a role in the ambush. Vikhail, Vardec and Goldare suffered a multitude of wounds from the fight. None were too serious, but they would be slowed down and vulnerable to anyone who might want some easy gold. Tigerius had suffered the most. Two of his wounds were lethal, one to his head and the other to his abdomen. Magnus was deeply concerned for the man's life, and he thought it especially despicable that Aeris had placed him at risk. Magnus, Goldare, Vikhail and Vardec were merely an escort. But Tigerius . . . he was supposedly her childhood friend.

Magnus looked over to the three men. Each was situated upon his bedroll about a farlo from the fire. Magnus stood up and approached them, knowing it was time that he told them what he had seen transpire between Aeris and the leader of the ambushers. The men listened intently as he spoke, and he watched as their expressions shifted from disbelief to anger as he finished recounting the events he witnessed.

Silence rang throughout the encampment for a moment before Magnus spoke again. "We need to bind her. She might try to escape when she discovers that we know about her allegiances."

Goldare shook his head. "I can't believe she allowed this to happen to Tigerius." He indicated towards the man who lay nearby upon his own bed pallet. His complexion was pale and his breathing shallow.

"We need ta get 'im to a priest as soon as possible," said Vardec.

Magnus nodded. "Daybreak will soonarrive. We will ride hard to Yortec all day and into the night."

Vikhail went to his pack to get a length of rope as the men went to where Aeris lay. Magnus took her hands and moved them behind her back, only briefly noting that the area around her wrists was sticky. He frowned for a moment, wondering what it was, but then the rope was being thrust into his line of vision. He took the rope, bound her wrists, and then went to her feet.

After he was done, Magnus stood and looked down at Aeris. She looked so vulnerable, lying there. He pulled his lips into a thin line and admonished himself. He must be strong and not give in to his weakness for her. "Isn't it strange that the priests left without her? If she was one of theirs, don't you think they would have taken her with them?" asked Goldare.

Magnus turned to the other man. "I don't know. Maybe they figured they didn't need her anymore."

"What did they attack us fer anyway?" asked Vardec. "They never took anythin'. They didn't even kill us when we was down. After a while, they jus' left."

Magnus frowned. Vardec had a point. Suddenly he froze. Perhaps it was him. The leader, Tholana, somehow knew him. She had indicated as much when she spoke to him whilst he was undergoing the paralysis. Perhaps the ambush was meant to get at him. But how?

Magnus didn't know what was going on, but he wasn't going to tell the others. All he knew was that Aeris was somehow involved. The young woman had taken the information that he had divulged to her in confidence and shared it with Tholana. Now the cimmerean woman was using it against him.

Magnus shook his head and glanced back around at the men. "I don't know. Maybe she will have some answers when she awakens. Come on. Let's get some rest before sunrise. We are going to need it."

CHAPTER 8

The men rode hard across the pampas. They stopped late every night and were early to rise the next morning. Alasdair was silent as they traveled, and Talemar and Cedric were the same. He knew that their thoughts were focused upon the same themes as his own: how Aeris was managing without them and what they would discover when they returned home.

Alasdair regarded Talemar from the corner of his eye. The other man had been especially moody, and he wondered if it resulted from leaving Aeris behind. He was aware of the history the two shared. They had studied together at the academy . . . he as a junior journeyman and she as an apprentice. Talemar was the son of Aeris' master, Dinim Coabra, and Dinim had paired them together for spell-casting sessions often. A friendship had already existed between them, for Dinim was an intimate friend of the family, and Talemar raised alongside Adrianna and Sirion's children. The friendship grew, and when the relationship naturally proceeded to the next level, the two found themselves caught up in the emotional tangle. However, they resolved the situation with maturity, mutually deciding that neither of them was ready to endeavor upon such a path. Their friendship continued, unhindered, and Alasdair thought that they were both the better for it.

However, looking at his friend now, Alasdair wasn't quite so sure that Talemar and Aeris were on the same page anymore. Talemar had been upset the evening Alasdair took Magnus up on his offer to escort Aeris back to Elvandahar, and had even told Alasdair that he should reconsider. But Alasdair knew that he was stuck. Deep within himself, he knew Aeris would not willingly come with them, and the next best thing was to give her an escort that he knew personally. Alasdair knew he could trust Magnus . . . the other man had proven himself when he placed himself at risk for Aeris during the skirmish with the caravan raiders.

Alasdair shook his head. Talemar had asked Alasdair about the relationship between Aeris and Magnus. Alasdair was quite forthright, telling Talemar that the two had been good friends, spending most of their days together on their journey to the small village of Grunchin. Alasdair said that he had started to think that there might be something more between them than simple friendship. However, those thoughts were nullified when Aeris left Grunchin without any word to Magnus. He sensed some tension between them now, but he was sure that they would work it out with time.

Alasdair sensed the vague disquiet emanating from the cimmerean man, noticed the hollows beneath his eyes. It was easy to see that the man was deeply worried. Alasdair shared his concern, but he definitely sensed something more. He had begun to realize that Talemar just might be in love with his little sister, and there was nothing that the man could do about it. Not only that, but Aeris was currently in the company of someone for which Alasdair professed she may have shared some feelings. Alasdair now wished he had said nothing of Magnus, for it would now be saving Talemar a heap of heartache.

Alasdair shifted his attention from Talemar to Cedric. The tall faelin tended to be the quiet one in the group, but with Talemar's spirits so low, he had recently been delegated to a mere second place in that arena. He was the son of their mother's sister, Sheridana Darnesse, and born not long after the Wildrunners' defeat of Lord Aasarak. He carried the physical features of both his mother and his father, not to mention their shared profession. Cedric was an excellent swordsman.

Alasdair regarded his cousin discreetly. He was tall for a faelin man, his body lean and muscular. His curly dark brown hair brushed leather-clad shoulders, and the lines of his face were well chiseled. Cedric wore his blades in crossed sheaths at his back and a long dagger at his waist. He sat his lloryk well, and his slightly canted green eyes diligently perused the landscape as they rode. Even now, Alasdair could swear that his sister's death weighed upon him even though she had passed several years before. Cedric and Fitanni had been close, yet he rarely spoke of her. It was almost like a part of him had died with her, and Alasdair could only imagine his pain. He would feel the same if something were to happen to Aeris.

Alasdair pulled his brows together into a frown. He had to stop doing this or he would drive himself to insanity. He had to trust that Aeris would be fine and that Magnus and the rest of the escort would take good care of her. He had to believe that as much for himself as he did for Talemar. His mother and father would be surprised when he returned home without their daughter, and he would have to convince them that he made the correct choice. He only hoped he was right.

***

Aeris slowly awakened to the sound of several voices. The pounding in her head kept her from focusing upon them right away, and all she could do was try and find a way to manage the pain. When she finally let out a soft moan, the voices stopped. She tried to move her arms, but she found that she could not, for they had been securely tied behind her back.

At this sudden realization, Aeris opened her eyes. The light from the fire almost made her want to close them again, but fear kept her from doing so. She was propped up against the trunk of a small tree, and she immediately saw that she had been taken captive. She heard footsteps approaching, and she looked up expecting to see Tholana standing over her. She was surprised to see that it was Magnus, followed by Goldare, Vikhail, and Vardec.

Aeris struggled against her bonds, confused as to why they had not released her. The emotion must have shown on her face, for Magnus knelt down beside her. "We know that you were in league with the ambushers. You were a fool to trust them, for they abandoned you when they left."

Aeris shook her head. "Ma . . . Magnus . . . wha . . . what are you talking about?" She continued to struggle against her bonds, the pain in her head keeping her from making the obvious realization. "Why am I tied up? Magnus, take these off of me."

Magnus shook his head. "Aeris, how could you do this? What were you thinking? What did you intend to accomplish? The woman knows me, yet she would tell me nothing. I shared my affliction with you in the utmost confidence. You have betrayed me, as well as every other member of this group."

Aeris stopped moving and took in Magnus' expression. By the gods, he was serious. She closed her eyes in response to the pain that continued to pound against her skull. She thought perhaps this was all a dream, and that when she opened her eyes again, it would be gone. However, when she did just that and opened her eyes once more, she was dismayed to find Magnus still crouched there beside her. His expression was an impenetrable mask, his emotions indecipherable.

"Magnus, what are you talking about? I would never betray you. Why am I tied up?" Aeris fought to keep her tears at bay, tried to keep her voice from cracking with the force of her emotion. He was scaring her, and she wished that he would stop.

"I saw you with the woman, Tholana, after she attacked me. She seemed to know you very well."

Aeris shook her head. "I have never met her before today." She refrained from telling Magnus that the woman seemed to know her mother. She did not want to add fuel to his fire, for he thought Aeris to be a traitor already.

Magnus' hand shot out and grabbed the front of her tunic. "I don't believe you. Does your brother know with whom you have forged your alliances?"

"Magnus, stop it. You are scaring me. Now, let me go." Aeris began to struggle anew against her bonds. They were tight, and were beginning to cut into her wrists. "Where is Tigerius?"

Magnus leaned close to her, his eyes devoid of emotion. "Don't you know? He lies on the other side of the fire, gravely wounded from our battle with Tholana and her followers. By now, he may be near death."

Once again, Aeris stopped. She stared at Magnus from wide eyes. No, not Tigerius. He was the only one that she could trust, the only one that would believe that she had nothing to do with the attack. Not only that, but he was no longer just Alasdair's friend. He was hers.

Aeris couldn't stop the tears from spilling from her eyes. Goldare, Vikhail, and Vardec all watched her dispassionately. They all believed that she was a traitor, that she had led them into Tholana's trap. "You have seen to him, haven't you? You wouldn't allow him to die as a result of my actions?"

Magnus rose and stood over her. "Not even I am that cruel. Yes, we have seen to him. Once the sun rises, we will ride as fast as possible to Yortec."

Aeris sighed inwardly with relief. She had incriminated herself in order to be sure that Tigerius would receive the care he needed. Now she would remain quiet. It was obvious that they would not kill her, for if they were going to do so, they would have done it already. She would suffer this indignity in silence, not give Magnus the pleasure he sought by making her his captive. She could not help but think that he did this to her out of vengeance. She had been successful in her attempts to keep her distance from him, and he had probably felt the rebuff. Only, she never would have imagined he would go this far to seek retribution.

**

Jonesy sang to the melody of the lyre. She had a beautiful voice . . . countless people had told her so over the years. They were people who visited her father's court, important people who came to see King Zerxes on business for the crown. And whenever he had important visitors, Zerxes always requested his youngest daughter to sing, for he was well aware of her aptitude. She couldn't count how many times she had cursed her ability, for she hated to sing for her father's visitors. But now she blessed it . . . for this night, it would earn her gold.

Before she knew it, the performance was over. The audience was silent for a moment before they abruptly erupted into applause. Jonesy had never heard such a reaction before, and her heart soared in her chest. These people sincerely enjoyed hearing her sing, and they weren't just some puffed-up visitors at her father's court. They were real, and their ovation was genuine. It was all for her, not just a show to garner her father's approval.

Several weeks ago, Joneselia Mondemer had packed her travel bags and left her father's home under the cover of the night. Dressed as a commoner, she had no problems getting out of the city of Velmist with one of the caravans early the next morning. No one questioned her as they traveled south through Karlisle, even when rumors of her capture by the same people who took her sister began to circulate throughout the realm. She took care not to bring undue notice to herself, and carefully averted the attentions of a couple of the swarthy denedrian men that belonged with the caravan.

When Jonesy reached the port city of Tambour, it was swarming with her father's men. She knew that her father had finally realized that she had not been taken captive at all, but had left of her own accord. She had rather hoped that his realization would have come a bit later, at least until she was out of Karlisle. With the gold that she had left to her, she booked passage upon a small ship. It was due to leave for Yortec the next day.

Jonesy was exhilarated when the ship sailed away from Tambour. She had succeeded in escaping the dreadful life she was beginning to live in her father's house, and now she could rest easy that her brother would be unable to hurt her. She was certain that her father's men would find her and drag her back to the palace. She dared not even contemplate the punishment she would be forced to endure, not to mention the harm her brother would find pleasure in rendering to her in retaliation for her attempt to leave.

Yet, when Jonesy stepped off of the ship onto the docks of Yortec, other fears came rushing to her. She had left the palace with only a measured amount of gold, only enough for her to get by a few days. She could have taken much, much more, but did not want to take the risk that someone would discover the large sum on her and realize her true identity. She belatedly realized she should have brought a little bit more, despite the risk. But she had not realized the expense it would take for her to reach Yortec.

Jonesy wracked her mind for the rest of the day, praying that she would find some way out of her predicament. That night, she was forced to seek refuge in a small stable. She sneaked up into the himrony loft and slept behind some of the bales. Early the next morning, before the sun rose, she left the building before anyone would be able to find her there. Her belly growled with discontent, for she had not eaten since she left the ship. She was tempted to filch a piece of fruit from one of the merchant's stalls, but was too afraid of being caught. By the gods, she had never been so tired, hungry, and dirty in her entire life!

But then it came to her . . . the answer to her problems. Jonesy came up with the solution as she walked past an inn later in the day. In front of it was standing a small group of people who were talking about the wonderful entertainment they had received at another inn farther down the street. One of the women spoke about the wonderful voices of the singers and the exceptional skill of the musicians. With the idea in her mind, she hurried down the street to the establishment about which the people had been speaking, the Silver Harp Inn. It was of high quality, and her spirits began to plummet. What if she wasn't good enough to sing at a place like this? Yet, she knew that she had to give it a try. Her welfare depended upon it.

It didn't take Jonesy long to discover the whereabouts of the small group of entertainers who were performing at the inn. When she approached them in the common room, asking if they needed another singer, the three of them eyed her speculatively. She knew what the two men and the woman must have been thinking, for her clothes were rumpled and strands of hair were coming out from under the scarf she wore. She told the group that she could prove her ability if they would allow her to sing for them. Nodding to one another, they obliged.

Jonesy chose a simple song, one that she had sung numerous times before. Despite her nervousness, she did not falter, and when she was through, she stopped to take in the astounded expressions on the faces of the entertainers. Moments later, they were shaking her hand and telling her that they would love to have her join them.

Now, as the audience applauded her, Jonesy smiled and bowed before them. On her way off of the stage, she passed Candis and the other woman gave her a delighted grin. It was her third night performing with the group, and everyone seemed so friendly and helpful. The inn gave her and the rest of the entertainers complimentary lodging on the days they performed, and she paid only half price for her meals.

Once behind stage, Jonesy went to the back door of the establishment and stepped outside. She breathed deeply of the cool air and looked up into the darkening evening sky. She was so pleased to have found a place for herself. Candis, Bowen, and Faisel had already offered to have her accompany them to Xordrel within the next fortnight or two. Jonesy was happy to accept the invitation. The farther she could get from home, the better.

Jonesy frowned when she contemplated her home, thoughts of Elinora filling her mind. Her sister had been abducted about a fortnight before Jonesy left. With the disappearance of his eldest daughter, the illness from which the King suffered began to manifest itself more readily . . . an illness that had also been borne by his father before him. He was touched with a bit of insanity, and it was no secret to Zerxes' advisors. Several months before, they had begun to prime Rigel to succeed the throne. However, her brother was young, and the administrators did not want the kingdom to be thrust into turmoil when they discovered the King's illness. Inasmuch, they kept his condition hidden, giving Rigel the impression that he was taking over much of the decision-making.

Jonesy snorted with derision. Zerxes' advisors had become Rigel's advisors. They exacted much of their influence over the younger man, not to mention that he was not much of a thinker to begin with. Not only that, but Rigel had many interests other than ruling the realm in his father's stead. They were drinking, gambling, and womanizing. She couldn't even begin to count the number of women she had seen leaving his wing of the palace on a consistent basis.

Jonesy swallowed the lump that suddenly formed in her throat. Her brother's habits with the women he took to his bed were appalling to say the least. She knew that he shared the women with his friends, and he had even gone so far as to try it with her.

Jonesy bit her bottom lip with the memory. Then, suddenly hearing someone on the other side of the door, she turned and went back into the establishment. It was Bowen, coming to tell her that it was almost time for her to take a turn back up on stage. Jonesy quickly composed herself, and she was ready when Candis passed by on her way to the back room. Jonesy pasted a false smile on her face as she walked back out on stage, but it was soon replaced by one of sincerity when the audience applauded her return.

***

The group rode through the city of Yortec. The place was similar to Xordrel, albeit much smaller. Aeris watched the hustle and bustle all around her with a stoic expression, one that she had maintained since her captivity the evening before last. Beside her rode Tigerius, much heartier in constitution than she would have imagined him to be. The others had been equally as impressed by his recovery. When Tiger got up from his bedroll that morning, claiming that he could ride, the others initially didn't believe him. However, when he proved that he was fit enough for the task, they let him do as he wished. Tigerius winked at her as he mounted his larian, and Aeris held back the grin that threatened her solemn countenance. Aeris had only some suspicions as to why Tigerius had been able to heal from his wounds so quickly . . . yet he knew that she would keep them to herself.

Tigerius was angry when he awakened to find that Aeris had been named a traitor and bound against her will. He called Magnus a fool for even thinking such a thing, and the others equally as foolish for believing the words of a man such as Magnus. To say the least, Magnus was irritated by Tigerius' declarations against him. He told Tiger that he wouldn't be surprised if he was a co-conspirator in Aeris' plot to get them ambushed. Tigerius subsequently spat at Magnus, just barely missing the target as he nimbly stepped aside. Tiger then uttered a string of epithets, none of which Aeris had ever heard spoke before. Such was for the better because they were obscene beyond comprehension.

Aeris caught herself from smiling at the memory. In Tigerius, she had found a staunch ally. How could she have ever thought of questioning him before? Had she truly been that blind? He was nothing what she thought him to be before Alasdair left. Already she had begun to feel the guilt of her past judgments upon him weighing her down. Tigerius' statements upon her behalf had made the others rethink their decision to keep her bound, and that morning she was released. They conceded that they may have been in error when they named her a traitor, but they still had their suspicions. Their allowing her freedom did not diminish that fact. Aeris kept her retorts to herself, knowing that she would rid herself of the lot of them as soon as she could upon entering Yortec.

As the group continued to ride through the city streets, many of the people paused to watch them pass. They were a rare sight: two faelin in the company of two humans and two halfen. Aeris hated the attention they invariably brought to themselves, but it just couldn't be helped. It was still too warm to wear hooded cloaks, and if they did, they would garner equally as much attention. Aeris rubbed her neck and chest, suddenly beginning to feel a burning sensation there. Her fingers caressed the crystal necklace her mother had given her. She thought it felt rather warm, but then forgot about it as Magnus led them up to the establishment at which he had chosen for them to stay. The Whistling Wayfarer Inn was a nice place. Aeris couldn't help but wonder why he chose it . . . perhaps he felt badly about his harsh treatment of her. However, Aeris couldn't quite bring herself to truly believe it to be the reason for his choice of inns. Most likely, he just had expensive taste.

The group dismounted in front of the inn, and the stable-hands were quick to lead their animals away. Aeris followed the men into the inn, meanwhile thinking of a good time that she would go to the rectory and have a message sent to Elvandahar. She would find herself, Mateo, and Tigerius a new escort home. Either that, or they would go in the company of any caravans that may be heading north. Aeris stood by as Magnus paid for their rooms. Aeris would share a room with Tigerius while Magnus shared one with Goldare. Vikhail, Vardec, and Mateo would occupy the third. Wordlessly, she took the key from Magnus' hand and then began to make her way towards the stairs. She could sense the men staring after her as she moved up the steps, but refused to look back at them. Gods only knew what they were thinking. She heard Tigerius say something in a chiding voice before he began to follow her up the stairs to the second story.

Upon entering the room, Aeris slung her pack off of her shoulder and tossed it onto the bed. Her body promptly followed. It was good to feel a sturdy pallet beneath her as opposed to the crummy bedrolls they used whilst they traveled. She then heard Tigerius enter the room. He relieved himself of his own packs before coming to sit next to her on the bed. He regarded her for a moment before he spoke.

"After the mid-day meal I will go in search of any caravans that may be leaving the city anytime soon."

It was almost as though he could read her mind. Aeris wouldn't be surprised if he had. She suddenly felt her lower lip begin to tremble, the events of the past few days rushing at her all at once. She heard Tigerius make a sound deep in his throat before he lay himself next to her on the bed and brought her into his arms. He held her as she cried for a few moments, and then stayed by her as she fell into the first sleep she had in gods only knew how long . . .

Aeris awoke to find Tigerius gone. Slowly she slid off of the bed, smoothing her tunic as she stood. By the light coming through the window, she could tell that she had not slept overly long. However, she doubted that the kitchens would still be serving any more food for a mid-day meal. She shook her head. Being tied throughout the past two nights, she had been unable to find sleep as she had been unable to find a comfortable position. And she must have been more tired than she realized in order to fall asleep in Tiger's arms.

Once more, Aeris found herself rubbing that place on her upper chest. It was like a burning sensation in the location of the crystal that rested there. Aeris took the crystal in her fingers, and when she felt the warmth emanating from it, she frowned. She unclasped the necklace and lowered it from her neck. She was surprised to find that the thing emanated a soft light.

Aeris held the crystal in the palm of her hands. By the gods, she never imagined it had arcane value. She hadn't sensed the magic from it before, but now it was difficult to miss. Not only did it shed an eerie pale light, but she felt it pulling at her . . . a compulsion to leave the establishment in the direction of the docks. Aeris shook her head in resistance to the pull. She couldn't just go wandering about the city by herself. She had to wait for Tigerius to return before she went lurking around, and even then, he would wonder what she was about. Upon seeing the crystal, he would probably become wary of it. Notwithstanding, she could see him wanting to investigate her compulsion as much as she.

Aeris heard a knock on her door just as she refastened the necklace. She thought to stuff it beneath the neckline of her tunic before her visitor entered the room, but she was too late in realizing that the chain was too short. Aeris frowned when Magnus stepped through the doorway. She covered the crystal with her hand as she watched him close the door.

Silence reigned as the two regarded one another across the room. Finally, Magnus walked over to her where she stood on the other side of the bed. "Tigerius said you were finally sleeping."

Aeris pressed her lips together. "Yes, it is quite difficult to sleep with one's hands tied behind one's back."

Magnus nodded. "Yes, I imagine so." He paused and then continued. "I came to see if you would be joining us for the evening meal."

Aeris shook her head. "No. I will be eating in my room."

"Are you sure? The inn-keeper says that the entertainment will be worth watching tonight."

Aeris nodded. "Quite sure. Besides, why would you care to dine with the woman who ensured a successful ambush? Someone could have died in our struggle against . . . what was her name?"

"Tholana."

"Oh yes. Tholana. My . . . how could I forget a name I am supposed to know so well?" Aeris spoke the last with a touch of rancor in her voice. She hadn't meant for it to come out . . . it just simply did.

Magnus cleared his throat. "Aeris, I am sorry for what happened. I didn't know what to think. For a time, I was so certain that you were in league with her. But now I realize I might have been mistaken."

"Yes, I would have thought you knew me better than that."

"Please, come join us for dinner. The others want to offer their own apologies."

Aeris shook her head once more. "No. Tomorrow I will be searching for another means to return to Elvandahar. I am no longer in need of your services. You can tell Goldare, Vikhail, and Vardec the same." Aeris dropped her hand from her chest as she turned away from Magnus. She walked over to the window and looked outside. It was late afternoon and soon evening would be upon them. She found that she was ravenous, and she wished that she had thought to eat something before she conveniently fell asleep.

"You really needn't do that. We are still willing to escort you home."

Aeris looked over her shoulder at him. "But I am not willing to have you as my escort. Your employment has been terminated. You are released of any obligation to me."

Magnus spoke quietly. "You forget, my Lady, that I am not employed by you, but by your brother. I will keep my word to him and remain to be your escort."

Aeris narrowed her eyes. By the gods, he actually dared to go there with her. "My Lord, I am sure that if my brother was aware of your transgressions against me, that he would terminate your employment himself."

"But Alasdair is not here, is he? You are stuck with me, Aeris Timberlyn, whether you like it or not. I will make sure that no others would be willing to escort you out of this city without me at your side. Do I make myself clear?" Magnus spoke the last with an edge of steel to his voice.

Aeris regarded him silently for a moment before responding. "Abundantly," she hissed from between her teeth. By the gods, she hated him, wished that she had never allowed Alasdair to give him responsibility over her. It was ultimately her fault, for she had every opportunity to voice her concerns. But she had been stubborn, so willing to allow her brother to go without her, just so that she could bring Mateo back to Elvandahar with her.

"Good. So, I will see you at dinner tonight. Order yourself a bath and anything else you might need. Take advantage of the luxuries now for we will be leaving the city the day after next." With that said, Magnus left the room.

Aeris stared at the door long after it was closed behind him. Tears burned behind her eyes, and she hoped that Tigerius would arrive back soon. She hated the thought of suffering through dinner without him, and even hoped that he would be able to get her out of it. Once again, Aeris felt the burning sensation on her chest. Damnation. What was causing the crystal to show her its true nature now, after so long? Perhaps she should find out.

Aeris left the vicinity of the window and made towards the desk situated against the adjacent wall. Upon it was a small tray of bread a fruit. Aeris approached it hungrily, realizing that Tiger must have left it there for her before he left. Damn, she hoped that he would be back before she was expected to make her appearance for dinner.

***

Giving orders to his crewmen to keep a skeleton watch on board the ship whist he took care of business, Cervantes disembarked the *Sea Maiden*, absently rubbing at his chest. The caravel was a good vessel, serving him well for the last three years. She was nimble and able to manage long ocean crossings . . . not to mention well-equipped to handle the occasional run-in with some of the denizens that plagued the immediate seas. She had a smooth hull, a full deck, a forecastle, a sterncastle, and three masts.

Cervantes jauntily stepped away from the ship and made his way to the nearest tavern. It was the place he frequented most often during his trips to Yortec, and he knew the proprietor rather well. He would conduct his business, unload his cargo, and then begin preparations for his next enterprise. Cervantes grinned to himself, pleased to have conducted another business venture without mishap. He was happy with the life he led . . . sailing from port to port, wenching where he could, and making more gold than he ever dreamed possible. The type of cargo that he transported, and the illicit means by which he obtained many of the items he used in trade, Cervantes was quickly becoming a wealthy man. The very ship he sailed was testimony to that fact.

Cervantes raised his face to the gentle wind that swept passed him, taking in the familiar salty scent of the sea. Without knowing why, he suddenly thought of a long-ago, almost forgotten, memory of his uncle . . . the man he had called his father. Cervantes was only about ten years old, but very much ahead in his years.

Cervantes ran into the small house that he shared with his uncle, aunt, and brother. Rohan was home between ventures, and Cervantes hoped to spend as much time as possible with his uncle before the man had to go back to sea. His uncle scooped Cervantes up in his arms and crushed the boy to his chest, tightening his arms until Cervantes was forced to cry out in forfeit. Then Rohan suddenly let him go, ruffled Cervantes' hair, and chucked him across the bridge of his nose.

"So what has my little man been up to?" asked Rohan with a grin.

"I've been working on my maps, Father. Come see them." Cervantes beckoned to his uncle with a wave of his hand, urging him to the rear of the house. He hoped they would meet with Rohan's approval, for he had worked diligently on them since having seen his uncle last . . . at least several fortnights ago.

Cervantes lead Rohan down the stairs and into the cellar, his aunt following behind. Of course, she had only a vague idea of what he was about to show his uncle, for she had very little interest in such things. However, despite their differences, Rohan and Isomalade loved one other very much. She mothered the boys that had been left to Rohan by his dead sister, loving them as though they were her own sons.

Entering the cellar, Cervantes lead his parents to the navigation table that Rohan had built in the center of the room. The man often used it as a place to lay out his maps and plot his next endeavor. Standing atop his stool, Cervantes would watch from his place at the other end of the table . . . listen as Rohan and his crew spoke about the route they would take and the bounty they hoped to acquire. His uncle had taught him all he knew about maps and how to read them in order to navigate the world. Now Cervantes spread his own maps out on the table, displaying them in all of their amateurish grandeur. For a boy who had only seen ten years they were good, and the expressions on the faces of his parents were testament to that fact.

Rohan approached the table and ruffled Cervantes' hair once more. "Good work, son. I have never seen any better."

Cervantes beamed at the praise despite knowing that the words his uncle spoke were not entirely true. Cervantes had seen the maps that were studied by the crew, and they were the most exquisite ones he had ever seen. Nevertheless, he saw the pride in Rohan's eyes when he saw Cervantes' maps, and that was enough for him.

Rohan placed a hand at Cervantes' shoulder. "You know, every great seafarer is famous for one thing, son. You must search out your own personal treasure and then hunt it down. Despite what most people say, the clues to the greatest riches are in books and scrolls. I have taught you to read manuscripts and maps alike, shown you the fundamentals of sailing a ship and how to lead men. One day, you must find that one great thing by which the world will remember you."

Cervantes smiled widely. "But Father, I have already found it. I know what I will be remembered for. It will bring our family much fame and fortune and our names will go down in history as the greatest who ever set sail," he said enthusiastically.

Rohan grinned. "Tell me then . . . what is this quest?"

Cervantes' face turned solemn. "I will discover the dragon continent."

Taken aback, his parents glanced at one another. Cervantes reached beneath the table and pulled out two more rolls. He then spread out a series of maps Rohan had never seen before. One was labeled, "The Mystical Continent of Dragons" in childish handwriting. Cervantes began studying the maps, deciding what he should show his uncle first.

Rohan stepped closer to the table and leaned in towards the maps. "Cervantes, where did you get these?"

"I drew them myself, Father. Aren't they grand?" Cervantes grinned, looked up at Rohan, and then saw the somber expression on his uncle's face. "Did I do something wrong?"

Rohan touched the edge of one of the maps with a forefinger. "How did you draw them, son?"

"They were from a dream. I was standing on the deck of a splendid sailing ship. In my mind I could see the path that I would need to use to make it to the continent. Then I was standing on a sandy beach, looking inland from the shore. It was the most wondrous place I had ever seen before."

Rohan frowned in consideration. "So how do you know that this was a mystical place instead of just another ordinary beach?"

Cervantes laughed lightly. "Because just as my dream ended, I saw a magnificent dragon flying overhead . . ."

Cervantes shook his head, drawing himself out of the memory. His uncle was long gone, but the things he had taught Cervantes were forever entrenched within him. Breathing deeply, Cervantes spoke to the winds, hoping maybe that his words would be carried to the only man he had known as a father. "By the gods, I wish you were here. I am so close that I can almost taste it. It is only a matter of time before fame and glory will be all mine."

CHAPTER 9

They called him Razlul Daemon-keeper. It was a fitting name, he supposed, if he were to simply hold on to the daemons with which he communed. However, such was not his way, and he simply saw Hell's denizens on their way once he escorted them into Shandahar. He knew that many of them didn't need him . . . that portals existed between Shandahar and at least four of the Hells, portals through which daemon-kind could infiltrate a world no longer barricaded by the Pact of Bakharas.

Razlul shook his head thoughtfully. The Pact had not been un-breachable. Many a daemon had been able to slip through undetected. Albeit they were lesser daemons, and caused little harm enough to set raise an alarm. Every once in a while, a dragon had been able to do the same thing. However, strangely enough, most had adhered to the Pact, daemon and dragon alike, alignment notwithstanding. And now there was Razlul, Mehta of the Daemundai, and the Pact rendered null and void. History had been made the day Adrianna Darnesse and her golden bond-mate brought a contingent of dragons into Shandahar to defeat Lord Aasarak's undead army. Not only had the Cycling of the world been broken, but so had the Pact. Now Shandahar was ripe for the picking, and Razlul would be at the head of the harvest.

The Mehta walked from the mouth of the cavern onto the overhang, and he looked down into the valley below. There he saw a group of new recruits . . . men who had answered his call for dragon-slayers. Most of them were shown to be worthless, but there were a few who proved to be a cut above the rest. Once passing the preliminary trials, they were brought before the degethozak. There the true testing began, and only those who strove to be worthy were chosen as companions for the dragons that Razlul had brought under his command.

Unconsciously, the Mehta brought his hand to the triad of glowing crystals that made a pendant at the hollow of his throat. *Dragon crystals.* It was they that gave him any authority he might have over the degethozak. Yet, if not for their propensity towards evil and chaos, Razlul still would not have had enough sway in order to persuade the dark dragons to his cause. The manipulative influence of the crystals was powerful, but it had limitations. It could not make the dragons act against their innate alignment, and he would be powerless to manipulate few, if any, of the helzethryn or rezwithrys races.

However, Razlul had to accede that the more crystals he had at his at his disposal, the more persuasive strength he was able to obtain. Even now he had a contingent of his priests out searching for dragon crystals. Lead by one of his most powerful mages, Sabian Makonnen, and guided by an unfettered crystal, his Daemundai scoured the largest cities and towns. Already they had a lead and were following a small group of travelers towards the port city of Yortec. With that crystal secured, the priests would need to find only one more to make another triad. With these triads, Razlul's influence over the degathozak would widen. Not only would he have more control over the ones already at his command, but he would have the power to sway more degethozak to his cause.

With a small smile, Razlul turned away and allowed his thoughts to shift to other concerns. With the fall of the gods, things had suddenly become even more interesting in the world. Very soon, the pecking order among the powers-that-be would be established. A small part of him wanted to be nowhere near the bloodbath that would ensue, happy with the power he had garnered on his own over the past several years. Yet, there was a larger part of him that hungered for more. By forging his alliances now, he would have access to other avenues of power that he might never have attained before. The venture would carry more risk, but what quest for power did not? It was an unfortunate aside that priests and clerics lost access to their powers, including his own Daemundai. However, the sacrifice would be small compared to what he could stand to gain if he chose the right powers with which to align himself. Of course, Verbaxor would be one of those. Yet, the daemon god had already made it clear that he would work only to further his own goals. Traditionally, Verbaxor was just that way, and Razlul knew he would only beseech the god if the need was dire.

However, Razlul's alliances were just one aspect of the plans he endeavored to bring into fruition. The other was something he had been contemplating for several years. With his abduction of the girl from royalty Karlisle, he had hoped to make headway in his enterprise to bring forth something Shandahar had never seen before. He had failed in this initial endeavor, but he would not be deterred. He had chosen the girl not only for her innocence, but for the chaos he knew would ensue when her family learned of her death. Now he searched for another innocent. They were not too terribly difficult to find, yet Razlul much enjoyed making a statement. He loved the turmoil he had thrust upon Karlisle and her neighboring realm, and it was his desire to accomplish something equally as entertaining upon his next abduction. It was only a matter of time . . .

***

Damaeris slowly walked down the stairs. She dreaded the evening to come, and had worked herself up so much that she lost her appetite. She had eaten little else as of late, other than the fruit and bread that Tiger left her earlier that day. Distraught about her 'capture', she had eaten nothing during the rest of their travel to Yortec. She had been forced to tighten the drawstrings to her trousers, not to mention, poke an extra hole through her belt. At this rate, she would wither away until the wind carried her away. *Perhaps far away . . .*

Tigerius had yet to return to the inn. Aeris was beginning to wonder about him, and she hoped that he was all right. She knew that if he did not come back soon she would begin to worry. She had hoped that he would be there with her for dinner, but by now she was accepting her fate. She would staunchly deal with it the best way she could.

When Aeris entered the spacious dining room, she quickly spotted Magnus and the others. They stood from their seats when she approached, and Goldare courteously pulled out the chair next to him. She made the effort to give Mateo a lopsided grin as she seated herself, and Vardec passed her a mug of mead. Silently she sipped it and realized it was quite good. Soon after, the meal was brought out to them. The bread was fresh, as was the cheese. The tubers were tender and the soup flavorful.

As they ate, the front of the room was being prepared for the evening's entertainment. There was a raised platform, or stage, upon which chairs and instruments were set. Lanterns were situated strategically about the room in order to maximize the effect of shadows. The bards came out first with more of their instruments. Aeris enjoyed the music they played. However, as the tables were cleared of the remnants of the meal, the bards were joined by a young woman. She wore her long chestnut hair in a rope down her back, and her eyes were colored a deep murky green. Upon seeing her, Aeris felt a tug of familiarity. When the woman began to sing, the entire room listened avidly to her words. Her voice was beautiful, and Aeris couldn't help but envy the woman her gift. She sang a ballad of love and loss, of life and death, and all of the things in between. The melody infiltrated every corner of the room, which Aeris suddenly realized had become packed with people. Magnus had been correct when he told her that the entertainment would be worth experiencing.

Aeris listened attentively as the singer blended her song into the next ballad. She did it well, so well that many would never know what she had done until several stanzas later. Aeris hadn't realized their absence until Vikhail and Vardec came rushing over to them. They whispered animatedly to Magnus and Goldare, something about 'the King's men' and that they were coming towards the inn. Momentarily, Aeris found her attention diverted from the singer.

"From what realm do they hail?" said Magnus with a frown.

"I don't know," replied Vikhail quietly. "I don't recognize the insignia."

"Are they human or faelin?"

"Human," said Vardec.

"They'll be here any minute," added Vikhail.

Aeris returned her gaze to the singer. What was going on? Whose men where these that the halfen didn't recognize them? Then she noticed that another woman had joined the singer and the musicians on stage and that she was speaking into the singer's ear. An expression of alarm suddenly crossed the singer's face and she fled from the stage. From out in the lobby, Aeris could suddenly hear a flurry of activity, and she knew that the men that Vikhail and Vardec warned them about had entered the establishment.

Aeris suddenly found herself jumping up from her seat. She hurried away from the table, her dinner companions none the wiser as they focused upon the commotion coming closer to the dining room. She rushed around to the back of the stage and saw a door that, most likely, led to the outside. Aeris went through it just as she heard the unknown men enter the dining room.

Once outside, Aeris quickly looked around. The sun was beginning to set, and the shadows of evening were lengthening. Soon it would be dark. She reached out with her faelin senses, hoping to get some indication of where the singer may have gone. From the front of the inn, she heard the sounds of lloryk and the men who tended them whilst their companions were inside the inn. It was easy for her to determine that their were quite a number of them. Aeris then focused upon the rear of the establishment, following the wall until it turned a corner. There, huddled against the stone, was the singer.

Aeris quickly walked over to the young woman. As she got closer, Aeris could see that she was very young, indeed, just barely out of adolescence. Upon seeing her, the girl's face first registered surprise, and then fear. The singer jumped to her feet and Aeris held up a hand. "Wait. I can help you."

The girl stilled her impulse to run, instead waiting for Aeris to approach her. "How? The King's men are everywhere," she whispered in a desperate tone.

Aeris held a finger up to her lips. "Shhh. I will show you. But you mustn't be afraid."

The girl stared at her warily for a moment before nodding her head. Aeris then began to cast her spell. It wasn't an illusion, for she knew very little about those types of incantations. It was an alteration spell. It would allow them to blend into their surroundings, and as long as they moved slowly, no one would be aware of their passage.

Once the spell was complete, Aeris took the singer's hand. Slowly they made their way towards the stable. By then, the King's men had surrounded the inn. Upon seeing the insignia, Aeris instantly became nervous. Karlisle. King Zerxes of Karlisle had sent his men to Yortec. She wondered if they were there searching for her. But if they were looking for Aeris, then why was the singer so afraid for them to see her?

Suddenly it all began to click together in Aeris' mind. Now she knew why the singer had seemed so familiar to her. This girl was the King of Karlisle's youngest daughter. Damnation! What in the Nine Hells was going on?

Once reaching the stable, Aeris quickly led the girl to a ladder that would take them up to the rafters. Once there, Aeris relaxed her concentration and the spell dissipated. She would cast it again later if she had the need. The twosome crawled behind some bales of himrony. It was the preferred grass of many hoof-stock, including lloryk and larian. There they crouched for several moments, neither of them saying anything.

Finally, Aeris turned to her companion. The girl still looked scared, and Aeris wondered why she was running from her own father's men. "I know who you are," she stated solemnly.

The princess of Karlisle turned to her with haunted eyes. "Are you going to turn me in?"

"No, I promised I would help you." The girl turned away from her, but not before Aeris saw the relieved expression on her face. "What are you running away from?" Aeris inquired.

"It is a long story," she replied shortly.

"So? We have some time."

The girl turned back to regard her from strangely colored gray eyes that seemed to have green undertones one moment and blue the next.

"What is your name?" Aeris asked.

The girl frowned. "I thought you knew me."

Aeris nodded. "We met once, when we were younger. My grandfather was meeting with your father in the beginning of talk that would, one day, come to be a treatise between our people."

Aeris saw the enlightenment in the girl's eyes. "Yes, you are the Princess of Elvandahar."

Aeris nodded again. "You are the youngest daughter of King Zerxes of Karlisle. However, I do not recall your name."

"Jonesy. You can call me Jonesy."

Aeris frowned. "It doesn't sound familiar."

Jonesy shrugged. "I don't like my given name, so I go by this one."

Aeris nodded. "All right."

"Your name is Damaeris. I remember because my father told me that I should strive to be more like you."

Aeris frowned. "Why did he say that?"

"You were so prim and proper standing next to the King of Elvandahar, and you seemed the utmost of sophistication. You impressed my father."

Aeris grinned. "Well, just so you know, it was all an act. I am neither prim, nor proper, nor sophisticated."

Jonesy regarded her intently. "So, what are you then?"

"I thought I was asking the questions," replied Aeris, knowing that the girl was referring to her spell-casting.

Jonesy only looked away.

"Once again . . . what are you running away from?" asked Aeris.

"My father is going insane."

Aeris was taken aback by the solemn statement. Was Jonesy serious, or was she only speaking out of anger. Did they have a squabble? Is that why she was running away from home? Damn, Yortec was a long journey from Velmist, the city where Zerxes and his family resided.

"Jonesy," began Aeris, "you can't just . . ."

"I am afraid of him. Please, don't try to tell me that I should go back. You don't know . . ." Jonesy stopped speaking, cutting her sentence short. It was obvious that she didn't want to say anything more, and she didn't need to. Aeris was already convinced.

Aeris put a hand on Jonesy's shoulder. "Like I said, I am going to help you. You can trust me."

Jonesy nodded, blinking the tears out of her eyes. She didn't bother to tell Aeris that the 'him' to whom she referred was not her father. Aeris began to hear some activity outside of the stable, and she was instantly on the alert. Within moments, Jonesy knew that it was her father's men, coming to search the stable for their quarry. Once again, Aeris cast her spell, the energies rallying to her call. Their bodies blended into the surroundings that made up the stable, and the men burst through the doors. The warriors searched high and low, but when they found no sign of their prey, they left. Two men had come to search the rafters, but they saw no one. Aeris and Jonesy remained still as the men searched, and it was only when the warriors were gone that they began to breathe normally again.

However, it was much longer before Aeris relaxed her spell, and even longer still before they emerged from their place behind the stacks of himrony. The twosome crawled over to the ledge of the rafter and looked over it. Below them were several stalls. Only a few housed any occupants, and most of those belonged to Aeris, Magnus, and the others. It was then that Aeris heard someone approaching the stable. She pulled Jonesy back away from the ledge as the doors were opened. A single person walked into the stable, followed by an animal. By the sound of it, Aeris guessed it to be a lloryk. Tentatively, Aeris peeked back over the ledge. The sight that met her eyes was a relief. It was Tigerius, finally returned to the inn.

Tigerius led his lloryk into his stall and was gave him some himrony. Deliberately, Aeris made a noise. Tigerius stopped his activity and looked around. Aeris made the noise again and Tiger looked up into the rafters. His expression became incredulous as he realized it was she.

"Aeris, by the gods, what are you doing up there?"

Aeris put her finger to her mouth, indicating for him to be quieter. She then motioned for him to join them. Tigerius climbed the ladder and then crawled over to them. "Aeris, what is going on? King Zerxes' men are in the city. Are they looking for you?'

Aeris shook her head. "I don't think so." She then turned to Jonesy. "I think they are here for her."

Tiger glanced at the girl speculatively. "Why?"

Jonesy spoke upon her own behalf. "I am the youngest daughter of the King of Karlisle. I am afraid of what my father has become. My brother has already begun to come into his own power, and there is no place for me in his house." She spoke the last with a resolute tone to her voice that brooked no argument.

Tiger only nodded. "We will wait a while longer for them to leave, then."

Aeris nodded. It wasn't until quite some time later that the threesome moved back down the ladder and into the stable proper. Tigerius looked out the door, and when he determined that it was safe, he beckoned Aeris and Jonesy to follow him out. Aeris rubbed at the place on her chest where the crystal lay, once more feeling its heat. It had glowed all day, but at certain times, the glow brightened and emitted heat. Now it bothered her. She had placed it on a longer chain so that she could hide it and she drew it out from the neckline of her tunic.

"Tiger, come and take a look at this."

Tigerius moved back into the stable and stood before Aeris. He took in the glowing crystal and then looked up at her. "Is that the trinket your mother gave to you?"

Aeris nodded.

"Why is it glowing like that?"

"I don't know. It just started today." Aeris paused and then continued. "When it glows, I feel a slight compulsion . . . a desire to make in the direction of the docks."

Tigerius was pensive for a moment and then sighed. "It's late. I don't know if we should go there now."

Aeris nodded. "I know. I thought about going there earlier, but I wanted to wait for you."

"Tigerius grinned. "I am glad that you waited."

Aeris smiled back. Jonesy simply looked from Aeris to Tigerius, and then back to Aeris again.

Tiger became thoughtful once again, and then an expression of resignation settled over his face. "Okay. Let's go," he said, "but we have to be extra careful."

Aeris felt her smile widen with excitement. This endeavor could prove to be rather fun.

Magnus, Goldare, Vikhail, and Vardec walked out of the Whistling Wayfarer Inn. Darkness had fallen, and the first moon, Steralion, was making her way across the sky. Angrily Magnus cursed to himself. Where in the Hells could Aeris have gone? She was there at the table one moment and gone the next. It wasn't until the king's men entered the dining room that he noticed her absence. Immediately, Magnus saw that they hailed from Karlisle, and he wondered if they had come for her.

It wasn't long before he learned that they were not in the city for Aeris. They were in search of other quarry, a girl that happened to fit the description of the young woman who had been singing on stage. Once they realized that Aeris was no longer in the dining room, Magnus and the others attempted to leave the inn. Much to their dismay, the men would allow no one to leave. They didn't want to take the risk that the girl would find a way out with others who would be leaving the establishment. So, they were forced to wait, and it wasn't until quite some time later that they were finally able to get out. By then the men had left, albeit without the girl, for they had been unsuccessful in finding her. Mateo was taken to the room he shared with Vikhail and Vardec, and then the men went out in search of Aeris.

They searched the periphery of the inn a few times before Goldare finally spotted her walking away from the stables in the company of Tigerius and another woman. Aeris turned when Goldare called her name and waited for them to approach.

"Where in the Hells have you been?" asked Magnus as he stepped up to her. He barely glanced at Tigerius and the other woman, his focus set entirely upon Aeris. She didn't dignify him with a response, instead shifting her gaze from him to the rest of the group. It was then that he noticed how quiet everyone was, and he noticed that they were all looking at the woman who stood by Aeris' side.

She was a girl, actually, just barely into woman-hood. Magnus noticed her as the singer from the inn, the one for whom the king's men had been searching. He frowned as he glanced back at Aeris. "You endanger us by keeping her with you. King Zerxes is offering a goodly amount of gold to have her."

"She is under my protection," Aeris replied.

"Where were you going?" he asked with a hint of petulance to his voice.

"To the docks," she replied with nonchalance.

"Are you crazy? You will get your throat slit if you go there at this hour." Magnus' gaze went to Tigerius. "You were party to this insanity?"

Tigerius shrugged. "We have ample reason to go. Besides, I am rather good at the dagger and sword. Aeris has her own . . . abilities so to speak. We can take care of ourselves."

Magnus felt the muscles in his jaws tighten. "Pray tell me what reason you have for going to the docks at night."

Aeris stepped towards Magnus, pulling the crystal from within the neckline of her tunic. His gaze was immediately drawn to the glowing object. He reached out and took the crystal in his fingers, turning it this way and that. It looked vaguely familiar, although he knew not why. He looked back up into her eyes. "What does this have to do with your excursion to the docks?"

"It tells me I should go there."

Magnus narrowed his eyes. "It speaks to you?"

Aeris raised an eyebrow and gave him a lopsided grin. "No . . . it is more subtle than that. It is a compulsion I feel when it glows at its brightest."

"Do you feel this compulsion now?"

"No. It is gone. But I felt it a short while ago whilst we were hiding in the stable."

"So, you were going to follow this compulsion to the docks. What do you expect to find there?"

Aeris shrugged. "I have no idea."

Magnus regarded her silently for a moment. "Alasdair would kill me if he knew I was allowing you to go to the docks at night." Then he sighed heavily. "Come on. We might as well go before it gets any later."

In silence, the group stepped out onto the street. It didn't take them too long to reach the docks, and once they were close, Aeris felt the compulsion anew. Aeris slowed her stride, felt the crystal burning on her chest. It urged her towards the tavern she saw down a street that diverged from the main thoroughfare. Aeris tugged on Tiger's sleeve, motioning him down the indicated street. As Aeris and Jonesy began to walk down it towards the tavern, the rest of the group followed suit. Once reaching the small establishment, they stopped to take in the sight of the poorly kept building.

Magnus shook his head. "There is no way we are going in there tonight. It reeks of treacherous things going on within." The other men only nodded in response. Aeris felt her hopes plummet. *Damnation.* She so much wanted to find out the reason why the crystal led her there.

Suddenly, the front door of the tavern swung open. The group scuttled around the side of the building, unwilling to be seen loitering in front of the place. After a moment, Aeris chanced a peek around the corner. A man stood in at the doorway of the tavern, looking out into the night. At first she couldn't see his face, for he was looking in the opposite direction. However, when the man began to turn, she was able to see his profile in the light cast by the lantern affixed to the stone wall beside the door. She then saw his face as he turned a bit more in their direction, and when he turned his body just slightly more, she was able to see the object that hung around his neck. It was a crystal, one that looked just like hers, gleaming brightly in the darkness of the night.

***

It was just afetr midday as Aeris walked towards the docks in the company of Magnus, Tigerius, and Goldare. They had left Vikhail and Vardec back at the inn with Jonesy and Mateo . . . afraid that the presence of the halfen would bring too much attention to them and that Jonesy would be recognized by someone out on the streets who wouldn't mind being paid a hefty sum for making her presence known to Zerxes' men, who continued to scour the city for her.

Truth be told, Aeris didn't quite know how she was going to approach the man she saw the night before. Tigerius had learned as much about the man as he could that morning before returning to the inn for Aeris and Magnus. She knew that his name was Cervantes, and he captained a ship that was moored at the docks close by. He was pleasant to look at, for she was able to see him clearly the night before. He was human with sandy colored hair, and his body was lean and muscular.

Aeris paused only momentarily before opening the door to the tavern. Once more, she felt the crystal burning at her chest and she knew that the man was experiencing the same sensation. Aeris stepped into the establishment and almost choked on the smoke-filled air. Even though there weren't many patrons at this time of the day, the air was still clogged with smoke from countless pipes and cigars that had filled the place not long before.

Aeris slowly began walking up to the bar. She suddenly felt very aware of herself, for her garb was not what she was accustomed to wearing. Before she ventured forth, she had altered her own garments to fit the clothing worn by many of the women who frequented places such as this one. She didn't quite dress the wench, but it was close enough. The tops of her breasts were bare, and the cinch belt tighter around her waist than usual. She wore the tunic and trousers she ordinarily used for travel, for their quality was less than that of many of her other garments.

Behind her, Aeris heard the door open and then close. It was Magnus, Tiger, and Goldare. They would discreetly seat themselves at another table. They were heavily armed and would come to her rescue if anything untoward were to happen. Aeris nonchalantly glanced around the room as she approached the bar. There, sitting at a table to her right, was the man she sought. She could feel the weight of his stare as she passed, and she fought to keep the smile from her lips. With her attire, she had hoped to lure him to her. She was glad to think the ruse just might work.

As Aeris seated herself at the bar, the tavern-keeper eyed her appreciatively. Aeris asked for a slab of bread with lard and a mug of fruity mead. Once brought to her, she began to partake of the nourishment. Both food and drink were barely tolerable, but she continued with the subterfuge. Much to her relief, it wasn't long before she found herself joined at the bar by Cervantes. It was a good thing because, not only could she cease partaking of the despicable food, but she had begun to get the impression that the barkeep might begin to have a hit at her.

Cervantes seated himself upon the stool next to her and asked for a mug of spiced ale. He then turned towards her, his gaze lowering to her breasts before it finally came back up to meet her unwavering gaze.

My lady," he drawled, "I haven't had the pleasure of seeing you here before."

Aeris gave him a charming smile. "Why Captain, that is so strange. I have seen you on quite a few occasions and happen to know very well who you are."

Cervantes leaned back and regarded her with a speculative grin. Aeris could see that her remark made him preen, that he was pleased by the fact that he had become so notorious. "Well, that is not fair. You know who *I* am, but I have no idea about *you*."

Aeris allowed her smile to widen. "Yes, I do seem to have that advantage."

Cervantes finally grinned in response to her mild flirtation. "Tell me your name, my dear. I imagine it must be as beautiful as your face."

Aeris had no reaction to the flattery. She was above such things, and knew where he hoped it would get him. She saw no reason to lie, so she gave him her real name. "My name is Damaeris, my lord Captain. I hope it meets your approval."

"Indeed, it does, my lady. It fits you, to be sure."

Aeris grinned and chuckled lightly. She saw Cervantes move an unconscious hand up to his chest to rub the spot where his crystal must lie. She wondered if he thought it curious that the burning sensation was now at its greatest, wondered if he imagined a connection between her and the crystal. She laughed when he made a joke about the barkeep, and she noticed that he had moved his stool closer to hers. Damn, how would she be able to find out anything about his crystal? She asked him about the ornamental dagger he had sheathed at his waist when she heard the front door open and then close again. She glanced only momentarily at the man who strode quickly over to the bar, but then returned her attention to the captain.

Cervantes started telling her the story of how he obtained the dagger. However, Aeris found her attention divided between the captain and the newcomer. The man was rather nondescript, clothed only in plain brown tunic and trousers devoid of any design. Aeris found her attention drawn to him nonetheless, for he had no hair, wore several rings in one of his ears, and sported a tattoo across the entirety of the side of his face closest to her.

Aeris kept her gaze on Cervantes, but heard the bald man speaking to the barkeep in strangely accented common. "Could you tell me of anyone who might be going to the eastern continent?"

The man spoke loud enough that she heard his question, and the barkeep replied in a voice equally as loud. "Sure I do. Cervantes sails to the eastern continent all the time." The barkeep indicated towards the captain, who stopped speaking in mid-sentence. Both Aeris and Cervantes turned towards the bald man.

"You have cargo that you need to have transported there?" asked Cervantes.

The man nodded. "Yes, as soon as possible."

"How much do you have?"

The man shook his head. "Not much . . . just myself."

Cervantes brows drew together into a frown. "I don't take passengers. You will have to find another ship."

The man patted his coin pouch. "I have gold. I will pay you handsomely for your services."

Cervantes shook his head. "I am sorry. I have no place for passengers on my vessel at this time."

The man sighed and inclined his head. "So be it, then. Have a good day." With that, the man left.

For a few moments longer, Aeris and Cervantes sat in relative silence. Then the captain rose from his seat. "I should go. It was a pleasure making your acquaintance, my Lady Damaeris. Perhaps we will meet again sometime."

Aeris smiled. "I look forward to that time."

Cervantes offered her a small smile in return, then turned and left the establishment. Aeris sat at the bar for a moment longer before quitting the tavern herself. She walked down the street and was soon joined by Magnus, Tiger, and Goldare.

Aeris shook her head. "Nothing . . . I learned nothing. We were interrupted."

Magnus concurred. "I saw. We will need to come up with another plan."

Aeris only nodded her agreement.

***

Evening was approaching when the group found themselves at the docks. The crystal had led them there after they decided to go in search of Captain Cervantes again. Once more, Vikhail and Vardec were left behind at the inn with Jonesy and Mateo. The group decided that it would be best this way. It was needless for them all to go there and bring unnecessary attention to themselves.

Aeris found herself approaching a ship moored between two larger ones. It was in good condition, and the words, *Sea Maiden*, were painted on the side. "The crystal is aboard this ship," she said.

Tigerius stepped up next to her. "Is the captain aboard?"

Aeris shook her head. "I don't think so." Looking at the ship, Aeris noted that there was no one on deck, and she wondered if anyone was aboard at all. However, they had to assume that there was. Besides, what fool would leave his ship untended?

Tigerius nodded. "All right. Wish me luck."

Aeris put a hand on his arm. "I would give you the crystal, but . . ."

Tiger shook his head. "No. It's best that you hold on to it."

"Be careful."

He grinned and patted her hand. "I will. Don't worry. I have done this type of thing many times before." With that said, Tigerius turned and discreetly made his way towards the ship. Aeris frowned. She highly doubted that he had attempted a heist aboard a sea vessel. He just said that to make her feel better.

Aeris, Magnus, and Goldare stepped away and moved to an area just outside the docks. Then they waited, hoping that Tiger would soon find what they were looking for. Aeris felt unusually restless. She turned her head this way and that, constantly on the lookout. Since her short meeting with Cervantes, she had been receiving mixed signals from the crystal. Sometimes it urged her towards the docks to the south, while other times it urged her in a new direction, one towards the city gates to the north. These new urges were accompanied by other feelings, and none of them were good. She couldn't shake the feeling that someone was coming, and her restlessness was testimony to that fact.

Aeris hugged herself from the sudden chill that swept through her and rubbed the tops of her arms. It was then that she realized she had wandered away from the men. It wasn't too far, however, for Magnus would surely have come to retrieve her if she had. Even now he had his eye on her as he talked with Goldare. Upon her chest, the crystal burned, and once again she found herself glancing to the north. Seeing nothing, she sighed and turned away, just to come face-to-face with Captain Cervantes.

Aeris jumped back in surprise, bringing her hand up to her mouth to muffle the startled cry at her lips. Cervantes steadied her with a hand at her arm. "My lady, what a surprise to see you here."

Aeris only stared at him from wide eyes for a moment before she replied. "Yes, my lord. I didn't expect to see you again so soon." Sudden fear for her friend rushed through her. *Damnation! Tiger, get off the ship!* Aeris screamed the words in her mind even though she knew he wouldn't hear her. Her childish speculation that he could read minds was merely that . . . speculation.

"'Tis getting late. The docks are not the safest of places for a lone woman."

Aeris nodded. She saw no other way but to point out her comrades, for he would think it strange that she was out there standing alone without an escort. She gestured towards Goldare and Magnus. "Yes, Captain. The two men yonder are my escort. We are awaiting a friend, and then we plan to accompany him to the tavern of his choosing."

Cervantes smiled and nodded. "I am pleased that we have met again. Would you care to share a drink with me? I know of a good tavern up the street from where we met today. Perhaps your comrades wouldn't mind awaiting your friend and then meeting us there."

Aeris grinned and was about to answer in the affirmative when she noticed a man approaching them. It was the bald tattooed man who had asked Cervantes for passage to the eastern continent earlier in the day. Aeris kept herself from rolling her eyes in irritation. This would be the second time that he would be interrupting her attempts to find out all she could about the captain.

"Captain . . . Captain Cervantes."

Cervantes turned when he heard his name. He courteously waited for the man to approach and then listened attentively when he spoke.

"Captain, I have asked everywhere for someone who can take me to the eastern continent. They claim not to take passengers, and always refer me back to you. Please consider having me aboard your ship." The man raised his fat coin ouch. "I have gold, enough for three trips to my homeland. I will give you all of it for only one trip."

Cervantes regarded the man intently, his thumb and forefinger cradling his chin. Finally he shook his head. "I am sorry. I can not take a passenger at this time. You will just have to wait for another ship."

Aeris glanced from one man to the other. She felt the restlessness begin to consume her and suddenly felt the incredible urge to leave the immediate area. However, she knew that such an action was not feasible. Tigerius was still aboard Cervantes' ship. She glanced at Goldare and Magnus, saw that they had wandered unobtrusively closer.

"Please, won't you reconsider, Captain? I must make the trip to my homeland as soon as possible. It is a matter of life, death, and . . ." The man's voice trailed off as he looked at a point past Cervantes left shoulder. "Who the Hells are they?"

Aeris looked in the direction the man indicated as Cervantes turned in place. She felt her eyes widen as the dark-garbed newcomers swept at them seemingly from out of nowhere.

Tigerius swiftly and stealthily made his way across the lower deck. He was not familiar with ships but encountered no problems finding the hatch opening to the stairs leading below. His senses were on full alert . . . extraordinary senses that he had only recently begun to realize he possessed. He knew that he had inherited them from his father . . . a man who had more than his own fair share of uncanny abilities. As of recent, Tiger had begun to wish that Triath were there to answer a few of the myriad questions going through his mind. However, it had been a long while since he was home, and he was sure that his parents were more than just angry with him by now.

Sensing no one near, he went down the steps. The ship was well-kept . . . the floors were clear of debris and the cargo organized neatly against the walls. Tiger first went towards the crew cabins, but quickly realized that the captain's quarters would be elsewhere. He hurriedly began to move to the opposite side of the ship, and when he found the cabin that was twice the size of the others and occupied by lavishly upholstered furnishings, he knew he had found the right place.

Tigerius entered the cabin with only a cursory glance at the door and its frame. It was unlikely that it would be trapped, for few corsairs would spend their ill-begotten gold to acquire such a safety measure. Their greed was often their downfall, and the only reason Tiger knew was because he had read about them in countless tomes when he was a young boy. He had been fascinated with seafaring and piracy, thinking it must be one of the most extraordinary professions in the world. But now that he was grown, his opinions had changed a bit. When he began to realize he was more than just an ordinary human man, it simply didn't matter anymore.

Tiger swiftly surveyed the chamber and was about to approach the desk when he heard a shout in his mind, *"Damnation! Tiger, get off of the ship!"* He could sense Aeris' fear for him. That fear was probably the only reason she had been able to transmit to him, for he had never heard her voice in his mind before.

Tigerius swept out of the cabin and almost didn't notice that there was someone approaching in his direction. He slid into the shadows just as the crewman came into view, and Tiger thanked himself for all of the hard work he had dedicated to such stealthy endeavors when he was younger. The man stopped, rustled around a bit in a nearby crate, and once finding what he was looking for, went back in the direction from which he had come. Once he was satisfied that the man had gone, Tiger again began making his way to the stairs. There was a sense of urgency that had begun to permeate his mind, and he could hardly wait to be off of the ship.

The first of the priests leaped at the bald man. With unusual speed and strength, he grabbed the priest's arm and slung him gracefully over his shoulder. The priest landed hard onto the ground. Still holding on to the priest's arm, the tattooed man twisted it and slammed his foot down onto the priest's face.

Nearby, Cervantes imagined he could hear the sound of crunching bone amidst the other sounds coming to life around him. Lady Aeris' escort had leaped into action the moment they saw the dark-robed men, the big one drawing a blade that matched him in size. He rushed towards the priests as they swept towards Cervantes and Aeris. The faelin man with black hair continued to stay back, but Cervantes could see that his mouth was moving although he was saying something.

Galvanizing himself into action, Cervantes grabbed Aeris' arm and pulled her out from the center of the burgeoning melee. He saw the bald man standing there, his hands inside his sleeves, a solemn expression on his tattooed face. It was almost as though he waited for something . . . Suddenly he was a flurry of activity. He spun around as he took his hands from his sleeves, small arcs of silver shooting from his hands. Insight dawned on Cervantes then, for he had seen weapons like that once before. He couldn't suppress the chill of apprehension that swept through him.

Cervantes deposited Aeris approximately a farlo away from the scene and then turned back towards the skirmish. He drew his long-knife from the sheath at his thigh and rushed into the fray. The ezekuls had struck the enemy with deadly accuracy, the star-shaped weapons protruding from heads, chests, and necks. Cervantes swept at these enemies first, helping the bald man complete what had been started. As he leaped behind the third one, savagely slicing his knife across the priest's neck, Cervantes noticed that one of the enemy lay upon the ground covered in frost. Black eyes stared out from an unnaturally hideous face, somehow frozen in death. By the gods, what type of power could make a man look like that?

Cervantes turned away just in time to see that another man had entered the melee. Like the bigger man, he was human, albeit much smaller in stature. Yet, he was quick on his feet and easily maneuvered himself amongst the combatants. He slashed his short-sword this way and that, injuring and maiming where he could. However, it was soon apparent to all that the battle was nearly over. Most of the dark-robed enemy lay on the ground, and soon enough, the last of their companions lay with them.

Aeris took in the scene around her. The priests lay sprawled on the ground while her companions suffered the aftereffects of the skirmish. Instead of staying where Cervantes left her, Aeris had gone back to the fray, entering just in time to get attacked by one of the dying priests. She had drawn her dagger, and as he collided into her, she sheathed it in his belly. He died quickly, but not before he gouged her with his own blade.

Briefly, Aeris looked at the wound on her upper arm. Despite the blood that flowed freely, she turned her attention to other concerns. The crystal beckoned her in the direction of the fallen priests. Slowly she began to walk amongst them. There weren't all that many, but she counted at least ten. Finally she came to the one she wanted. She knelt down next to him, turned him over, and recoiled when she saw the face revealed by the hooded robe. It was twisted with darkness and evil, and she wondered if all of the Daemundai were so ugly. However, despite her contempt, she searched the body. Coming across a crimson pouch looped through the priest's sash, Aeris cut it free. Then she opened it and turned it upside down. Into her waiting palm fell a crystalline shard.

Aeris breathed deeply as she curled her fingers around the crystal. Suddenly, she found herself swept away. In her mind's eye she saw more of the dark robed priests . . . at least fifty strong. Led by a man who wielded a gnarled black staff topped by a glowing red orb, they were quickly approaching the city. Aeris came back to find herself still kneeling next to the fallen priest. She looked around and found herself the focus of everyone's attention.

"Who in the Hells are you?"

Aeris glanced over to Cervantes, who was looking at her with a disgruntled expression on his face. "Do you know who these people are? By the gods, what is going on?"

Aeris regarded him impassively. She could sense his unease, and she didn't blame him for the belligerence. She shook her head. "We don't have time for this conversation right now. There are more of them entering the city as we speak. They will search until they find us. They want the crystals." Aeris took in the entire group as she spoke.

"Then we have to go back to the inn for Jonesy, Mateo, Vikhail and Vardec," said Goldare.

"Did we get most of our supplies?" asked Magnus.

Goldare nodded the affirmative.

Aeris looked from Magnus and Goldare back to Cervantes. "You are in grave danger. We know that you have one of the crystals. If you know anyone else who has one, they are in danger as well. I don't know how many are in existence, but the Daemundai are on a mission to claim as many of these crystals as they can."

"We must leave the city as soon as possible," added Magnus.

Cervantes cursed eloquently. Aeris quietly waited for him to finish his tirade and then spoke again. "I am hoping that we can use your ship to escape the city. Most likely, the Daemundai will expect us to flee by land. We have a better chance of losing them, at least for a little while, if we travel by sea."

Cervantes cursed again and stomped his foot on the ground. Aeris watched him for a moment, but suddenly found herself overcome by weakness. She weaved on her feet and almost stumbled but for the helping hand at her back. It was the bald man. When he put his hand on her wounded arm to steady her, she moaned with the pain his touch solicited. He pulled back the torn fabric of her sleeve, and when he saw the deep laceration, he put a hand into the bag at his side and quickly withdrew a clean length of cloth.

"This wound needs to be cleaned," he stated brusquely.

Aeris nodded as the man proficiently bound her arm. Magnus, Goldare, and Tigerius approached them and then watched until he was finished. "We need to head back to the inn," said Magnus.

"Make certain she has not been compromised," stated the bald man. "The Daemundai are known for their poisons."

Aeris looked back to Cervantes. The captain frowned and put his hands on his hips. He clearly was not happy about the situation. He shook his head as he spoke. "I will prepare my ship and crew. We will be ready to sail as soon as possible."

CHAPTER 10

Sabian Makonnen paced the periphery of the chamber. He had been close . . . so close. He and his priests had just reached the city when he saw the departure of their quarry through the red eye of the tanjavian orb situated at the head of his staff . . . sailing away in a wretched caravel captained by a simple lowlife mercenary. Inwardly he seethed, his anger only manifesting itself in the tightening of his jaw and the quickening of his pace. He hated the loss of the *dragon crystals*, but even more the loss of one of the men who shared close proximity to them.

As Sabian had made his way closer to the city and watched the battle at the docks through the tanjavian orb, he began to realize the prize that was almost within his grip. A daemon-spawn was with the group he had been following, and only now that Sabian was so close could he begin to feel the vibrations given off by the young man. Sabian knew who the man was, for only one other gave off vibes such as this one. This was the son of Triath Solanar.

For many years the Daemundai had been searching for the daemon-spawn known as Triath. A couple of decades ago, the man seemed to fall into some oblivion, never to be seen or heard of again. There was rumor amongst the fold that he had sired a child upon a mortal woman, but nothing had ever been verified. Knowing the strength of the circles in which Triath kept his company, Sabian was not surprised that he had found a way to remain undetected. And the only reason Sabian knew this much was because he had once traveled with Triath himself.

Angrily, Sabian slammed his gnarled black staff onto the floor. He hated to remember that time . . . a time in which he had experienced his greatest failure. As a member of the Wildrunners, it had been easy to have access to Triath. Yet, things had not gone as Sabian hoped. The struggle between the human and daemon aspects of Triath had begun to destroy him. Once in Krathil-lon, a druidical stronghold in the far north, the Wildrunners had finally divined Sabian's true intentions and then struck him from the group. The druids with whom they left his fate would not kill him, but they sent him to a place where they felt that death was a near certainty.

Sabian paused in his path, staring ahead pensively. The druids had brought healing upon the beleaguered Triath, showing him how to come to terms with the duality of his new nature. And obviously the rumors of a child were truth.

That child now sailed away from him across the Biske bay, and Sabian could do nothing to intercept him. The seeing power of the tanjavian orb could only operate through the eyes of other Daemundai priests, and already Sabian could feel the waning of the vibrations given off by the daemon-spawn.

Once more Sabian felt the sting of failure, knew that Razlul would be disturbed by his inability to bring him that which he most desired. With a daemon hybrid such as Triath or his son, the Mehta might be able to determine what made the human/daemon fusion possible. The discovery would be momentous for the Daemundai, and once they were able to replicate the phenomenon, they would rise to heights never known before. And Sabian wanted to be pivotal in that occurrence . . .

***

31 Cisceren CY633

The *Sea Maiden* sailed south through the Biske Bay. Cervantes glanced about deck, saw his crew hard at work, and nodded in satisfaction. He was glad that no one gave him a hard time about the alacrity of their departure, and he remembered why he had hired them in the first place. These men put their captain, ship, and crew-mates above all else.

Within the last two days, Cervantes had deeply contemplated their destination. He was sorely tempted to simply sail east to the realm of Izran, unload his unwanted passengers at the port city of Jerbic, and then go about his business. Yet, he recalled the girl's words to him . . . that he was in danger because of his possession of the crystal that customarily hung about his neck. Cervantes rubbed at his chest, remembering the heat that emanated from the crystal when the girl was near. Now the crystal no longer hung there, but instead remained locked away in his cabin.

Cervantes sighed heavily. *Damn.* He wished he could just dump them in Jerbic and be done with them. But that wasn't usually his way. It had always been one of Cervantes' downfalls . . . his tendency to be sympathetic to the plight of others. The captain then ran a hand through this light brown hair. Besides, those monsters probably had the same thoughts. For all he knew, they would be waiting for them at the docks. Inasmuch, he would be placing himself at risk as well. It would perhaps be safest to proceed around the foot of Izran to the port city of Carmey.

Glancing around once more, Cervantes noticed a few of his passengers on deck. One of them was the lady, Aeris. She was being supported by the only other woman aboard the ship, the one they called Jonesy. For the first two days, Aeris was terribly ill, unable to keep down any food or drink. Another passenger, Tigerius, was in the same situation. Cervantes only shook his head.

It was obvious they had never set foot on a ship before, and the movement of the vessel over the waters made them sick. But now it appeared that Aeris was well enough to venture above deck. It was a good sign, and Cervantes could rest easier knowing that she would not die aboard his ship.

In spite of himself, Cervantes found himself making his way across the deck. Even though their initial meeting had been under false pretenses, Aeris was still a very beautiful woman. Cervantes wasn't above having her in his bed, and he would find a means to that end, even if it meant portraying himself as the solicitous captain.

The two women watched Cervantes as he approached. He schooled his expression into a pleasant one as he stopped in front of them. He inclined his head first to Aeris and then to Jonesy. "Good day, ladies. I hope you are enjoying the pleasant weather."

"Thank you, Captain. 'Tis about time I ventured above deck," said Aeris.

Cervantes nodded. "I am glad to see that you are recovering from your malady."

"I feel Tigerius is having a rougher time of it than I. If he does not improve within the next day or so, I will begin to worry for him."

Cervantes shook his head. "Do not fret. I have seen illness such as this before. Even for him it shall pass."

Aeris smiled and then lowered her head. "I know how difficult this must be for you, Captain Cervantes. It seems that we have literally fallen into your lap. Even though it is genuinely no fault of mine, I am sorry."

Cervantes just shook his head again. "That is all right. My luck was bound to run out at some point, anyways. 'Tis just as well it was accompanied by you."

Aeris felt her face flush. "When I am fully recovered, we must set aside some time to talk about the situation in which we have found ourselves."

"Indeed. Come to my cabin tomorrow afternoon. We will talk then."

Aeris nodded. "Thank you, Captain. I will do that."

Cervantes bid the women a pleasant afternoon before he left them. His congenial expression shifted into one of intense speculation as he made his way back to the stair that would take him below deck. It had been easier than he thought it would be to get Aeris to agree to come to his cabin. It would be effortless for him to manipulate her, and he would discover all he could about these crystals that were in such hot demand. If he happened to get her in his bed, that would be nice too.

As Cervantes strode across deck, his thoughts went to Levander. He had accepted the bald man upon his vessel after the skirmish with the Daemundai, realizing that he would be transporting passengers anyway. Right from the start, Cervantes had recognized the tattoo the man sported on the side of his face, a pattern worn only by the members of an elite brotherhood that resided throughout much of the eastern continent. He had heard much about the Kronshue, and none of it was good. He was warned to always steer clear of them, and he had heeded that advice up until the point when he knew that he would be giving passage to Aeris and her comrades. The bald man offered him a good sum of gold for his own passage, and Cervantes suddenly found no good reason to pass it up. He would keep a vigilant eye on the man, and had even made his point clear as Levander stepped aboard his ship with his possessions in tow. Levander had only nodded to him in acknowledgment, but it was all Cervantes needed.

Discarding his thoughts of Levander, Cervantes glanced about deck and took note of his newest crew member. The man was young, with black hair and strangely colored silver eyes. Cervantes had been keeping watch over Jaxom, but as it was turning out, he need not keep such close tabs on the man. Despite his peculiarity, Jaxom was a good worker and learned quickly. He would one day make an excellent ranking crew-member.

Once reaching the stairs, Cervantes climbed below deck. He made his way to the master's cabin, and once there, he entered and seated himself at the desk. From out of the drawer, he extracted the crystal. It burned the palm of his hand as it responded to the close proximity of the other crystals. Cervantes smiled to himself. Damn, he could only imagine its worth, especially accompanied by the other two artifacts.

Cervantes sighed and returned the crystal to the drawer. He then removed the key from its hiding place within a nearby empty wine decanter and locked it. Then he pocketed the key and slumped back in the chair. He couldn't keep Aeris' words out of his mind . . . *You are in grave danger. We know that you have one of the crystals. If you know anyone else who has one, they are in danger as well. I don't know how many are in existence, but the Daemundai are on a mission to claim as many of these crystals as they can.*

Cervantes stood from his seat and made his way over to the bed. Once reaching it, he sat down and leaned back on the pillows. Several months ago, he and his crew had boarded a small cargo ship. They had stolen all of the goods on board and when Cervantes left the captain's quarters, he departed with a large bag of gold and two glowing crystals. A few weeks later, when he returned home, Cervantes gave one of the crystals to his brother, Cortes. Truth be told, he had thought them to be the only ones in existence. Once apart, the crystals lost their luminescence, but Cervantes liked the idea that he would always know his brother was near when his crystal began to shine.

However, Cervantes began to suspect that the crystals were not alone when he noticed his own glowing once more. He knew that his brother was nowhere close, for he had only recently left Cortes back home. Just to be sure,

Cervantes went out in search of the man. His brother was nowhere to be found. But then a woman came, a woman whose presence made his crystal shine all the brighter. Cervantes felt himself drawn to her, and he knew it was more than just her beauty.

Now, Aeris' warning echoed through his mind. Cervantes knew that he needed to get home as soon as possible. His brother still had the other crystal . . .

***

Desolation swept through her like a wave, a flood that would not recede. Her pain was like a wet cloak that clung to her after a heavy rain, weighing her down. Torment sang through her mind like a scythe that was relentlessly accurate, cutting at the foundations of her sanity.

Aeris stood upon a forested hill that looked down upon a valley that was shadowed by the predawn darkness. Her body seemed somehow unlike her own, heavier than she knew it should be, yet empty of something she could not quite determine. She felt so alone, standing there. Yet, she knew that her comrades rested not far away. Unshed tears threatened to emerge from eyes that had seen more than they should have, eyes that would be never be the same again. Her mind would forever be haunted by the horror she had witnessed, the absolute evil that could encompass a person so completely . . . to the exclusion of all that was good and right in the world.

Suddenly hearing a noise behind her, she turned. It was a dragon, a magnificent silver dragon. His scales glittered like a million multifaceted gems in the light of the moons, and his eyes beckoned to her to come with him. This time, resistance was futile, and she knew it the moment she climbed onto his shimmering back. She could hear his voice in her mind, a deep, resonating voice that brought calm to her turmoil. She felt herself trusting in him and pressed herself against the smooth back. Beneath her, she could feel a sudden tension, a gathering of physical power. And when the dragon launched himself into the air, it seemed that all of her woes were left behind . . .

Aeris suddenly awoke to the sound of someone knocking on her cabin door. Quickly looking over to the other bed, she saw that Jonesy was not there. The remnants of the dream clung to her for a moment as she shook her head. Then, just as she muttered a command to enter, Magnus opened the door. Aeris sat up and rubbed the sleep out of her eyes as he stepped inside and closed the door behind him. Magnus walked over to the bed, stood there for a moment, and then seated himself.

Aeris regarded him as he sat there. She couldn't help but notice how handsome he was. However, she knew that she had to keep that separate from the other things she knew about him. Magnus had labeled her a traitor and then bound her against her will. Even after it was determined she was not a traitor after all, he continued to control her. That is, until now. After the attack from the Daemundai, Aeris had taken control of the situation. No one had disputed her, and no one had any better ideas.

"Aeris, we need to talk."

Magnus stated the obvious and Aeris found herself beginning to frown. However, she found that she was no longer angry with him. It was against her nature to carry anger for so long, and she liked to find the good that existed in most people. Despite his many shortcomings, Magnus did have his good qualities. She just needed to find them again.

Aeris turned away and nodded. "All right." She waited for Magnus to speak again, but the cabin only rang with silence. What, did he want her to say something more? Aeris was about to question him when he spoke.

"We are sailing away from our destination. It was my duty to return you home, but now we are traveling in the opposite direction."

Aeris nodded and rose from the bed. "Yes, I know. However, I could see no other way."

Magnus also stood. "I am not questioning the decision we made. It was necessary for our survival."

Aeris regarded him once more. "You should have walked away when you had the chance. Now the Daemundai consider you an enemy. Even after they confiscate the crystals, they may hunt you down and kill you."

Magnus frowned. "Yes, I could have left you." He suddenly closed the distance between them and took her wrist in his hand. "But, I knew that there was no better escort. If I had allowed you to end my service, you might be dead by now." Magnus paused before he continued. "Besides, who is to say that the Daemundai will accomplish their task?"

Aeris turned away from Magnus, pulling herself free of his grip. She slowly walked across the small cabin until she reached the far wall. There she stopped and spoke over her shoulder. "The Daemundai are very powerful. Eventually, they will have what they want."

"Then why did we bother to escape them?" asked Magnus gruffly.

"Because I still have hope," Aeris said in a quiet voice. "I want to see my brothers again . . . my mother, and my father. Because, despite the odds, I find that I want to live." Aeris stopped speaking for a moment, suddenly overcome by emotion. Then, "If they find us again, they will kill us."

Aeris whispered the last so quietly, Magnus almost didn't hear her. Once more, he stepped up to her. This time he took her by the arm and pulled her around to face him. "Aeris, I know that you wanted me to let you go that day. If it had been me in your situation, I would have felt the same. I didn't let you go because I knew that no one would protect you the way I will. No one." Magnus growled the last words vehemently.

Aeris stared at him from wide eyes. She could feel the determination in him, the will to overcome the odds against them. She found herself suddenly believing in him, and a part of her began to feel some semblance of safety. Aeris nodded, and it wasn't until she brought a hand up to her arm that Magnus seemed to realize that he still held it.

Magnus dropped his hand away from her. "I know that you haven't been feeling well, but when do you plan on speaking to Cervantes about the crystals?"

"I will be going to his cabin tomorrow afternoon," she said.

Magnus frowned. "Be careful. I do not trust him. I see the way he looks at you."

Aeris narrowed her eyes. "And how is that?"

"Like a hungry animal," he replied.

Aeris sighed. "Magnus, you are just going to have to realize that you need to trust me. I can take care of myself."

Magnus' frown deepened. "Aeris, you are going to have to learn to trust me as well. As a man, I know what he is thinking."

Aeris put her hands on her hips. "And what *exactly* is he thinking?"

"Only about getting you in his bed."

Aeris laughed. She knew for a fact that Captain Cervantes was thinking about more than just getting her into his bed. He wanted to see how much information he could get from her first. "Let me deal with the Captain. Besides, I have been doing a pretty fine job of it already, don't you think?"

Magnus pressed his lips into a thin line. Yes, he had to accede that Aeris had done very well with the Captain thus far. That was why he had come to ask her when she would be speaking with the man about the crystals. Otherwise, Magnus would have done it himself. Despite his attempts to avoid it, Magnus realized that he had become quite jealous. He hated the fact that Aeris was forced to play the vixen for that scoundrel of a captain, and he hated it even more that she did it so well.

"Fine, but I will be keeping a close eye on him."

Aeris grinned. "*Fine*, but don't give away my game. Besides, I am having fun."

"Humph, it won't be so *fun* when you find yourself in an uncompromising situation."

"Like I said, Magnus. You will just have to learn to trust me."

Magnus only sighed. Yes, it was one of the things he was quickly learning about himself. He had a hard time trusting anybody.

***

Joneselia looked out across the sea. The water lapped lazily against the hull and the ship swayed easily with the waves. She leaned over the rail, let the wind carry her hair alongside her face, and smelled of the salty spray. She imagined that she saw things just below the water's surface, strange creatures that lived within the depths of the sea. Once she thought that it might be more than just her imaginings, a huge shape that appeared beside the ship, shadowed by the bluish green waves. It stared at her from one dark eye and then disappeared, never for her to see again.

Jonesy continued to lean over the rail until her feet no longer touched the deck. She had no fear of going overboard, although she knew she should. Yet, she had discovered that she bore a certain liking for the sea, enjoyed the time she spent aboard ship. She realized it during her first seafaring experience . . . when she took a ship from Tambour to Yortec. Of course, this journey was much longer, but she found that she enjoyed it even more.

It was several moments later before Jonesy turned away from the sea. She leaned her back against the rail and glanced around. All the way across deck, at the stern of the ship, the helmsman was easily navigating the vessel, manipulating the wheel as needed. His name was Gerol. She had learned it, as well as the names of all of the other crewmen that Captain Cervantes had aboard the *Sea Maiden*. Currently, Dramid was above deck. He was the captain's first mate and tended to be there whenever Cervantes could not be. Jonesy brought her lips up into a grin. She knew *exactly* where the Captain was.

Jonesy began to walk around the periphery of the ship. She had always considered herself to be a perceptive individual. She had a propensity to read people and tended to know their intentions even before they themselves did. She had become quite fascinated by the people with whom she had chosen to keep company, the complexity level within the interpersonal relationships intriguing. Right from the start she could see Aeris as the hub, and all of the others seemed to radiate around her. Over the last few days, she had begun to piece together the connections between these people, and her conclusions served only to put a smile on her face.

First there was Tigerius. He was Aeris' rock, that steady place within her realm of upheaval and indecision. She knew that she could count on him, but had no idea that he had once harbored strong feelings for her, and perhaps still did. Then there was Mateo. He was a student, a boy that started out as a simple assignment, but now had become so much more. Since their initial meeting, Jonesy had quickly realized Aeris' profession . . . she was a sorceress, a witch with the ability to call upon magic to do her bidding. And Mateo was a fledgling warlock with the potential to do just the same. Despite the negativity that surrounded persons of their ilk, it didn't matter much to Jonesy, for Aeris had saved her life. She was a friend now, and Jonesy found that she rather enjoyed Aeris' company.

Jonesy continued to walk along the rail. The wind gently buffeted her and tiny droplets of water began to fall. She looked up to find a blue sky, marred only by the puffy clouds that floated overhead. One of them was marginally darker than the others, and she assumed that it was the cause of the rain. She shifted her thoughts back to Aeris, Tigerius, and Mateo. Somehow, the three of them had acquired a following. Jonesy would have to remember to ask Aeris how it came to be that Vikhail, Vardec, Goldare, and Magnus came to be in her company even though it was easy to determine why . . . it was not safe for a woman, a single man, and a boy to travel across the plains without either an escort or access to a caravan.

Jonesy glanced about deck once more. She saw that Magnus had emerged from below deck and that he stood astern of her. Jonesy stopped moving in that direction and instead contented herself with her present location. Out of the foursome who comprised Aeris' escort, Magnus was the most interesting. It was easy for her to see that he was attracted to Aeris, for he watched her when he thought no one noticed. The expressions that crossed his face were many and varied, and Jonesy quickly realized that he loved her. Jonesy's heart went out to the man, for Aeris seemed unlikely to return the favor. Instead, the woman went to see the captain in his personal cabin.

Jonesy found her lips turning up into another smile. Yes, Aeris was the reason why the captain was not present above deck. He was much too preoccupied with his lovely visitor to pay much heed to anything else. Jonesy knew that there was a specific reason for Aeris' visit, knew that she and Magnus were privy to some important pieces of information that the others were unaware. It had much to do with the Daemundai attack she had heard about, and the reason why they fled the realm of Torimir completely. It was the reason why Aeris now visited the Captain below deck, despite the gossip that would ensue.

Jonesy watched Magnus from the corner of her eye. Most likely, Aeris' visit was driving him crazy. She had seen the way Cervantes watched Aeris, and she was sure that Magnus had noticed the same. The Captain was a handsome man, which made the threat all the more palpable. Just like Cervantes, Magnus was a dominant individual. If it came down to it, he would fight for her, much as a lloryk stallion did for his mares. Despite her refined upbringing, Jonesy acceded that she would not mind viewing such a fight. And she would certainly enjoy seeing the consequences.

***

Aeris walked across the lower deck to the captain's cabin. Many of the crewmen were above deck, but there were a few who were there to watch as she

143

made her way to the other end of the ship. They stared at her speculatively, and she knew what they must be thinking . . . that she would be their captain's whore for the duration of the voyage. Aeris simply passed them by. Who cared what these men thought? Besides, it just might serve her purposes for them to view her as nothing more than a common wench.

As Aeris passed, one of the men caught her eye. Uncharacteristically, he was of faelin descent . . . she knew very few of her race who chose the sea over their land-bound homes. And he was handsome, quite different from the other crewmen who worked upon the ship. His black hair fell to his shoulders and his eyes were a strange hue of gray that she might describe as silver. He stared at her as she passed him by, but not the same way as the other men. His gaze went straight for her eyes, as though he hoped to catch a deeper glimpse of her soul. Aeris found herself regarding him as well, but when she passed, she did not stop. Hells only knew what the other men would think if she did.

Only a few moments later, Aeris arrived at the master's cabin. She knocked on the door, and it wasn't long before Cervantes was ushering her within. He looked out before he closed the door, and she could only imagine the look that passed between him and the crewmen who saw her enter. Cervantes invited her over to the small table that dominated the center of the cabin. Once she was seated, he poured two mugs of reddish liquid. He offered her one as he made himself comfortable in the chair next to hers. She took the mug and smelled of the contents. It had a mild, spicy odor. When she finally drank, she realized that the beverage was rather good.

Aeris lifted the mug in Cervantes' direction. "This is nice. What is it?"

Cervantes grinned. "Don't tell me that you have never tasted murg before!"

Aeris shook her head. "Never."

Cervantes shook his head. "You have been missing out, then."

"Indeed," Aeris replied in agreement before she took another drink from her mug.

Cervantes smiled to himself. It would be easier than he thought to intoxicate her. Then he would begin to obtain the things he wanted from her . . . first some information, and then perhaps a tumble in the furs.

Aeris replied to the small-talk that Cervantes initiated as they drank the murg he provided. It wasn't long before her mug was empty and Cervantes was refilling it. She found herself quickly becoming less inhibited, and their conversation more lively. He told her funny stories about some of his crewmen, including their interesting, and oftentimes unsavory habits. Aeris found herself responding in kind about her own comrades. She began with Vikhail and Vardec, and once the deluge began, she saw no reason to stop it.

Aeris regarded Cervantes with a grim expression. "Those halfen brothers, Vikhail and Vardec . . . they could drive me to the brink of insanity. At the end of every day, they sit, smoke, and tell their stupid stories. Goldare, Tigerius, and Mateo think they are funny, but I honestly can't find the humor. I suppose they are good in a fight, and they can prepare some edible food, but other than that . . ."

Aeris trailed off as Cervantes filled her mug once more. She noticed that Cervantes did not refill his own, and she took the decanter from his hand and poured it for him. He chuckled as he took a deep swig from his mug and then gestured for her to continue.

"Oh yes. Next there is Goldare. Needless to say, he is much like the halfen, only much bigger. He is a good fighter, but he can't cook worth a damn. At least he doesn't smoke as much, and the lloryk and larian seem to like him. "Tis just as well. I suppose everyone must have a strength somewhere.

"Then I have Mateo. By the gods, I hope that his Talent is as good as they say it to be. It is the only thing going in his favor. The boy is useless, especially when it comes to Jonesy. He stares at her all day like a love-sick cub. It makes it difficult for me to teach him anything."

Aeris shook her head. Despite the effects of the brew, she still had the mental capacity to refrain from telling the captain too much about her profession. She knew that he didn't know about it, for she had kept much of it from him during their skirmish with the Daemundai. She felt no qualms about telling him her feelings about the group, and she wasn't about to stop there.

"Tigerius is my good friend, but I must say, he has some of his own foibles. He needs to get his own life instead of following me around in mine. He is a terrible womanizer, and I must say, I don't think I have ever seen him succeed in taking a woman to his bed yet. But, at least I haven't seen him take a man, either." Aeris grinned at her own joke.

Cervantes laughed and poured some more murg into her mug. This time, he didn't hesitate to pour some into his own as well. He regarded her over the rim of his mug as he drank deeply. He could tell that she was intoxicated. Her cheeks were flushed, and her eyes bright. Her inhibitions were intriguing, and he found that he loved to listen to her light banter. However, she had yet to mention the one man whom he had been waiting to hear about. It was the cimmerean man, Magnus.

"Yes, but what of Magnus? Is he a ladies man or a man's man?"

Aeris almost choked on her murg. She stifled her laughter and put a modest hand to her mouth. "Captain, why do you ask?"

Cervantes shrugged. "He seems to have a stick shoved so far up his buffelshmut, I can't tell."

Aeris made a sound in her throat and her eyes watered with merriment, not only with the question, but with the captain's use of the childish term. "I must say, I am not so sure."

Cervantes narrowed his eyes at her. "Are you certain? I have seen the way he looks at you."

Aeris then narrowed her own eyes. This conversation was beginning to sound all too familiar. "And how is that, my lord?"

"Like a wemic hunting his prey."

Aeris chuckled. "That is silly. He does no such thing. Besides, I happen to know that he bears quite a disliking for me."

Cervantes guffawed. "I beg to differ. As a man, I can tell you that he thinks nothing of dislike when you are near."

"Pray tell me, Captain . . . what is he thinking?" Aeris couldn't keep herself from asking the question. She was curious to know what Cervantes thought, even if she would not believe him.

"Only about having you in his bed," he stated solemnly.

This time Aeris was not successful in her attempt to keep the laughter at bay. She cackled with glee, more as a result of the murg than anything Cervantes said. Yet, his statement was, indeed, hilarious to say the least.

"I assure you, having me in his bed is the last thing on Magnus' mind."

"Then he *is* a man's man," replied Cervantes.

"Of course not!" she heartily exclaimed.

Cervantes grinned. "He must be. How could he not want you warming his furs at night?"

Aeris pursed her lips. "Now you are flirting with me. He told me that you would."

Cervantes frowned. "He did, eh? What else did the man say?"

Aeris grinned. "That all you wanted was to get me in *your* bed."

Cervantes was silent for a moment before he burst out in laughter. Aeris followed suit. They continued for a moment before he finally caught enough breath to speak again. "So, have you anything more to tell me of your wayward companions?"

Aeris shook her head. "Not much, only this captain that I have met recently. I think he must be a scoundrel, for he is an awfully good flirt. However, I can hardly shake the feeling that he just might be a womanizer too, much like my good friend, Tigerius."

Cervantes only stared at her for a moment. Hells, she was so pretty, sitting there next to him. She thought nothing of picking fun at him, much unlike most of the other people in his life. His crewmen would never dream of it, and neither would his customers. Damn . . .

Suddenly, he was reaching out to her. His fingers found her sides, and he began to tickle her relentlessly. Aeris giggled and immediately began to squirm beneath the barrage. She fought to push his hands off of her, but he responded only by increasing his efforts. Still laughing, Aeris stood from her seat hoping to escape, but Cervantes followed. Finally, he grabbed her around the waist, lifted her, and then carried her the short distance to his bed. He tossed her down upon the blankets and resumed tickling her. It wasn't until tears were streaming down her temples, and she was calling for mercy, that he stopped. By then, he was lying next to her on the bed, and his face hovered just above hers.

Aeris felt her breath catch in her throat. His breath was warm against her face and when she looked into his eyes, she felt herself becoming lost in their deep blue depths. She then felt his lips enveloping hers, and a rush swept through her body. She could smell the spicy odor of murg as she returned his kiss. When he pulled her more closely to him, she slid her fingers behind his neck and into his hair. Cervantes ran his hand down the length of her body, over her back and side, down to her hip and around the curve of her buttocks. She pressed herself into him, reveling in the gratification his touch brought.

Cervantes felt himself swept away in a sea of passion. Her flavor was the sweetest he had ever tasted, and her body was curved in all of the right places. He brought his hand from her buttocks back up to her waist and then to her breast. He felt her body arch slightly in response, and his own body was quick to reply. His made a trail of kisses down to the curve of her neck and then he flicked his tongue onto the soft flesh behind her ear.

Aeris felt a warm sensation begin to settle low into her belly. Magnus was right, she had found herself in an uncompromising situation. However, contrary to his belief, it was not one out of which she found herself in a hurry to depart. Still, she knew that she should not give in to her base emotions. It would not benefit her cause to sleep with the captain, and may even serve to do the opposite. She needed him to respect her as a person, and if she gave her body to him this easily, he would find it difficult to do so.

Aeris reluctantly pulled away from Cervantes. He cast her a questioning glance, and was about to resume kissing her, when she placed her hand over his lips. With a resigned sigh, he allowed her to make some space between them and then propped himself up with his elbow. The effects of the murg slowly began to dissipate, courtesy of her faelin heritage. If she had been any more human, she would already be in the throes of passionate lovemaking.

"I suppose we should get down to the reason behind your visit." Cervantes spoke into the silence that pervaded the small cabin.

Aeris nodded. His eyes had become suddenly guarded. His gaze scrutinized her where she continued to lay next to him.

"You came so as to persuade me to give you my crystal." Cervantes spoke bluntly as he got up off of the bed. He knew that he wouldn't be able to have his way with her, and he was more than a bit piqued. He still wanted Aeris to give him her own crystals instead, for he entertained thoughts of their worth. He had hoped to seduce them from her, but he now knew that such a tactic was out of the question. She had shaken off the effects of his murg like a wemic does water after a swim. It was something he had never seen before, especially with a woman who barely made it up to his chin. However, he had experienced only minimal contact with the faelin race, despite his extensive travels.

Aeris sat upright on the bed and nodded. She had considered denying it, but then decided otherwise. Cervantes was an intelligent man. She would not be able to fool him easily. "Magnus and I have researched the crystals. However, texts will only tell so much. With the addition of your crystal, we may be able to more easily divine their true nature. Then we will discover why the Daemundai want them so much." Aeris forbore from telling him that they already had an idea why the Daemundai wanted the crystals. She didn't want to offer too much information just to regret it later. However, she knew that she needed to tell him something. So she gave him the basics.

Cervantes listened to her words. He respected the fact that she was honest with him. It was surprising, especially in his profession, where most people lied for a living. Inasmuch, he had learned to determine whether or not they spoke the truth . . . and Aeris had definitely done so. He knew that there were some things she was not telling him, but he respected that as well. It proved to him that she was not a fool willing to trust just anyone.

However, by right the crystal was his. Cervantes had stolen both it, and it's sister, fairly from their previous owner. Since procuring the crystals, Cervantes had thought of nothing but his dream of discovering the dragon continent. Then, when he had rummaged through Aeris' belongings and discovered the book about dragons, his hopes were galvanized to greater heights. In his heart, he believed that Aeris and her companions might be the means to realizing his dream.

Cervantes went over to his desk and opened the drawer. He reached within and pulled out the crystal. He then turned towards Aeris and held it between them. It dangled from its golden chain, beautifully reflecting the light beaming through the small portholes. "Here, take it then. However, I have just one condition."

Aeris was surprised to have Cervantes offer her the crystal without an argument. She nodded when he stated that he had a condition, and she waited patiently for him to speak it.

"In return for giving you the crystal freely, I would like to know what you discover. I am aware that you have not told me everything, not even close. But some day I would like to be a part of what is going on. Hells, these Daemundai people are after *me* now. You even went so far as to tell me my life is endangered. I now ask for the same respect I have offered to you."

Aeris took in his words. She didn't have to think about it very long before she was nodding in agreement. "All right. I will let you know." She took the golden chain holding the crystal from Cervantes' hand.

The captain nodded. "You had better go. Your watch-wemic is probably wondering about you by now."

With such a description of Magnus, Aeris couldn't help the grin from turning up the corners of her mouth. "I wouldn't be surprised."

Cervantes found himself smiling as well. He led her to the door of his cabin and then opened it. Before stepping out, Aeris carefully placed the crystal into the pouch she had hanging from her sash. Cervantes guided her above deck, and once there, he turned to her. "We are partners, then?"

Aeris nodded. "Yes. We are partners." She put out her hand, and when Cervantes took it, he pulled her close to him.

"We must seal it, then."

Before she could respond, Cervantes' lips had claimed hers. Without hesitation she returned the kiss. When he finally pulled away, she grinned widely. "Indeed, you *are* a scoundrel."

"The worst kind," he replied with a twinkle in his eyes. He then turned and made his way back down the steps below deck.

CHAPTER 11

Magnus broodingly leaned against the railing as the men who served as the evening's musical entertainment struck up another bawdy song. Jonesy sang accompaniment when the halfen brothers would not, and Magnus realized early in the evening that he much preferred her voice as opposed to theirs. The revelry was complete with a barrel of ale on deck. Everyone took turns at the dartboards that had been secured to the wall of the forecastle, and Magnus could not help but notice that Aeris was pretty good at the game, especially for someone as inebriated as she seemed to be.

Magnus narrowed his eyes at Aeris yet again. He then shifted his gaze to Cervantes and frowned. By the gods, he had come to despise the man, for Cervantes had proven to be exactly what Magnus warned Aeris he would be. However, much to his consternation, Aeris didn't seem to mind the Captain's degenerate ways. He saw the kiss they shared on deck earlier that day, and her response had been anything but dislike. Hells, for all he knew, she had shared his bed already. Although, he did have to concede that she was able to obtain the crystal.

Hells! Magnus tightened his grip around the mug in his hand. He hated the thought of her in the rogue's bed, but there was little he could do or say to change it. He watched as she threw another dart at the board, and when she almost hit the center, Tigerius clasped her hand. When Cervantes stepped up and threw his own dart, it struck just inside of hers. Tigerius cursed and Aeris chucked the Captain good-naturedly on the shoulder. Then they all doubled over in laughter, too far in their cups to realize how ridiculous they looked.

Magnus took a deep drink from the ale. Sometimes he found himself wishing that he could let go . . . just like the Captain, his crew, and their passengers did this night. He wondered what it would be like, to have no care and to simply live for the moment. It was difficult to imagine, for he didn't think he had ever done it before, even in his past life.

Magnus turned his attention back to the musicians. Two of Cervantes crewmen seemed to be pretty well versed, and Jonesy began to sing a ballad. It was a change from the fast-paced bawdy tales he had been hearing for most of the evening. However, no one else seemed to notice the change in music except for Levander. The other man seemed to perk up when he heard the change in tune. Once the Captain decided to take Aeris and her comrades aboard his ship,

Cervantes didn't seem to have a problem taking the gold the bald man initially offered and allowing him to receive passage as well. Like Magnus, Lev seemed to have no intention of joining the revelry, and instead seemed content to view it from a distance.

Magnus returned his attention to the festivity. Vikhail and Vardec were smoking something pungent, for the aroma seemed to be everywhere. If Magnus was right, it was something mind-altering, although not in the debilitating sense. It would simply allow them to release their inhibitions even more than they did with ale alone. A couple of members of the captain's crew were smoking it as well. Magnus knew he would hate to see it if something were to come up and Cervantes made to rely upon these men to perform some specific function.

Magnus heard another round of laughter from the dart-throwers and turned to see Cervantes with his arm around Aeris' shoulders. She was leaning into him with a familiarity that bespoke years worth of friendship. Tigerius was on her other side, almost doubled over at something that had been said. Dramid, the captain's first mate, and another of his crewmen looked on in astonishment, as though it was a rarity for them to see their captain partaking in so much frivolity. Goldare threw another dart and it missed the board entirely, instead hitting the wall of the forecastle. The laughter began anew, this time on his account. Goldare had the sense to look abashed.

Magnus looked away from them, slightly shaking his head. He then noticed another of Cervantes' crewmen. The man was staring at the group, and when Magnus followed his line of vision, he saw that the crewman was looking primarily at one person in particular. It was Aeris. His silver eyes were intent as they fixed upon her, but it wasn't of the lustful type. It was different than that. The gaze was almost speculative, almost as though the man was trying to figure something out. Magnus regarded him pensively. There was something familiar him, but Magnus couldn't quite put his finger on it.

Magnus stepped away from his place at the railing and acquired himself more ale from the barrel. He drank it down with barely a breath in the middle, and when he was finished, he became conscious of being watched. He turned to find the young woman, Jonesy, regarding him. It was only then he realized that the halfen brothers were singing again, and he almost cringed at the auditory impact.

Jonesy walked over to him, and when she stopped, she held out her mug. Wordlessly, Magnus accepted the mug and subsequently filled it with ale from the barrel. When he handed the mug back to her, she grinned and took a long swig. When she finally lowered it, she wiped her mouth on her sleeve. "I hope that you know how to dance, my lord."

Magnus inclined his head. "Indeed, I do."

Jonesy nodded. "Good. Despite the bad music, I would love to have a partner."

Magnus raised an eyebrow. "Are you inviting me for a dance, my lady?"

"What, are you really that surprised?"

Magnus took a deep breath and thought about it for a moment. "No, not really."

Jonesy awarded him with another smile. "Good. So take the lead already. I have been hoping to find a decent partner all night. You were the only one who appeared to be even half capable."

Magnus cleared his throat and offered her his arm. "Should I take that as a compliment?"

Jonesy nodded. "Oh yes. By all means, 'tis a compliment."

Magnus led her into a dance, one that he thought best matched the type of music being played. For the rest of the evening, he played partner to the princess of Karlisle, and he was finally able to take is mind away from Damaeris Timberlyn.

***

Aeris sat upon her bed, the book splayed across her lap. Beside her were the crystals, each one wrapped within its own strip of fabric. She could feel them calling out to one another, longing to be one. She had ceased wearing the one her mother bestowed upon her when she obtained the second crystal from the Daemundai. Within such close proximity to the other, the first crystal only served to burn her flesh where it rested against her chest. And now that she had the crystal from Cervantes, the glow was all the brighter.

There was a swift knock at her door, and before she could issue the call to enter, Magnus was opening it, stepping into the small cabin, and closing the door behind him. Seeing Aeris on the bed, he made his way over and seated himself opposite her. His eyes were immediately drawn to the three cloth-enclosed crystals, and she knew that he felt their power just as strongly as she. Aeris slid the book over to Magnus and bade him look at the text. "It doesn't give very many particulars about the power of the crystals. We know that they are made of dragons, but not by whom and for what purpose. It tells us that the crystals must be activated in order to be used at their fullest potential. The power of the crystals increases with propinquity, but there is no indication as to what exactly what that power is and what it entails."

Magnus read over the text, his brow creasing to form a frown. After a few moments, he looked up at her. "I can't help but think that these crystals were used as a weapon *against* dragons, not *for* them."

"What makes you think that?" Aeris regarded him intently with a solemn expression on her face.

Magnus pressed his lips into a thin line. He then pointed to the text. "Here it tells that the crystals will *'bring the dragons into alignment . . . that they will have no thought for themselves, but only for the song of the crystals'*."

Aeris nodded. She had recently arrived at the same conclusion herself, but needed the opinion of another to justify her beliefs.

"It might explain why the Daemundai want the crystals so much. Daemon and dragon-kind have been at war for centuries. These crystals would give daemons an upper hand," said Magnus.

Aeris nodded again. "I thought about that."

Magnus regarded her downcast expression for a moment, wondered why she seemed so affected. He then glanced at the folded cloths again. "Maybe we should try to glean some information from the crystals ourselves. We have three of them right here. Let's see what we can learn about them. Obviously, the writer of this book had none of his own."

Aeris turned her eyes to him, took in the boyish expression on his face, and grinned. Sometimes he could surprise her, much like he did now . . . abandoning his persona of absolute seriousness to take away her melancholy. She picked up each of the three pieces of fabric and emptied their contents between them on the bed. The crystals glowed brightly, each one beckoning to the others.

Aeris reached out and picked up one of the crystals. The warmth it radiated was intense, and she knew that it would soon begin to cause discomfort. She then picked up another one. She slowly brought them together, immediately feeling the dynamism of the connected pair. She suddenly remembered the vision she experienced after taking the crystal from the dead Daemundai priest. Now she knew that it was a particular property of the crystals . . . to give the wielder an ability to see immediate threat. Once more, Aeris was all too aware of the Daemundai's efforts to locate her and others who had similar crystalline artifacts within their possession.

Aeris studied the crystals closely. They had fused to become one crystal and she could scarcely see the seam that separated them. It was like they were meant to be together, yet their yearning was for something even more. She reached over and picked up the third crystal. She felt a pulse sweep through her and the larger one began to hum with expectancy. Glancing up at Magnus, she could see that he heard the same sound. Slowly she started to bring them together, but Magnus put a staying hand over hers.

"Wait. Let me do it."

Aeris nodded and placed the smaller crystal into his open palm. He was concerned about what could happen. They knew next to nothing about these crystals, yet they were handling them with no protection. It was against what they had been taught, but they needed to know the true nature of the crystals and what they were up against with the Daemundai. Magnus handled the crystal for a brief moment, angling it this way and that. He then slowly began to bring it closer to the one Aeris held within her own hand.

The moment the third crystal touched the other two, her mind rocked with something that was almost beyond her ability to comprehend. At first she saw only a jumble of images, but they quickly melted into one another to form a single picture. But the vision was more than just a series of images that could be seen . . . she could *feel* them.

The golden dragon landed at the opening to the cavern. She paused for a moment . . . loathe to enter. She felt the danger lurking inside, but the compulsion was strong. It gripped her mind like a vise, taking away her will to resist.

Folding her wings against her sides, she succumbed to the insistent pull tugging at her mind. It wasn't long before she reached the chamber. In the center there was a faintly glowing ring of stones upon the floor, and at the periphery stood several humanoid figures. Deep within her mind she could still feel the desire to flee, but it was nothing compared to the force that compelled her into the circle. The moment she stepped inside, she felt a noose settle around her neck just below the jaw. It was then she suddenly sensed the presence of the dragon who had come before. Flaring her nostrils, she could smell the maleness of the dragon, as well as the blood that was spilled.

With a surge of strength, she reared upward, her voice shaking the cavern walls. She sought to unfurl her wings, but found that they had nowhere to expand, the chamber walls keeping them bound against her. The noose tightened about her neck, cutting into that vulnerable place at her throat where the armor of her scales was predominantly absent. Yet she fought . . . fought against the bonds of the cavern, the noose, and the compulsion. But it was to no avail. Already she could feel herself waning, her will once more receding deep within her soul.

Hopelessness settled into the crevices of her mind. The pressure of the noose forced her back down into the ring. Her partially unfurled wings scraped against the cavern walls and she could feel the myriad of tiny cuts they had sustained when she fought to escape. She brought them in close and then crouched to the ground, wrapping her tail tightly around her body. She then slowly lowered her head until it rested upon her front feet.

The dragon watched the man as he approached. His black robe just barely swept the ground as he moved. His companions fanned out behind, and once they were close, situated themselves around her. Their voices began as a low murmuring, but then picked up strength and volume. At first she heard their voices just in her ears, but before long they were in her mind. The first man unsheathed his blade. It glowed eerily lavender in the gloom and she could feel the power it held. It was a dragon-slayer, *a sword she had never seen, but only heard about in legends. She never really thought they existed, but now that it was before her, she felt nothing. She knew that death had come for her, and she felt sadness that she hadn't the opportunity to live her life to the fullest. She would never have her first mating flight, nor bear the clutch that would result in that union. She would never have the chance to find her bond-mate, nor to see her offspring grow.*

She felt the dragon-slayer *slice into the soft flesh of her throat. Her life's blood poured out of the fatal wound. Only dimly did she see the large flasks and jars as they passed before her eyes. She didn't know how long she lay there, only that she felt herself becoming more and more weak as the time passed. Her heart slowed, and it wasn't until it took it's last beat that she saw the crystal. She felt the last of her blood drop onto the shard. Darkness enveloped her vision, and she suddenly thought that she should perhaps be afraid . . .*

Jaxomdrehl suddenly awakened from a restless sleep. He felt a disturbance in the air, something that made him edgy and restless. He glanced around in the darkness, saw his fellow crew mates all sleeping on their bed pallets. The ship swayed with the motion of the water, nothing in the movement that would have made him awaken. Focusing his senses, he could neither hear nor smell anything that could be a potential danger.

Yet, there was *something* there. It pulled at him, urging him to come. Jaxom felt inexplicably drawn, and he stood from his pallet. He slowly walked among the bunks to the door of the cabin and then quietly opened it. He made not a sound, and no one stirred with his passage. Jaxom left the forecastle and he began to make his way across the deck. He remained in the shadows, not wanting the night-watch to notice him. Not that it really would have mattered . . . but he didn't want to bring unwanted attention to himself. They would wonder why he was walking about above deck in the middle of the night, and he didn't feel like coming up with an adequate response. Although, he supposed it wouldn't be too terribly difficult. They were only humans, after all.

It wasn't long before Jaxom found himself standing at the steps that led below deck. He felt the urge to continue, but he resisted. With no small amount of agitation, he wondered what was wrong with him. He was awake in the middle of the night, following some invisible mystical force that had some kind of hold over him. He wanted to turn away from the steps and go back to his pallet, but the compulsory need for him to proceed was strong.

With a resigned sigh, he went down the steps. Once below deck, Jaxom walked towards the passenger cabins, those usually reserved for the officers. He felt a thrum in the air, tinged with a hint of expectancy. He moved stealthily and slowly; he felt the hunter without knowing what it was he hunted. He grinned mirthlessly and shook his head. This was ridiculous . . .

Then, suddenly it was gone. The compulsion vanished as though it had never been. Jaxom sensed a veil lift from over him, and he began to feel some semblance of normalcy. He found himself standing before the door to one of the cabins. He could sense someone within, two someones actually, a male and a female. It was effortless for him to determine that it was the young woman they called Aeris and her companion, Magnus. They started speaking, but he didn't bother to stay to hear what they were saying. He shook his head, turned away from the door, and began to make his way back to the forecastle.

By the time he returned to the crew cabin, Jaxom's mind had begun to clear. He didn't really understand what had happened, and whatever memories that he had of the event were slowly starting to fade from his mind as though it were a dream. As he settled back down onto his bed pallet, he thought about the young faelin woman with red hair. Aeris. There was something about her that he found intriguing, and now he wished that he had stayed at the door to hear what she may have been discussing with Magnus. However, it wasn't long before all thoughts of his recent experience melted into the back of his mind as he began to fall into sleep. It had been a long day, and another was soon to come.

**

"Seascrags! Prepare for assault!" Cervantes shouted his orders above the activity going on aboard his ship. The crewmen had already begun to rush to their stations . . . the tell-tale signs of approaching seascrags sending everyone into a flurry of activity. The Migallon Mechanism being released into the water was the next sound to be heard. The large spiked bars fell into the sea, and upon impact began to heat the surrounding water. The bars were attached to chains that ran into the bowels of the ship, which in turn, were wrapped around four large turning wheels. Once manned, the chains could allow the bars to drop, or to be pulled up, after a battle. The mechanism was designed to defend a ship against the most prevalent threat in the seas surrounding Ansalar, the pestilence known as the seascrag.

Many years ago, Cervantes had known a man by the name of Mercer Migallon. He was a brilliant inventor with no small amount of Talent. Cervantes didn't quite remember how he met the man, only that Migallon once asked Cervantes to make a visit to his family at a time during which he sailed to the port city of Tambour relatively often for business. The captain agreed to do Migallon this favor in exchange for a discounted price on his most valued invention. Agreeing to the terms, Migallon gave Cervantes a message for his family.

Unfortunately, once making port in Tambour, Cervantes discovered that the family of which Migallon spoke had succumbed to a malady that swept through the region many fortnights before. Neither the woman nor her two children had survived the sickness. With a heavy heart, Cervantes returned to Darban with the devastating news.

Unexpectedly, Migallon had kept to his word. Within only a few days, the *Sea Maiden* was fit with the mechanism. The only drawback was that the ship would no longer have the capacity to carry heavy artillery. Should the ship be attacked, there would be no cannon aboard to protect them against other corsair ships. As such, Cervantes set out to find a crew that had a strong background in archery and other offensive techniques. They would never have the ability to sink an enemy ship, but at least they would have their archers and the Migallon Mechanism.

After touching the nearest chain and muttering the strange 'incantation' Migallon had taught him in order to activate the mechanism, Cervantes watched as the spiked bars fell beneath the bubbling waves. They would heat the surrounding water, making it virtually impassable for the approaching menace. The seascrags were vulnerable to shifts in water temperature . . . any changes that made it too hot or too cold were intolerable. As such, they tended to attack in the dusky hours as the sun was setting and the first shandaharian moon making her ascent.

Leaning over the railing, Captain Cervantes watched as the bubbling became more turbulent. Damn, there was a large number of them this time. It was possible . . .

Cervantes suddenly reared back as a host of seascrags leaped out of the foamy waves. They landed aboard the *Sea Maiden*, their clawed feet scraping against the polished deck. They were hideous to behold, their striped and mottled skins colored sickly green and yellow. Their maws were wide, containing several rows of small sharp teeth. They had four arms and two legs, large pale-colored eyes, and sharp spines that rose in a line down the center of their backs. The striped variety was more intelligent than the mottled one, and Cervantes suddenly found himself glad of the fact that he saw more mottled skins than striped ones.

Grappling at his belt, Cervantes took hold of the rod sheathed there. Drawing it out, he thrust it before him as the first of the seascrags leaped at him. Too late, he thought that perhaps he should have equipped his passengers with the electrically imbued devices he and his crew called "shock-sticks". There were plenty aboard the ship, for Cervantes spared no expense when it came to the safety of the *Sea Maiden* and her crew. The devices were magically enhanced, and as such, very expensive. Cervantes happily spent the coin he had for them . . . he had experienced too many skirmishes with 'scrags to think twice about it.

After a vicious thrust of the shock-stick into the abdomen of the seascrag, Cervantes turned from the wounded creature and rushed towards the forecastle. Along with many other integral supplies, it was where the surplus shock-sticks were kept. He ran alongside the ensuing fray, subconsciously taking note of the positions of his crewmen, and then that of his passengers. He was quite taken aback by the number of seascrags that had boarded the vessel . . . the Migallon Mechanism was usually much more useful a tool. Most likely, the mechanism had been dropped just a few moments too late; or perhaps there were simply so many 'scrags, that many more were able to breach the defense.

Jonesy dodged one of the sickening creatures just as Cervantes rushed past. They were grotesque to say the least . . . bipeds that stood about two feet tall with milky gray eyes bulging from fishy faces. They had gaping, foul-smelling mouths filled with tiny sharp teeth, four arms each with a hand having four fingers, and slimy striped and mottled skins varying from pale greenish yellow to a deep murky green.

Jonesy crouched behind a crate. Gods only knew why it was there and what was within it, yet she saw no reason to be choosy. She took deep ragged breaths, and then wondered where the Hells Cervantes was going in a situation such as this. She squelched the urge to scream when one of the creatures suddenly fell next to her, it's rank body smoking from whatever weapon had been used against it. The creature didn't move, yet Jonesy wasn't quite convinced it was dead. Already, within the short amount of time the little monsters had been aboard the ship, she had seen their regenerative qualities.

For a moment Jonesy simply stared at the dead body. Then she hazarded a look around the corner of the crate she used as her hiding place. She saw Vikhail and Vardec hacking and slashing at the creatures with axe and hammer. Goldare used his massive broad-blade. The men tried to cut down the creatures until the fishy things reached a point where they could no longer regenerate. These creatures died upon the deck of the *Sea Maiden*. Unfortunately, many others simply scampered away to regenerate a lost limb or to close a massive laceration that would have been the end to any human, faelin, or halfen.

Glancing in the other direction, Jonesy saw Ragon, Marion, and Gerol. The men were using some device against the creatures that took them down better than any sword, axe, or hammer. It was a glowing rod that, upon contact, sent an electrical current through the enemy. The creatures were powerless against it, for with only a touch or two, they were laid out upon the polished deck. Not only that, but it seemed much cleaner than the disemboweling techniques that Goldare used, for hardly any blood was shed with the use of this wondrous rod.

Jonesy focused her gaze beyond Cervantes' crewmen. She saw even more of the creatures. It was difficult to focus properly at this distance, but it seemed that many more of them were prone upon the deck as opposed to upright and fighting. She saw Magnus and Aeris, each one casting their spells one right after the other. The electrical beams seared the creatures where they stood, making them fall in a greenish, crumpled heap. It was an awesome sight to behold, for one did not see such things on a common day. It was the first time Jonesy had seen the spell-casters in action, and she was momentarily enthralled by the scene.

Jonesy finally sat back in her place behind the crate. She was about to turn and look in the direction of Goldare and the halfen brothers when she began to smell the presence of something behind her. She felt her heart stop in her chest for a moment, and her breaths stilled in her chest. She felt the tingling sensation of impending danger just as she shot to her feet and turned around.

Jonesy felt the weight of the creature upon her in an instant, and it raked wickedly sharp claws along her back and forearm. She couldn't help but scream, pain intermingled with fear making a voice for itself. Jonesy fell backward with the impact, the creature landing on top of her. The back of her head hit the deck, and her vision wavered. In a feeble attempt to shield herself, Jonesy raised her arms before her face. The creature bore down upon her . . . and then there was nothing.

***

Aeris slowly walked above deck. The men had worked hard all day and into the next cleaning it of seascrag guts. Aeris had offered to help, but Cervantes only waved her away. She found the gesture a bit vexing, but she said nothing and simply went about her business. Hells, she had offered to help because it seemed that they could use as many hands as possible. By no means did she really *want* to scrape seascrag gore from the deck. However, she was a passenger aboard this ship. As such, she was bound to perform any duties that might be required of her. She supposed that this wasn't one of them. Aeris knew why the captain had turned her away . . . she was a woman, and most likely not up to the task. Well, the man had another thing coming if he thought he could keep her sitting around doing nothing for the entirety of the voyage.

For the rest her life, Aeris would never forget the evening before as the *Sea Maiden* sailed away from the scene of the 'scrag skirmish. As the last rays of the sun disappeared upon the horizon, Aeris watched as the crew pulled four large, spiked bars out of the sea. The water was littered with the bodies of seascrags that had succumbed to the heat generated by the weapon Cervantes called the Migallon Mechanism. There were at least a hundred of the sickly green carcasses floating haphazardly in the waves, and that didn't count dozens more whose thick blood slicked the deck of the ship. Already the air was thick with the scent of death . . . in particular the death of dreadful fishy beings who seemed to have emerged from out of the pages of some storybook Aeris may have read many years ago.

Yet, Aeris didn't loiter at the hideous scene for too long. Tigerius had been severely wounded in the attack and lay below deck . . . subject to the healing skill of the strange bald man known as Levander. At first she was reticent to allow the man to see to her friend, but when Lev quickly proved to her that he knew how to help Tiger, she allowed him to work. It wasn't long before her friend was taped and bound to the fullest and then allowed to rest without disturbance. Aeris was impressed by Lev's ability, and knew that they were fortunate to have him aboard the ship.

Yet, although Lev was able to help Tigerius, there was one man that was beyond even his skill. One of Cervantes crew-men, Tegmet, died of wounds sustained in the skirmish. The tears at his throat were the ones that ultimately led to his death. It seemed that, much like Tiger, sheer numbers had overwhelmed the man and brought him down.

Aeris sighed and leaned herself against the railing. The waters were calm, and the ship was moving swiftly and smoothly. At this rate, they would reach Cervantes' home port, the city of Darban, within another fortnight or so. Aeris turned when Mateo joined her at the railing. He smiled a greeting and then looked out across the water. Grinning to herself, Aeris continued to watch him from the corner of her eye. His disheveled brown hair blew in the wind, revealing the slightly pointed ears customarily hidden beneath. Once noticing them, Aeris suddenly realized why it had been so easy for his family to cast him aside. He was a bastard . . . a child bred from nothing more than a simple affair. Most likely, his mother had been with a faelin man, become pregnant, and borne the child out of wedlock. For both mother and son it meant nothing more than a hard life. And when the mother finally found a man that would have her, he found it difficult to accept the child that came along with her.

However, Aeris kept her thoughts to herself. She was sure that Mateo was very aware of the intricacies of his upbringing. Nevertheless, despite his propensity for remaining distant from those around him, he sustained a relationship with Aeris and even risked an attraction for Jonesy. Over the past several days, it was easy to see his romantic interest in the young woman. Yet, in spite of the closeness of their ages, she kept him at arm's length. Aeris thought it might have much to do with the differences in their social class, but she couldn't be entirely sure. Jonesy didn't seem to treat Mateo as though she were above him . . . only that she was the elder sister to a wayward younger brother.

It wasn't much later that Aeris found herself turning at the approach of Jonesy herself. Courtesy of Captain Cervantes, she had suffered little from the seascrag who singled her out during the skirmish. Just as the creature was about to bite into her throat, Cervantes had closed in on it, kicked it away from her prone body, and then electrocuted it. The only wounds she had to show were the cuts on her back and arm.

Jonesy nudged Aeris' shoulder with her own as she placed herself at the railing next to her. Smiling, Aeris nudged her back, glad of the camaraderie they had come to share together. The friendship brought some light into Aeris' existence, for she found herself bogged down with knowledge she had only recently acquired. For some reason, she was being hunted by the Daemundai. They seemed to be after the crystal within her possession. Captain Cervantes had a similar crystal, one which he had surrendered to her. Magnus bore a strong distrust of her, enough for him to take her as his prisoner, and Jonesy had secrets which she had yet to divulge. Then, to top everything off, Aeris had terrible dreams and visions that sought to take her very breath away. These things, and more, weighed upon her; yet she could wait another day to divine the truths she needed. Only another day . . .

***

Cervantes looked out across the calm sea. The horizon was only a thin line that separated two shades of blue. The air was sticky with moisture, and he swept a hand through the matted strands of his hair. He breathed deeply with anticipation and no small amount of anxiety. There was a storm coming; he could sense it. It was a big one, and he had never been wrong before.

Cervantes turned away from the rail and made his way to the helm. There, Gerol was deftly manning the wheel. Not far away, Neil was busily sewing a tear in one of the sails, and Hardow was checking the rigging for any signs of weakness. At the other end of the ship, near the bow, Ragon and Marion were scrubbing the deck. Cervantes stepped up to his helmsman. Gerol turned to him attentively and when Cervantes didn't say anything right away, the man spoke. "Anythin' ya need, Cap'n?"

Cervantes was quiet for a moment, hating to be the bearer of bad news. "I can sense a storm coming, so you need to be on the alert."

"How close is it?" Gerol looked up at the blue sky above, devoid of any sign of the approaching storm.

"Three, maybe four hours away." Despite the clear sky above, Cervantes didn't doubt that Gerol believed him when he said a storm was coming.

"Do ya want me to inform the rest of the crew, Cap'n?"

"No. I will do it. Stay at your post."

Cervantes turned from the helm. Damn, they were so close. The port city of Carmey was only two days at a brisk sail. Now, with the impending storm, they could be swept entirely off course. Depending on the strength and duration of the storm, they could be taken deep into unfamiliar waters. Keeping the alarm out of his voice, Cervantes called out to his men to meet him below deck. Any good captain would never translate his fears to his crew. It was bad form, and might result in panic that would hinder the work he needed from his men.

Once below deck, he told everyone about the approaching storm. Afterwards, there was a flurry of activity as preparations were made. Cervantes went back above to survey the horizon, and it wasn't long before he sensed a shift in the winds. Glancing down, he could see that the water lapping against the hull was slightly agitated, yet had not become powerful enough to make it felt on deck. By his deductions, the storm was coming from the port aft. He briefly considered trying to outrun it, but quickly decided that it would be a futile attempt. The storm was simply approaching far too fast.

It wasn't until a gray smudge appeared on the port horizon that Cervantes finally informed his passengers of the impending ordeal. He watched as each person took note of the severity of their situation. Varying degrees of alarm then passed over their faces, and he left them to contemplate their fate on their own. Cervantes was comfortable with his own mortality, but was very aware that most others were not. He much preferred to not be witness to sudden outbursts of emotion.

Less than an hour later, the first large waves began to strike the ship just as Aeris and Magnus began to climb below deck. The ship leaned with the impact, and the water washed over them, rushing into the opening to pour below deck. Aeris fell into Magnus and he clutched her about the waist, keeping her from falling the rest of the way down the steps. She sputtered as she inadvertently inhaled the water and felt her stomach roll with the lurching of the ship.

"Get the Hells to your cabins!" shouted Cervantes from the top of the stairs. His hair hung in drenched strands down the sides of his head, and the water literally poured off of him. He then slammed the hatch shut, most likely wanting to keep as much water as possible out of the bowels of the ship.

They had barely made it off the stairs before the next wave hit. Once again, Aeris was thrown against Magnus and they found themselves tossed to the floor. Cargo slid by, threatening to hit them as it passed. Magnus' body cushioned the brunt of her fall, and he pulled her out of the way of a sliding crate before it could strike her. They hurriedly struggled to their feet and stumbled towards the cabins. Magnus' was the first one on the right, and just as he opened the door, yet another wave rocked the ship.

They were thrown roughly into the cabin as the ship was pressed to its side from the weight of the water. Aeris found herself torn from Magnus' grip, and she was the first to hit the wall. Her head barely missed hitting the bunk, and when the ship lurched back into its vertical position, nausea overtook her. She grabbed the chamber pot just in time to vomit into it. She held her sides as she retched, and when she was finished, she looked up to find Magnus crouching there beside her. The ship continued to buck and heave, and she knew that she would soon be using the chamber pot again.

"Are you all right?" Magnus asked over the sounds of the storm.

All Aeris could do was shake her head. Already her body was beginning to tremble with the effects of the sea sickness she endured when first coming aboard the ship. Magnus scooted himself until he was sitting next to her, and then he put his arm around her shoulders. With her body wedged between the bunk and Magnus, when the next wave struck, she went nowhere. Yet, she gripped the leg of the bunk tightly and when she vomited into the chamber pot once more, her knuckles turned white.

The storm raged relentlessly, tossing the ship madly about. Aeris had passed out by the time Magnus heard the captain and what remained of his crew take refuge below deck. There was nothing they could do as the ship spun out of control, entirely subject to the whimsy of the storm. Magnus pulled the chamber pot over to him and he finally retched into it as well. He only hoped that it would be over soon, and that he would still be alive when it was.

***

The degethozak soared over the small city of Rotham. Farenze felt the beat of his heart accelerate in anticipation of what was to come. He glanced at his comrades astride their own dragons. Dark scaled hides glistened in the rays of the afternoon sun . . . magnificent beasts that had succumbed to the lure of the crystals that Lord Razlul kept in his possession. Farenze knew little about the leader of the Daemundai, and even less about the crystals. Yet, he faked knowledge before his companions, garnering their unwavering respect and awe. He reveled in the power his simple lies brought, and sometimes he imagined he could feel his dragon respond to the emotions that surged through him.

His dragon. Yes, Farenze supposed that Sifrozelnik was his. It seemed like only yesterday that he had arrived at Razlul's stronghold in response to the call for dragon-slayers. Farenze thought it would be as good a profession as any other, not to mention that he was a good fighter. He stood within a crowd of many other men . . . all hoping for a similar opportunity. And once the competitions were begun, Farenze had beaten all of his opponents in all of the trials. Only he and a handful of others stood in the arena. A few days later, they were introduced to the degethozak. Two men died during that initial meeting, and two more during the training that ensued after the dragons and their riders were paired. Farenze had assumed that he would be slaying dragons, not riding them. However, he realized right away that he didn't really care as long as he was being paid.

And now here they were. Rotham was the third city in just thrice that number of days. They had been ordered to incite anarchy and fear within the realms, and if they happened upon a helzethryn or rezwithrys, they were commanded to slay the gold and silver dragons immediately. Farenze could hardly wait for the day they faced their first draconic opponents. He grinned to himself as Sifrozelnik banked to the right and began his descent upon the city. The other dragons followed suit and prepared for their first pass.

Farenze readied his cross-bow as they approached the city. Below them he could see that the dragons had been seen, and people were running through the streets. Just a couple of moments later and they were close enough that screams could be heard. Farenze felt another surge of anticipation, and he imagined that it was more than just his own. However, he wondered about that for only a moment before the first wave of flames washed over the people in the streets. The screams shifted from fear to torment as the fire enveloped them, burning the flesh from their bones. The scent of seared meat swept into his nostrils, and Farenze inhaled deeply of it. He could suddenly *feel* the terror of the residents of Rotham, and the sensation brought him to a level of elation he felt only at times such as this.

Sifro beat his massive wings and lifted them up and away from the city proper. Farenze took in the damage that had been wrought in only a single pass. Several buildings had caught fire, and the blackened corpses of tens of people littered the streets. Sifro rumbled deep in his throat, the vibration traveling throughout his body. Farenze felt it too, accompanied by the emotion itself . . . immense satisfaction.

Farenze tightened his grip on the harness straps. He was not fool enough to think that the dragons were entirely under their control. Since being permanently paired with Sifrozelnik, he had come to realize that the power of the crystals worked only so far, and that it was the disposition inherent within the degethozak that made their mission easy. The dark dragons took pleasure in chaos and bloodshed . . . they thrived on it. If it had been helzethryn or rezwithrys that they attempted to control, Farenze doubted they would have been able to make the dragons commit the atrocities they had made within the past fortnight.

The dragon-riders prepared for their second attack. Farenze noticed that the city guard had mobilized. Catapults lined the defense towers, and they were being equipped with projectiles. In the streets, the wounded were being dragged out of harms way, and men bearing long-bows and cross-bows took their place. Farenze felt the corner of his mouth turn up in a grimace of malice. These people were stupid to think they could stand against the assault. In the end, they would die just like all of the others.

As Sifro began his descent, Farenze felt the dragon inhale deeply in preparation for his next breath attack. It was an awesome sight to see the dragons spewing fire from their massive maws, the flames deadly as any ordinary fire. Farenze aimed his cross-bow at the men in the streets, gratified to see them fall when his bolts struck. He had quickly learned to shoot accurately from the back of the dragon, and he was adequately praised for his efforts.

Farenze knew when the catapults were fired. He could hear the sound almost as though he were right there on the walls next to them. The rocky missiles flew through the air, and the dragons were forced to dodge out of the way. Sifro spat another wave of flame upon those remaining in the streets, and the nearby buildings became engulfed in fire. Hearing a commotion behind as they swept past, Farenze glanced over his shoulder. A group of people rushed out of one of the buildings and onto the street. The last was a man ushering a young woman and her infant before him. The woman screamed in terror as the gray dragon, Ramzexis, snatched the man up in his maw. The rider cackled with glee as Ramzexis lifted his head and swallowed the man whole.

Farenze turned back as Sifrozelnik lifted away from the city once again. He heard the shouts of his fellow dragon-riders as they derived pleasure from the wanton destruction they had wrought. Farenze felt his own heart soar in response, and he lifted a closed fist into the air. He let out his own battle cry, one that emerged from deep within. Sifro answered the cry with a mighty roar . . . a call to ultimate victory. Farenze felt it reverberate through to his very soul . . . felt himself become one with the dragon beneath him. Apart, each of them was powerful . . . but together they would be much, much more.

CHAPTER 12

Aeris found herself suddenly startled awake. The sound was terrible as the hull of the ship scraped against . . . something. Aeris could feel the trauma of it reverberate throughout the body of the ship . . . the massive crunching and grinding of wood against rock. The vessel lurched onto its side and she could vaguely hear the shouts of the men on deck. It then righted itself. The sounds of the storm were significantly less than they had been before, and the ship rocked less forcefully with the action of the waves. It was then that Aeris realized she had no idea how much time had passed since the storm started.

Shaking herself free of the effects of sea-sickness, Aeris realized that she was lying within the shelter of Magnus' arms upon a bed pallet. She turned to him and found that his eyes were open as well, most likely awakened by the same terrible sound. Magnus turned his head to face her, and she found herself suddenly overly aware of the arm that cradled her back and the hand at her waist. Magnus simply regarded her from dark lavender eyes, his expression inscrutable.

For a few moments they lay there, looking into one another's eyes. Time seemed to slow down and Aeris felt herself holding her breath. Her body was warm where it touched his, and she suddenly felt the intimacy of their situation. Despite his unreadable expression, she could sense something from the man beside her . . . she just didn't know what. She waited for Magnus to pull away from her, but he seemed to be content where he was. The air became thick with suppressed emotion, and Aeris felt her heart begin to accelerate in her chest. She wet her lips with the tip of her tongue and then watched as his eyes drifted from her eyes to her mouth. By the gods . . .

All of a sudden Aeris heard the scraping sound yet again. The ship once more tilted to the side, and she heard more shouting from the men above deck. She waited for the ship to right itself, and when it did not, she felt her body become tense. The loud scraping sound continued, and a sickening feeling stole over her. The ship was foundering.

Suddenly the noise stopped. The ship was quiet. All she could hear was the lapping of water. Magnus slowly extracted himself from her, and she saw the flicker of regret in his eyes as he pulled away. Aeris sat up in the bunk and slowly swung her legs over the side. She put her feet down and felt a cold wetness envelope them. In shocked surprise, she recoiled and then looked down. The cabin was flooded ankle-deep with water. It was then that she heard the sound of the water sloshing all around, and she was chagrined to realize she had not noticed it sooner.

Magnus stepped down into the water that had flooded the cabin. He looked back at Aeris and took in her expression of dismay. His intention was to go above deck, see if his fears were a reality. The ship had ceased moving, and he was almost certain that they were stranded somewhere. It was obvious that the ship had been damaged. Otherwise, this much water would never have succeeded in infiltrating the lower deck. It meant that it was a good possibility the cargo hold was completely submerged.

Magnus waded towards the door and opened it. It was difficult, especially with the ship tilted as it was. Aeris was quick to follow behind. They made their way to the steps leading to the main deck. The hatch was closed, and Magnus pushed it open when he neared it. He stepped out on deck, and then reached out his hand to pull Aeris up to join him. He noticed the pallor of her complexion, and knew she had reached the same conclusion he had just made himself. The sight that met his eyes almost took his breath away.

The *Sea Maiden* had foundered upon a rocky beach. Beyond it was a large swath of forested land. The air was sticky with warmth, and Magnus knew that they had been swept south with the storm. He glanced about the deck and saw the disheveled appearance of Cervantes and his crewmen. There were less than he remembered, and he knew that the men must have been lost in the storm. They looked exhausted, and now to be shipwrecked in the middle of nowhere on an unfamiliar island, was almost too much to comprehend all at once.

Aeris stared at the beach upon which they rested and then at the jungle that lay beyond. It was intimidating to say the least, and she wondered how they would survive. Glancing at Cervantes, she took in the weary slant of his shoulders and the intense fatigue etched into the lines of his face. She knew that he and his crew had fought the storm to the best of their capabilities and failed. Yet now, even in their dire situation, she knew he would show no weakness.

Sensing movement behind her, Aeris turned to find the rest of the group making their way up the steps. Tigerius was the first, followed by Jonesy, Goldare, Mateo, Vikhail, Vardec, and then Lev. Initial expressions of disbelief were soon replaced by those of solemn acceptance as everyone took in the situation.

"Secure and lower the ropes," Cervantes commanded in a forceful voice. The tired crew swung into motion, and it wasn't long before all of the passengers were standing upon dry land. Aboard the ship, Cervantes continued to work alongside his crew as they went into the flooded hold to acquire as much cargo as they could and unload it onto the sandy beach. Meanwhile, Aeris walked towards the jungle that lay not far from the shore. Once standing before it, she stared into the dark depths.

"It seems awfully foreboding," said a voice at her side.

Aeris turned to look at Tigerius. He looked much like she felt. His eyes were red-rimmed and his complexion pale. She remembered that he seemed to suffer much as she did whilst they traveled by sea. She suddenly felt her throat beginning to close up. "Tiger, what are we going to do?"

Tigerius heard the catch in her voice and put a comforting arm around her shoulders. "We are going to find a way home."

Aeris shook her head. "I wish we were there now. I was such a fool to allow Alasdair to go without me . . . without *us*. By the gods, I am so sorry . . ."

Unable to stop her sudden influx of emotion, Aeris put a hand to her face, hoping to stop the tears that threatened. Tigerius frowned and pulled her around to face him. "Don't you dare apologize to me. It was my choice to stay with you, and I haven't regretted it once. This was beyond your control; you had no idea that anything such as this could possibly happen. Aeris, you are only mortal."

Aeris looked up at him from tear-filled eyes. "Why . . . why did you stay with me Tiger?"

He only shook his head. "Because I knew that you would need me."

Aeris wrapped her arms around his neck, and Tigerius pulled her close to him. He held her as she cried, and when she finally pulled away, she was quick to compose herself. "We have to set up some kind of shelter for ourselves, find potable water, and then something we will be able to eat."

Tigerius nodded. "You probably know more than most of us. You will need to tell us all how we should go about surviving in this place."

Aeris gave him a wavering grin. "Oh, no. There must be someone who knows more than I do." Aeris gestured towards the rest of the group and then to the men aboard the foundered ship. "Look at all of these men. There is bound to be someone."

Tigerius only shrugged. "Perhaps, but I wouldn't hold my breath if I were you. Not to mention that they were not trained by one of the greatest rangers in western Ansalar."

Aeris' grin widened. "My, you have quite an opinion of my abilities. Remember, I am no ranger."

"Yes, but you received at least some training from the legendary Sirion Timberlyn. That has to mean something."

Aeris shook her head. "What about Goldare, Vikhail, or Vardec?"

Tiger raised an eyebrow. "You *are* joking, right?"

Aeris' grin faltered and turned into a slight frown. "No. I had rather hoped . . ."

"'Hope' is the operative word there, Aeris. Most likely, the three of them put together know less about survival than you do."

"Then we may be in for some more trouble than I thought. I had every right to cry like a small child with soiled wrappings."

"Every right," agreed Tigerius.

The comrades turned and walked back towards the ship, reaching the rest of the group just as the last of the crates were being lowered to the sand. Cervantes and his crew joined them on the beach soon after. Aeris counted only five of them, where before there had at least been ten. The captain had lost half of his crew in his battle with the storm, and Aeris could only feel the weight of their precarious situation settle more heavily about her. She was sure that Cervantes felt much the same.

"We will need to repair the ship. The hull has been breached in several areas, and it will take all of our efforts to make her sea-worthy again."

"About how long will it take?" asked Magnus.

"A fortnight . . . maybe more," replied Cervantes.

Magnus frowned. "How do you expect us to live that long in this gods forsaken place?"

Cervantes planted his hands on his hips. "Listen, I am only giving you the facts. I am only one man with four crewmen who are still alive after our ordeal. There is only so much that can be accomplished in one day."

"We will starve to death before your repairs are complete."

"We have food stores available from aboard the ship. We can use some of those," said Cervantes irritably.

"Then what will we use on our return trip?" asked Magnus, also putting his hands at his hips.

Cervantes threw up his hands. "Hells, I don't know. Think of something! There must be some plant or animal worth eating around here." Cervantes glanced up and down the beach and then at the jungle that lay not far away. "At least we won't need to build a shelter. The ship is stable enough that we can sleep above deck, and when the weather becomes inclement, we can take shelter in the forecastle."

"That still doesn't solve our problem about food. We will also need water. The barrels you have on board will not be enough, especially in this heat."

It was only then that Aeris noticed how hot she had become. When they first emerged from below deck, it was early morning, and the sun had just barely crested the horizon. Now, it was creeping high overhead as mid-day approached. It was becoming warmer by the moment, and she had the incredible urge to begin shucking her clothing. She asked the question that should have been asked at the outset. "Captain, where are we?"

Cervantes shook his head. "I am not sure. The storm raged around us for at least two days. It could have carried us anywhere, especially with the force it projected."

"Do you at least have any ideas?"

Cervantes sighed. "Perhaps something uncharted in the southern half of the Drujasu Sea. There are many islands that have not yet been explored, and this could very well be one of them."

Aeris nodded and lapsed back into contemplative silence. For a few moments, no one said anything more. But then Cervantes spoke again. "Allright, let's get started. It feels like it is only going to get hotter out here. We might as well use whatever time we can to get the essentials. Dramid, you go with Goldare and Tigerius to find something to eat. Marion, you go with Magnus and Mateo to find a water source. Gervais, you go with Vikhail and Vardec to find the materials we will need to begin repairs on the ship."

Aeris stood by as Cervantes shouted his orders to everyone. He very conspicuously left herself and Jonesy out, and she suddenly realized that, once again, he felt them incapable of any type of real contribution. She was about to say something when Magnus' voice cut through the air. "What in the Hells do you think you are doing?"

Aeris' eyes flew from Magnus' angry countenance to Cervantes. His features darkened considerably as he considered his reply. "What does it look like? I seem to be the only one out here who can decide what needs to be done."

Magnus narrowed his eyes. "You have no jurisdiction over us now. We are no longer aboard your ship, Captain, and we are not within your employ. I am the decision-maker in this group, and I will decide what tasks to give to which persons."

Cervantes threw his hands up into the air. "Fine," he spat. "Just get the work done. I don't care how it's executed or who does it."

"You just mind your own responsibilities, such as getting that ship of yours repaired, and leave the rest up to us. We are relying upon your skills to get us out of here," snapped Magnus.

Cervantes abruptly turned away from the cimmerean and addressed his crew. "You heard the man. Let's get to work. We have a lot to accomplish . . ."

***

Jaxomdrehl sat upon the empty barrel, far removed from the others. They were preparing for the night, their first night in the wilderness in which they found themselves. Strange noises emanated from the jungle not far away, and he wondered what was out there. Not that it would have mattered. If there was any real danger to himself, he would shift into dragon form within moments and rend the menace with tooth and claw.

Jaxom shifted his weight on the barrel. He was becoming rather accustomed to his faelin form, and was even beginning to like it. He was glad he had left Honshae when he did, for he had begun to weary of all of the training. Most likely his father was angry, but Jaxom could not find it within himself to truly care. Trebexal had other sons and daughters. Let them carry the burden of the dragon-riders.

Jaxom scanned the group before him. Within but a moment, he had picked out the object upon which he wished to focus. It was the faelin girl with red hair. There was something about her, something captivating, something that made him want to resign himself to her. He resisted the impulse, fearing that he would lose himself. He had heard the other dragons talk, that when one found his or her bond-mate, they felt many of the same sensations Jaxom did now.

He shook his head. No. He could only hope that such was not the case with him. He did not like the idea of a faelin as his bond-mate, hated that he would feel compelled to return to Honshae to undertake the training that went on there. With a faelin as a bond-mate, he would be expected to bring her with him, and then undergo the most rigorous of the training. As bond-mates, they would be able to function as other dragons and their ordinary riders could not . . . at an accelerated capacity that far exceeded most others.

Yet, he could not just ignore her. Jaxom had seen her watching him a time or two, an expression of contemplation upon her beautiful face. Now she sat next to her companion on deck, a human female. They calmly watched the men as they prepared the area. Wet bed pallets had been brought from the lower deck and allowed to dry in the sun throughout the day. All of the food stores aboard the *Sea Maiden* had been placed within the forecastle. They would be divided among all and eaten sparingly. The water and ale barrels had been brought up from the hold, and they currently rested upon the sandy beach. They would be forced to use these until potable water was found.

Preliminary forays into the jungle had proven to be unsuccessful. Magnus and his group were forced to return to the ship. When they realized they needed something to cut down the dense foliage they encountered, just enough to make a narrow path in order to allow passage, Cervantes grudgingly gave them the use of a few of the fauchards he kept in the master's cabin. They were weapons he and his crew used when they encountered the worst situations. Jaxom felt that the only reason he allowed himself to part with the fauchards was because of the alliance he shared with Aeris. Perhaps as well the fact that he relied upon Magnus and his group to obtain some type of nourishment during their excursions into the jungle.

Jaxom sighed to himself. He knew that he could not continue to ignore the connection he felt with Aeris. Despite his fears, he needed to talk with her, perhaps find out why he felt so compelled to be near her. He hoped it had nothing to do with Bonding, for he so much wanted to find himself a dragon bond-mate one day. Perhaps he should look upon the brighter side of things. Maybe she would prove to be a good friend. Jaxom looked back to the young woman, saw that she was watching him intently from dark eyes. *No, it was much more than that . . .*

***

Aeris walked slowly among the trees behind Magnus. She watched his bare, muscular back as he moved, saw the sweat as it trickled down to his lean waist. There it stopped at the line of dark trousers that rested low upon his hips. She allowed her gaze to travel even farther down to the swell of his rear. She couldn't keep the appreciation out of her mind, but she was soon looking away. She shouldn't be having these thoughts, especially about this man. Yet, she couldn't keep Cervantes' words out of her mind . . . *I can tell you that he thinks nothing of dislike when you are near . . . how could he not want you warming his furs at night?* There was a time that she may have agreed with the captain; she remembered the kiss she and Magnus had shared the night of the festival in Grunchin. However, much time had passed since then, and even more separated them.

Aeris wiped an arm across her sweaty forehead. Damnation, it was hot, even more so beneath the canopy of the jungle. The insects were voracious, and they settled upon her at every opportunity. She slapped at them constantly, and when one happened to bite into her, she squelched the urge to yelp. For a while, she had continued to wear her long sleeved tunic, but as the heat began to wear upon her, she finally took it off. Now she wore only her pants and camisole. She felt quite the wench, walking around with so much exposed; but half of the time, she found that she didn't really care.

Aeris heard a curse from behind her and recognized the voice as belonging to Tigerius. She grinned to herself, knowing that he was hating life right about now. In front of Magnus, Goldare was wielding a fauchard, a large curved sword with a wide blade that was able to slice through the vegetation with relative ease. He used long sweeping strokes to cut down the tall grasses and thick bushes that impeded their passage. Although the men took turns, Goldare had the most upper-body strength and was able to endure a bit longer than the others. Aeris stopped to look behind her, saw Jonesy following behind Tiger, and then Mateo and Lev bringing up the rear. Vikhail and Vardec had opted to offer their services to Cervantes, who seemed to need the help in repairing the ship. It was probably just as well, for she didn't think they would have been much help out in the middle of the jungle.

Magnus stopped when he realized that he was no longer being followed. He turned to look back at the procession and saw that Aeris was stopping to do the same. His gaze perused her slender body, taking in the thin camisole that barely covered her breasts and torso. By the gods, within the space of only a day or two she had become transformed into the indiscriminate woman he saw before him now. Her skin glistened with tiny droplets of perspiration, and her cheeks were flushed with heat and the effects of physical activity. He swung his fauchard up over his shoulder and patiently waited, content to simply look at her.

Seeing that everyone appeared to be keeping up with the pace, Aeris turned back to the front. Magnus was watching her intently, one hand at his hip, and the other holding the fauchard he had resting against his shoulder. He regarded her intently as she continued forward. A moment later she was standing before him and he had not moved. He continued to look at her, his lavender expression fathomless. She returned his gaze, unwilling to back down from him. "Should we stop?" he finally asked.

"No. Everyone is fine."

Magnus turned one corner of his mouth up into a small grin. He then stepped away from her and turned in the direction in which Goldare had gone. "Goldare, it's my turn to take over."

Aeris heard a shout in the affirmative from the narrow path ahead. A moment later, a sweat-laden Goldare was walking towards them. Magnus clapped him on the shoulder. "I will take over for a while. Give your fauchard to Tigerius; he is next."

Aeris shook her head. She wanted to try to help, even if it was just a little. "No. I want to take a turn."

Magnus turned to look at her, his expression registering surprise tinged with no small amount of humor and tolerance. He shook his head. "This isn't the type of work you need to help with. Goldare, Tigerius, Lev and I can handle it."

Aeris drew her brows into a frown. "No, Magnus. I told you I want to help." She held out her hand for the fauchard.

Magnus shook his head. "Aeris . . ."

"Come now. Give it to me. Or must I wrestle the fauchard away from you?"

Magnus paused. He suddenly realized that she was the epitome of seriousness, and that she would not hesitate to grapple the weapon away from him. He had to admit that he was not so averse to such a turn of events, and even found himself anticipating it. However, he was quick to catch himself. He knew that he should not be entertaining thoughts such as those, especially in regards to a woman who wanted nothing to do with him.

"Fine. Here it is." Magnus handed the fauchard to Aeris. He watched as she manipulated it with two hands, the weight of it slowing her movements. She then stepped past him and began to make the strokes she had seen the others make as they cleared the path. She held the weapon awkwardly, causing her cuts to be rather ineffectual. For a moment Magnus watched her, but quickly decided to volunteer some assistance. He knew that it was likely that she would reject him, but he would offer anyways.

Magnus stepped up behind her. "Aeris, wait. Let me show you a better way to hold the blade."

Aeris abruptly turned at the sound of his voice behind her, giving him the impression that she was startled. He closed the gap between them and placed his hands over hers upon the fauchard. She did not resist, and she was amenable to him moving her hands into a different position upon the handle of the weapon. He became suddenly aware of her closeness, the feel of her back at his chest and her hands beneath his.

"Now, move the fauchard like this," Magnus demonstrated. "It will maximize your swing, place more power behind it." With his hands over hers, he slowly manipulated the weapon, arching it first one way and then the other. Her hair tickled the side of his face, and her shoulder moved against the inside of his arm.

Aeris performed as he instructed, and when she seemed to have a grasp of it, he released her hands. She then stepped forward and cut into the vegetation. Magnus followed behind, watching her as she moved. It wasn't long before her body was soaked in sweat, the thin fabric of her camisole sticking to her chest, sides, and back. Her form was fully outlined by the wet garment, and Magnus could not help his gaze from raking over her again.

It wasn't long after that she began to falter. Magnus was there to grab the fauchard when it appeared to be too much for her to wield any longer. "Here, let me take that for you."

Aeris dropped her hands from the weapon and turned to him. "You were right. This is hard work."

Magnus nodded. "But I still appreciate your desire to help."

She only nodded and then looked away from him. "Yes. Well, it isn't enough."

Magnus put his fingers beneath her chin and turned her face back to him. "Aeris, it is always enough."

She then offered him a small smile, one that he could not quite decipher. The mystery of it stayed with him until Tigerius came to take over for him, and then even longer afterward.

22 Thaliren CY633

Aeris sat before the fire, waiting for the water to complete boiling. It hadn't taken them very long to find it, for the jungle was rife with a myriad of fresh-water springs and lakes. It was only slightly brackish, so they boiled the water so as to release the minerals. Moreover, it served the dual purpose of making it free of potential disease.

Hearing a shout behind her, Aeris looked towards the deck of the foundered ship. The men were working diligently day in and day out to make the vessel seaworthy as soon as possible. Now, in addition to using whatever aid that Vikhail and Vardec could provide, Cervantes had recruited Goldare, Tigerius, and Mateo. Even Jonesy was lending a hand with the less arduous tasks. With their help, the work seemed to be going a bit faster.

After waiting several moments longer, Aeris removed the large pot from over the fire and set it on the sand to cool. The mission of finding edible food was currently up to herself, Magnus and Levander. Just that morning, they underwent yet another foray into the wilderness. Lev was a wealth of knowledge and information. He was a master herbalist and familiar with a variety of the plants they encountered. Many of these were inedible, yet he was able to pick up a few unfamiliar ones that seemed promising. Once returning to the beach, he opened his pack and began to work over the vegetation he collected, telling them he would know of its edibility later the next day.

Aeris dug her toes into the sand, watching as it slid from the tops of her feet. She was hungry, but she knew that she couldn't take any more of the rations allotted to her. Fish had been found in one of the lakes they discovered a couple days earlier, and two of Cervantes' crewmen were taking time away from repairing the ship to catch them. Tomorrow, she, Magnus, and Lev would be responsible for the fishing. They would have done it today, but she wasn't all that good at it, and Lev was busy determining the edibility of the plants they found. It was good that Cervantes' men went to the lake, for there were too many hungry people that relied upon a good catch. Magnus accompanied them, and she hoped that he would be able to show her some of the methods they used to obtain the aquatic creatures.

Aeris stood up from the log that she was using for a seat. It was similar to the others that were situated in a circle around the fire. Soon it would begin to get dark, and another fire would be placed in the pit located a few feet from the one she currently used. She turned when she heard someone call her name and smiled when she saw Magnus, Marion, and, Gervais coming towards her with several strings of fish. She waved and started towards the ship to get Vikhail and Vardec, who were quite proficient with preparing food. Once everyone on deck was aware they would be eating fresh fish for the evening meal, a round of applause erupted. The workers began to put their tools away, and it wasn't long before everyone was climbing down the ladder to the beach.

Soon the second fire was built and everyone was sitting around and enjoying the company. An ale barrel was breached, and it wasn't long before everyone was partaking of the contents. It was the first time Aeris had seen anyone really relax since before the storm, and she was glad that she could be a part of the merriment. A toast was made to the five men who lost their lives to the sea, and everyone drank to their afterlife. It wasn't much later that the first of the fish was released from the spit and the flesh divided among all. As more fish were cooked to completion, the conversation lulled as the group ate. Sensing someone watching her, Aeris looked up and glanced across the fire. It was the man with silver eyes. There was something about him, something she could not quite place. She felt strangely drawn to him, but as of yet had made no action in response to her impulse to approach him.

Jaxom looked away and Aeris focused her gaze upon the man that sat next to him. Cervantes offered her a tired grin, and Aeris smiled in return. In the captain, she had found a good friend. A fortnight ago, she would never have imagined it. Now she sought out his company for a while every evening. Despite Magnus' reservations, she had faith in Cervantes. She believed that one day they would sail away from this island and never look back.

***

Alasdair paced the wide balcony, a small roll of parchment clutched in his hand. He had read the scroll over and over again, a message that was written a scant nine days after he had left Xordrel. The letter was written in the fine handwriting of his sister, and the contents worrisome to say the least.

Dearest Ami and Babu,

> *We have hit some trouble in Yortec. I do not want to worry you, so I won't go into detail. There is no choice but the sea, but we hope to be back on course as soon as possible. I will send another message when I can, just to let you know of my whereabouts. I hope everyone is well. May the sun shine upon you.*

> *Damaeris*

Alasdair turned on his heel and made his way back across the balcony. *Damnation!* He should never have left her behind. Only a few days after entering Elvandahar, they were accosted by Sirion and Adrianna. His parents prayed that their daughter was safe within his company. When they saw she wasn't with Alasdair, Cedric, and Talemar, they focused the full force of their wrath upon him. Sirion had thrust the message at him, and barely gave Alasdair a chance to read it before demanding an explanation. When Alasdair gave it, his words sounded weak. He had already realized the gravity of his mistake, and his mind reeled with the implications of his actions.

Reaching the other side of the balcony, Alasdair pulled back his fist and slammed it into the nearest support tree. Several splinters of bark flew in all directions, and the impact left a dent in the trunk. He didn't even bother to cradle the hand despite knowing he had broken it. The pain that arced up his arm only served to anger him all the more, anger that he could only direct at himself. The expressions on the faces of his comrades after they read Aeris' message for themselves haunted him, and his hope was to leave Elvandahar as soon as possible to go in search of her. Due to the severity of their sibling's circumstances, Alasdair and his company were released of their obligation to the king of Karlisle.

Alasdair thumped his way back down to the opposite side of the balcony. He knew that it would be a waiting game. He had no idea where in Shandahar Aeris was, and he would simply have to wait for another message before he could go in search of her. It would be pure torment, not only for him, but for his mother and father as well. He could already see the effect that it was having on them. Adrianna had lost weight, and Sirion sported dark circles beneath his eyes. Alasdair wished that he could turn back time . . . correct the mistake he had made. His sister would be home with him now, despite her protestations, and his parents would not be suffering.

Once more, Alasdair spun on his heel and made back across the balcony. He didn't realize he had company until a voice stilled his movement. "They have you all in a tizzy, don't they?"

Alasdair's head shot up, and he saw his brother standing at the balcony entrance. He knew that Asgenar was coming . . . had been waiting for him only gods knew how long. But still he had been startled, and now he sought to calm the rapid beating of his heart. "Do I not deserve it?"

Asgenar walked out onto the balcony, keeping his silence until he reached the balustrade. He put his hands on the railing and then looked beyond. Finally, he turned back to Alasdair. He shook his head. "No. You made the best decision you could at the time. Aeris is quite strong-willed. Not to mention, she is a woman in her own right. Gone are the days when we made decisions for her. I learned my lesson the hard way the last time I tried to exact my influence over her. I will not repeat the same mistake."

"She is out there, somewhere, in trouble. She needs me."

Once gain, Asgenar shook his head. "She needs to learn to rely on herself. She wants that . . . needs it even. She has been struggling against us for a long time now."

"You think that we should just leave Aeris to her fate?" Alasdair regarded him incredulously. How could Asgenar be so cold? Had he no care for her?

"No. I agree that she needs our help. However, I do not agree that you should have forced her to come with you against her will. You would have broken her spirit and led her to believe that no one has faith in her to conduct the responsibilities that have been delegated to her."

"If I had brought her back, she would be safe right now . . . right here with her family."

Asgenar regarded him intently. "But at what cost? I have already spelled it out for you. Would it really be worth it . . . to deny her a place in this world simply because she happened to be third born and a woman to boot?"

It was then that Alasdair began to understand the words of his brother. Indeed, Asgenar had become wise beyond his years. If he had taken Aeris against her will, she may have lost the impetus to do other things on her own. She would be only a shadow of the person she could become, and no one would be to blame but him and the others who loved her so much they wanted to see no hardship come to her.

Seeing the acceptance passing over his brother's face, Asgenar gestured towards the alcove. "Come, let us retire inside. I have much to discuss with you, things that are best spoken behind closed walls."

Alasdair nodded. He had nearly forgotten that there were other troubles besides those concerning Aeris. They were troubles concerning more than just their family, but the entire realm of Elvandahar. He followed Asgenar into the alcove and then seated himself upon the sofa opposite his brother. Looking at Asgenar now, he could see the lines of strain written upon his handsome face, lines Alasdair did not recall seeing there before. Within the span of only a few months, his brother had aged several years. Things must be worse than he anticipated.

Asgenar was silent for several moments. Alasdair's hand ached abominably, throbbing to some unheard cadence. Finally he gave himself leave to cradle it, bringing it close to his body for support. The gesture was not lost on Asgenar. He stared at Alasdair from piercing eyes, wondering when his brother would mention the wound. However, Alasdair said nothing and focused as much of his attention as he could upon Asgenar. "So, how is the state of affairs between Elvandahar and Karlisle? How goes the search for the Princess Elinora?" he asked.

Asgenar eyed his brother speculatively. It was obvious that Alasdair had not heard the news. He wouldn't have . . . especially traveling at the pace he and the others set to make it back to Elvandahar in record time. They had foregone any luxury by passing by all of the towns and villages they would have seen on the way home . . . all for the call of supreme royal duty. After meeting Sirion and Adrianna, they had traveled a few more days to the Sherkari Fortress, but somehow the word had escaped them.

Asgenar shook his head. "Elinora is dead. Her head was delivered to her father barely a fortnight ago."

Alasdair felt his eyes widen in shock. Only someone with a lot of power would even consider murdering a member of the royal house of a kingdom as influential and powerful as Karlisle. Either that, or someone who was very stupid.

Alasdair said nothing, only waited for his brother to elaborate. "It was the Daemundai . . . the high priest they call Ruzlul Daemon-keeper. He sent a message to her father, one that detailed the way Elinora was sacrificed. Razlul told Zerxes that she was a pleasure to torment . . ."

Asgenar's voice trailed off. Alasdair could only imagine how his brother must be feeling. After all, the lady was to have been his future wife. Despite having only met her upon a handful of occasions, Asgenar had accepted his marriage to the Princess of Karlisle, and he had even come to like her. Elinora was a good person, and easy on the eyes. Now the young woman was dead, and it was obvious she had suffered a hideous death.

Alasdair whispered a prayer to the gods . . . one that he hoped would be heard . . . one that would ease her soul. Then he continued his silence, knowing by his brother's expression that there was more Asgenar needed to share.

"However, that is not all of it. The youngest daughter of Karlisle has also gone missing. At first, it was thought that Razlul had taken Joneselia as well. However, upon further investigation, it was discovered she had simply left home. She was tracked to the port city of Tambour, but then her trail was lost. It is thought that she took a ship to Yortec, but no one is entirely sure."

Alasdair shook his head in wonderment. "How is Zerxes holding up?"

"Not good. It has been brought to my attention that the King suffers some type of mental illness, and that he is slowly losing touch with all reality. I feel that some have known about it for years but said nothing. However, in the wake of one daughter's death and the other's disappearance, the illness has intensified and can no longer be kept hidden. Zerxes' advisors are corrupt and favor the ascension of the son, Prince Rigel. In my estimation, the young man is a wastrel and will be easily influenced. I am sure that these same advisors have been making regular decisions concerning the realm for the past couple of years."

Alasdair grew thoughtful. "Yet, they have not been able to adversely influence the merger of our two realms?"

Asgenar shook his head and looked down at the hands clasped before him. "No. Not until now. That was one thing about which Zerxes has remained adamant. It was always his intention to see our two kingdoms at peace and united through blood."

Alasdair sighed. He could only imagine the turmoil going on within Karlisle right now. Even more, it would soon begin to influence Elvandahar. If Zerxes was indeed going insane, Prince Rigel would have been better to stay by his father's side, despite his desire to see his sister home . . . for whatever reason. The throne could easily become fair game for any of the other houses comprising the nobility, especially those with bloodlines closest to Mondemer. By leaving the throne unprotected, Rigel left himself open to be usurped. Of course, the way Alasdair saw it, that reality might not be such a bad one.

Asgenar looked back up at Alasdair. "Razlul has made his home where the hills and mountains come together north and east of the Siskrit Desert. Elvandaharian rangers have been able to discover his approximate location with the help of some highly trained scouts from Karlisle. Against our father's better judgment, Zerxes wants to mount an attack against the Daemundai that have set up residence in those hills. He wants vengeance for the death of his daughter."

Alasdair nodded. He understood the King's sentiment; however, a full-blown open attack against the Daemundai was foolhardy. The cult was powerful, and had only grown in numbers since the time of the Wildrunners. It had become a force to be reckoned with, especially under the leadership of Razlul. Gaknar, Razlul's predecessor, had been nothing compared to this man. Zerxes was setting himself up for failure, and the force from Elvandahar assigned to the attack would surely follow the same desolate path.

CHAPTER 13

*J*onesy ran through the verdant field. The blossoms were beautiful at this time of year, and the climate was mildly warm. Laughter burbled from between her lips, the bewitching trill of a child at play. The multilayered skirts of her dress swished around her legs, weighing at her. Yet, Jonesy paid them no heed, focusing all of her attention ahead. Before her ran Elinora . . . her beautiful, golden haired sister. Ribbons trailed behind the older girl, held fast in a flawless pale hand. Jonesy reached out her own hand, her fingertips just grazing the longest of the vibrantly colored swatches. She laughed again when Elinora pulled them just beyond her reach, reveling in the game her sister played. Jonesy felt herself nearly bursting with love and affection . . . all for the older girl who showered her with attention.

Suddenly, the scene began to shift. The game had come to an end, and the cerulean blue sky had darkened. Before them stood five boys, all older than Jonesy but none more than Elinora. One of the boys stepped forward, grabbing Jonesy roughly by the arm. Rigel grinned malevolently down at her with a glint of malice in his dark eyes. Her brother said something she couldn't hear, something she would remember only when she awakened. They were words meant to torment her, to insidiously intrude upon her most peaceful of dreams. A flash of fear rushed through her, followed by a prickling upon her skin that warned her of danger.

But then Elinora was there, removing Jonesy from her brother's cruel grip. She shouted at him with words Jonesy would not recall even in her waking moments, an onslaught that caused Rigel to retreat. The boys left them alone, but not before Jonesy saw the silent message in her brother's gaze . . . the battle had been won, but the war would continue to be waged. One day, Elinora would not be there to champion her.

Jonesy suddenly sat upright upon the pallet. Glancing around in the darkness, she could just make out the sleeping form of Aeris beside her. Jonesy was drenched in sweat . . . knew it was more than just a result of the tropical climate in which she found herself. She focused upon her breathing, slowing it to a more normal pace. Jonesy crossed her legs beneath her, rested her elbows at her knees, and then placed her head into her waiting hands. She could still feel the residual effects of her fear, a fear that was not only the stuff of dreams, but based upon reality.

The dream was real, but then again not. It was not an accurate rendition of what happened that day in the field, nor did it portray an isolated event in her life. There were several more situations such as those in which she had found herself, each one more terrifying than the last. When she was young, Elinora was there to cool Rigel's foul temper and divert it away from her. However, as Jonesy grew older, Elinora began to accept her own responsibilities within the household. Jonesy was forced to fend for herself, glad that she was successful in many of her attempts to keep Rigel at bay. But then there was that night . . .

Jonesy breathed deeply of the still night air. In the near distance, she could hear the nocturnal sounds emanating from the jungle. By the gods, how she missed Elinora. Her sister was her senior by several years, but they had always been close. Their mother died of an illness soon after Joneselia's birth, and Elinora had mothered her as no one else could. Despite being the middle child, Rigel was the only son of King Zerxes and thus favored by the household. Yet, he had always been the odd one, often sullen and withdrawn. Jonesy knew that he always had a dislike of her, for whatever reason. She never thought to ask him why, nor would she have cared to inquire. To her, he had never really been what a brother should be, so why would she care what he thought?

But with Elinora it was different. The older girl seemed to somehow be able to influence him . . . to reach inside of Rigel and subdue the beast that raged within. Something about Elinora quieted him, bade him retreat and pursue his crusade another day. Jonesy was always grateful for that, for it gave her that much more time to grow and mature enough to be able to learn to avoid him. It had probably saved her from a fate far worse than she had suffered, and for that she would always have her sister to thank.

Jonesy slowly lowered herself back down onto the pallet. Despite her fatigue, she continued to stare into the darkness. Unbidden thoughts of home came to her, in particular, her father. She remembered the days before his illness began to affect him, when he would sit her upon his lap and listen to her childhood woes. He would stoke her hair with his fingertips and kiss her on the tip of her nose. He would tell Jonesy how much she resembled her mother . . . and that he had loved his wife so very much.

It was only a couple of years ago that she started to realize her father was going insane. His behaviors became somewhat erratic, and although he would still have his 'normal moments', they became fewer and farther between as the months passed. By the time she discovered the awful truth about her brother, Jonesy knew that there was no use in going to the king. She would have gone to Elinora, but it was the following night that her sister disappeared from her bedchamber, never to be seen again.

Jonesy closed her eyes tightly, willing the memories away. Yet, they were small compared to what was to come. Her body gave an involuntary shudder, and she swallowed convulsively. She barely escaped her brother and his ruffians that ill-fated night a few weeks later, and it was the next morning that she realized she had to leave. Her father would not protect her, and Elinora was no longer there to act as a restraint for Rigel.

Jonesy's fingers went to the golden neck-chain at her throat . . . an object that had saved her and doomed her at the same time. She wore it as a token to make her remember the threat she left behind when she fled Karlisle. She had been petrified when her father's men almost caught her in Yortec. She imagined that she could sense her brother's presence within the city, but later tried to pass it off as simple fear-induced paranoia. Despite his hatred of her, and his desire to be sure she kept his secrets hidden, it would have been foolish for Rigel to come after her. He would put his rights to the throne in jeopardy.

Jonesy began to feel herself slipping once more into sleep. She liked to think that Rigel would be consumed with his desire for the power that ruling the realm of Karlisle would bring. She liked to think that he would just let her go despite the secrets she harbored. She liked to think that whatever illness had stricken her father was not also embrace his son and that his mind was of rational thought. However, Jonesy could be sure of none of these things. She could not shake the feeling that Rigel would not rest until he had her within his control once more, no matter what the cost.

***

Aeris trudged along the beach back to the fire-pits. Beneath one arm she carried a load of wood from a few of the dead trees they had found at the tree line not far away. They would be able to burn it later that evening and for a few more evenings to come. Once the sun set upon the horizon, the darkness fell quickly despite the rising of the moons. Aeris thought that it must have something to do with the island they were stranded upon, but Magnus felt it to be something that existed just in her mind. He claimed that the darkness stole upon them the same way upon the mainland as it did on this vague island out in the middle of the sea. Aeris refrained from telling him that she thought he was wrong.

Once at the camp-site, Aeris deposited her load onto the sand near the fire pits. She then stretched her aching arms and legs, muscles that were unaccustomed to the physical labors she had been forced to endure since their arrival. She knew that much of it was a result of her own stubborn nature . . . for she had insisted upon cutting through the jungle just a few days ago. Magnus had good-naturedly given into her whimsy, and the next day she felt the physical consequences of her actions. She obviously wasn't designed for such arduous labors, and she reminded herself of that upon several occasions over the last few days. But at least she could collect the firewood.

Cervantes and his men continued their work upon the *Sea Maiden*. The repairs were going well, but they took a lot of time. Every morning the men awakened early with the light, and they only stopped in the evening when there wasn't enough light left by which they could see in order to continue their work. For most of the day, Levander spent his time in the jungle searching for edible fruits, tubers, and legumes for everyone to eat along with the fish that were caught by Magnus and Marion. Aeris spent much of her time seeing to the fire pits. There was almost always something cooking within one or the other. It took quite a bit of work to keep the remainder of Cervantes' crew and those of her company fed and watered for the course of the day and into the night. Boiled water had to always be available, as well as beverages prepared from the plants Lev brought back from the jungle. Despite his quiet nature, Aeris delighted in Lev's companionship. Concurrently, he seemed to enjoy teaching her how to make the varied teas and food items he created from the plant-life he discovered upon the island.

Everyone partook of their evening meals together, eating and drinking under the canopy of a darkening sky lit only by the pale glow of Steralion. Afterward, everyone retired to bed-pallets that had been situated amongst the debris still aboard the *Sea Maiden*. They slept under the stars above deck, for the bowels of the ship still contained water. And the nights passed, often fraught with the eerie sounds that could be heard emanating from the jungle just up the beach.

The next day would dawn, and the work would begin once more. Some days were hotter than others, and it was difficult to refrain from tearing every bit of clothing off her body. Aeris noticed Jonesy dealing with the same temptations, and she was glad that she wasn't the only one. For the men it was much easier. They could walk around in their loincloths and not get a second glance. It was difficult for a woman, for everyone seemed to be watching when Aeris passed by with her sleeveless chemise and cropped trousers. She initially seethed with the unfairness of it all, but after a few days she became accustomed to the stares. From the corner of her eye, she saw Cervantes knocking about a head or two, and she was glad to know that someone was on her side. The knowledge that the captain would offer his protection in addition to that offered by Magnus and Tigerius was enough for her. It seemed to take away much of the aggravation she felt, and she was able to live her days more easily.

Yet, as those days passed, Aeris found herself becoming weighed down by the knowledge that her family must be worried about her. Alasdair was likely beside himself by now, and her parents almost ready to kill him for taking the risk of having their daughter so far out of reach. For that alone, Aeris regretted not allowing Alasdair to take her home that day the king's men came to collect him and Talemar. She loved her bother dearly, and the hardship she knew he endured was something that brought her close to tears. Yet, at least she was alive and able to look forward to the day she would see him again. She continued to believe in Cervantes and his promise to take them home.

***

As she had been doing for a few fortnights now, Tholana looked through the eyes of the boy. Through him she had kept track of Tallachienan and the rest of the group . . . saw their skirmish with the Daemundai, their watery escape, and their subsequent marooning on a deserted island in the middle of the Drujasu Sea. Tholana had been dumbfounded by the turn of events, and had even begun to regret letting Tallachienan go when she had him within her grasp. But she had wanted to experience the thrill of the chase, to make him wonder about her identity, and eventually make him lust for her the way she had countless other men in her acquaintance. Without any recollection of his own identity, TC had no memory of Tholana either, and it gave her a rare opportunity to potentially ensnare him within her web.

Before her suddenly swam the image of Aeris Timberlyn. It didn't surprise Tholana, for Mateo was her underling. Yet, the goddess still hated the sight of her pretty face. To pass the time, Aeris had chosen to teach Mateo the quarterstaff. For some reason, the girl forbore to instruct the boy upon the basic intricacies of the dimensionalist mage, and Tholana could only assume that she left the task up to her masters. If it had been Tholana, the teaching would have been done by none other than herself, no matter who might have been in charge. But that was just the nature of Tholana's personality.

The goddess lay low within Mateo's consciousness. It had not been difficult to penetrate the boy's mind that day at the lake, much unlike that of his superior counterpart. To her utmost anger and resentment, Tholana had been unable to breach the defensive barriers of Aeris' mind, and it did not take Tholana long to realize that the girl had been trained to withstand mental intrusion. Angrily, she had turned her attentions to Mateo. While Aeris crumpled to the ground in a lifeless heap, Tholana penetrated Mateo's mind and insinuated her intricate webs. They allowed her to keep track of him without the effort of scrying, and it gave her the added benefit of being able to make mild *Suggestions* to the boy in order to achieve her goals.

Tholana had much hoped to be able to insinuate herself within Aeris' sub-conscious. It would have been intensely gratifying to break down the girl's mind, and then 'push' her to do things that she would not ordinarily contemplate. Yet, the goddess had been delegated to take advantage of other alternatives. Adrianna was smart to fortify her daughter's mind. It seemed Aeris was quite unaware of the conditioning, and that was even more frustrating for Tholana. It made the girl stronger somehow, and Tholana would have to work hard to break her. However, she just didn't have that kind of time.

187

So here she was, looking out the eyes of a boy Talent just barely into puberty. But at least Tholana was able to keep track of her primary target. Tallachienan was all that really mattered. Aeris was only a bonus, a prize to be claimed only when the time was right. And Tholana would be waiting . . .

***

Jonesy bit at her lower lip, focusing intently upon her task. She was never good at sewing, not like her sister had been. Elinora's embroidery was quite the marvel, and many times she tried to teach her young, wayward sister the skills associated with being a proficient seamstress. Zerxes had rather hoped that both his daughters would bear such proficiency. Yet, Jonesy had never taken to the art.

Now she sat with her back against the hull of the foundered *Sea Maiden*. Her arms were full of the thick fabric that comprised the main sail of the ship, assiduously bending to a task she had offered to accomplish despite her shortcomings with the bine. The instrument was much like the needle, only thicker and stronger in order to poke through the canvas. She had offered to mend the torn sail, quite a feat even for one with adequate proficiency. Yet, as the time passed, she found that she had just enough knowledge to learn quickly. It took her a while to understand exactly what was needed for the mending, but now she worked the bine with swift strokes.

So engrossed as she was upon her activity, Jonesy didn't realize she was being watched until the captain cleared his throat. She looked up to find him standing there, his arms crossed at his chest. He leaned casually against the side of the ship, surrounded by his customary debonair aura. The corners of his mouth had turned up into a grin as he watched her, and Jonesy felt her heart skip a beat.

"My men certainly wouldn't have done so well with that sail," he said.

Jonesy shrugged. "It wouldn't have taken this long if I had really been any good at this myself," she replied with a smirk.

Cervantes chuckled. "I think you underestimate yourself. You seem to be adept enough with that bine even from over here."

Jonesy shrugged again. "All right . . . then consider it one of my only requisite skills. It's the only thing I could think of to help."

Cervantes guffawed and slapped a hand against his thigh. "Oh, come now. There must be *something* else you know how to do that can be termed useful."

Jonesy schooled her expression into one of melancholy. "I assure you, my dear Captain, that I have no other skills to offer. Now please, allow me to get back to my work." Jonesy made a show of refocusing her attention on the sail, mindful to keep the smile off her face. It seemed he had come to harass her, and she refused to be sucked into whatever game he wished to play . . . even if there was a part of her that wouldn't really mind it.

Cervantes shook his head. "What about cooking? Surely you can cook."

Jonesy shook her head, keeping her eyes on the sail in her lap. "No, I can't cook. I never have, and probably never will."

For a moment there was silence and then, "Okay, then you are good at weaving . . . a weaver of magnificent tapestries, plush rugs, and billowing pillows."

Jonesy laughed lightly. "No, I am no weaver . . . especially of anything 'magnificent'."

Another pause and then, "All right. Since you cannot cook, perhaps you are the one who knows how to catch the meat that goes into the stew-pot. You must be a falconer or an archer."

Jonesy sighed heavily and then looked up from her task. "No, Captain Cervantes. I told you . . . I have no other biddable skills. I was not jesting when I told you so."

With a hand at his chin Cervantes regarded her for a moment. By the gods . . . the girl was serious. She looked at him through wide hazel eyes, her expression the epitome of seriousness. "Well, we must fix that," he said.

Jonesy frowned. "What do you mean?"

Cervantes planted his fists at his hips. "I will teach you another salable skill."

The girl pursed her lips and her eyes danced with merriment. "And what, pray tell, might that skill be?"

Cervantes glared at her. Damn, she didn't believe him. The thought irked him for a moment, but then he realized that perhaps she had found very few people in her life who would bother to give her the time. And why should *he*? What did this girl mean to him that he should put any type of effort into teaching her anything? Why did he care?

Cervantes narrowed his eyes. "The cutlass . . . I will teach you the cutlass."

Jonesy's eyes widened. "Oh no. I can't do that. I haven't any experience with weapons."

Cervnates stepped towards her and then offered her a hand. "So? There is a first time for everything."

Jonesy shook her head. "No. No I couldn't . . ."

"Why not? Are you afraid?" Cervantes asked, knowing what the response would be.

Jonesy cast him a look of indignation. "Of course not! It's just that . . . that . . ."

Cervantes grinned. "So get up. There's no reason why I shouldn't teach you. Besides, it's a dangerous world. You should have at least the basic knowledge of how to protect yourself."

Jonesy's gaze went from his face to the proffered hand. A moment later she grasped it and allowed the Captain to pull her up, the canvas falling into a heap at her feet. They both stood there for a moment, each one taking in the other. Cervantes watched an errant lock of her hair blow in the breeze, took in the cut of her jaw, and the shape of her nose. He then took a hold of himself. "So, shall we get started?"

***

Aeris and Jaxom approached the small lake. It was one of those that had been discovered by Marion and Gervais . . . one they found hosted the tastiest fish. They hunted there once every couple of days, unwilling to deplete the lake too quickly. Jaxom glanced down at his wrapped hand and grimaced. He had cut it yesterday while working on the rigging, slicing it deep enough so that Cervantes bade him take a rest from such strenuous activity the following day. So now here he was, hunting for fishes with Aeris. Initially, he thought he might be anxious in her company. However, once they set out in the direction of the lake, he found the opposite to be true. He felt content and at ease . . . almost happy to be in her presence. He felt at harmony with himself for the first time since he set his eyes upon her, and he felt himself entering a state of relaxation.

Aeris and Jaxom set down their packs. Then they removed their boots, Jaxom rolling up the legs of the trousers he wore. Aeris wore only a sleeveless tunic, one she had fashioned for herself from out of those she found buried within her travel pack. She cut off the arms and shortened the hem, making it more tolerable to wear in the heat. Jaxom had noticed the other men eying her appreciatively, including the ones who claimed to be her friends. Jaxom could only shake his head. Humans and faelin were such sexual creatures, allowing thoughts of copulation to intrude upon other, more pressing, situations.

Spears in hand, Jaxom and Aeris waded into the blue-green waters. The lake was smaller than others he had seen, but the location was good. Along the far side it was bordered by a steep rocky slope, a place where lizards and toads could bask in the sun. And the sands were so pale they were almost white. Once in place, Aeris and Jaxom kept still and waited for the fishes to venture close. When the time was right, they thrust their spears at the unsuspecting creatures, and then brought the blue striped fish out of the waters, their shimmering bodies flapping on the end of the spears. Aeris had become rather proficient with her spear, and although she was not the best hunter, she was certainly passable.

Once they had a sizable pile, Jaxom and Aeris left the waters and began placing their catch into cloth sacks they removed from their packs. They were almost finished with their task when Jaxom sensed something from the periphery of his senses. He stopped his activity and went on the alert, his eyes and ears attuned to the jungle surrounding them. Then he heard it again, something stealthily approaching them from the trees not far away. His instincts cried out to him of approaching danger, and he had to suppress his initial urge to shift into dragon form. It would be a mistake for him to shift, for he would give himself away. No one knew of his true identity, and he planned to keep it that way.

Aeris stopped what she was doing to glance at Jaxom. His silver gaze was staring into the jungle to his left, and she noticed the rigid tension of his body. It was easy to see that something was wrong. She stilled her movement and focused on Jaxom and the trees nearby. At first she sensed nothing amiss, but within moments she began to hear something coming towards them. Suddenly it was emerging from the trees . . . a long yellowish-green body with tens of legs and an elongated snout full of needle-sharp teeth. It was at least as long as two or three men, and she couldn't even see the entirety of the body, camouflaged as it was within the jungle surrounding it.

Jaxom slowly took Aeris' hand and began to creep backward towards the lake. The dark blue eyes of the creature bore into them, almost hypnotizing in quality. It was then she heard Jaxom's quiet voice near her ear, "Don't look into it's eyes".

With some degree of effort, Aeris tore her gaze away from the serpentine animal. She had never seen anything quite like it before. The cool water of the lake closing around her feet and ankles helped release her from the trance, and she tightened her grip on Jaxom's hand. It was then that the creature made it's move. In a flash of speed, it rushed for them, paused only momentarily at the water's edge, and then slipped within.

"Damn . . ."

Aeris heard Jaxom's curse just as she felt him dragging her deeper into the lake. Then he was swimming towards the rocky wall at the other side. She followed close behind, glad of the instruction given by her father. Sirion had insisted that all of his children learn how to swim well. All of a sudden they had reached the rock, and Jaxom was grabbing her by the hand. Taking a deep breath, Aeris didn't hesitate to follow as he dove beneath the surface. She could sense the creature gaining on them . . . felt the disturbance of the waters behind her. She refused to allow panic to overtake her, merely concentrated on maintaining the speed that Jaxom set.

Just as Aeris was sure the creature would surely catch them, she found herself slipping into a narrow tunnel. She increased her speed, not only hoping to escape the predator, but to bring herself into the air once more. Her chest ached with the lack of it, and she felt her lungs beginning to burn. Behind her she suddenly heard a loud thump, followed by a cessation of activity. Yet, she dared not look back . . . couldn't take the time to find out if the creature still followed.

Just as she thought she would pass out, Aeris crested the surface of the water. Jaxom quickly pulled her onto a rocky ledge, and she gasped for air. The twosome scrambled back from the water, widening the distance as much as possible. Aeris coughed and shuddered . . . continuing to gasp. Jaxom smoothed his hands over her back and sides, helping to calm her so that her intake would be greater. It was only then that they realized the creature was not following them. Nothing disturbed the surface of the water from which they had just emerged. Glancing around, they saw that the only reason they could see the water at all was because of the gentle glow emanating from the walls of the cavern in which they found themselves.

Standing upright, Jaxom took Aeris' hand and helped her rise. They wrung the excess water from their clothing and ignored the cold rock underfoot. They then approached the cavern wall. With a tentative fingertip, Aeris gently touched the wall and was surprised to find that it felt fuzzy. Some type of fungus adhered to the rock, a fungus that happened to have illuminating qualities. Aeris couldn't help but smile at the discovery. She glanced at the man beside her, and he seemed equally as captivated.

Aeris and Jaxom began to walk around the chamber in which they found themselves. A corridor branched off of it, lined by the glowing green fungus. They glanced at one another for only a moment before stepping into the passageway. They might as well explore the place since neither had any intention of re-submerging in the waters from which they had recently come.

For a short time the pair walked in companionable silence. Jaxom continued to hold Aeris' hand, and she seemed content with that. He regarded her from the periphery of his vision, a sense that remained to be acute even in his faelin form. Her profile was flawless, and as her coppery red hair began to dry, it curled around her face and shoulders. He watched as she brushed it back from her eyes a time or two, noticing the exasperated expression that passed over her features. His lips twitched with amusement, for he found the action rather endearing. He suddenly began to wonder things about her . . . simple things. He wondered where she was from, if she had brothers and sisters, and what were her likes and dislikes. He wondered what her dreams might be. Were they were lofty ones, or those that were more land-bound? Jaxom felt himself wanting to ask, hesitated for a moment, and then wondered why he was afraid to initiate the conversation.

"I wonder where this passage will lead us." Beside him, Jaxom felt her startle slightly at the sound of his voice, for it had come rather unexpectedly.

"Perhaps it will lead us to some treasure," she replied in a lilting voice. "Mayhap someone left it here a long time ago, intending to return for it one day."

Jaxom glanced at Aeris once more. Her lips were turned up in a small smile. "You seem to be quite the optimist," he replied.

Aeris only shook her head. "No . . . not really. I said it only to see how you would respond." She looked back at him solemnly.

"So you are an academician, then."

Aeris frowned. "Why do you say that?"

Jaxom shrugged. "You are studying me. You say something to see how I will make my reply. You file my response away and then generate another comment to learn more about me."

Aeris regarded him unwaveringly. "It was nothing less than what you are doing yourself. Are you an academician, then?"

Jaxom huffed slightly. "No . . ."

Aeris turned away from him. "Then don't make assumptions about *me*."

Jaxom was quiet for a moment. "I hope you are not upset. I didn't intend to offend you. I just wanted to . . ." He suddenly stopped, not wanting to tell her too much. For all he knew, she didn't want to talk and didn't care to know anything about him.

"I'm not upset," she answered. "I just wanted to set you straight." With a slight smile she glanced back at him, a mischievous glint in her dark brown eyes.

Jaxom grinned in return, her charisma enveloping him in it's embrace. Now he had some inkling of why the others followed her. Suddenly remembering what had prompted him to speak to her in the first place, he asked her where she was from. They continued to talk as they slowly made their way down the passage. At his insistence, she told him all about her home, her family, and her friends. She graciously dodged questions that seemed as though they could lead to others about her professional background. It soon became obvious to him that she was hiding something, but he didn't mind. Everyone had their secrets.

It wasn't long before they began to hear the sound of running water. Increasing their pace, Jaxom and Aeris followed the rest of the corridor into a large chamber. In front of them was an extensive shimmering pool. To the right, water fell from a wide tunnel near the top of a rock face. To the left was another corridor, leading only gods knew where. Across the water they could see the signs of the outdoor world just beyond a thick screen of vines and other vegetation.

Aeris looked around herself in wonder. The place was beautiful, like something out of a dream. From the narrow streams of light filtering in through the veil of vegetation, the water glistened as though littered with thousands of gems. The sound of the waterfall splashing into the waiting pool was a soothing background. She and Jaxom began to walk around the periphery of the chamber around the pool in the direction of the waterfall. As they approached, Aeris began to realize that the falls appeared somewhat broken . . . that the cascading waters were hitting some protruding rocks.

Finally they reached the waterfall. The path continued behind it, and she enthusiastically stepped behind the sparkling curtain. The sight that met her gaze stilled Aeris in her path, and she felt her eyes widen with awe. She felt Jaxom step up behind her and heard his sudden intake of breath.

Aeris had never seen anything like it ever before. It was in the shape of a huge bird, one wing reaching up to the cavern ceiling and the other buried deep in the ground. The body was at least three lloryk long, and beneath the ages of grime and plant growth, traces of a metallic sheen could be seen. Swallowing heavily, Aeris stepped towards the unnatural object only to feel Jaxom's restraining hand on her shoulder. She glanced back at him, but seeing the determination in her eyes, he took his hand from her shoulder and brought it down to embrace hers.

Together they approached the fallen bird. Aeris could feel her heart beating in her chest, sensing that something was about to happen. Stepping up to the thing, she tentatively reached out her hand and pulled some of the creepers away. The act revealed more of the structure. It had a mottled appearance, as though the thin outer shell had began to deteriorate. Beneath that thin exterior was the gleam of dull metallic gray.

Aeris proceeded to pull away more of the vegetation. Jaxom set to work beside her, and it wasn't much later that they were viewing the bird in its entirety. Most of it was composed of the strange metal coated with a material that flaked away when it was touched. Pieces of it had come loose when they removed the vines, and it littered the ground at their feet. However, much of the top of it was made of another substance. It was thick and appeared as though it had once been transparent. The years had taken that facility away, causing the material to become cloudy and discolored. Yet, when they pressed their faces close to it, they could see the vague outlines of things that lay within the bird.

Aeris stepped back and regarded their discovery. Her body shook with excitement, wondering how they would find a way within. She knew the bird could be opened, but had no idea how. Not long ago, she had joshed with Jaxom as they walked through the tunnel, telling him that they would find a treasure. Now that it sat there before them, she didn't even know how to breach it.

Aeris' gaze followed Jaxom as he slowly walked around the large object, his eyes scrutinizing everything about it. He ran his hand over the body, taking in every plane with his touch. He then disappeared on the other side. Aeris put her hands on her hips and pressed her lips into a thin line. By the gods, where did this thing come from? It was old . . . very much so. She could sense an ancient-ness about it, despite the advanced techniques it took to build it. The body appeared to be constructed from a single piece of metal, but she knew that was not possible. The material that composed the top was alien to her, for she had never seen anything quite like it before.

Suddenly something began to happen. Aeris heard a disjointed bleeping sound and then the top of the bird was moving up and back. It moved slowly, as though it took a great effort. It struggled for a moment and stopped, but then it moved along once more. In awe, Aeris just stood there and watched the movement. When it was finished, the bird lay open before her. Jaxom came rushing around from the other side. "Aeris, come over here."

The pair rushed over to the other side. "I was right here." Jaxom pointed to a flat panel along the body. It was glowing a dull red. "I passed over this spot with my hand and the top suddenly slid back."

Aeris regarded the glowing panel, and then placed her own hand before it. Nothing happened. Shrugging her shoulders, she climbed onto the top of the bird. Where the clouded translucent cover had once been, there was now an open pit, and the bowels of the bird could be clearly seen. She could make very little out of the strange things she saw within, however one thing was certain. Near the front there were two seats where people could easily sit.

Aeris slid down into the bird. Immediately she was enveloped by a strange odor, most likely resulting from a long time without fresh air. Jaxom followed behind, saying nothing as he inspected his surroundings. Aeris continued back into the bird, taking in the strange symbols on the walls and the debris on the floor. She saw a couple of glowing lights and slowly approached them. Nothing happened when she passed a hand before them. She even touched one, and when nothing happened, she turned away from them.

It was then that she saw it. At first, she thought that she must be mistaken and that shadows were playing tricks on her eyes. However, stepping towards it, she realized that the skeleton was really there, leaning against the far wall. Swallowing heavily, she made her way over to the remains. Somehow they were still intact; even the skull remained attached to the neck bones. She had seen skeletons before, but somehow this one was different. Most of the bones were very familiar: the arms, legs, chest, and spine. However, the planes of the skull were unusual, yet similar to other humans.

Aeris knelt before the skeleton. Somehow, she sensed that it must have once been male. Oddly, she felt a connection with the man . . . a man that had obviously been dead for many years. Behind her, she could sense Jaxom's approach. He was silent as he knelt beside her, taking in the form before them.

Aeris took a few more moments to contemplate the remains. She wondered about him . . . what he may have looked like in life, what kind of person he may have been, if he had a family and friends, and what had ultimately happened to take his life. Why had he been sitting in the stomach of this bird . . . this strange structure built of materials she had never seen before on Shandahar. What had he been thinking when he died, alone in the middle of nowhere?

Sorrow for a man she had never known suddenly flooded Aeris, and she reached out to the skeleton. Her fingertips just barely touched the cheekbone, and she imagined she could feel the warmth of living flesh. In her mind's eye, she could see blue eyes set within a handsome face . . . a face like none she had ever seen before. The hair was a light brown, the front of which fell just above the eyes. There was a cleft in the chin, and the nose bent in such a way that she knew it must have once been broken. Her eyes traveled from the face, down the smooth curve of his neck, and then to his chest. Setting upon the unfamiliar style of his tunic, she noticed a golden chain. The links were tightly woven in a rope-like design, and suspended from it was a dark orb . . .

Aeris shook herself free of her reverie. Before her rested the skeleton. Lying across the chest-bone was the golden chain. Her eyes followed it down, and then came to the bones that comprised a hand that lay over the lower portion of the chain. She gently moved the hand, and when the bones came apart she startled slightly. But it was nothing like the shock she felt a moment later. It was the orb she had seen in her imaginary scenario. How could she possibly have known it was there when the skeletal hand had been covering it the whole time? Aeris slowly moved her own hand to the orb and took it in her grasp . . .

CHAPTER 14

The group followed Aeris and Jaxom through the jungle. They walked in silence, each one engrossed with his or her thoughts. The tale that the twosome told upon their return to the beach the evening before had been overwhelming to say the least. They decided to return to the cavern from which Aeris and Jaxom had come the next morning, everyone wanting to see the large bird spoken about in the story.

Aeris clutched the dark orb within the palm of her hand. She had been compelled to take it from around the neck of the skeletal corpse, unwilling to leave it within the cluttered remains of the fallen bird. There was something about the orb, something that called out to her of some hidden power, a magic that remained elusive to her. The sleek golden chain dangled from between her fingers, and she imagined that the man who had worn it before was somehow connected to her through it.

Jaxom pulled aside the veil of vegetation at the entrance to the cavern. Aeris stepped within, closely followed by Magnus, Cervantes, and the others. There were murmurs of appreciation when they saw the splendid waterfall flowing like a shimmering rainbow river from a tunnel high above them. The group slowly walked around the periphery of the crystalline lake. Tiny fishes darted about within the clear waters. Once reaching the edge of the fall, the group stepped behind the watery curtain.

Magnus' eyes widened when he saw the massive vessel before him. It reminded him of some type of ship, something he had read about in a book a long time ago. There was once an academacian by the name of Alensis Grundy who had fashioned a submersible to be used in underwater exploration. Of course he had some Talent, and even though he despised his innate abilities, they ultimately shone through in his works. There was a sketch of the craft in the book, an object that looked comparable to, yet very unlike, the thing he saw now. Actually, Magnus had no idea why the submersible had come to his mind in the first place, for the two were so dissimilar.

Magnus stood aside as the rest of the group approached the object. His mind burned with his desire to inspect the vessel closer, but he suddenly found his attention diverted. He looked around just in time to see the unspoken communication between Aeris and the young man, Jaxom. They regarded one another in silence for a moment before they fell in behind the rest of the group.

It was easy to see that they shared something together, something intangible and just beyond his reach. Perhaps it was simply the harrowing encounter they had experienced together, but Magnus felt it to be much more than that.

The group slowly circled the fallen bird. Most were extremely wary of it, keeping a wide berth. However, others such as Cervantes, Tigerius, and Goldare took the risk to move in closer. Despite the intriguing nature of the structure before him, Magnus kept much of his attention focused upon Aeris. He couldn't help it . . . over the past several days his attraction for her had only grown. Since the shipwreck, he had received the opportunity to view a different side of her, and he liked what he saw. Aeris' show of strength and dominance when they were cutting through the jungle, her willingness to embrace the duties bestowed upon her, and the positive attitude she had towards their grim circumstances had given him a tremendous respect for her. It made him remember how he felt about Aeris before her desertion in Grunchin, before he had proclaimed her a traitor outside of Xordrel, and before he had discovered her to be an heir to the realm of Elvandahar.

Magnus glanced towards the man who had made the knowledge of Aeris' heritage known to him. Of course Magnus had known that she and her brother hailed from Elvandahar, but he had no idea of their lineage before Tigerius spat it in his face. The man had been severely wounded after the cimmerean ambush, and he just may have been a bit delirious. Yet, Magnus knew the words Tigerius spoke to be truth. Foolishly, he had continued to believe that the woman he held was a traitor. Or did he?

Every day since that time, Magnus wondered if he had made more that just a simple mistake when he took Aeris as his prisoner. He questioned himself . . . wondered if he had truly believed Aeris to be in cahoots with the cimmereans, or if he just made himself believe it. That way, he could punish her for the torment she had put him through when she left Grunchin without so much as a simple letter. Magnus hated to think that he could stoop so low, but he was man enough to at least realize that the possibility existed.

Yet, Aeris had incriminated herself when she asked Magnus about his willingness to let a man die because of his allegiance to one such as her. With that statement, she had fortified Magnus' belief that she was in league with Tholana and her followers. Now, Magnus realized Aeris would have said anything in order to be sure that Tigerius was spared any ill-treatment he might suffer upon her behalf. Magnus still could not be sure of her intention, but he could only imagine . . .

Magnus continued to watch the recondian man. Virtually oblivious to the reticence shared by most other members of his company, Tigerius stepped up to the large object that Aeris had referred to as a 'fallen bird'. Indeed, it had wings like one; yet nothing else about it appeared bird-like at all. The top of the thing was open, just like Jaxom had described it in his story the evening before. And despite the shelter of the cavern, pieces of the outer surface were chipping away with the elements.

Tiger shook his head. By the gods, what in the world was this? Never had he seen anything like it, even in all of his dealings with sorcerers, sages, and others of their ilk. Tentatively, Tiger stretched out a hand toward the bird. The moment his fingertips touched the cool surface, his mind was swept away, showing him a vision of a Time of which he had no knowledge . . . of a world he knew was not Shandahar.

The world was enveloped in a dark haziness. The sun was only a muted orb where it hung in a sky tainted with acrid smoke. Thunder rumbled in the distance and upon the horizon he could dimly see lightening from the approaching storm. Below there were people . . . people making their way through constructs he could only assume were cities. Many of them walked among immense, closely spaced buildings that were so tall they could touch the gray clouds . . . along winding roads upon which traveled multi-hued, enclosed carriages with eyes that glowed in the darkness and propelled by some unseen entity.

Tigerius' vision skimmed across the landscape, one that shifted onto scenes outside of the cities, places where the sun could shine a bit more brightly and where the cloud-scraping buildings were replaced by other, low lying types. Vegetation grew, varieties that were akin, yet different from those on Shandahar. Regardless, the storms were still close, their thundering not far off in the distance. There were more people . . . human people. To him they seemed so odd with their strange clothing and even stranger behaviors. How they made their livelihoods was an enigma to him, for only a few seemed to have any apparent profession. However, despite the differences, there were similarities. Aggression and sexuality were manifest, the people of this world having many of the same characteristics as those upon Shandahar.

Tigerius' vision skipped again. This time it focused upon a particular group of people, men and women who convened in secret, those who rallied together in order to fight a threat. But there was something special about these people. In a world without magic, they seemed to have abilities that were against the norm, abilities that put them at risk. And the threat against which they fought was something that Tiger would never have thought possible, a danger that went beyond this world and into another.

Daemons walked this world. They were powerful and free, having gained a foothold in this place . . . something they had not been able to accomplish upon Shandahar. At least, not yet. And these people, these rare individuals, had developed the ability to fight them. However, they did not realize that it was too late. Already the world was dying. The ravages of something gone wrong, whether it was human or daemon induced, had destroyed this world. The storms were a physical manifestation of that . . .

Tigerius staggered back from the shuttle. He knew the word for the bird without knowing why. He had seen the images given to him by the *Impression*, but there was no sound that accompanied it. He turned his head to look upon the one who had torn him away from the *Impression,* and Mateo's worried face came into focus. As Tiger sank to his knees, he heard the boy call out to the others. He felt so tired . . . so drained of energy that he could no longer support his own weight. He vaguely remembered his father telling him about *Impressions* before, that they would steal one's strength until one learned how to limit energetic output. It had all sounded like trash to Tiger then, but now . . . now . . . Tiger pitched forward just as Aeris reached his side. Her beautiful face swam before him for barely a moment before his world shifted to black.

***

The ship heaved again and Aeris struggled to maintain her composure. She could feel the sickness simmering just beneath the surface. Much more movement than this and she would be forced to retrieve the bedpan from beneath the bunk. It would be embarrassing and undignified . . . and why in the Hells couldn't she contain her stomach like everyone else? Well, mostly everyone. Just like the first time they had sailed, Tigerius suffered the sickness as well.

Aeris closed her eyes. She was tired, and she knew that she just needed to find a way to get some rest. Since discovering the fallen bird, she had received little sleep, tossing and turning all night on her bedroll, her dreams fraught with strange images . . . things she would never have thought existed. She could scarcely make sense out of the scenes, for her sleep was broken, and the dreams were vague and disordered. She imagined they had something to do with their strange discovery, but she told no one of her dilemma.

It was only a fortnight after the group had gone to see the metal bird that Cervantes announced the *Sea Maiden* was once more worthy to sail. Everyone prepared for the voyage by taking all of their remaining resources from the beach and bringing them back aboard ship. Food and water were collected and stored in the appropriate places. Aeris helped as much as she could with the preparations, but much of her mental energy was focused upon Tigerius. Levander had inspected him after the incident in the cavern and proclaimed him to be unharmed. For two days Tiger slept, and she remained by his side until he finally awoke. With no prior indication, his eyes suddenly opened. She recognized the expressions of disorientation and confusion, followed by a flicker of fear. His expressions then became guarded as he focused his gaze upon her. Since then, he had been quiet and withdrawn. She knew that something had happened to him that day in the cavern . . . she could see it reflected in the blue of his eyes and the way he seemed to view the world about him differently. Perhaps it was much the same as she had come to view it after her dreams . . .

Aeris began to realize that the bucking of the ship was slowing. Yet, she allowed several more moments to pass before daring to lift herself from the bed. From atop the desk that sat against the far wall of the small cabin, she retrieved her travel pack and returned to the bunk with it. Aeris stretched out across the narrow bed on her stomach and rummaged about within the sack until her fingers touched what she was looking for.

Aeris withdrew the golden chain. Suspended from it was the dark orb. She recalled the image it had conjured of the man who had once worn it, the skeleton of whom still lay within the structure they left behind several days past. He was the same man who dominated her dreams. By the gods, what was happening to her? Aeris shook her head. She recalled asking herself that same question once before, and it seemed like years ago when only a few months had passed. Her life had spun far out of her control, and she didn't know if she would ever find some semblance of normalcy ever again.

Aeris pondered the small orb. The circumference was about that of a quarter pence. The surface was smooth to the touch and unblemished with age. The color was a monotone smoky gray; there appeared to be nothing special about it. Yet, she had been compelled to take it from a skeletal man in the bowels of a fallen bird that was not really a bird. She had received a vision of that man, and he now dominated dreams that she could scarcely remember in the light of day.

Aeris heard footsteps outside the cabin and looked up as Jonesy entered. The girl closed the door behind her and regarded Aeris speculatively for a moment before she spoke. "You seem to be feeling better."

Aeris nodded solemnly. She thought about saying something but then refrained, not exactly sure what she wanted to communicate to Jonesy. She knew that the young woman had her own problems to think about and felt loathe to burden her with these. Nevertheless, Jonesy seated herself next to Aeris on the bunk. The cabin became hushed once more as the two mused over the dangling orb before them.

Several moments crept by, and the silence enveloped them within its embrace. Beside her, Jonesy could feel a calmness about Aeris, a serenity that always seemed to shroud her like a cloak. The woman was good at maintaining her cool exterior . . . one that fooled many into believing that she was thinking nothing at all. But then Aeris would act, the calm demeanor would fall away, and a formidable adversary would be standing there, replete in all of her glory. Jonesy could not help but feel the utmost of respect for the lady and would always be in her debt. Aeris had believed her at a time when she needed it most.

Jonesy took her eyes off of the dark orb and focused them onto her friend. When the two were together, she felt the tension between Aeris and Magnus. It was a tension that hung so thickly in the air, she could cut it with a knife. Not only had she seen the way Magnus watched Aeris, but also the way she watched him. It was not obvious . . . never apparent to those who were not looking for the subtle indications. But Jonesy had been waiting . . . and she knew that she should say something to her friend. She just didn't know what.

Jonesy cleared her throat. "The captain says that the winds are good. He hopes to be in familiar territory within two, maybe three fortnights at the most."

Aeris looked up, her dark eyes locking onto Jonesy's own. The faelin woman regarded her intently for a moment with a probing gaze. Jonesy got the impression that Aeris was searching for something, but then she was glancing away back to the suspended orb.

"He still plans to celebrate tonight?"

Jonesy nodded. "Everyone has been looking forward to opening the last barrel of ale."

Aeris grinned. "Especially Vikhail and Vardec, I am sure. Their thirst is unquenchable."

Jonesy tried to suppress a giggle. When she realized the futility, she allowed it to slip past her lips. "Aeris, you look so serious."

Once more Aeris pinned Jonesy with a solemn stare. "I *am* serious."

Jonesy sighed. "You shouldn't poke so much fun at their expense. They are good men."

Aeris shook her head. "I never said they weren't." The corner of her mouth began to twitch until a grin appeared. "I only said that they smoked and drank too much. And their singing is *terrible* . . ."

Jonesy found herself giggling again, a hand over her mouth to muffle the sound. Both women laughed for a moment, enjoying the camaraderie. Finally they collected themselves, and Aeris spoke once more. "I hear that they have developed quite a propensity for sailing, and they have taken on some duties aboard the ship."

Jonesy nodded. "Mateo helps out too. I think that Tigerius would if he were well enough. He was quite an asset when we were repairing the ship."

Aeris raised an eyebrow at her companion. "We? My, when did this come about?"

Jonesy felt her cheeks flush. Truth be told, she had preferred to stay aboard the ship to aid Captain Cervantes with his repairs. At first it had been the mending of the sails . . . but then other tasks he and his men found around the ship within her physical capability to perform. It wasn't very long before she found that she was quite interested in the workings of the ship, and she realized that she rather enjoyed Cervantes' company. And she had gotten to know some things about him during those times he took her aside to teach her a 'salable' skill.

Jonesy shook her head. "What do you mean by that?" she asked defensively.

Aeris' eyes narrowed speculatively, and they regarded her intensely. "You know what I'm talking about." Aeris grinned as she took in Jonesy's discomfiture. "You *like* Captain Cervantes."

Jonesy swallowed heavily. Her sharp retort rested on the tip of her tongue, but she knew that Aeris would only see through the lie. Her friend was right . . . Jonesy was attracted to Cervantes . . . very attracted.

Jonesy looked away from Aeris. She knew that the captain had a fascination for the young faelin woman. But what man didn't? Aeris was the dream of every male on this ship . . . everyone perhaps with the exception of Lev. But Jonesy was inclined to believe he was a man-lover because he was the only male she had met who didn't look at Aeris as though he wished she were in his bed.

Jonesy suddenly felt a warm hand on her arm and she looked up into Aeris' solemn face. "I am sorry. I didn't mean to make you feel badly. I am not a very good friend."

Jonesy shook her head. "No, that's not true. It's just that I know that he doesn't feel the same way towards *me*."

Aeris frowned. "How do you know?"

Jonesy gave her a piercing look. "Sometimes a woman just knows these things." It was because the captain was so smitten with Aeris. But she didn't want to tell her friend the truth, knowing that the other woman wouldn't believe her. Aeris was so modest . . . oblivious to the affect she had on the people around her, most notably those of the male gender. Jonesy only wished that she had it so easy.

"Then he is a fool," Aeris replied in a factual tone.

Jonesy grinned at the outpouring of loyalty. Aeris was a better friend than she realized. She was just the medicine that Jonesy needed in order to feel better about the situation. Jonesy considered bringing up the subject of Magnus, but somehow felt that it wasn't the right time. She didn't know when that time would be, but she hoped she would recognize it when it finally arrived.

***

Aeris stood back and took in the revelry all around her. Just as Jonesy had said, the men were quick to breach the last ale barrel the moment the sun began its descent upon the horizon. Despite the absence of half of Cervantes' original crew, they bent to their celebrating wholeheartedly. Vikhail and Vardec followed suit, striking up the beginning of a long series of bawdy seafaring tales that encouraged wenching, drinking, and brawling. Mateo helped Goldare set up the dart-board, and Tigerius and Cervantes brought the platters of food that

Simon had prepared. Since the loss of Hardow, he had taken over kitchen duty, and although Simon wasn't as good a cook as the other man, he did his best.

From her relatively secluded spot, Aeris watched Mateo. He was busy looking at Jonesy like a love-sick cub. She felt the corner of her mouth turn upward in a solemn smile. It was interesting how people tended to gravitate towards those who would be the least likely to want them. It was unlikely that Jonesy would ever care to see Mateo in any way except as a sister for her wayward younger brother. It was easy to see that she cared for the boy, but nothing romantic existed between them.

Aeris then shifted her gaze to the captain. She wondered if it was the same way for him. Could he ever have feelings for Jonesy? They were so disparate . . . not only in upbringing, but in the way they viewed the world. She was the daughter of a king and he the son of a sailor. What could there ever be between them? Yet, Jonesy had revealed her feelings for Cervantes. She loved the way he stood at the railing and looked out upon the sea with a tender expression . . . much like the way a man would look at his wife. She loved the way he took care of his ship, his crew, and the business enterprises upon which they embarked. And she loved to watch him pour over his maps . . . his brows furrowed in an expression of intense scrutiny.

After several moments, Aeris returned her gaze to Mateo. In the time they had known one another, he had begun to realize that she accepted him for who he was and that the Talent he possessed was a big part of his identity. He had come to accept his lot in life and to find some semblance of happiness despite the desertion of his parents. Despite all of her attempts, Aeris had found herself unable to describe it any differently, and she knew that he must be thinking of them in the same light.

Since leaving the island, Aeris had continued to teach him the quarterstaff. Mateo had finally begun to make some significant progress, his initial clumsiness making way for more refined movements. She could finally see some potential in him, especially since he had begun to embrace her teaching. She could see it in the stance he took during their sparring matches, the power he placed in the swings of his staff, and the determination in his eyes when he met her across the ring. She couldn't help but feel some measure of pride, for her efforts to prime him for arcane training with one of the masters at the academy were beginning to show

Aeris finally slid her gaze away from Mateo to focus upon the tattooed man, Levander. He was quite interesting to say the least, with his flying stars and his bald head. He was a good fighter . . . she could not contest that fact. He was also good with finding edible food, and his knowledge of herbal lore was impeccable. But there was something more to the man that remained hidden. Cervantes knew his secret, for she had seen the glances the captain cast in

Lev's direction a time or two. If the rest of the crew knew anything, they said nothing that Aeris could hear . . . and she was rather good at hearing things. Vikhail, Vardec, and Goldare also knew nothing about the man. He was an enigma to her, and she disliked that.

Aeris found her attention diverted with the shift in musical ability. Jonesy's voice had replaced that of the halfen brothers, and it was a good thing. Their interpretation of song left nothing to be desired, but people accepted it because it was so obvious that they were enjoying themselves. Anyone with a good heart would never think of taking that away from them. Except, perhaps for Magnus.

Aeris brought her gaze to rest upon the handsome cimmerean. Like always, he remained away from the activity . . . an outsider looking in. No one even attempted to draw him out of his shell anymore. They all assumed that he just simply didn't know how to have fun . . . either that or he simply didn't want to. Regardless, it was written within his personality to be so monotonous. Only Aeris knew the truth. She had known him before any of the others, back at a time when mere survival was not more than a luxury.

Pressing her lips into a thin line, Aeris looked away from Magnus. Not for the first time, she wondered how circumstances had settled her there upon this ship. Why were the Daemundai so desperate to have the crystals, and how had they tracked her so easily? They must be more widespread than anyone had thought in order to have moved upon her so quickly. And what trick of Fate had caused the ship to be wrecked upon an island far out at sea . . . an island that harbored the remains of what Tiger referred to as a shuttle?

Shuttle. Aeris soundlessly mouthed the strange word. Just the mere thought of it evoked the eerie memory surrounding her discovery of the skeleton. And then there was the vision she had seen when she touched him . . .

Aeris swallowed convulsively. She would have thought she was going crazy if not for the *Impression* that Tigerius received from the shuttle. In more detail, he had seen the place from which the man had come, and had even caught glimpses of the man himself, the same man that Aeris had seen when she knelt before the skeletal remains. Only upon her insistence had had told her anything about the *Impression* at all, and afterwards he had been more sullen towards her than ever.

Unconsciously, Aeris' gaze sought out her friend and found him in the company of the captain. It appeared that the two men had become comrades, for she had seen them often within one another's company even before they set sail from the island. This fact did not surprise her, for they were so much alike in so many ways. Cervantes was just as much a rake as Tiger, and Tiger just as much a scoundrel as the good captain. Aeris grinned in spite of herself. She did not condone their objectionable behaviors, but she would not judge the men for them either. No matter what, both were her friends and she would look past their unwholesome faults.

Aeris finally allowed her eyes to slide past Cervantes and Tigerius to touch upon Marion, Gervais, and Simon. They played a rather competitive game of darts with Goldare. As of yet, no one had proclaimed himself the winner. She glanced around, expecting to see Jaxom somewhere nearby. Yet, he was nowhere to be seen. She had found an unexpected friend in the pale young man, and she had rather hoped she would see him this night. She had caught precious few glimpses of him since they set sail, and she was beginning to wonder if he was avoiding her. Narrowing her eyes, Aeris realized that the notion hurt more than she thought it should. It wasn't as though she really knew him very well, or even for any length of time. It was simply that she had felt something between them, something indefinable, that fateful day they escaped the clutches of a voracious monster. She wondered if he had felt it too . . . and that if it was perhaps the reason why he might be avoiding her.

Aeris noticed that her gaze had finally returned to Magnus. Meanwhile, she had also come to the realization that Jonesy was no longer their source of vocal entertainment, for she was standing next to the cimmerean man. They appeared to be in the midst of some lively conversation. Her eyes were alight with merriment, and Magnus wore an expression of cheerfulness upon his customarily stoic face. Aeris found herself wanting to know what they were speaking about, but somehow could not muster the will to move out of her seclusion. After another moment, she settled herself back down, adjusting herself to simply watching the people before her. She did not join them, and she found herself unable to participate in their frivolity. Her thoughts weighed upon her soul, thoughts concerning the things she had recently experienced, coupled by those of the family who must be worried sick about her. She knew that she had to find a way to get a message to them, but feared that if they were too far away, a messenger bird would do no good. The creatures were only useful when one needed to send a message either to a neighboring realm, or one with which the visitor realm had a business relationship. She doubted that any such affiliation existed between any realm within the eastern continent and the western side from which she had come. *Damn.* There had to be another way. She just had only to discover what it might be.

Jaxom watched Aeris from his position behind the ballista platform. The weapon was no longer perched atop it, for the *Sea Maiden* would have been unable to sustain both the weight of the cannon and the Migallon Mechanism. Aeris could not see him, and he preferred it that way. He harbored an internal struggle against a destiny he did not want to accept. He willed himself to stop thinking about the red-haired faelin girl . . . commanded his subconscious to cease dreaming about her. He did not wish to acknowledge the possibility that it was *Suresh* . . . the Calling. It had beleaguered him every moment of every day since he had set eyes upon Aeris for the first time. And now it was worse, for they shared something together. He had caught a glimpse of her innermost person, and his heart was beginning to beat in synchrony with hers . . .

Damnation! These things didn't happen to rezwithrys! They were above the helzethryn, those to whom it had happened upon more than one occasion. He had thought the golden ones weak . . . not understanding why they would yoke themselves to bipeds who lived barely even a half of their lifetime. But then this faelin girl had walked into his life.

Jaxomdrehl turned away and put his back against the empty platform. He leaned back on the mortar, closing his eyes and breathing deeply. He did not want this . . . did not need a bond-mate such as her. He refused to believe that his soul was set upon this creature who knew naught about his kind or the world from which he came.

Jaxom allowed his back to scrape along as he slid to the floor. He barely realized the discomfort, but noticed that the deck had been freshly cleaned. The wood was smooth against his palms, devoid of the salt that built up when it wasn't scrubbed for a few days. He put his head back until it touched the cool metal support that would have anchored a ballista. His gaze took in the multitudes of stars in the sky and two of the three moons that hovered near Shandahar. The third would soon begin her emergence, a pale comparison to her brighter sister, Hestim. He tried to use these as a diversion to his true thoughts . . . thoughts that continued to focus upon that which he tried so hard to escape.

***

Cervantes slowly walked towards the passenger cabins. It wasn't often that he came this way, so he found his gaze darting this way and that, just to be sure that no one saw where he was going. And if someone did happen to see . . . who cared? It was *his* ship. He could go wherever he damn well pleased. And he would tell them so . . .but only if someone saw him . . .

Cervantes stopped before the cabin he knew to be occupied by Aeris. He hesitated a moment before the door, and then set his knuckles to it. She had been different since leaving the island. Cervantes shook his head. No, the change had occurred before then . . .since she and Jaxom discovered the structure everyone referred to as 'the fallen bird'. Something had happened to her since then, something that made her introspective and withdrawn. Cervantes could see that Magnus noticed it as well, for he caught the cimmerean man watching her a time or two, an expression of pensive worry on his face.

"Come in."

Cervantes opened the door to find Aeris sitting on the bunk situated at the far side of the small cabin. She looked up as he entered and smiled a greeting. He noticed that the smile didn't quite reach her eyes, and he regretted that not even he could bring any real semblance of happiness to her. He took the chair situated in front of the small desk against the adjacent wall, and then seated himself. He had forgotten precisely how cramped these cabins really were, and he was suddenly grateful for the cabin he himself inhabited on the other side of the ship.

Cervantes regarded the young woman for a moment before he spoke. Her dark eyes stared at him from a face paler than he remembered, and the dark smudges beneath them attested to the fact that the journey home had been hard on her already. More times than he could count, Cervantes wished he could make her voyage a more endurable one. Yet, even with all he knew about the sea, Cervantes had yet to come across a drought that could save a person from seasickness.

"How are you feeling?" He asked the question merely as a formality, a way to get the conversation started. Aeris knew it right away and she raised an eyebrow.

"How do I look?"

She asked the question to be facetious, but Cervantes heard the admonishment lurking just below the surface. He acceded to her mild rebuke and asked the question that was on his mind . . . the reason he had sought her out in the sanctuary of her cabin.

"I was wondering if you have discovered anything about the crystals. While stranded on the island, I didn't have much time to think about them. However, now that we are back on course, I was hoping you might have learned something."

Cervantes immediately noticed a guardedness about her, a response he had hoped to avoid. He knew that she was sickly and weak, hence the reason for his initial efforts to lighten the mood in the cabin. Yet, she had seen past those efforts, and now she looked at him as though he were an intruder upon his own ship. Cervantes sighed to himself and then rose from the chair and approached Aeris where she sat upon the bunk. He situated himself next to her and put an arm around her shoulders. She seemed thinner than she did upon their initial journey, and he felt his own worry for her begin to bubble to the surface of his consciousness.

"Aeris, I know that you are thinking that the only reason I care about this is because we made a deal, a bargain based upon some benefit I perceive connected to the crystals." Cervantes paused and sighed. "I am going to be honest with you . . . I would still love to hear you say that we are going to become immensely wealthy simply by being in possession of these crystals .

. . that they will somehow lead us to riches we can only imagine in our most wondrous of dreams.

"But I am not a fool. I know that you will tell me no such thing. You are going to give me the short version of a long string of bits and pieces of a strange and convoluted story you think might belong to these crystals. And the reason I know this is because I have realized that nothing with you has been easy thus far . . . and why should that change now?"

Cervantes stopped and looked over at the woman he had begun to know as his friend. Strangely enough, he had allowed her and her comrades entry into that place within himself he could only call "heart". Sure, he was still a corsair . . . a sea rover. . . . a buccaneer. He still relished the idea of a good pillaging and perhaps even his way with one of the local women. Yet, he knew that he wouldn't be able to bring himself to swindle the woman who sat next to him on a crummy cot in the middle of the sea. By the gods, wouldn't his brother be surprised when he saw him?

"Aeris, the past few fortnights . . . with everything we have been through . . ." Cervantes stumbled upon the words, unknowing of how to explain to her the newfound emotions he had begun to realize within himself.

Slowly, Aeris turned her face and brought her gaze up to look at him. Somehow, she knew what he wanted to say. She didn't smile, but he could see the understanding in her eyes, knew it by the softening of the lines about her face. At first she didn't say anything, but simply took the hand that rested in his lap and held it.

"You are right." Aeris spoke slowly and with very little emotion. "I thought to tell you the condensed version of what I have come to believe as the truth concerning these crystals." Then she sighed heavily, as though the weight of the world suddenly rested upon her slender frame. "But I am so afraid that I might be doing you some kind of injustice, that perhaps I might, albeit unintentionally, be placing you at risk by not telling you everything we have learned.

"I have struggled with myself for days now, wondering when you would come to seek me out, and what I would tell you when you were finally before me. I imagined that we had become close, especially in light of what we have all shared together in the recent past. A part of me was anxious as to what you might say when you finally came.

"But now you are here. You have shown me a part of your true self and given me the courage to tell you all that I can, despite what Magnus says." Aeris turned her body to face him and then placed her other hand upon his cheek. "I believe in you, Cervantes."

For a moment he simply stared at her, an angel sitting within the dark bowels of his ship. Her physical radiance was muted, but the way she made him feel shone through him like a brilliant flame. He cupped her face and kissed her gently on the mouth, an affirmation of the friendship they shared. Not to mention, she had just made him feel like one of the wealthiest men upon all of Shandahar.

***

Tigerius looked out across the sea. The wind blew into his face, a crisp wind that carried the promise of cooler temperatures to come. North. They sailed due north with very little variance. The sea had cooperated with them thus far, yet no one brought attention to that fact, at least not out loud. It was almost as though everyone was afraid that if the wind heard them speak of it, then it would tell the sea. The sea would subsequently take their good fortune away. Tiger grinned to himself. He knew it was silly, but he wasn't about to say anything either.

Tiger leaned into the railing, basking in the sudden chill of the cooler air. His thoughts had shifted to what they left behind, and he wondered if that chill really was from the air, or if perhaps the dreams he endured during their last days on the island. He inhaled deeply, and then breathed out with exasperation. More often as of late, he had begun to wish he listened to his father more often. At the time, Tiger didn't really know why Triath spoke to him of those things . . . of abilities that he possessed. Tiger had never really understood that his father thought he may have passed those abilities to his degenerate son.

Tiger pressed his hands into the railing. He was finally approaching the realization that he had been quite difficult on his parents. He had been a spirited child, always getting into trouble and expecting others to get him out of it. He had always treated his mother unfairly and was constantly giving her a hard time. When he was finally old enough to rescue himself, he heard that Tianna had almost died giving birth to him. For that he blamed his father, instinctively knowing that it was something about Triath that was incompatible with his mother. The thing that Triath had become was too disparate from the human he had once been. Of course, now Tiger knew that Triath could never have known that he placed his wife at risk by impregnating her.

When Tiger was old enough, Triath told his son the story . . . that during his early days with the Wildrunners he had fought against a daemon, and upon its death, the creature had somehow infused its essence into that of its adversary. Triath eventually healed from the skirmish, but as time progressed, the spirit of the daemon began to take a hold over him. He began to realize that he was no longer quite human, and that he harbored abilities that no ordinary man should ever possess. Triath fought against the essence of the daemon within him, and he slowly began his path towards death. It was only with the aid of his friends that he was able to accept what he had become and thwart the inevitable.

But what did that make Tiger? Before leaving Sangrilak, he had never really noticed anything about himself that separated him from other men. Yet, since then he had heard the voice of another within his mind and received an *Impression* from an inanimate object. The first he had never heard his father speak about, but the second was an ability that Triath had told him about upon several occasions. An *Impression* was an ability upon which one could glean the history of an object without having ever seen it before. Triath had told Tiger that it could be a rather disconcerting experience, but Tiger had no idea what his father was talking about until he experienced it for himself. And now he would never be the same.

However, the *Mindaware* and the *Impressions* were not the only abilities Tiger had begun to notice he possessed. It was little things, actually, such as being able to see better in the darkness. Another he wasn't quite sure about . . . but he could swear that he was starting to be able to tell when danger was near. Now that he looked back on it, he remembered feeling ill-at-ease prior to the attack of the seascrags and then again before the storm struck no more than three days later. And then there was the last thing. *Healing.* His body was able to heal itself at twice the rate of any human or faelin. The first time he had noticed was after he was wounded after their skirmish with the priestess with which Magnus later thought Aeris may have been in league. The second was after he had been injured during that same incident with the seascrags. On both occasions he had been in bad shape, but within days was up and about, doing many of his regular activities.

It just wasn't normal.

Once more, Tigerius took a deep breath of the cool air. The *Impression* he got from the fallen bird had rocked him to the core, and he didn't quite know what he should do with his newfound knowledge. A part of him wanted to tell Aeris more, knowing instinctively that something had happened to her upon the fallen bird as well. However, he didn't really know how to broach the subject. Not to mention, he wouldn't have any idea of what to tell her when she asked specific questions about him. Already, he had come to realize that she had her suspicions about him, but she had no real sureties. And then he faced the possibility that she just might consider him something well beyond her desire for friendship. He knew that one day he would have to talk to her, but he needed just a little bit more time. Just a little . . .

CHAPTER 15

Magnus slowly approached Aeris where she stood against the ship's railing. The wind blew the crimson waves of her hair away from her beautiful face, a face more gaunt and pale than he liked. Yet, Cervantes promised that there was an end in sight . . . he had finally entered familiar waters, and the captain assured Magnus that they would be land-bound with the seven-day.

Magnus stepped up to stand beside Aeris at the railing. She didn't turn, but the corner of her mouth curved up into a faint smile. Magnus gazed at her profile for a moment before looking out to the sea. He knew that this might be one of their last moments alone together before they reached port. Despite his disliking for Cervantes, Magnus believed the captain when he said that they were getting close to the mainland. Somehow, that rogue had brought them home, and Magnus was just becoming acclimated to that fact.

So many times now, Magnus had wanted to approach Aeris about things that had transpired in the past, events that he didn't quite know how to broach. Perhaps it simply wasn't his way . . . or mayhap something simply beyond his ability to execute. Nevertheless, the subject of their past had never come up. A part of him was content with this arrangement; but another part of him, that part that detested unresolved issues, would not allow it to simply *be*.

"I suppose you told Cervantes about the crystals." Magnus made the statement just as much out of the necessity to have something about which to start a conversation as his need to know all of the facts. He probably could have chosen a better topic about which to speak first, but he was not one for intricate social graces.

Aeris turned, her dark eyes regarding him intently. She revealed very little emotion, and he cringed inwardly. *Damn.* He wondered if she had been this hardened before she met him, or if her life's experiences since then had made her such. "Yes, I told him."

Magnus had figured as much, but he just wanted to be sure. "And you told him about the orb as well?"

Aeris shook her head. "No. I didn't mention it. None of the group even knows of its existence except for Jaxom and Jonesy."

Magnus nodded. There was no reason why anyone should know about it, and it was probably best if it remained that way. Since procuring the dark object, they had discovered some very intriguing things about the crystals, and Magnus didn't really know what to make of it.

After the group returned to the beach after viewing the fallen bird, Magnus had followed Aeris to her cabin aboard Cervantes' ship. She often went there to sleep, and Magnus could only imagine that she found more security resting within the walls of the *Sea Maiden*. He found it to be a bit peculiar, for her lineage was mostly hinterlean, and most faelin of that race had a propensity for open spaces. He found her with a neck-chain dangling from her hand, and at the end of it was a small, dark orb.

"Where did you get that?" His presence at the doorway had startled her, and he was confused by the fact that he had been able to approach without her awareness of him. Her faelin senses should have picked up his intrusion before he ever got close to the cabin.

Aeris beckoned him over to the cot upon which she had seated herself. She continued to allow the orb to dangle from the chain. Magnus seated himself across from her, the small sphere swaying between them. "I found it aboard the fallen bird," she said quietly, her gaze fastened upon the orb.

Magnus frowned slightly. She should have told him earlier, before they went to investigate the structure. He would have been on the lookout for other, similar, objects that may have been of use to them. Notwithstanding, it was too late now. Sure, he could go back to the steel bird, and he just might do that. But, to be honest, the thing had given him an eerie feeling that he didn't like, and he did not relish the thought of returning there.

Magnus pursed his lips. "Where?"

Aeris finally brought her eyes up to his face. Her gaze was almost piercing in its intensity. "It was around the neck of the skeleton man."

Magnus felt a chill creep up his spine. He vividly recalled the skeletal corpse of a man, but had chosen not to investigate. It had added to his disquiet upon the vessel, and he didn't want to perpetuate what discomforting feelings he was already experiencing.

Magnus sighed. "What is it?"

Aeris shrugged. "I don't know."

Magnus held out his hand. "May I see it?"

Aeris shook her head, almost as though to diffuse any feelings of disorientation or muddiness. "Sure, of course."

Magnus took the chain from Aeris' hand. He allowed the orb to rest against his palm. It remained dark. He didn't know what he had been expecting . . . for all he knew, the thing was simply an item whose only intent was for decoration.

But he doubted that.

By the time Magnus handed the chain back to Aeris, she had already removed one of the crystals from her travel pack. He didn't realize what was happening until she had been thrown backward into the wall behind the bunk. It was as though a force had suddenly come between them, a powerful one. To say the least, he was quite alarmed, and it took a repetition of the occurrence in order for him to understand what was happening.

Magnus raised a hand to bid Aeris stay where she was. He looked down at the orb dangling from his hand and saw that it glowed a deep blue. The crystal within Aeris' grip shone a bright yellow. It seemed that the two objects repelled one another, and that the response was magnified when such objects were in the possession of two different people. No such repulsion existed when the crystal had remained buried within Aeris' travel pack despite being within much closer proximity when Aeris was in possession of both the crystal and the orb.

Now, standing at the ship's railing, Magnus could see the memory reflected in her eyes. Both of them realized the benefit of keeping their findings to themselves . . . at least until they could learn a bit more about both crystals and orb. The group didn't need any more uncertainty than what they had experienced already.

The two stood in silence for a while. There were things Magnus wanted to say . . . things he *needed* to say. He looked away from the sea to look down at the railing, saw his pale hands next to her golden ones. Impulsively, he placed one of his hands atop of hers . . . felt her tremble slightly as she always seemed to do at the feel of his touch. He had always wondered at this reaction, but not for long. He never knew what to make of it, and he hated for his imagination to get the better of him.

Aeris swung her gaze up to meet his. He saw the questions in her eyes, questions he wished he had the answers for. So many times now he had been a fool, and he knew that there would be many more of those times.

"The Captain says that we should be landed within the seven-day."

Aeris nodded. "I know. He told me this morning."

Magnus nodded. He had known as much. But he didn't know how to begin to say what was really on his mind, and sought only a means to start their conversation anew. He then shook his head and cast his gaze back out to the sea. "It seems so long, does it not? So much has happened since we met one another for the first time."

There. He said it. May the gods smite him where he stood.

Aeris kept her gaze fixed on him. He turned back and gave her a rather lopsided grin. Actually, *too* much had happened within that span of time, and it seemed like forever had passed since he had first set his eyes upon her.

"Things seemed so much easier back then, didn't they?" He continued to speak without really knowing what to say. She wasn't making this easy for him, and perhaps he shouldn't blame her. She finally looked away from him, casting her gaze down to the railing to eventually focus upon their combined hands. He thought surely that she would pull away, but when the rejection never came, Magnus found the strength to glance back at her.

Aeris continued to stare at their hands for a moment. He had never reached out to her this way before. Why now, after so much time had passed? He had never bothered to ask her the reasons for her leave-taking so long ago back in Grunchin, choosing instead the path of anger and resentment. Yet, she somehow knew that he cared about her, and she thought that perhaps if he did not, that perhaps he might not have been so angry.

Yet, mayhap that was just wishful thinking on her part.

Aeris nodded in response to his last statement. Yes, things did seem to be much more on the simple end of things back then. She never had the need to defend herself so assiduously, against friends and foes alike. She had never been forced to think solely of her survival, and then that of her family. Tigerius had become that much to her. And then there was Mateo . . .

"Why did you do it?"

The question took her unawares, making her look back up at him. For a moment, he seemed almost as surprised as she did. But then he regarded her as though in wait for a response.

Aeris shook her head in confusion. "Do what?"

"I know you weren't in league with the cimmereans," he said. "Why did you do it? Why did you make it seem like you were?"

Aeris suddenly knew to what event Magnus was referring. It was the ambush . . . when he had erroneously thought she was allied with the cimmereans and their queen. And that she had betrayed him . . .

"It would have been easy for you to continue denying affiliation with them," he continued. "You had to have known I would never harm Tigerius. Why did you incriminate yourself?"

Aeris looked up at him through haunted eyes, shaking her head once again. "No. You would never have believed me. I could see it in your eyes. You were so set against me, that you would never hear the truth. You had become another man, a stranger, and I could not be entirely sure that you would not harm my friend."

She spoke the last words in a whisper, and he was forced to bring his face close to hear what she said. He closed his eyes with the pain he had caused . . . for in the end, it was he who had betrayed Aeris, not she him. She was right. He would never have believed her, and the realization sickened him.

Yet, he would not have ever considered laying harm upon Tigerius. She would never know that.

Magnus put his face even closer to hers, and then a hand upon her cheek. "I am so sorry for what I have done. I hope you can find it in your heart to forgive me," he said softly.

Aeris lay her hand atop of his where it rested against her face and then shook her head. "There is nothing left to forgive, Magnus. Remember, we have been through so much since then."

He nodded slowly. "Yes, I remember . . ."

***

29 Chanteren CY633

Aeris trembled as the group prepared to disembark. Her heart hammered in her chest with excitement. She couldn't believe it was over. Despite the vile twist of Fate that rendered them lost at sea, Captain Cervantes had brought them back to the mainland. For that she would be eternally grateful. And even though they weren't in familiar territory, she still felt a little bit like she had returned home.

The plank was lowered, and it landed with a thud onto the pier leading to the main dock. Aeris' legs shook as she bid them walk her forwards. She struggled for a moment, but looked up when she felt a hand envelope hers. It was Tiger. He had remained withdrawn from her whilst they sailed, but now he was beside her, a bastion to lean upon should she need it. Unexpectedly, he gave her a small smile and, she grinned tremulously in return. She was glad of his presence, and it was strange how he seemed to have known that she needed him more than any other member of their group..

Slowly the comrades left the *Sea Maiden.* Aeris and Tiger followed behind Vikhail, Vardec, and Goldare. The three were almost running down the plank, so eager to be on dry land they could scarcely contain themselves. Not to mention that there was ale that waited to be drunk in the nearest tavern. Somewhere behind them Aeris could hear Cervantes chuckling at their antics. She knew that he itched to join them, but he knew his responsibility towards the ship and remaining crew. He would see to the documentation needed for the dock-master, and then focus on his crew to be sure that they had the ship safely docked. Only then would he see to his own wants and needs.

The group convened at the dock gates, as the sun began to sink below the horizon. Vikhail, Vardec, and Goldare had gone ahead to the nearest tavern and were probably well into their first tankard of ale. Cervantes lead them through the streets of Darban to the Gritty Murg Tavern. It was a shady place, but the first one past the docks. The threesome would surely be there. Once opening the doors, Cervantes found his thoughts to be correct. The human and two halfen had claimed a sizable table and awaited them with tankards in hand. Beards were wet with spiced ale, and the talk was merry as the rest of the group situated themselves around the table.

Aeris glanced nervously around the tavern. She felt conspicuously out of place and had not failed to notice the attention that she and Jonesy brought to the table. She didn't like it, and it put her on edge. Not to mention that most of the men would soon be drinking themselves into oblivion and unable to help should trouble arise. However, she noticed Cervantes was a bit more quiet than usual and he drank slowly from his mug. His gaze slowly perused the establishment, and Aeris felt her fears calming. The captain would protect them should anything go wrong.

Cervantes glanced unobtrusively around the tavern. A part of him almost wished that Goldare had not chosen this place despite it being one of his favorite haunts whilst he was home. Thing was, he knew the type of patronage the Gritty Murg attracted, and it was definitely not the place for women such as Aeris and Jonesy, or boys such as Mateo. He thought to tell the others that they should move on after their tankards had been emptied, but he couldn't help his thoughts from drifting to other matters. He knew he had to see his brother as soon as possible, but he didn't want to desert the group on their first night in Darban.

For several more moments, Cervantes continued to glance about the disheveled establishment. Not much had changed during the year he had been gone. He recognized many of the men sitting around the tables . . . men who had a hunger not only for the murg, but for the women and game the tavern had to offer. In the past, Cervantes had sat many a game, some stakes low and some high. He was not the best player, but also not the worst. There were some whom he had beaten well, but also some to whom he had lost. Tavern wenches walked among the tables, offering spiced ale and strong murg. Most of them were rather buxom, one of the several conditions to being hired by the owner of the establishment. And if a woman didn't have big breasts, she had best have other qualities that suited a man who was looking for a good time.

Cervantes finally turned his attention back to the table. *Damn.* Everyone had ordered another round and all were well into their flagons and tankards. Now he would have to wait even longer to take them away from the Gritty Murg before it started to get late. That was when the place became a bit rowdy. He glanced over at Aeris and Jonesy and saw that both seemed to be well situated. Cervantes noticed the attention they garnered upon first entering the tavern, but that had died down significantly. They now only received the occasional glance.

Cervantes suddenly found his attention diverted when he heard a commotion on the other side of the room. A group of men sat around a rather large table, and it appeared that one of them was winning at the game that they all played. There were shouts of encouragement interspersed with those of disgruntlement. He mused that it must be a game of rather high stakes for everyone to get so worked up.

And then the game was over. Many people were congratulating the winner while others were groaning over their loss. A buxom blonde stood atop the table and shouted "Grunthor, we have a winner over here!" Cervantes' eyes widened with recognition at the sound of the voice, and he focused the intensity of his stare at the woman. Hells, what was Jezibel doing in Darban?

Cervantes stood from his seat and shouted across the room. "By the gods, is that my woman Jezibel?"

The blonde swung her head towards the sound of Cervantes voice, her lips curving into a wide smile and her eyes lighting up with joy. Catching sight of him, she maneuvered herself off of the table and rushed into Cervantes' waiting embrace. He kissed her soundly on the mouth, and then buried his face in her ample bosom. He reveled in the familiar scent. It was just what he needed after all he had recently been through.

Finally Cervantes pulled away from her. Jezibel was not a small woman. She was buxom and curvy in all the right places . . . her breasts, hips, and thighs. A man could lose himself in her softness, and he had done so on several occasions on his trips to Gridiron. What Jezibel was doing in Darban was beyond him, but he would find out later when they could find some time to be alone.

Cervantes turned back to the table, curving his arm around Jezzie's ample waist. Goldare, Vikhail, and Vardec saluted them with their mugs, sloshing the contents upon the ale-laden table. Mateo had his head down, most likely sleeping after his mug. Aeris, Magnus, Lev, and Jonesy all gave him questioning stares. He introduced them to the woman with whom he had shared more than just a bed, but also his hopes, dreams, and aspirations. For a time, he had even entertained thoughts of marrying her one day, but those were short lived. Not even Jezibel Pyratt could keep him tied down . . . not even close.

Jonesy couldn't take her eyes off of the woman Cervantes introduced to them. She was pretty, with curling blonde hair and large blue eyes. She had big breasts, a cinched waist, and curving hips and buttocks. Jezibel was the epitome of what a man desired most in a woman, and Jonesy disliked her for it already. She hated herself for feeling that way but she couldn't help it. Cervantes seemed so pleased with Jezibel's company, and he wrapped his arm so possessively around her, Jonesy couldn't help but feel that any chance she may have had with him was slipping away.

". . . and this is Jonesy." She inhaled sharply as Cervantes' gaze stopped to linger for a moment. Fearing that he would somehow divine her thoughts, she quickly looked away. Damn . . . she couldn't believe it had come to this. Feelings of inadequacy welled within her and she swallowed convulsively. After a moment she raised her eyes once more, but he had moved on, beckoning to a serving wench to bring them more ale and situating Jezibel more soundly upon his lap.

Feeling someone watching her, Jonesy turned to find Aeris regarding her from across the table. She could see the sadness reflected in her friend's eyes, sadness that Aeris felt upon her behalf. Once more she looked away. She knew that Aeris felt hurt because she cared about her so much, but she didn't want Aeris' pity. She just wanted to stop feeling this way . . . like the world would come to an end if Cervantes didn't somehow feel the same way about her as she had come to feel about him.

***

Levander walked through the streets back to the Amber Anchor Inn. It was the place they had finally decided to stay after their initial night at the Gritty Murg Tavern and Inn situated near the docks. He was glad they had found another inn, for he was uncomfortable with the one that was initially chosen. He had bad vibes about that place, and by the guarded expression on his face, so did Cervantes.

Lev had just come from the aerie-keeper in order to send a long overdue message to his uncle in Gulshaan. After all this time, he had finally made it home, and Lev could see to his responsibilities. He was aware of the possibility that it was too late; but until he heard otherwise, he would continue to believe that his bother had not yet made any rash decisions.

Regardless, Lev knew that he had to make his journey to Gulsahaan as soon as possible. There wasn't the possibility of his staying in Darban to receive a response from his uncle. His message had simply been one to inform the man that he was close, and that within the fortnight he would be in Gulshaan. On the morrow, Lev would be leaving the group in order to make the journey.

Levander entered the establishment and then made towards his chamber. He momentarily thought about the people he would be leaving behind. They had quite a fight ahead of them if, indeed, the Daemundai had them within their sights. He felt a pang of regret to leave his comrades behind, for he knew they could benefit from his expertise. Yet, the welfare of his family came first, and if that meant leaving the group to their own devices, so be it.

Levander shook his head with the absurdity of it all. He was on a mission he never imagined he would be forced to embark. He needed to dissuade his own brother from attempting to join the Kronshue. Over the years, Severus had begun to prove that he was rather impetuous and head-strong. Not only that, he had his youth against him as well. All these things set the stage for hardship Lev had always hoped to avoid. But now, it was inevitable.

It had been quite some time since he had seen his brother last. He remembered the last time he made a visit to Gulshaan, vaguely recalled being surprised at how tall Severus had grown, how much the boy had begun to resemble a man. That should have made Lev realize that time was swiftly passing him by, and that precious little of it remained. He remembered how adamantly Severus fought to have Lev take him back west, and then the expression of devastation when Lev turned him down for the final time.

Lev shook his head. *Damnation!* Severus had gone to pursue the only thing Lev had asked him not to have. Lev could have demanded many things from his younger brother, but this was the only thing. And now Severus had possibly gone and done it anyways. Damn the boy. Severus was too stubborn . . . too much like himself.

***

Tholana brought her mind back into herself, disengaging from that of the boy Talent they called Mateo. It had taken them more than a few fortnights, but Tallachienan and his band of rag-tag companions had finally made it back to the main-land of Ansalar. She grudgingly accepted that the captain just might not be the idiot she had originally thought him to be. She supposed it had to take at least some bit of skill to repair such a ship, and make her sea-worthy once more, with only the most basic of materials.

Tholana stood from her seat within the comfort of the heated spring. Naked, she walked across the chamber and into the adjoining one. She stopped to pick up a jar of scented oil, poured it into her hand, and then began to rub it over her body. One of her priestesses could have easily seen to this task, but Tholana preferred to do it herself. Only when she participated in the evening orgy did Tholana allow another to apply the oils, and of course in that situation, other things took place during the application.

However, this evening she would prepare herself to accept the Mehta of the Daemundai. Tholana smiled to herself. Razlul had become quite solicitous towards her as of late. But she was not a fool. Tholana knew that it was more than his lust for her . . . he needed her for her ability to track the group in a way that he could not. She didn't yet know the precise reason, but the daemon prince had quite a vested interest in the group, and it had nothing to do with Tallachienan Chroalthone.

Truth be told, Tholana didn't much care why he had such an interest. With time, she was sure that she could easily learn the information. All that mattered was that he treated her with the deference she deserved. He had been visiting her citadel periodically for quite some time now, coinciding with when the group escaped his minions at the docks in the city of Yortec. Through some reliable source, Razlul had learned that she was able to track the group, and when he came to her that first time after the group became sea-bound, Tholana had been fascinated by his desire to please her. It was beyond what she had experienced with him before, and she wondered how much of it had to do with any newfound respect she may have inadvertently procured when she was able to do something that he could not. It told her how important the group was to him . . . and Tholana loved knowing a person's weakness, whether he be ally or enemy.

The goddess finished her bodily ministrations, donned a sheer camisole, and then made her way to the adjoining bedchamber. It was the one she used most often in the company of the daemon prince. Upon entering, she received a nod from the priestess waiting within, telling Tholana that her guest had arrived and was awaiting her. She nodded in reply and the priestess quickly left the chamber. Tholana made her way to the plush bed pallet and fell onto it. She curled herself amongst the pillows, knowing that Razlul enjoyed seeing her thus when he visited her. It was easy to please him as he pleased her, and it made their union that much more intense. Tholana smiled in anticipation . . .

***

Cervantes walked up to the tavern. It was old, having seen many more years than most of the others in Darban. The Sea Wharf had always been the one of choice for he and Cortes, even as young men just out of adolescence. It was a place that catered only to the local populace, and those of unknown identity were asked to vacate the premises upon initial entry. The locals were glad for the fact that they had a place all to themselves, and the tavern was almost always at least half full of patrons.

Cervantes confidently walked into the Sea Wharf Tavern. He nodded at the thug that sat the door and made his way to the bar. Once there he ordered a tankard of murg and downed half of it before he turned to look around for an empty table. He spotted only one and began to make his way over to it.

"Is there not one man here who can beat me?" Cervantes paused at the sound of the burly voice. "Not even one? Has the Sea Wharf turned into an establishment catering only to mindless whelps?"

There were guffaws all around the tavern, but no one stood to accept the challenge. Cervantes altered his route and arrived at the table. The man was a brawny one, with dark curling hair and matching goatee. He sported piercings in both ears and his nose, as well as tattoos that climbed up his arms to disappear behind his tunic. He was not an attractive individual, and some might even call him monstrous.

"What's the game?" Cervantes asked.

The man looked hard at him. "Shockwave, the untamed version," he responded gruffly. "Hard murg over here, wenches," he bellowed. "And keep 'em coming."

Cervantes seated himself at the table and the cards were dealt over stones scattered between them. Cervantes drank and placed his wager, thus starting the first round of the game. For quite a while it continued, each man seeking victory over the other until finally it was apparent that Cervantes had achieved the upper hand. He could sense the animosity that had begun to emanate from his opponent, but it did not stop Cervantes from taking yet a third hand in consecutive victory.

Suddenly the table was being overthrown. Cervantes jumped out of his seat only to find himself confronted by the big man. "Fraud . . . charlatan!" he shouted. Heads turned in their direction. The sound of wood scraping against stone could be heard all around the tavern as people made sure that they were out of the way of any harm that could befall them from the brawl that was about to ensue.

His opponent threw the first punch and a long-winded fight began. At first the scuffle was simply a fist-fight, but in the end, the men grappled at one another like two wenches might, scratching at one another's faces and pulling hair. They fell in a tumble of arms and legs to the sticky murg-laden floor and wrestled about for a few moments. Finally the big man grabbed a broken table leg and brandished it over his opponent. "Cervantes, I'll make you regret cheatin' me you old seascrag."

Cervantes snatched up a plate and slung it at his adversary. It hit him in the middle of his forehead. The man reeled from the impact, giving Cervantes the time he needed to rise from the floor and slam his body into his rival. Both men fell back to the floor, this time with Cervantes on top.

"Now Cortes, I never cheated you. I never have in the past, and I never will in the future. You always do this when you know I'm winning. It's not fair, and I demand that you stop this foolishness."

Suddenly the big man put his thick arms around Cervantes. "I have missed you, brother. Why did it take you so long to return this time?"

Cervantes felt the anger drain out of Cortes. He couldn't really blame his brother; Hells, all they had was each other. Cortes had every right to be upset.

"We hit a big storm and it foundered the ship. It took us a while to make the *Sea Maiden* worthy to sail once again." Cervantes paused and then continued. "I am sorry that you worried about me."

Cortes shook his head as Cervantes released him and stood. "No, I shouldn't have been so angry. You know that I have a hard time with that." The big man also rose and the brothers embraced once more, pounding each other heartily on the back. "Now I am only glad to see you home, Cervantes."

Cervantes nodded and gestured to the mess that had been made. "Let's pick this up and talk for a while. It's been quite a time."

The brothers picked up the tables and chairs that had been overturned in the scuffle, followed by bowls, mugs, and tankards. They reimbursed the tavern-owner for any damages they may have caused and then set themselves down at a table at the farthest side of the room. Sitting over full mugs of murg, they regarded one another for a moment.

"So, tell me about this storm, Cervantes. It was a big one, eh?"

Cervantes shook his head and spoke in a low voice. "Cortes, the storm isn't important. I need to talk to you about how I got caught up in it in the first place."

Cortes' thick brows pulled together into a frown. He could suddenly feel the tension in his brother, saw it reflected in the intensity of his gaze. This was serious. He had rarely seen Cervantes like this, and it was never a good portent.

Cortes leaned forward to hear what Cervantes had to say next. "I didn't come to Darban with just my ship and crew. There are others."

Cortes nodded. He was aware of the people about whom Cervantes was speaking. One of the reasons he had been so angry was because Cervantes had not come to see him the previous evening, his first night home after being away for so long. And Cortes had felt more than just anger. He had been hurt as well.

"And they are the reason why I was unable to find you last night." Cervantes paused and then continued. "I met them in the port city of Yortec a couple of days before I was due to set sail back to Darban. I had taken care of most of my business, and the cargo was safely stored in the hold. Somehow I got caught up in their troubles, and before I knew it, my situation had become deadly."

For a moment the table was quiet. Cortes stared at Cervantes. "Why didn't you just leave them?"

Cervantes shook his head and lowered his voice even more, leaning towards Cortes as much as the table allowed. "You know that crystal I gave to you? The one that glows when it is near mine?"

Cortes nodded. "Yeah, I'm wearing it now. But it's not glowing."

Cervantes nodded. "These people have another crystal, just like ours."

Cortes' eyes brightened. "So where is it? Show me!"

Once again Cervantes shook his head. "These people . . . remember I mentioned that they had trouble? Well, it followed them to Yortec and to the docks outside the ship. The trouble is called the Daemundai, a sect of priests and mages that cater to daemon-kind. These Daemundai were hunting the group for the crystal they carried via the link that sister crystals share." Cervantes pulled his lips into a thin line. "But the Daemundai were not just drawn to their crystal, but to mine as well."

Cortes just sat there, saying nothing, the ramifications of Cervantes' words refusing to settle into his mind. "Brother, I still don't understand how you got caught up in this. I . . ."

"The Daemundai were hunting to kill, Cortes. They were not going to leave Yortec without the crystal. And once they realized there was another crystal nearby, they would have come to kill me too. That is the main reason why I am here, Cortes. They will stop at nothing to have as many crystals as they can. As long as you have that crystal, your life is at risk, as well as everyone else's around you."

Cortes felt his eyes widen. "But how do you know that? How would these priests have any idea of where we lived? Why didn't you just leave these people back in Yortec to deal with their own problems?"

Cervantes covered one of Cortes' hands with his own. "I believe that the Daemundai are far-reaching. It would only be a matter of time before they found us." Cervantes paused and his gaze intensified. "But that is not the only reason. Remember the vision I told you I had when I picked up our two crystals for the first time? The vision of the dragon continent? I can't help but think that Fate brought these people to me. Somehow, I just know that they are a link to my vision. They are going to help me realize my dreams, Cortes."

Cortes sat back in his seat, regarding his brother. Cervantes had that bright look in his eyes, the look he always had when he spoke of the dragon continent. Cortes had come to realize that it was obsession, but he couldn't help getting caught up in Cervantes' fervor. What if Cervantes was right? What if the dragon continent held more riches than a man could ever dream? And what if these people were a path to that kind of wealth?

"Well, then I am going with you." Cortes made the statement almost belligerently, preparing himself for the argument that he imagined would probably ensue.

Cervantes smiled. "I wouldn't have it any other way."

CHAPTER 16

It was their second evening in the city of Darban and Aeris sat upon the bed situated in the middle of her room at the Amber Anchor Inn. Resignedly, she regarded the crystals spread out on the covers before her and felt a momentary sense of déjà vu . . . like she had been there before. And she had, indeed, been there before, albeit at a different time and a different place. She remembered what had happened the last time she brought the crystals together. How could she possibly forget a vision like that? But despite her reservations, she had to know the location of the Daemundai and if the group was yet out of danger.

Aeris had been surprised by the turn of events the evening before at the Gritty Murg Tavern. She had been unaware that Darban was Cervantes' home port and was taken aback by the woman, Jezibel. Cervantes seemed to favor the wench and Aeris hated that Jonesy cared so much for the reprehensible captain.

Aeris sighed, rose from the bed, and made her way to the window. She looked out upon the street below and saw that not many people were out, most having gone home for the day. The shadows were lengthening with the approach of the night, and just as she was about to turn away, something caught her eye.

Aeris squinted into the dusky shadows. A young man had left the premises and upon first glance it had looked like Mateo. Aeris stared at the backside of the man until he disappeared along the bend in the road. No, it couldn't be him. Mateo would not be leaving the inn at this hour, not to mention that he seemed rather uncertain about the new city the evening before when they left the ship. Vikhail, Vardec, and Goldare had succeeded in drawing Mateo out of his shell, but Aeris was convinced that he would not leave the sanctuary of the inn without a comrade.

Aeris walked back towards the bed and stood over it for a moment. Since arriving in Darban, Cervantes had surprised her more than once. Earlier that afternoon he brought his brother back to the inn, and Aeris was not the only one of the group whose expression registered astonishment. Cortes was a giant of a man, standing at least a foot or two above Cervantes. It was readily apparent that the man was not entirely of human descent, his orocish parentage shining through. Not only was he large, the man had a plethora of facial hair that she was sure included his chest and back. And the cut of his jaw and the length of his incisors were also an indication.

But despite his heritage, Cortes seemed to be a friendly sort. He treated her with nothing but deference, and it was the same with Jonesy. With the men he was cordial and seemed to gravitate especially towards Goldare, Vikhail and Vardec. It didn't surprise her; those three could befriend a tree and it would come to join them for the evening meal. She wondered about Cortes for the rest of the day, how he and Cervantes were related . . . if it was by blood or only simple friendship. And if they were bloodbound . . . what was their story?

Aeris sat down once more on the bed. The three crystals glowed eerily in the gloom. She knew that she had to stop procrastinating and simply pick up the crystals to see if they would show her what she needed to see. And if they didn't, she would hopefully be none the worse for wear, and Magnus would never know that she tried it without him there.

Aeris grinned lopsidedly. Magnus. He had been sullen since arriving in Darban, picking up where Tiger had left off since leaving the *Sea Maiden*. She couldn't help but wonder what he was about, but she knew she needn't become too concerned. By now she had come to expect such dourness from Magnus, and knew that it was just a part of who he was. And he was protective . . . very much so. He would be quite put-out if he knew that she used the crystals without him present.

Aeris sighed and picked up the first crystal. It glowed warmly in her hand. Closing her eyes, she thought about the information she hoped to divine, and then took up the second and third crystals.

Immediately, an image surfaced in her mind. She expected to see some kind of image of the dark hooded priests she had come to know as the Daemundai. However, she saw something far different. It was dragons. There were six of them, all colored deep green and black. She had never seen the likes of these before, and she realized they must be degethozak. They were flying, and upon their backs were riders strapped within harnesses similar to the one Xebrinarth had fashioned for her mother. She couldn't get a good look at the riders' faces, but she thought that they all seemed like they were probably men. She began to feel a sense of foreboding surrounding the pairs, and she couldn't help but wonder . . .

Aeris opened her eyes and the imaged faded away. She swallowed convulsively, continuing to grip the crystals in her hands, shards made of the blood of gold and silver dragons. What the *Hells* were these dark dragons doing with riders, and why did she have this residual feeling of malcontent? A tear escaped one eye and it fell onto one of the crystals. It glowed even brighter for a moment and then settled.

Aeris slowly brought her knees up to her chest and wrapped her arms around her legs. She allowed herself to cry, her first outpouring of emotion since arriving on land. She felt helpless, despite the strength of the men with whom she had made her company. And she feared for them because she could not see how they could possible escape the might of the Daemundai and their dread master.

But it was more than that. It was the crystals she held in her hands. They were terrible things created from the life-blood of a race of beings she had come to love so much. She thought of Xebrinarth, her mother's bond-mate. His kindness was boundless, and she knew that he would always be there to protect her, just as he did Adrianna. As a child, Aeris had never borne fears of the night, for she knew that Xebrin would always be there to chase the monsters away. And Xebrin had friends, awesome friends who could be called at a moment's notice.

Aeris always knew she had a propensity for dragons . . . drawn to them much as her mother was. She was enamored by them, reading as many books as she could about them, asking Xebrinarth about his home world, and even drawing sketches of them on her parchments. Xebrin used to look over her shoulder as she drew, his head cocked, thin wisps of smoke rising from his nostrils. She remembered the amusement she saw in his eyes, and the feelings of delight that often suffused her mind.

Xebrinarth had been pleased that she chose to draw his kind, happy that she loved him so much. And now, to have the crystals in her hands, she felt that she somehow betrayed him. Yet, she couldn't help being drawn to them. The thought repelled her because she knew the suffering it took to create them. And if she didn't feel that she needed them so much, she would have discarded them over the side of Cervantes' ship long ago. But she somehow knew that they were important . . . very important. One day soon she would find out why.

***

At a table removed from the general revelry, Jaxom sat and sipped at his ale. Ordinarily he did not partake of such drink, but this evening was an exception. From his secluded spot, he watched the rest of the group. He was glad that Cervantes had taken them to a more reputable tavern. They tempted Fate at the Gritty Murg, a place where scoundrels and thugs just in from the docks went to get their first night of drink and wenches after a length of time at sea. Trog Tweila Tavern served better murg and ale, a hearty meal, and clean floors, tables, and women.

Inconspicuously, Jaxom regarded Aeris. She sat at a table with Jonesy, Tigerius, Mateo and Levander . . . watching as Goldare, Vikhail, Vardec, and Cortes played a lively round of darts. Nearby at the bar, Cervantes flirted with a serving wench. By the expression on her pretty face, Jaxom was sure that the captain would have her charmed into his bed before the end of the night.

Watching Aeris, Jaxom saw that her color was returning. She had appeared a bit pale when she met up with the rest of the group before heading over to Trog Tweila, and Tiger had asked after her welfare. She insisted she was fine, but Jaxom knew better. It felt strange being privy to information about her, and Jaxom couldn't even begin to understand what he had experienced earlier in the evening.

Jaxom had been out most of the day, simply taking in the sights and sounds of the port city. He enjoyed such excursions since he had become employed by Captain Cervantes, and he had even begun to look forward to them. He liked the bustle of the marketplace, the quietude of the temples, the ring of steel at the smithy, the brawling at the taverns, and even the strange smells of the apothecary. He knew that this made him rather unique for his kind. Most rezwithrys didn't care for such things. But Jaxomdrehl had always been different . . .

It was at the close of the day that it happened. He was making his way back to the Amber Anchor Inn, when suddenly she was in his mind. It was like a splash of icy water, the shock taking him aback. He felt his backside hit the wall of one of the buildings lining the alleyway, and he gripped his head in his hands. He felt all of Aeris' thoughts and emotions like they were his own. Foremost was a great sadness, followed by helplessness and fear. He could sense that she was crying . . . great gulping sobs that made her ribs ache. He could feel the warm wetness of tears, long tendrils of hair sticking to her face, and something clutched in her hands.

But Jaxom also felt another emotion, one underlying all of the others. And when he realized what it was, he gasped with the significance of that emotion. It was love. Because she loved the members of her company, she feared for their lives. The Daemundai were close, and she felt helpless to stop them. And she loved her family so much, she feared what would happen if she were to lose her life in her efforts to escape them.

The next realization rocked Jaxom to his core. He wouldn't have believed it if he hadn't experienced it himself . . . it was her love for dragon-kind. Aeris wasn't just crying about her hopeless situation with the Daemundai . . . and her chest wasn't aching just as a result of the strength of her sobbing. She felt like her heart was breaking.

Jaxom saw everything then . . . the information hitting him like a wave. Within her memories, he saw the visions she had been given. He saw the making of the crystals and realized it was these that she clutched in her hands as she cried. He saw the image of her mother's bond-mate . . . felt her love for him and for all dragons. He sensed her feelings of betrayal and the loss that accompanied it. She felt that she didn't deserve a friend like Xebrinarth, and that she would surely lose him forever if he knew about her predilection for the crystals.

Jaxom suddenly felt overwhelmed. As her emotions finally began to recede from his mind, he scraped against the stone until his buttocks hit the ground. It all seemed to make so much more sense to him now, why he was so drawn to her. He felt his own tears sliding down his cheeks, humbled by what he had just experienced. Aeris loved so generously and with such sincerity . . . love that went well beyond her friends and family. It extended to a whole other race of beings.

Jaxom looked up at the darkening sky, fighting to control his emotions. Despite his newfound knowledge about Aeris, he still felt the urge to fight his instincts. He wanted nothing to do with a faelin bond-mate, wanted nothing to do with the program his father had founded upon a land separate from Ansalar . . . a continent they called Thelandiron. He wanted nothing to do with that life . . . the life of a virtual outcast. Draconic society wanted little to do with those dragons with faelin bond-mates, and even though Jaxom was living outside of dragon society now, at least it was by his choosing.

Sitting at his isolated table at Trog Tweila Tavern, Jaxom brought himself back to the present. He gazed at Aeris for just a moment longer before tearing his eyes away from her. He was right to remove himself from her presence as often as he could. Without her near, it was easier to resist the temptation to do something he might regret. Jaxom picked up his mug and downed the contents. He then stood from his seat and quickly made his way out of the tavern.

***

Cervantes slowly opened his sleep bleary eyes. Something had awakened him, and he wasn't quite sure what it was. Then he heard it again, a light tapping at his door, and then the muffled whisper of a woman outside it. "Cervantes, let me in."

Cervantes forced his eyes open wider. He felt movement beside him and looked to see it was one of the serving wenches he had been seducing the night before. The weight on his other side told him that the other wench he had been seducing was there too, and he smiled with satisfaction as the memories slowly began returning to him.

The tapping became more insistent, as did the voice on the other side of the door. "Cervantes, please wake up. They are after me."

It was then that he realized that the voice was familiar and that it belonged to none other than Jezibel. By the sound of it, he could tell that she was afraid. Pulling his brows into a frown, Cervantes climbed over one of the women and left the bed. Snatching up trousers that had been discarded on the floor the night before, he pulled them up over his backside as he made his way to the door.

The moment Cervantes opened the door, Jezibel swept into the room. Raising an eyebrow, he closed the door behind her. "Cervantes, you have to help. They found me, and I don't know what to do. I'm afraid they might kill me." The last she said with a catch in her voice.

Cervantes shook his head. "Jezzie, who is after you? You aren't making any sense." He walked back over to the bed and sat upon it. From under the covers, a pair of arms circled his waist and pulled him back down. Muffled giggling could be heard, as well as some other sounds that Jezzie knew could easily lead to activities that she did not particularly wish to be privy.

Grabbing his arm, Jezibel pulled him back up. "Cervantes, I'm serious. They are already here, waiting downstairs as we speak."

Her voice had developed a pitch that he had never heard before. Cervantes regarded her for a moment, suddenly realized the tension she exuded and the fear reflected in her blue eyes. "Jezzie . . . *who* is downstairs?"

Jezibel swallowed convulsively. "Men from Gridiron."

Once again from beneath the furs, arms came to circle his waist. Cervantes laid a staying hand. "Ladies, it's time to get up."

Muffled moans could be heard. And then, "But Cervantes . . ."

But Jezibel had had enough. She flung the covers off of the girls, reached down, and grabbed one by the arm. "My dear, I am sure that Cervantes wants nothing more than to offer you the pleasure of his manhood once more, but this is important. So please . . ." Jezibel hauled the girl out of the bed, pulled her to the door, opened it, and pushed her out. Jezzie slammed the door shut behind her. By the time she made it back over to the bed, the other girl had vacated, and was standing beside it in shock. Just as with the first one, she grabbed the girl by the arm and shoved her out the door to join her comrade.

Once more, Jezibel slammed the door shut. Then she locked it. The doorknob rattled and furious exclamations could be heard outside. Then, realizing that both girls were naked, she gathered up as many clothes off the floor as she could find, reopened the door, and threw them out into the hallway. Renewed exclamations could be heard and Jezzie rolled her eyes as she closed the door for the third time.

Cervantes simply stood there, watching the interplay. This was a side to Jezibel he had never seen, and it intrigued him. Finally the girls left the vicinity of his room and Cervantes spoke into the silence. "Jezzie, why are men from Gridiron after you?" He moved to the other side of the room, adjusting his trousers and fastening his belt. He then picked up his shirt off of the foot of the bed and began to put it on. Realizing that Jezzie hadn't answered him, he looked over to her. Her expression was fearful.

A sudden thought crossed his mind and he couldn't help smiling. He knew he was making light of the situation, but he couldn't help it. She had to be over-dramatizing things. Who in their right mind would have followed her all the way from Gridiron? "What? Did you sleep with the governor and steal his money?" He chuckled at his own joke, and proceeded to button up his shirt. It was only when his statement was met with more silence that he began to feel some concern.

Looking back up at her, Cervantes' concern shifted to worry. The expression on Jezibel's face was not very assuring. "That isn't what happened . . . was it?"

Jezzie's lower lip began to tremble. "Oh Cervantes, don't be mad at me. I couldn't help it. He was young, and handsome, and newly assigned to his position. You know how attracted I am to men of authority!" Jezibel threw her hands up into the air and began to pace the room.

Cervantes strode over and grabbed her arm. "Jezzie . . . what did you do?" he growled.

"He was at the inn that night, celebrating his new assignment. He and his men started buying all of us women some drinks with the hopes of getting lucky. Well, he took a liking to me and took me up to his room. After all was said and done, I didn't think that he would connect me with the stolen gold. He was so far in his mugs, I didn't think he would even remember me. He passed out right after . . ."

Cervantes raised his hands and shook his head. "Okay, I don't need all the details," he said testily. He didn't really want to know about the interplay between this man and Jezibel. He was surprised by his possessiveness, even after so long, and it over-rode his curiosity about how well the man performed in bed.

Jezibel stopped and simply stared at him. Cervantes ruminated over the information she had provided. Finally he asked the inevitable question. "Jezzie, how much gold did you take?"

Jezibel swallowed heavily. Cervantes narrowed his eyes. He then asked the question again. "Jezibel . . . how much?" He felt his palms begin to sweat, and he knew the answer wasn't going to be to his liking.

"Eight hundred gold."

Cervantes felt his eyes widen with incredulity. He couldn't believe the number Jezibel had just spoken, and knew with certainty why the men were hunting her down. With that amount of gold a man could almost buy a small town. Almost.

"Whaaat? You must be joshing me. Jezibel, seriously, how much . . ."

Jezibel shook her head. "No Cervantes. I am telling you the truth." Her lower lip began to tremble once more. "They are going to kill me, aren't they?"

Cervantes grabbed her arm once more. "What in the Hells were you thinking, woman? Are you out of your mind? What possessed you to do such a stupid thing?"

Jezibel shook her head and tears began to fall down her cheeks.. "I don't know. All I saw was the money. I didn't think he would trace the theft back to me. I didn't even think he would remember me . . ."

"Of course he would remember you!" Cervantes spat. "Who wouldn't? I don't know a man who would forget you being in his bed."

Jezibel said nothing in response to the compliment. Cervantes simply stared at her for a moment. Was she really that naive? Of course the governor would trace the theft to her. He would remember having the gold when he got to his room that night.

"Jezibel, just hand it over. Give the gold to the governor's men, and any extra they might want for their troubles, and be done with it."

Jezibel shook her head. "I can't."

Cervantes' hand tightened around her arm. "What do you mean 'you can't'?" His voice held an edge of warning.

"I hid the gold in my own room back at another establishment in Gridiron. A thief broke into the room and stole all but two hundred gold. I used it to get myself here, and I have been working for the owner of the Gritty Murg Tavern ever since," she said.

"If you didn't think that the governor would trace the theft to you, why did you leave Gridiron?"

Jezibel shrugged. "I don't know. Maybe there was a part of me that realized the danger."

Cervantes sighed heavily, releasing her arm. He then rubbed his hands over his face. *Damn.* Eight hundred gold was a lot of money. He hated letting go of that much hard-earned gold, but he would do it for his Jezibel.

"Okay, Jezibel. I will give you the money." The moment he spoke those words he could see her visibly relax. "Just give me a chance to finish getting dressed so I can go get it."

Jezibel's expression suddenly became concerned. "You don't have it with you?"

Cervantes chuckled. "Only a fool carries that much gold. Of course I don't have it on me. I have it hidden on the *Sea Maiden.*"

Jezibel shook her head. "No no no. You don't understand. They want the money *now*. Once they have me in custody, they might not wait that long. Please Cervantes, don't let them have me." Jezibel's voice caught again.

"Hush, hush." Cervantes soothed her, enfolding her in his arms. "I'll not let them have you. I will ask my comrades if they have the gold amongst them and then reimburse them once I get back to the ship later today."

"Are you certain they will let you have the gold?" Jezzie sniffed."

Cervantes chuckled again. "Of course I'm sure. Besides, I will be paying them right back. Don't you worry about it."

Cervantes rubbed Jezzie's back reassuringly. The only one he worried about was Magnus, but the man would do anything Aeris asked him to do. Magnus was ever a thorn in his side, but surely the man would see reason and let Cervantes have the money until he could compensate everyone for their losses . . . once he obtained his gold from the *Sea Maiden*.

***

Jonesy awoke late in the morning. Once out of bed, she washed her face and hands at the wash-basin and then donned her tunic and trousers. As she combed her hair, she wondered why Aeris didn't wake her earlier. She shook her head in mild consternation and finally left the room. Jonesy was about to make her way down the stairs when there was a sudden disturbance outside one of the rooms down the hall. It didn't take long for her to recall that the room belonged to Cervantes.

Jonesy stopped and simply stared at the commotion taking place. Outside of the closed door there were two young women, both wearing not a stitch of clothing. Neither could have been any much older than she. They shouted obscenities at the closed door, and when it opened to reveal another woman's arm, tossing clothing out into the hallway, Jonesy inhaled sharply. What in the Hells was going on?

The girls muttered to themselves as they gathered up the scattered clothing. They noticed Jonesy standing at the top of the stairs and stopped to regard her disdainfully. "What are you staring at?" one of them spat haughtily.

Jonesy only shrugged. "Just a couple of whores scampering around for their rags out in the hallway," she replied.

The girls sneered scornfully and stalked away in the opposite direction. Jonesy stared after them for a moment, and then regarded Cervantes' closed door. By the gods, she wouldn't have believed it if she hadn't seen it for herself. Captain Cervantes was very much the man he claimed to be . . . a mercenary and a womanizer. Of course, he hadn't said it in that many words, but she caught the general gist.

Jonesy felt her heart ache at the realization. She shook her head at her own stupidity and began to make her way down the stairs. She just needed to understand that Cervantes was nothing but a scoundrel, undeserving of anything she might have been able to offer him. And it was just as well, she being the daughter of an inland king, and he being a seafaring rogue. Their lives were too disparate . . . what could they possibly have offered one another?

Jonesy stepped off of the stairs and walked into the common room. It was only then that she noticed anything amiss. Several armed men stood at the bar looking out across the common room. Jonesy's breath caught in her throat, and every instinct bade her turn and run. Their livery was maroon and forest green . . . the same colors as those worn by her father's men back in Karlisle. But then she saw the insignia and her senses came back into focus. The crest was different, as was the lining of the men's cloaks. It was silver instead of Karlisle gold.

Gathering her composure, Jonesy glanced quickly around the room. Several patrons seated haphazardly around the area, each breaking his or her fast. Magnus and Aeris sat closest to the bar. She saw none of the others of their group in the room. Vikhail, Vardec and Goldare were probably still sleeping off the effects of the murg and ale they imbibed the evening before. Unfortunately, she also knew how Cervantes was occupying his time.

The leader of the men looked carefully around the room. "We are here to take into our custody a woman by the name of Jezibel Pyratt. She is a criminal and we have been charged to bring her back to the city of Gridiron for sentencing. Anyone found to be keeping information about her or harboring her in any way will be dealt with by the full extent of Gridiron laws. Sources here in Darban have led us to this inn, so we know that she is here."

The room was silent for a moment. Then, "Why are you looking for her? What crime did she commit?" asked the barkeep.

The leader turned to face him. "She is wanted for stealing from the governor of Gridiron. We are here under his service to either bring her back to him, or the gold she stole. Have you seen this woman?"

The barkeep raised his hands and shook his head. "No, my lord. I just wanted to know the severity of the crime that brings you so far from Gridiron."

The leader drew his brows together into a frown. "She stole *a lot* of gold." He emphasized the words with a growl in his voice.

Jonesy chose that moment to enter the common room. The leader's eyes were instantly drawn to her, and with the flip of his hand, two of the men were striding purposefully in her direction. Jonesy stopped in her tracks, suddenly frightened by the hostility of the men approaching her. She timidly stood her ground until they reached her side.

It was then that the front door of the common room swung open. As another two patrons stepped into the establishment, the men from Gridiron were rushing to detain them. The area was suddenly alive with a flurry of activity. Aeris and Magnus were quickly making their way over to Jonesy, followed by the leader of the men from Gridiron. He reached her just as Magnus and Aeris did. "We are here looking for a woman by the name of Jezibel Pyratt. What might you know of her?"

Jonesy hesitated for only a moment before shaking her head. She didn't like Jezibel, but it was for entirely selfish reasons. As a woman on the run herself, she knew she would never knowingly condemn another to a fate she could only imagine might one day be hers to face.

Magnus maneuvered himself into a more protective stance beside Jonesy, Aeris' hand held tightly within his. "You are quite far from home to hunt down a woman merely for stealing. What more could she possibly have done to deserve this much man-power out looking for her?"

The leader's eyes narrowed as he regarded Magnus. "Like I said, she stole a large sum of gold from the governor of Gridiron. He would like to have it returned to him." The leader paused before continuing. "Where is she?"

Magnus cocked his head and chose his words carefully. "I didn't say I knew her. I was simply asking a question, my lord."

The leader's eyes flashed dangerously. "She is a thief and a whore. She must either be brought back to Gridiron to stand before the governor for her crime against him, or return to us what she stole so that we may return it to him. Now I say again . . . *where is she?*"

Magnus opened his mouth to make a reply when they heard a commotion behind them. The group turned to see Vikhail, Vardec, Goldare, and Tigerius descending the stairway, the halfen brothers laughing raucously at something one of the others must have said. The leader shouted to his men, and as the foursome stepped off of the staircase they were surrounded.

"Do you men know the whereabouts of Jezibel Pyratt?"

The four glanced at one another in confusion. Jonesy held her breath, hoping that none recalled Jezibel's face or name. She found herself counting on the fact that her comrades had been too far in their mugs the night Cervantes introduced Jezibel to them that they wouldn't remember anything about her.

Finally, all four shook their heads in the negative. The leader looked from one man to the other, taking in their bloodshot eyes and pale complexions. Jonesy could sense his frustration and wondered if she imagined the slight rolling of his eyes skyward. He and his men stepped aside to allow Tiger, Goldare, and the halfen to pass and then faced the common room once more.

The leader raised his hands and his voice rose above all others. "From this point onward, no one may leave or enter this establishment until Jezibel Pyratt is found. Someone had best step forward and inform me of her whereabouts right now, or my men will tear this place apart in our search of her. Am I making myself clear?"

Jonesy swallowed nervously, watched his eyes pop out of his face as he spoke his last words. The leader wasn't joking around and she was loathe to find out if he would actually carry through with his threat. It was then that she heard Cervantes' voice from behind her.

"She is right here, so stop your shouting." Cervantes and Dramid stepped into the common room followed by Jezibel. As the men from Gridiron began to rush the threesome, Cervantes pulled out his crossbow and Dramid his cutlass.

The leader chuckled as the Gridiron men slowed. "Drop your weapons now. You don't have a chance for you are severely outnumbered. We could have you down within moments."

Cervantes and Dramid stoically held their position. The leader raised his hand to bid his men proceed towards their quarry when there emerged another voice from the staircase. "I wouldn't do that if I were you."

Jonesy almost smiled when she heard Levander's voice. She turned to look towards the stairway and saw him standing with his elbow resting over the railing. In the crook of his arm rested a small metallic device that looked like a tiny crossbow. He had it trained on the leader.

Levander spoke again in a calm and concise voice. "I assure you it is fully loaded. I can fire five zivets before your men even began to lift their weapons to my comrades. I advise you to rethink your next move."

The leader's complexion had visibly paled. He pursed his lips into a thin line, and with barely a nod his men lowered their weapons. Cervantes and Dramid followed suit, trusting that Lev would keep the situation under control.

"I am aware of why you men are here and I am prepared to give what you want. All I ask is for a few moments of time so that I may confer with my companions," said Cervantes.

The leader hesitated. The tension in the room was high, and Jonesy knew it would take very little for the situation to take a very bad turn. He was suspicious of Cervantes and didn't want to see his prey get away. Finally the man gave a wary nod. Cervantes glanced around the common room, gesturing for everyone to join him on the far side away from the men from Gridirion.

Once everyone was together, Magnus was the first to speak. "Captain, what the Hells is going on?"

Cervantes shook his head. "Listen, there isn't a lot of time for me to explain everything to you. But just know that my friend is in a lot of trouble and has asked for my help. As it happens to turn out, most of my gold is stashed on the *Sea Maiden*. I have every intention of getting it; however, it seems that these men might do Jezzie some harm in the meanwhile." Cervantes paused and looked around the group. "I ask you this favor as a friend. Please give me the gold to pay these men off, and when the deal is done, we will immediately go to the *Sea Maiden* so that I can reimburse you for your losses."

Magnus frowned. "How much gold do we need?"

Cervantes sighed. "At least a thousand. These men won't be happy simply with the eight hundred taken from the governor. They will want restitution for the efforts they have gone through to find Jezibel."

Tigerius almost choked. "That is a lot of gold, my friend."

"If each of us puts all he has to the cause, we might have just enough," said Goldare.

The halfen brothers were the first to put their gold on the table, followed by Goldare, Dramid, Tigerius, Jonesy, Magnus, and Aeris. Digging into his own belt pouch, Cervantes added his own money to the mix. In the end, they had just over the thousand gold they needed. Cervantes swept all of the gold into a single large pouch and turned back to the men from Gridiron. They had stood silently by, carefully watching the group to be sure no plans were made to stage a coup and flee the establishment. Cervantes presented the gold to the leader. Feeling the weight of the bag, and then peering inside, he nodded with satisfaction as he realized all the gold promised lay within. Raising his hand for his men to follow, he promptly left the establishment.

The common room was silent for a moment after the men left. Lev stepped down from the stairs and approached them, tucking his weapon into the folds of his clothing. Cortes then walked through the front door of the inn and ignorantly waved them a good morning. Cervantes turned to his companions and grinned. "Now on to the *Sea Maiden*!"

***

Cervantes Conradi could hardly remember a time that he didn't know the story. His uncle had told him about Cortes, the brother that gave Cervantes so much pleasure, yet so much more pain. Cervantes knew that Rohan had wanted to keep the truth from him, hoping to protect him. But by the time Cervantes had suffered his third beating on behalf of his bastard brother, Rohan had seen fit to bequeath the painful truth to his sister's son, despite the agony it might bring.

By the time that Cervantes was of age, Penelope had been long gone. Cervantes recalled his mother only in the vaguest of memories, a sweet face framed by the darkest of brown hair. Somehow, he remembered even the sound of her voice . . . but only within the deepest of his dreams where the harshness of reality could never go. The only real mother he remembered was Isomalade, the woman who was Rohan's wife. She had been good to both himself and Cortes, and Cervantes couldn't have asked for anything more.

Yet, it didn't take someone very smart to notice that his younger brother was much different than any of the other boys. Cortes was a bit large, much larger than Cervantes despite the two years seniority, and his appearance was much different from that of anyone else. His body hair was much more thick and proliferative, and his canines a bit longer. At first, it made him simply an outcast from the other boys, but when they discovered that Cortes was a push-over, despite his size, they teased him mercilessly. And only the diminutive Cervantes was there to champion him.

So Rohan told his son the terrible truth; his mother had been abducted by an oroc raiding party and raped by the males in the troupe. She had barely survived her escape. Even before the labor pains started, Penelope somehow knew she would die during the birth of the child conceived during her captivity. She beseeched her brother to care for both her children as though they were his own, for the baby was simply the innocent byproduct of a corrupt union and didn't deserve to be rejected. Despite the parentage of the younger child, Isomalade embraced the responsibility. She loved children and had been unable to produce any of her own.

After that, Cervantes never looked at Cortes the same way again. Yet, nothing really changed between them. Cervantes loved his brother as he always had, tempered only by knowledge and understanding . . . even after knowing that it was Cortes' birth that brought about his mother's death. What made it all so easy was that Cervantes knew how much he was loved by his brother; it was all that really mattered. And when Cervantes grew into a man and walked in the footsteps of their uncle, becoming a corsair in his own right, he could always feel the affection of Cortes, no matter how far he roamed . . .

CHAPTER 17

The group disconsolately rode out of the city of Darban. Spirits were low, and no one spoke, each simply following the others in single file. Even the horses had adopted the prevalent morose attitude. They hung their heads as they slowly walked through the gates and into the waiting countryside, the air coming from their nostrils pluming into the cold air.

Aeris inconspicuously glanced at each of her companions. Directly ahead of her rode Mateo. She could tell that he felt somewhat responsible for the events that had taken place the day before, despite her telling him that it couldn't possibly be his fault. After handing all their gold over to the men from Gridiron, the group had made their way to the docks. They had almost made it there when they saw Mateo stumbling up the street towards them. He had been badly beaten . . . one eye was swollen shut, his upper lip badly cut, and his nose broken. His hair was matted to one side of his head, testimony of a head injury. People regarded him sadly as he passed, and one man even reached out to try to catch him as he fell.

Aeris was suffused with guilt as the group rushed over to the beaten boy. She had not stopped to wonder of Mateo's whereabouts that morning before their episode with the men from Gridiron, nor did she consider him as they made their way to Cervantes' ship. Truth be told, she had completely forgotten about him. Once reaching Mateo, Lev easily picked the boy up and began to carry him back in the direction of the inn. Aeris and Magnus followed, waving for the others to proceed to the docks with Cervantes.

It wasn't much later before Vikhail and Vardec were rushing into Mateo's room back at the inn. Lev had seen to the boy's injuries as soon as they arrived, and Aeris had tried to help where she could. She immediately knew something was wrong by the expressions on the halfen's faces, but was still stunned when she heard the news: Cervantes ship had been stolen during the night. Everything that had been left on the *Sea Maiden* was gone.

Cervantes was in a rage. Aeris had never seen him like that before. He was a crazy man, accosting everyone who came to the docks. He asked if anyone saw the thieves who had taken his ship, despite knowing the truth in the gut of his stomach. It was Simon, Gervais, and Marion . . . the very men he had trusted with his life out at sea.

Cervantes would surely have killed the dock-master if Cortes had not been there to stop him. The other man pleaded ignorance to the fact that the ship had been stolen right under his very nose, and Aeris couldn't help but believe him. He had been confounded when Cervantes rushed into the dock cabin that morning, for he thought the captain of the *Sea Maiden* had simply broken protocol and sailed out with the dawn. Upon questioning, the master remembered very little of the evening and early morning. He denied having drunk any spirits or smoked any herbs that may have hindered his ability to perform his duty. Aeris smelled nothing on him and was wont to believe the man despite the fact that he seemed strangely dazed.

For the remainder of the day, Cervantes was unapproachable. The group was left to make preparations without him, for they knew they could not remain much longer in Darban, especially in the wake of Aeris' information about the approach of the Daemundai. Magnus was perturbed to discover that she had used the crystals without him, and after the events that had taken place already that day, this only served to fuel anger he felt already. Aeris almost expected him to shout at her for her foolishness, but he simply turned away and ignored her.

With his savings in gold, Cortes bought the horses and other basic provisions they would need in their travels. They had decided to ride north to Gulshaan, for it was the largest city in eastern Ansalar. It also happened to be home to one of the largest libraries in Shandahar, holding the most complete collection of literary and historical archives. There, Aeris and Magnus hoped to learn more about the crystals and the dark orb now in their possession.

Now, with nothing but the clothing they wore, winter cloaks, travel packs, meager food rations, and horses, they began their journey north across the plains comprising the Tanze Peninsula. Aeris' gaze moved to the man that rode beside her. It was Tigerius, his eyes fixed on the boy that rode before them. Aeris only vaguely remembered her opinion of Tiger before their adventure started . . . haughty and imprudent. However, it seemed that she was wrong, for he had turned out to be a good friend and staunch ally. He could still sometimes appear to be a thoughtless scoundrel, but she knew better. And she found that she rather liked that.

It was obvious that Tiger cared about the boy that had come to be placed within their custody. It was often that Aeris noticed him looking out for Mateo, always asking of his whereabouts and generally concerned about his general well-being. It was the same with Goldare and the two halfen, they having taken Mateo under their sturdy wings. Aeris did not always agree with their principals, but she would manage. Mateo needed the male influence they offered, and Aeris would not begrudge him that.

But much as she found herself wondering about Tiger, she thought about Jaxom as well. She had once thought she found a friend in him, especially after the experience they shared discovering the fallen bird. But since then, Jaxom had avoided her like a sickness he hoped never to contract. At first she had been stung by his attitude towards her, but now she felt only remorse. It must have been something she did to push him away despite her efforts to the contrary.

Aeris finally settled her gaze onto Cervantes. He had changed since discovering the theft of the *Sea Maiden*, and it wasn't for the better. She could sense a recklessness about him, a volatility that she feared could somehow influence the welfare of the group. He was like a loaded crossbow, ready to discharge at any moment and at any provocation. She wanted to keep her faith in him, but she would just have to gage his behavior over the next several days to see if she could continue to trust in his abilities.

Suddenly feeling the sensation that she was being watched, Aeris turned to find Magnus gazing at her intently. His expression was brooding as he regarded her, and she couldn't help but feel disconcerted by the weight of his stare. She then looked down at the withers of the beast she rode, hoping to evade him. She found herself doing a lot of that lately, wondering what he was thinking about her to make him glance in her direction so often. She wondered if it was something she was doing that garnered so much attention, or perhaps something she was wearing. She even took a look at herself in a looking glass the day before last, thinking perhaps she had a blemish on her face.

But there was nothing about her that Aeris could find that might be different. Except perhaps for the bronzing of her skin that seemed to have taken place during their stay on an island far south of the mainland they now found themselves traversing. Taking a chance, Aeris peered back up in his direction, hoping Magnus' attention had been diverted elsewhere. But to her consternation, she found him still watching her. Upon seeing her shy glance, the corner of his mouth pulled up into a grin. Flooded with embarrassment, Aeris looked away from him once more. What in the Hells was he doing? She shook her head to herself, allowing a smile of her own to creep onto her face. Sometimes Magnus could still surprise her, despite all they had been through.

Magnus continued to watch Aeris. He couldn't keep the smile from his face; she was such an enchanting creature. Aboard the *Sea Maiden*, he had kept many of his emotions at bay. But now that they were back on land, and he felt some semblance of control over his life, Magnus felt his feelings for Aeris once more coming to the forefront of his mind. Not that he had forgotten them whilst they were at sea . . . quite the contrary. He had simply found it easier to keep them in check.

Magnus continued to watch Aeris long after she turned away and focused her attention elsewhere. Now that they were land-bound once more, the desire to see her safely to Elvandahar was paramount to him. He knew that her family must be very worried about her, and he felt failure in his duty to bring Aeris home in a timely manner. Yet, they still continued to be tracked by the Daemundai, and his mind continued to return to the cimmerean woman who had accosted them on their journey from Xordrel to Yortec. What had she truly wanted from them? She toyed with him and subsequently left him to ponder the events that had just taken place. He accused Aeris of being Tholana's accomplice, and he later regretted his hasty decision to make Aeris his prisoner. But now it seemed that the young woman had forgiven him this transgression . . .

Magnus finally looked away from Aeris. His gaze skimmed over the rest of the group, and he noticed that another member of their party watched her. Magnus had noticed Jaxom's interest in Aeris before, and he could not help but wonder about the other man's intentions. As of yet, Magnus had not seen him make any advances towards her, and he wondered what Jaxom was about. Regardless, Magnus would keep an eye on the man. There had to be some reason why he was interested in her.

***

Travel-weary, the group wandered into the city of Gulshaan. The horses walked with lowered heads, their hooves barely disturbing the dusty street. Everyone was hungry, for they had eaten all of what remained of the travel rations the day before. They had used them sparingly, for they had not the gold to buy more, nor had they even a decent hunter amongst the lot of them, especially in this cold. Goldare was the best; however, it was obvious that archery was not his profession. It had been easy enough for Lev to find edible plants and roots, yet it did not replace the meat. Everyone was a bit smaller now than they were when they left Darban, and that thought weighed heavily upon Magnus' mind.

The cimmerean turned to look behind him. The rest of the group trailed haphazardly behind. They needed to decide what course of action they would take next, for they had not the gold to secure lodging, not to mention that much needed meal. After a few moments more, Magnus guided his horse down a side-street and then stopped and dismounted. The others followed, and finally all of them had congregated there. Magnus looked from one face to the next, sensing the fatigue in all of his comrades.

"We have to decide what we are going to do. We have made it here, but we have no gold. Cervantes, do you know anyone who might offer us lodging for a night or two?" Magnus could only hope the answer to be in the affirmative.

The man ran a hand over his unshaven face and then brought it to the back of his neck to rub at the sore muscles there. He shook his head. "I don't know. My cousins move around so much, I can't be certain that they are still here."

Cortes only nodded in agreement while the rest of the group glanced at one another disconsolately. It was only a moment later when Tigerius spoke up. "I will get us some gold. It might not be very much, but at least enough for some fresh fruit and bread."

Magnus narrowed his eyes as he swept them over the other man. He had always suspected that Tiger was capable of being a good pick-pocket, especially when the man convinced Aeris of his ability to heist one of the crystals from Cervantes' ship. Magnus watched as she turned towards her friend.

"Tigerius, I don't like you going out and stealing peoples' purses. It makes me nervous. What if you get caught?"

Tiger turned his lips up into a grin. "So you *do* care about me. I have been wondering all this time . . ."

"Shut your face," Aeris replied. "I need an escort home, remember? I might not make it without you."

Despite the lighthearted nature of the banter, Magnus felt stung. He thought that Aeris had come to trust him during their last few weeks together. Now he realized that might not be the case.

Tigerius' grin widened. "Come now, my lady. I know the *real* reason behind your concern."

Aeris sniffed in mock disdain. "Don't give yourself airs. You are an indiscriminate rake. How could you ever think that I could fall for you?"

Tigerius stepped up to her and brought his face close to hers. "You can't help it. I am so debonair; you can't keep your thoughts away from me. Confess . . . you are in *love* with me, Damaeris Elora Timberlyn."

Aeris grinned, put one hand upon his shoulder and the other at her forehead. "Why Tigerius, how is it that you can read my mind so well? I could just swoon at your feet this very instant. Please, take me in your arms now before I fall."

Very dramatically, Tigerius swept his arms around Aeris' slender waist. Magnus watched the interplay with stoic indifference. Glancing around, he saw that the show put smiles on the faces of the rest of the group. They were good . . . very good. It was selfless for them to put on such a display solely for the benefit of the others in their band. However, Magnus could not help the emotions that welled up inside of him. He could only wish that it were he that held Aeris within his arms.

"My lady, I must depart in order to carry out my duty. Kiss me now before I go. It will remain with me as I perform my crimes against society, pull me up when I am down, and carry me upon wings of haste should I be discovered."

Unhesitatingly, Aeris pressed her lips against Tigerius'. Magnus could sense the sudden tension of the man's body, his response to her more than just cursory. When they parted, Magnus saw the effect it had upon Tiger. "I still bid you not to go. I wish you to stay at my side and decide upon another way to obtain that which we need."

Tigerius released an explosive sigh and Magnus frowned, disliking the turn that events had taken. A moment later, Cervantes chuckled and the two looked towards him. "Damn. That was good. For a moment, you two had me going."

Jonesy gripped Aeris' arm. "I know how we can get the gold!" She was so full of excitement that she could barely contain herself.

Aeris frowned in pretend anger. "You better not be on his side. I forbid it."

Jonesy shook her head. "I can't believe I never thought of it before. We will *work* for our gold."

Goldare shook his head, knowing where the conversation was going. "We aren't like you, Jonesy. None of us possess the abilities that you have at your disposal."

Jonesy stared at his from wide eyes. "I beg to differ. The performance I just heard was great. With my voice and their drama, I think we could get a job at one of the inns."

Cervantes stepped forward. "Hey, I have a pretty decent voice myself. Maybe we can do something together."

Jonesy nodded and then gestured towards Magnus. "I know that this one can dance. I bet we can think of some kind of performance for him as well."

Tigerius suddenly snapped his fingers and grinned widely. He turned towards Aeris, who was suddenly shaking her head in denial. "Yes, I seem to remember seeing a display of Magnus' skill. Aeris has much experience as well."

"I don't think so," began Aeris. "Magnus is a much better dancer than I am. I bet . . ."

Tiger shook his head. "No. I remember that night in Grunchin. You two were great together. It would be a wonderful performance. With Jonesy's voice, it could be magnificent."

Aeris shook her head. "I don't know . . ."

Tiger interrupted. "Well, it looks like I will be stealing coin purses, then." He turned as though to walk away when Aeris grabbed his arm.

"Wait. Maybe you are right. Perhaps we should do it." She looked up at Magnus to find his gaze already settled upon her, watching her intently.

"Well, then. What are we waiting for? Let's find an inn that will have us," said Cervantes.

Jonesy only smiled with triumph.

***

Xebrinarth walked down one of the main corridors of the Medubrokan Academy. He made his way to the lanai, for he knew his friend liked to sun himself there. Many times it had been Xebrin's favored spot as well, but he was glad to relinquish it to Pylarith when he came to stay with them in Elvandahar. He had thought about simply communicating with his friend telepathically, but Xebrin rather liked the mundane and decided to hunt Pylar down by foot.

Xebrinarth opened the door that led out onto the spacious veranda. And just as he thought, Pylar was there, his vibrantly crimson form stretched out as long as it could, his tail curved loosely about the balustrade. A smile momentarily turned up the corners of Xebrin's mouth, for it was good to see the older dragon relaxing himself. Yet, the pleasure was soon gone. He had disturbing news to share with Pylar, and it was nothing to grin about. Only then did Xebrinarth reached out to Pylar with his mind. Immediately the other dragon was at mental alertness, raising his head and turning towards him.

Via the connection, Pylar could sense that Xebrin had serious business to discuss. He wondered at the nature of it, but did not choose to extend a probe to his friend's mind. It was discourteous, and usually reserved for times when two dragons could not speak face-to-face. Pylar was anxious to hear about the information that Xebrin had to impart, but he could practice patience. He would wait and give Xebrin a chance to tell him what weighed upon his mind.

The rogue degethozak are moving closer to Elvandahar. Already they have attacked southern cities in the realm of Karlisle said Xebrin.

Pylar sighed. He had rather hoped that these renegade degethozak would give up their fool's mission and cease the wanton violence. He didn't know what had initially spurned the attacks, but nothing that humans or faelin could have done deserved the destruction that had been wrought.

*But that is not all. It isn't just dragons that are participating in the attacks. There are humans as well. *And they are riding astride the degethozak.*

Pylar reared his head back in astonishment. Through the open link, Xebrin could sense Pylar's mystification. He grappled with the idea of a man riding astride a dragon, wondered why it would be done and the implications of such a thing. Xebrin immediately shielded himself to his friend. Too many times had Adrianna ridden upon his back, not to mention that they both enjoyed the experience. He now knew that Pylar would never understand . . . that he and his own bond-mate did not have the same type of relationship as Xebrin did with Adria. He could sense that Pylar thought the act of a rider sitting astride a dragon as rather shameful, and Xebrin did not wish to be less in his eyes.

By the gods . . . I can't believe the degethozak have allowed it. Pylar became pensive. *It seems we have entered a new era . . . dragon-riders. I never thought I would live to see the day . . .*

Xebrin stood quietly by. He was glad that Pylar was so distracted. This way, he would not sense that Xebrin was hiding something from him. Yet, the magnitude of their situation weighed heavier than Pylar's opinion of him. Pylar was right . . . they had entered an era where humans and dragons were combining their efforts for a shared cause. And that cause happened to be one driven by Razlul and the Daemundai.

All of Elvandahar is concerned. The Silverwood will be an easy target, despite what magicks reside within. This is unprecedented, and no one knows what to think.

We need to muster a defense said Pylar. *What about your friends, Saranath and Mordrexith? Could they help?*

Xebrin shook his head. *I don't know. They have others that rely heavily upon them for their livelihood.*

Pylar nodded. *Oh yes. I didn't intend to forget the younglings. Might I offer my apologies?*

Xebrin shook his head. *None are needed my friend. These are hard times. It is natural to try and think of any aid that might be possible.*

Pylar nodded and was silent for a moment. *Perhaps we should attempt to waylay them . . . divert them from their path to Elvandahar. Maybe we will be able to make enough of an impression to keep them away . . . at least for a while.*

Xebrin nodded in agreement. It wasn't the best strategy, but at least it was something. Maybe it would give Adria and Dinim more time to figure out what to do in the interim. Or perhaps Elvandahar and Karlisle would be reconciled enough to work together against this new menace.

We will make our way to the southern swath of the Denegal River tomorrow said Pylar.

Once more Xebrin nodded. He then shifted into dragon form, and he lay next to Pylar on the lanai. At least they would rest well until the morrow. He wouldn't divulge his intentions to his bond-mate until he was ready to depart. He knew how Adrianna was about such things, and she would try to keep him from going. He would have more resolve if she didn't have so much time to dissuade him. Curled loosely about one another, the two friends slept in the sun. They would conserve their strength until they needed it most.

***

The audience was silent as Aeris positioned herself upon the stage. Nervously, she glanced around. She had never done anything quite like this before, and she felt vulnerable. She heard the musicians begin the melody to which she was to begin her dance, and she felt suddenly overwhelmed. She was not an entertainer. She hadn't even been able to practice the dance before putting herself on a stage with over a hundred people staring at her.

It was at the third inn they visited that the group received a chance to show someone the skill they could bring to the stage. The decision was ultimately up to the owner of the establishment and the group of musicians who played there on a regular basis. Watching Aeris dance, followed by Magnus, they agreed that a performance could be developed. Then, hearing Jonesy's singing voice, as well as Cervantes', a bargain was struck. The group would perform at the Falcon's Crest Inn for the remainder of the week. If they did well, they could stay as long as they liked.

Aeris suddenly felt herself freeze. Her throat closed up, and she was afraid she wouldn't be able to breathe. The music was familiar, as were the voices of Jonesy and Cervantes. Hells and damnation . . . she couldn't believe that the captain had such a strong, resonant voice. But then again, he probably couldn't believe that she could dance like the gypsies . . .

Forcing herself to move, Aeris began to dance. She moved slowly, endeavoring to make her steps in sync with the music. Her dark green gown swirled against her legs as she moved . . . an old one that had been bought cheaply and modified to capture the attention of an upper-class audience. The reactions of her comrades to her attire had been of astonishment, and it only served to make her feel self-conscious. The dress was low-cut, displaying the tops of her breasts, and the slits up the sides showed most of her legs. She hated to leave so much of her body exposed, but she reminded herself that it was for her livelihood that she did it. Then she remembered what she wore in the heat of a jungle located on an island far to the south. She gave a mental shrug and let the issue go . . . it simply didn't matter anymore.

Within a few moments, Magnus was joining her on the stage. Apprehensively, she watched him approach, taking in the tightly fit trousers and finely woven shirt lent to him by one of the musicians who played in the background. She was acutely aware that she would be forced into close proximity to him, a situation she had been trying to avoid for as long as he had been hired as her escort. Yet, now it was inevitable. She was no longer in a position to make choices based upon her feelings alone, and she had to act in the best interests of the group.

Stepping up to Aeris, Magnus grasped her hand lightly within his, and then put his other hand at her waist. He could feel the stiffness of her body, and looking upon her face saw an expression of grim determination. Her eyelids had been outlined with kohl and her lips painted. The contrast made her complexion appear paler than usual, but he knew that it probably had much to do with her unusual situation as well. Magnus was aware of her reluctance to perform the dance, and that she felt trapped into doing it. She had set aside her personal reservations and agreed to do it for the sake of her friends. Magnus admired her for that.

Magnus took the lead and Aeris promptly followed suit. By the gods, he had prayed for this moment, the time when she would be in his arms once again. As the mesmerizing gypsy music infiltrated his mind, he studied the profile of her averted face. It was a face that haunted him in his deepest dreams . . . dreams tied to a larian that would never tire. Aeris turned in his arms, creating an arc of energy between them. He knew she could feel it, for she inadvertently grasped his hand more tightly. It was the way she moved in the logic of all those dreams, and no perfume had ever tortured him more . . . A fire burned deep within him, the flames playing in the shade of his desire. He could only dream of loving her . . . and he struggled to stop Time from slipping away between his fingers.

With the slow seductive movements dictated by the gypsy dance, Aeris moved against him. Her sweet scent was intoxicating, and he fought to restrain himself. Suddenly, Magnus gripped Aeris about the waist and pulled her into him. She adjusted herself to the shift in movement, realigning her body against his in order to maintain the steps of the complex dance. Magnus lowered his face to the curve of her neck, deeply inhaling her fragrance. She was like a desert arzahalia, the most aromatic of the flowers that blossomed upon the western side of the continent.

In response to his cue, Aeris turned back towards him. She glanced up at Magnus with wide questioning eyes, wondering why he had altered the structure of their dance. It was the first time she had really looked at him since he approached her upon stage. He caught her gaze and held it. Despite her attempts, Aeris could not dispel what had arisen between them. She felt it just as strongly as he, only she was much better at escaping from it.

Magnus continued with the dance, hoping it would please the audience. Meanwhile, he treated Aeris to his caress, resolute in his decision to seduce her. He saw her eyes close as he slowly lowered his face to the curve of her neck once more. He brushed his lips against her flesh, and he felt her body tense with his gentle touch.

Aeris couldn't believe that he was doing this to her. Not only had Magnus altered the dance they had agreed upon, but he continued to torment her with his touch. First it was his hands, and now it was his mouth. She could feel the warmth of his breath against her neck, and she felt herself exposing it to give him easier access. By the gods, what was she doing? What was Magnus doing?

Aeris felt herself giving in to the moment. How much would it hurt if she succumbed just this one time? Besides, it was just a dance, performed for the benefit of those who paid for such entertainment. Why not endeavor to make it all she could?

With her fresh attitude towards the circumstances, Aeris decided to plunge herself into the finer nuances of the dance. She would play with Magnus at his game. She slid her hand down his chest and then onto his hip until it finally rested upon the hand that held her waist. Placing her hand atop his, she eased his hand from her waist to her backside.

Aeris suddenly felt a sudden exhale at her neck, the warm breath washing over her over-sensitized skin. She grinned to herself . . . realizing that she may be able to beat him at his own game. But then she felt herself tensing yet again, for he never ceased to amaze her. She felt his lips replacing the warm breath, and tiny quivers of anticipation fluttered through her belly. By the gods, he was kissing her . . .

Aeris spun out of Magnus' reach, more out of a desire to escape him than to follow the dictation of the dance. However, it was only moments later that she was back within the circle of his embrace. Locking his gaze to hers, he didn't bother to rest his hand at her waist this time, but immediately placed it at the curve of her buttocks. Following his lead, she increased the intensity of the dance, melding her body to his as she moved. She caressed the side of his face before sweeping her hand through his hair, and when he moved a hand from her hip, over the mound of her breast, and up to her face, she felt her heart beat faster in her chest.

Magnus prepared for the finale of the dance. He hated for it to end, but he knew that all good things must. He felt a tightening in his loins as Aeris ran a light hand down his back and over the curve of his rear, circling to rest at his hip for a moment before quickly coming up to grasp his hands. She then spun away from him once again and returned only to complete the end of the dance. She leaped towards him, and he caught her about the waist, lifting her high before lowering her once more. She wrapped her arms about his neck as her feet settled onto the floor, and she arched herself backwards. Magnus supported her at the waist as she performed the maneuver, curving his body over hers. Then, as she slowly began to straighten, Magnus pulled her into him, placing his lips at her throat. He kissed her most sensitive place, and when she had enough leverage to support herself, he awaited her response.

Aeris bared her throat to him, reveling in the sensations his kiss elicited. She felt the naked emotion emanating from him, knew that it was more than just his desire to give a good performance. She wondered how far they should go with it as she brought her head forward, and when she felt his lips suddenly closing over hers, she felt her body startle.

Aeris opened herself up to the kiss as her body completed the last steps of the dance. It was briefer than she hoped it would be, for he ended it once the dance was complete. To her, it was only the barest hint of a caress, and when it was over, he trailed his lips across her jaw to settle behind her ear. Aeris suddenly heard the applause of the crowd, forced herself out of her reverie to turn away from him and towards the audience. The adulation was more than she could have ever expected, more than she could ever dream. Now she understood why Jonesy spoke the way she did when she described the emotion she felt when they applauded after her performances.

Aeris bowed to the audience, and taking hold of her hand, Magnus followed suit. She felt the power of his grip, somehow knew by the way that he grasped her hand that he was restraining himself. She could feel the passion emanating from him . . . passion for her. She felt tears spring to her eyes and they coursed down her face, unchecked. It didn't matter how desperately she fought to keep herself from him . . . nor for how long. Despite her vague memories of another, she knew that she was in love with Magnus. Now she only regretted that she had not allowed herself to come to the conclusion sooner.

Aeris breathed deeply and bowed once more to the assembly. No longer did she care about a man she could only remember in her deepest dreams. No longer did she wait for a man who seemed to have no intention of coming for her. There was another who was right there before her, one with whom she had shared the most extraordinary of adventures, one whom she had told many of her greatest fears and most profound dreams. Long ago he had accepted her for who she was. Now she would accept him. She had finally realized that she loved him more than any other . . . she had only to find the way to tell him.

***

It was late as the group sat around the table. They were the only ones left in the common room, all of the other patrons having gone to their quarters for the night. Goldare took another massive swig of his ale, wiping the back of his hand across his mouth when he finally lowered the tankard. The halfen brothers followed suit, not to be outdone by a human, no matter how big he was. Cervantes and Cortes had obtained more from the barrel back in the kitchens, having promised the innkeeper that they would pay for what they took. Mateo was drunk . . . Aeris had given him free rein to celebrate the success of their performance. His head rested on the table, for he had passed out after the first two rounds. Even Magnus showed signs of inebriation, laughing heartily at something Jonesy said behind a concealing hand.

Aeris took one last look around the table and then rose. She enjoyed the camaraderie she felt amongst her companions, but she was suddenly feeling tired and knew that she should try and get some rest. Besides, she had much to think about, her revelation weighing heavily on her mind. She needed to decide what course of action she should take, if any, and when she should do it.

Tigerius stood from his seat as Aeris pardoned herself from the table. "Aeris, you can't leave yet. We are still in full swing." He gave her a lopsided grin.

"You know I would, Tiger. But it has been such a long day . . ."

"Oh, come now. Just a little while longer."

"Yes, you must stay, my dear," said Cervantes. "You were the star of the show."

Aeris shook her head and glanced momentarily at Magnus. His eyes had settled intently upon her and she could feel the heat of his gaze. She could not take all of the credit for their success, for his skill equaled hers. Tearing her eyes away, she looked back to Cervantes and then to Tigerius. "I can't stay. I need to be up early to go to the library to conduct my research. Remember, I have other responsibilities besides the performances."

Tiger drew his lower lip into a pout while Cervantes frowned. "Oh yes. I am suddenly reminded of how important you are," he said sarcastically.

Aeris sighed and put her hands on her hips. "Do *you* want to do the research?"

Cervantes' expression instantly changed and he shook his head. "Oh no. Such things are best left up to you, my lady. I wouldn't want to pick up the wrong books, perhaps pick a lock that is trapped . . . you know . . . by magic. I wouldn't want to fry myself."

Aeris narrowed her eyes in mock scrutiny. "Hmm. I don't know. Maybe you need to be a bit scorched here and there. Perhaps you would begin to understand the responsibilities of others in this group."

Cervantes shook his head vehemently. It was obvious he had partaken of too much ale. "You misunderstand me . . . I have much respect for you, my lady. Please excuse my earlier statement to the contrary."

Aeris grinned. "Apology accepted. Now I shall bid you all good night. Most likely I will not see any of you until the mid-day meal." With that said she swept away from the table, her green gown swirling about her legs as she left the room and began to move up the stairs that were visible from the table. Everyone watched her as she left, their eyes following her until she was out of sight.

Magnus could only smile to himself. These men . . . they all had a bit of a lecherous side to them. He stayed there for only a short time longer before, he too, pardoned himself. He would be accompanying Aeris upon her errand on the morrow and he did not want to be overly tired to perform their task. He smiled and waved at the others as he left the room.

Watching Magnus disappear up the stairs, Tigerius slouched thoughtfully down in his chair. He had seen Aeris and Magnus' portion of the performance. It was more than he could ever have expected, the passion radiating from them in waves. It would be easy for him to say that it was nothing more than a show, a drama created for the sole purpose of captivating the audience. However, he had begun to notice the way Magnus watched his friend, and also saw that Aeris sometimes watched him in a similar fashion. Suddenly sensing someone's eyes upon him, Tiger turned to find Dramid regarding him. The sailor raised an eyebrow and then gave him a knowing smile. "He's in love wit 'er. I'll wager he'll 'ave 'er in 'is bed by the end o' th' fortnight."

Tigerius let a slow grin creep across his face. "Are you serious?"

"Shoor as I'm sittin' 'ere."

"Did you see that performance? They were sensational! It was like . . ."

"Like they was makin' love," supplied Dramid with a wink.

Cervantes frowned as he heard the words of his first mate. Hells, what did Magnus have that he didn't? Sure, he and Aeris had an awesome friendship, but he had always made it known to her that he wouldn't mind making it more. Damnation, Magnus didn't deserve her.

Cervantes shook his head. "No. He won't get her."

"How do you know?" asked Tiger.

"I just do."

"I don't know. Maybe Dramid is right. I have seen him watching her . . ."

"Yeah, me too. But she won't have him. He isn't the man for her," growled Cervantes.

"But I have seen the way she looks at him, too," replied Tiger.

"And how is that?"

Tigerius shrugged. "Like she's falling in love with him."

Jonesy grinned and nodded. "I noticed it too."

"Naw," guffawed Vikhail. "I seen 'er lookin' at anoder young man in Darban."

Vardec turned towards his brother. "Are you crazy? She weren't lookin' at anyone else."

Vikhail nodded. "She was, I tell ya."

Vardec only rolled his eyes. Goldare shook his head. Tigerius looked over to Lev, who had been silent for most of the night. "What do you think, Lev? Will he have her within the fortnight?"

Levander gave him a small smile. "Perhaps."

"What do you think, Goldare?" Tiger turned towards the denedrian man.

Goldare was pensive for a moment, then shrugged his broad shoulders. "Na. I don't think so. She's in love with someone else."

Tiger frowned. "Who?"

Goldare shrugged again. "Don't know. It's just a feeling I have, is all."

"I say we wager on it," said Cortes with a tone of anticipation.

"Fine. All right. Who thinks he will have her?" said Tigerius. Shaking his head, he thought of how silly all of this seemed, for this was the first gold they had seen in several days. They had obtained this gold only that night after the performance, and here they were gambling it all away.

Dramid, Jonesy, and Vardec put their gold on the table.

Tiger nodded. "Who thinks not?"

Cervantes, Goldare, and Vikhail placed their own coins on the table.

"Come on, Tiger. You have to wager, too," said Jonesy.

Tigerius thought about it for a moment. There was that small part of him that still hoped it wasn't true. Yet, deep within his being, he knew that Magnus was in love with Aeris, and that she shared his sentiment. Tigerius placed his gold in the pile with that belonging to Dramid, Vardec, and Jonesy. Cortes placed his own gold in the opposite pile, and Lev inconspicuously stayed out of the wager. The group was divided, but by the end of the fortnight they would know who the winners would be.

CHAPTER 18

A eris followed Magnus into the extensive library. She had never seen one quite as large as this, for it even exceeded the one in Grondor. The floors were covered by plush rugs and never-ending shelves of books and scrolls that climbed the high walls to reach the vaulted ceilings. Lighting was scarce, for no one wanted to take the risk that a fire should break out and consume the place. Many valuable literary works had a home in this library, parchments that were original to all of those that came to be read by any of the public who could and chose to do so.

At first the search was random. They hunted through catalogs, looking through cards that held key words specific to their investigation. They found only small clues when they found information on jewelry and charms and even less when they researched minerals and gems. They then moved along to a section that contained tomes that paid attention to objects of the arcane variety. Once again they found some vague references to something they called "dragon" crystals, but not much else.

At Aeris' insistence, they then moved to some literature that focused upon the dragons themselves. Not surprisingly, they found several books on the subject. Aeris frowned in dismay. It would take them the better part of the day and into the next to look through them all. Beside her, Aeris heard Magnus give a heavy sigh. Throughout their search so far, the companions had said barely a few words to one another. Aeris couldn't keep their dance from the previous evening out of her mind. It somehow seemed to hang in the air between them. Simultaneously, they advanced towards the shelves. Their hands touched as they reached for the same book, and both slightly recoiled from the shock.

Aeris glanced towards Magnus. His eyes were dark pools of lavender. She could see the tumult within those eyes, barely restrained emotions held in check by only the most tenuous of threads. She suddenly realized, without knowing why, that this was a man accustomed to getting what he wanted. She had never grasped that about Magnus before, but the unexpected clarity made her recognize it as truth.

Nervously, Aeris looked away from him, her mind flooding with more recollections of the night before. She remembered the passion of their dance, the way his arms felt as they embraced her, and the touch of his lips at her throat and mouth. She remembered his body as it moved in synchrony with hers, his hands at the curve of her waist, and the feel of his chest beneath her palms. She remembered feeling the warmth as it poured off of him, stirring a need that arose within her . . . a need that had stayed with her all through the deepest hours of the night. She wanted . . . needed to tell Magnus her revelation about him, but she found herself troubled. She feared what would happen when he finally knew the feelings she had been keeping from him all of this time. But even more . . . she anticipated it.

Aeris tore her thoughts away from the memories, distracting herself by selecting another book from the shelf. She gathered as many as she could carry and then took them to a secluded table. Magnus followed suit, choosing the tomes that seemed to have the most potential. He seated himself in the chair beside her and they both began to quickly scan over the pages. Some books were easily reviewed and subsequently re-shelved. Others took a while longer to sift through the knowledge contained within. Pertinent information was written down upon parchments brought for that purpose, parchments containing other bits of information that they had been collecting over time.

Struggling to maintain her focus, Aeris read through the books. By the gods, there had to be *something* worth finding here. Setting aside yet another tome, she reached for another. It would be the last one she picked up this day, for not only was she tired, but her mind wasn't where it should be. It was not conducive to thorough research, and it would be better if they simply waited until the morrow to continue their search.

The book was ancient. She could smell the age when she opened it. The pages were yellowed around the edges, and they had even begun to crack. She turned them almost reverently, her eyes scanning over the strangely styled lettering of the words written within. It wasn't long before she realized she was reading a document that was beyond any of the others she had perused before. It was intriguing, for there were references to 'the world before Shandahar'. It spoke of daemon-kind, the Pact of Bakaharas, and another pact that had been made long before Bakharas.

Aeris continued to skim the text despite her desire to study it. She was on to something, she could feel the tingle of it along the surface of her skin and then deep within the core of her body. And then it was there . . . the passage she had been waiting for. She held her breath as she read it once, and then again a second time.

" . . . *but the Shadow-walkers weren't enough. So they developed something new, something so innovative . . . so cutting-edge that the Detectors couldn't help but be impressed. The orbs were engineered by biologists and chemists, manufactured in secret so that the demons would never know. Then they would be used by the Shadow-walkers, a tool to aid them as they fought against an evil to which there seemed to be no end.*"

From the corner of her eye, Aeris looked at Magnus. He had ceased studying his own book and had focused his attention onto the one before Aeris. His brows furrowed into a frown and he let out an explosive breath as he finished reading the selection.

"Just as the crystals were made to be a weapon against dragons, the orbs were made to be used against daemons." Aeris almost whispered the words, afraid to speak them too loudly.

Magnus acquiesced. "Perhaps it is the reason why they repel one another. If the essence of the dragon rests within the crystals, and something of the daemon exists within the orb, perhaps it would be expected."

Aeris nodded, yet her mind wasn't entirely focused upon his words. It had begun to reminisce about the man she had discovered whilst upon the structure Tigerius referred to as 'shuttle'. She couldn't really say it was a vision, for nothing had happened. It was only that she had seen the image of a dead man as though he would have been in life. She then envisioned the strange dark orb before she had ever beheld it in her reality.

Aeris inhaled sharply. *Her reality.* It was a strange choice of words. She still had yet to share the full extent of her experience upon the shuttle with anyone. So far, it had remained her secret.

"Aeris, are you alright?"

Aeris came back to herself at the sound of Magnus' voice. He regarded her with a concerned expression, and she couldn't help but smile. "Oh, Magnus. You worry too much."

Magnus grinned in return. "Only because you bring that quality out in me."

Aeris chuckled and shook her head. "I beg to differ. You fret about everything, my dear. You have only to ask any other member of our company to realize this truth."

Magnus' smile widened. "Well then perhaps you bring it out better than any other."

Aeris laughed again, this time putting a hand over her mouth. She didn't want to be too loud. The sound of her mirth echoed among the massive bookcases, and she could only hope no one would suddenly turn the corner to tell her to be quieter. She finally began to calm herself and it was then that she realized it was there again . . . the strange something that had hung between them when they first began their search. She could see that Magnus sensed it too, and his demeanor became somewhat pensive.

The silence that followed was pregnant with suppressed emotion. There were things that Aeris wanted to say, she just didn't know how to begin. She liked to think that perhaps it was the same with Magnus, but she had never been very successful at gaging his thoughts.

"It's been a long time since we last laughed like that," Magnus said in a low voice. His gaze swung up to meet hers, and it caught and held.

For a moment Aeris simply stared at him. She remembered the time about which he spoke. It was at the festival in Grunchin several months ago. It felt like aeons had passed since that time, yet nothing had changed. She felt the same way about him now as she had back then. Aeris tore her gaze away, knowing what she was going to say without really wanting to. She couldn't seem to stop the words as they tumbled from her mouth. "I didn't mean to leave like that."

Silence reigned once more. She knew that more was required, that there needed to be some type of explanation . . .

"It seemed the easiest thing to do at the time." Aeris paused and then tentatively looked back up at Magnus. His gaze was guarded, yet she could see the emotion her words evoked within him.

He slowly began to shake his head. "When did you begin to take the easy path?" He stopped for a moment and then continued. "I don't understand what would urge you leave without any word . . . not even a simple message."

Aeris knew that she would be confronted with the question in one form or another. She had never decided how it should be answered. She shook her head, closed the book resting on the table before her, and stood from her seat. "Fear sometimes does that, I guess."

Magnus reached out to take hold of her arm. Startled, Aeris glanced back at him to realize he had risen to stand with her. "By the gods, what were you afraid of?"

She swallowed against the heaviness that came to her throat. Once again she was faced with the same old fear, only this time she would face it. "It was the way I had begun to feel . . . the way I had begun to feel towards you."

Aeris then swept the book off the table, grabbed her cloak and pack, and rushed out of the library. She didn't bother to realize that she had taken the book until she reached the inn. By then, it didn't seem to matter. Only the fact that Magnus had not followed had any significance.

***

Cervantes watched the woman as she made her way to the other side of the room. Her hair was dark and her eyes a pleasant shade of blue. The combination perhaps a bit unusual, but nice. She walked behind the bar and disappeared into the kitchen beyond. He then turned to his table companion. "That, my dear boy, is how you get a woman to notice you. It is the first step towards getting her into your bed. And by the gods, if you are good enough, you won't have to pay her for your pleasure. After only a single night she will beg you to come back to her."

Cervantes grinned at the dumbfounded expression on Mateo's face. The boy was more than just a virgin . . . he was daft when it came to *any* relationship that existed between men and women. Cervantes had chosen to take it upon himself to educate the poor soul, for no man should live without the simple comfort of a woman in his bedfurs.

Cervantes was about to expound upon the intricacies of love-play when a shadow suddenly loomed over the table. He looked up to meet the thunderous gaze of Tigerius. Cervantes glared at the interruption, but found it in his heart to give his new friend some consideration. Perhaps Tiger wished to discuss some matter of importance.

Tigerius slammed the flat of his hands down on the table between Cervantes and Mateo. "What in the Hells do you think you are doing?"

Cervantes frowned and narrowed his eyes. "What are you talking about? I am merely teaching the young man the particulars of bedding a woman." Cervantes gestured towards Mateo, who quietly cleared his throat and sank back in his seat. "What's your problem?"

Tiger's brows drew together into a scowl. "What is *my* problem? My problem is you, Cervantes. That is the second woman you have diverted from me in just as many days." Tiger gestured in the direction of the dark-haired wench.

Cervantes straightened in his seat and shook his head in denial. "Tigerius, I was unaware of your endeavors. I have only been focusing upon my own, which has been to show this boy the best way to obtain the attention of the women he wishes to bring to his bed."

"Well, perhaps you should take more notice of what is going on around you." Tiger lifted his hands from the table.

"Perhaps you need to be more certain of a woman's interest in what you have to offer," replied Cervantes.

Tiger planted his fists at his sides. "What is that supposed to mean?" The tension in the air became suddenly elevated, and Mateo shifted uncomfortably in his seat.

"Only she wouldn't have regarded me so hotly from those blue eyes of hers if she had been entirely certain that she wished to visit your bed tonight." Cervantes gaze was unwavering as he regarded his friend.

"Is that so? Well, for your information, her eyes are not blue. They are green. And her response to sharing my bed was not cursory. She had every intention of coming to my chamber this eve."

"Her eyes are blue, and why would she agree to share *my* bed when she had intentions to share *yours?*"

Tiger shrugged his shoulders. "I don't know, but her eyes are green. You are a fool to think she would come to you when she has me."

Once again, Mateo shifted uncomfortably. His eyes darted from one man to the other, both whom were obviously very certain of their sexual prowess. He hated to watch them go on like this and sought to end the confrontation, despite the repercussions it could have upon him. "Excuse me . . ."

"They are blue, and you are more the fool to underestimate me. I am your senior by at least ten years and as such, have that much more experience."

"Excuse me . . ." Mateo continued to try to get a word in edgewise.

Tigerius shook his head. "Her eyes are green. That is just it. You are getting old. What woman would want a scurvy old bag like you when she can have the best pick of the crop, like me?" Tiger grinned mirthlessly.

Mateo sighed explosively, so loudly that both men turned towards him. For a moment he was taken slightly aback, but refused to back down. "By the gods, her eyes are hazel! It explains why one of you sees blue and the other green."

Both men stared at Mateo. After a moment they glanced at one another and then back to the young man. "You didn't have to shout, boy. We are sitting right here," said Cervantes.

"Yes, that was quite rude," added Tiger.

Mateo looked from one man to the other in astonishment. Indeed, they were both going insane. Did they really see no fault in themselves?

Cervantes turned toward Tigerius. "I propose a contest. Whoever wins shall have first pick of all of the women that enter this establishment. Agreed?"

Tigerius regarded Cervantes for a moment. "We will need to work out the details of this contest."

Cervantes inclined his head. "Of course."

Tiger regarded the captain for a few moments longer before he put his hand, palm down, on the table. "Agreed."

Cervantes grinned profusely and placed his own hand atop of Tiger's. "This is going to be so much fun. Not to mention that I will prove to you that I am not the old man you think me to be."

Tiger smiled back and simply nodded. Yes, this was going to be quite amusing. He would see whether Cervantes was as on top of his game as he thought he was.

***

Levander slowly rose from his place on the veranda of the Falcon's Crest Inn. His muscles ached from having sat so long in one place, and he took the extra time needed to loosen his limbs. He found that he was tired . . . extraordinarily tired, actually. He had traveled so long and undergone so much adversity only to be met with dismal failure.

Lev made his way across the veranda and entered the establishment. On the way to his chamber, Lev ordered a bath, and once in the room he stripped himself of his clothing and waited. Despite the time he had remained seated outside the inn, his thoughts remained the maelstrom they had been the moment he left his uncle's house. His brother refused to be deterred from his path of destruction, and Lev could only sit by and watch the last person he loved lose his life to the evil of the Kronshue.

With a knock on the door, the bath was brought by two burly men and set onto the floor. He watched as the women filled it, the water so hot he could see the mist rising as it was poured into the waiting tub. Most likely they were the same women who served their ale and stew every evening. It wasn't long before the task was complete, the women backing out of the chamber, and Lev lowering himself into the steaming pool. He then leaned back and allowed himself to relax. He thought of the young brother who had become a man, and the anger he seemed to harbor deep within himself.

Long ago, Levander had once been a member of the Kronshue, an elite brotherhood of individuals known for their military might, unequivocal cruelty, and technological expertise. He had been young when he was brought into the fold, barely fifteen summers. He had completed the requisite testing with accolades, and he became known as an elite within the elite.

But one day something happened. After an accident that left him near death, Lev came to realize the full extent of the cruelty of the Kronshue. He was given a rare chance to see the agony that had been inflicted upon countless people through the experimentation that was required in order to develop the technology they used so flagrantly. After that, Lev made it his mission to derail the Kronshue in any way he could.

Inevitably, there came the day he was discovered. Overnight Levander became a hunted man. It was a principle of the Kronshue that they only pursue a man for up to fourteen days after his crime was discovered. Yet, anything and everything that might be held dear to him would be forfeit. Lev's family was not spared. His mother and father both died to protect his whereabouts. Only his very young brother was left of the family he loved so much. Having seen only five summers, Severus couldn't entirely grasp what had happened.

Several years passed. Placed in the care of his father's brother, Severus grew into adolescence. Every so often, Lev would come to visit his young brother with tales of the people from the west. He always came bearing gifts, things that would never be found this far east. Despite the disappointment that always came whenever Lev left, Severus was always happy to see his brother upon the next visit.

However, things began to change. The time came that Severus had grown enough that he began to wonder where Lev went when he wasn't in Gulshaan, and why Lev didn't simply stay with him. Lev tried to explain that he had many enemies and that it was safer for him to stay away. Severus begged to go away with him, but Lev would never hear of it. He knew he could never give the boy those things that which his uncle provided. And the one thing he always asked Severus never to do was to join the Brotherhood of the Kronshue.

Levander didn't know how long had passed before he received the ill fated message from his uncle. Severus was starting to rebel, and had even begun to set his mind upon joining the Kronshue. Lev was suddenly beside himself, desperate to reach eastern Ansalar before it was too late. He was finally given permission to join the others that were aboard Cervantes' ship, and it was a brutal twist of Fate that landed them upon an island far from their original destination.

Finally, once at the port in Darban, Lev sent a message to his uncle. He told the man that he was on his way to Gulshaan, having every intention of parting ways with the rest of the group. But then the *Sea Maiden* was taken. The group decided to leave the city to make their way to the very city Lev needed to be. Thanking the Fates, Lev accompanied the group to Gulshaan, and once there he almost immediately went to the house of his uncle.

But it was too late. Severus had already made the decision to begin the requirements necessary to become a member of the Brotherhood. Lev was astounded by the anger and animosity Severus bore towards him. Now that he was of age, Lev offered to take Severus with him, but it was to no avail. Levander had become an object of hatred by his own brother, and he had no idea as to what he could do to make Severus see reason and to stop him from ultimately choosing the life that would bring him destruction.

This morning, Lev had chanced going back to his uncles' house once more, hoping that perhaps Severus would change his mind. Again, he was met with open hostility. It wasn't long afterwards that Lev was dejectedly making his way back to the Falcon's Crest. Now, he sat in a tub of water that was beginning to cool. He rose from the tepid pool, dried himself with the nearby cloth, and donned fresh tunic and trousers. He then went to the window and looked out upon the street below. In his mind's eye, he imagined his brother down there, waiting for Lev to emerge from the establishment. Lev embraced Severus, thanking the gods for his brother's return. They then entered the inn together, each one leaning upon the other.

But there was no one there standing in the street. All he saw was the lengthening shadows cast by the nearby buildings. Only a mangy canine loped down a nearby alleyway. Lev pulled himself back into the dimness of the chamber. His thoughts continued to flux around his brother. He wished that, at a time when Severus still wanted him near, Lev had made himself more available. Now it was too late. Too much time separated them, and Lev just now realized that their connection had begun to fray long ago when he chose the life of a wandering man over that of one who would stay to care for his family. Now he would pay the ultimate price for his transgressions against the Kronshue. It seemed that, in the end, they had taken everything from him after all.

***

Aeris stared at the wall of the small chamber. She had gone through her short list of options, and all of them seemed to have less promise than this one. However, the one she now contemplated was not all that great. Most likely she would fail, and her strength would be sapped by the force of the spell. But she had to make this attempt, for she would not rest until she had done all she could to reach her family.

Just as she had expected, there were no messenger birds that flew as far as Elvandahar. The aerie-keeper had never even heard of the place, and it was his apprentice who had spoken up to tell him that it was the largest of the hinterlean realms and situated in central Ansalar. Aeris then spent the rest of the day inquiring around the city if anybody knew of someone who might be planning a journey to the mid-west. Once again her suspicions were correct, and she found no one who had even contemplated traveling so far.

Aeris was forced to return to the inn with nothing to show for her efforts. Passing through the common room, she met up with Jonesy and Cervantes who were busy planning their next performance, which was to take place the following evening. They wanted it to be even better than the last one with some modifications to their costumes and some additional lighting and musical effects. Aeris feigned interest for as long as she could endure it, and then excused herself from their presence. Her thoughts had become so wrapped up in her desire to contact her family that she could think of nothing else.

Upon reaching her chamber, Aeris took the spellbook from her travel-pack and opened it upon the bed before her. She quickly found the spell she was looking for, but knew before she read it that it was of a caliber much beyond her present skill level. Not only that, but she had never before attempted to cast a spell of this type. Much to her present detriment, she had a tendency to focus more upon spells that could be used in an offensive capacity.

The spell was of the teleportation variety. It would be years before she would have the skill and strength to teleport herself, much less another living thing. However, this one was much more simple that that. It would open a tiny portal through which she would be able to push a small, inanimate object. Of course, Aeris had opened many portals in her lifetime, those that allowed her to obtain the energy she needed to cast her spells. The use of runes, arcane components, and concentrators lessened the drain the spells had upon her physical self and made them easier to cast. Yet, even with these tools, many upper level spells would wane her strength. As it was, she was still only a novice and had much to learn.

However, Aeris could not help but recall the story. It was that of her mother and the man who brought forth a contingent of dragons that would turn the tide of battle in their favor. There had been no reason why Adrianna and Dinim should have been able to open a portal to another world, despite the advanced skill of the latter. Not to mention, the ability to bring living beings through it. They had no spell components or concentrators, and neither one of them had attempted a spell of that magnitude before. They had only Adrianna's bond with Xebrinarth and an intense will to beat the overwhelming odds. Dinim had used all of his strength to create the portal and keep it open for as long as he could. For the first two days afterward he lay near death. He then slept for several days more within relative stability. It had happened to many a spell-caster before . . . those who attempted to cast spells that were many zacrol out of their skill range.

Aeris focused her gaze back onto the open book before her. She had studied it for the better part of the afternoon and into the evening. She knew the incantation as well as the runes she should draw as she spoke it. She was a fast learner; Master Dinim had always told her so. Her classmates had detested her for that fact, and they liked to imagine that she was favored by him because she was the daughter of his partner. What they didn't realize was that he expected more from her because he knew from whom she had been bred. Because of the extraordinary abilities of the mother, Dinim had a glimpse of what things the daughter was capable. Inasmuch, he pushed her to her very limits . . . and she had often hated him for that.

Nevertheless, she loved him too. More than he was her Master, he was her uncle. Aeris never grew up thinking that she was not loved. She had so many people around her that adored her so much, she could never forget it. Every waking day, her parents, brothers, cousins, and friends showed her how much they cared about her.

A tear splashed onto the page of the spellbook before she had a chance to wipe it away. She rubbed her damp hand along the side of her tunic and sniffed at the wetness that invaded her nose. In that instant she made her decision. She could not allow her family to speculate about her any longer, wondering if she was sick or injured . . . alive or dead.

Aeris took a deep breath . . . then slowly exhaled. She closed her eyes and began to concentrate. Upon the open book before her was a small slip of folded parchment within which she had written her message. Her goal was to push it through the portal into her mother's bedchamber. With the attention Adrianna paid to the smallest of details, Aeris knew that her mother would notice it right away. That is, unless she was so ridden with worry for her daughter that she . . .

Aeris stuck such thoughts from her mind. They had no place there now, for she had to put all of her efforts into the spell she was about to cast. She briefly contemplated consulting Magnus on the matter, but then discarded the idea. She hadn't seen him since their foray to the library. She didn't quite know how to approach him, especially considering what she had said, followed by her hasty exit.

Taking another deep breath, Aeris lifted her finger and began to write the runes into the air before her, complex runes that helped to focus the magical energies she called. A small wind swept through the room, but Aeris took no heed. The spell had already begun to carry her away upon wings of brilliance, and she found herself caught in a zephyr of power she had never experienced before.

***

Magnus swept his hands over his face and into his black hair. He suppressed much of the forceful breath that exploded from between his lips as he leaned back in the chair. For hours he kept vigil over her, and for almost as many he contemplated what she had done. By the gods, the woman was an imbecile! Why in the Hells didn't she come to him for aid? What possessed her to attempt to cast a spell well beyond her capabilities?

Just that morning, Jonesy had entered Aeris' chamber to find the young woman lying in the middle of the floor. When Aeris would not be roused, Jonesy came to find Magnus. His heart pounding in his chest, he ran to Aeris' room. Once there, he picked her up from the floor and carried her to the bed. Despite the commotion, she had not moved. Her complexion was pale, her breathing shallow, and her pulse faint. At the time, he had no idea what calamity had befallen her, and he sent Jonesy to find a priest. He knew that the clergy had lost their powers, but they still had knowledge and skills that could help Aeris.

It took longer than he expected for such a person to be found. It wasn't until much later, when he finally had a chance to ask Jonesy about it, that he learned that most clerics and priests had left the city. People claimed that since the gods had fallen, the clergy left to go in search of them. Jonesy recounted her strange tale of nearly deserted temples that now housed only beggars and street urchins. The only priest she could find was an old man who was too crippled to make a journey out of the city.

Magnus was taken aback when the priest could find nothing wrong with Aeris. She seemed to be in good health despite the paleness of her skin and weak pulse. He could see no reason why she would be comatose, for he found no skull trauma that would bespeak such a condition. He then mentioned that he had witnessed something like it only in the Talented when they had over extended themselves. Their minds and bodies were often too weak to perform the tasks presented, and once the duty was completed, both simply shut down. The priest assured him that many times it was temporary; yet he had to admit that there were times the casters never awakened from their spell-induced sleep.

The old man departed soon after, and Magnus was left at Aeris' bedside. Somehow, the clergyman's words rang true. It was as though a revelation had come over him, and he knew that she had attempted an upper-level spell that was beyond her ability to cast. Once discovering their comrade was ill, the rest of the group came to see her. They arrived in groups of twos and threes, all asking Magnus what ailment had beset her. Not knowing how to explain it to them, he simply lied and told them he did not know. He could see that this answer distressed them, for they feared that she would not become well if they didn't even know what affliction had befallen her. Yet, Magnus told them nothing. He hoped that Aeris would eventually awaken and that she would be forced to give the explanation herself.

Now it was late. The performance that had been scheduled for that evening was canceled. The owners of the establishment were kind to allow them to stay until their comrade was hale once more. Magnus was grateful for the generosity, for there were few people who would extend such a welcome to others they hardly knew. He could only hope that they would be able to repay the owners in some way.

Magnus hoisted himself forward and planted his elbows above his knees. He then rested his chin in his hands and simply watched the woman who lay before him. Not for the first time, he noticed the ring that circled the middle finger of her right hand. The central stone swirled with pale blue and green color. With a tentative hand, he reached out to touch it with the tip of his forefinger. Just like the last time he had made contact with the ring, it evoked a sense of familiarity. It seemed to call to him somehow, and sometimes he could feel its pull even when Aeris was in another room.

Magnus moved his hand from the ring up to Aeris' forehead. He swept away a lock of hair that rested there. She was so beautiful, the contours of her face exquisite in their design, the corners of her eyes slightly canted, and her nose small and dainty. Then there was her mouth, perfect in every detail. He remembered the dance they shared . . . the feel of her body beneath his hands and the sensation of her lips against his. He had taken liberties with her that he normally would not have done. Yet, she had played games with him, only galvanizing him to continue with his own.

In the end, Magnus liked to think he had won. She succumbed to his seduction and responded to his kiss in the way he wanted. She said nothing of the dance during their visit to the public library yesterday afternoon, yet she had given him a part of the reason why she had left Grunchin without letting him know where she would be going. Her words had stunned him. Magnus was tempted to follow her out of the library, but he held back. He didn't know what was going on with her, but he could find out after she had some time to herself.

Magnus ran his fingertips lightly across her jaw to her lips. He gently traced their blushing softness, and an urgency to kiss her suddenly encompassed him. He leaned forward and hovered for a moment before brushing his mouth over hers. He then slipped out of the chair and onto the bed beside her. He pulled the blankets up over them both, and then curved his arm protectively over her. Once again he was overcome with worry, and he hoped that Aeris would soon awaken from her coma. Despite their differences, and the difficult circumstances in which they had found themselves, he could not imagine spending the rest of his life without her. No longer did he care about who he had been and what type of past that he had once led. All that mattered was the man whom he had become, and that he spend the rest of his years with the woman who lay beside him.

***

Adrianna read her daughter's message for what may have been the hundredth time. She didn't really need to, for she had burned the words into her memory within the first few times of reading it. She had been astounded to find it, for Aeris should not have had the skill or the strength required to cast such a spell. It was one thing to bring the elements to oneself through a portal, but quite another to send or receive objects. Adrianna put the matter quickly to rest when she realized that another spell-caster must be present within Aeris' company. It relieved her to know that her daughter traveled with one who was so powerful, and a Dimensionalist at that.

Dearest Ama and Babu,

I am hoping that this message finds you both well and that you have not been overly concerned for my welfare. After a long time at sea, we have found ourselves finally land-bound once again and residing within the city of Gulshaan. I would have sent a message earlier, but I hadn't even considered the possibility of sending something by my own devices until I realized that there was no messenger that could get a letter to you quickly enough . . . or at all for that matter.

Regardless, I am hale and whole. The company with which I have shared my travels is good and we have plans to begin our journey back to Elvandahar as soon as we have acquired all that we will need. And, of course, after some time to rest after a tumultuous excursion at sea. When I am home I will have to tell you about it. I love you both dearly. Send my affections to Alasdair, Talemar, and Cedric. Oh, and perhaps Asgenar as well.

Damaeris

Adrianna shook her head. It was difficult for her to realize that Aeris knew nothing of what transpired in Elvandahar since her leave-taking. Xebrinarth and Pylarith had left to patrol their border with Karlisle at the Denegal River. It was mostly in response to the dragon attacks that had been taking place all across the southern realms of Selintan and Bekbor. More recently they had begun to infiltrate Karlisle, and it was only a matter of time before they reached Elvandahar.

Karlisle. The name of that realm had been upon the lips of many an Elvandaharian over the past several fortnights. Asgenar spent much of his time treating with King Zerxes to no avail. It seemed that, with the murder of one daughter, the possible abduction of the other, and the son traipsing about the realms in search of her had set the man over the edge. Most recently, Zerxes was even beginning to blame Elvandahar for many of Karlisle's problems . . . . especially the resurgence of Razlul and the Daemundai. Adrianna did not understand the rationale of his arguments, but they stood nonetheless. Now the two realms were at the brink of war. It was a far cry from the unity they were seeking to achieve by the marriage of Asgenar and Elinora. She couldn't help but think that Razlul had them right where he wanted.

Adrianna folded the parchment. She could not concern herself with these things. Her duty now was to bring her daughter home. Already Alasdair, Cedric, and Talemar were in preparation for the journey. She would have gone herself, but she was needed in Elvandahar should the tenuous situation with Karlisle suddenly erupt. Sirion was currently hard at work with many of the rangers, training them to perfect their skills for the war that seemed so inevitable. She and Dinim did the same with the apprentices, journeymen, and masters currently residing at the Medubrokan Academy.

At least Adrianna could console herself with the fact that the journey would not be a long one. At the advent of the academy, Master Tallachienan constructed a well much like the one he had designed at his citadel. It would transport Alasdair, Cedric and Talemar to the familiarity of the portal chamber in Krathil-lon. Once there, the men would be able to use the portal system to teleport them to a location not far from where Aeris currently resided. Then they should only have to travel a couple of days on foot to reach the city.

Adrianna sighed and pocketed the letter within the folds of her robe. She could hardly wait to see her daughter again . . . had missed Damaeris in ways she never could have imagined. All of these weeks she had hoped and prayed that the young woman would soon be home . . . that she would look upon the beauty of her daughter's face and feel the security of Aeris' hand within her own. She had even dreamed of it. And when the time came, Adrianna would thank Fate and the fallen gods for her safe return.

***

Cervantes narrowed his eyes at the three men sitting across the room from him. For what seemed the hundredth time over the past two nights, one or the other of the men had staked competitive claim upon one of the women with which he had made seductive overtures. He knew that they were aware of their actions, for none hesitated to look in his direction every time he may have earned the upper hand with one of the women. And Cervantes found himself beginning to work extra hard to get the attentions of such women. Cervantes hated that. And that was not to mention the wager he had made with Tiger.

Cervantes glanced at the rear of the tavern when the door opened to admit some patrons. It was Goldare, Cortes, and Jonesy. Being that the Falcon's Crest Inn was just across the street, it was easy for them to come over to the Twisted Tankard Tavern and get a change in pace from the calmer atmosphere offered by the inn.

By the gods, Jonesy had finally torn herself away from Aeris' bedside. Immediately Cervantes chastised himself. Aeris was dear to him, and he had to realize that she meant the same to many of the other members of the group. He shouldn't be so quick to degrade the actions of those people. Not seeing him, the three comrades seated themselves at another table, one closer to the three men whom Cervantes had just been pondering. He wondered where Vikhail and Vardec might be, for he rarely saw Goldare outside of their company. And he also wondered of the whereabouts of Diamid, who had a tendency to keep with Cortes.

However, Cervantes found his thoughts diverted when he noticed that one of the three men that had become Cervantes' competitors take an interest in Jonesy. She had stepped up to the bar, most likely to order some ale for her comrades. The most refined of the three men had approached her and was initiating some conversation. Cervantes felt his hackles rise as he watched the interplay. Not only were these people making moves on wenches upon which he had staked competitive claim, but they were now doing the same with the women in his group.

Cervantes remained still as he watched. Jonesy smiled at something the man said, and a flush rose to her cheeks. She said something in response and the man moved slightly closer to her and leaned in. Cervantes gritted his teeth. He was not blind. It was readily apparent that Jonesy was an attractive girl, and it bothered him to see that another man noticed that fact. If it had been Jezibel standing there, it wouldn't have perturbed him so much. But it wasn't Jezzie . . .

Even after they were back at sea, Cervantes continued to train Jonesy with the use of the cutlass He was busy as the captain of his ship, especially since he had barely even a skeleton crew, but with the help of the halfen brothers and Goldare, they fared rather well. It also gave Cervantes the opportunity for leisure time. Jonesy was smart, and quick to learn despite her lack of self-confidence and physical conditioning. He was more than surprised to discover her knack for sword-play, and wondered at the reason why she had never been offered training before. Regardless, Cervantes enjoyed the time he spent sparring with his new student, and even more so because Jonesy was so eager and enthusiastic to to learn from him.

The training had begun to slow after they made it back to the mainland, and a distance sprang up between them. He only vaguely took note of that fact when he made the realization he had formed a bit of an attachment to the girl. He enjoyed her company very much, and began to regard her in an almost possessive light. Cervantes had always borne the propensity towards such possessiveness, not just with people within his realm of influence, but objects and places as well. It was just something about himself he had learned to accommodate as needed, and to quell when the necessity arose.

Inasmuch, Cervantes had to restrain himself from getting out of his seat when the man lay a hand on Jonesy's arm. He felt anger rush through him, fueled by jealousy. He didn't stop to wonder why he felt quite this volatile about the interaction between Jonesy and the other man, only that he felt outraged. That man had no right to touch her, despite the distance that had grown between them in recent days.

Cervantes was only able to start calming himself when the two finally parted ways. Paying the barkeep, Jonesy took up the tankards and carried them back to the table. Cervantes saw Goldare and Cortes josh with her about the man who approached her at the bar, and the color rose to her cheeks once more. Annoyed by her response, Cervantes looked away only to find his gaze settling on the three men. They were all watching Cervantes, and each sported a smirk on his face. They knew that Jonesy was a companion, and they reveled in the rise they hoped to get from him.

Once more, the anger coursed through him. He found himself smiling in return, a smile that bespoke the thoughts going through his mind. He would see them all to the Hells before any of them had Jonesy in his bed. Cervantes only looked away from the men when he noticed someone sitting down on the opposite side of the table from him. He turned to Tigerius, and when his friend saw the thunderous expression on Cervantes' face, the smile of greeting receded. "What's happened to put you in this kind of mood?"

Cervantes slid his gaze over to the men. "Them."

Tiger discreetly glanced in the direction Cervantes indicated, saw the men, and turned back to his friend. "Those men again? Come now, Cervantes. You are needlessly allowing them to get to you."

Cervantes' tightened his jaw. He knew Tigerius was right, but he couldn't help being exceedingly irate over the men. At another time and another place, he would have simply shrugged off such offensive behavior and walked away. But now . . . now he couldn't . . . now he *wouldn't*. He felt the energy just building up in him, waiting to be unleashed. It was only a matter of time.

CHAPTER 18

Jonesy completed the last of her preparations for the performance. She looked over to see that Tigerius was almost finished as well. It was getting late, and by now Aeris should be getting ready for her dance. After three days of slumber, the woman had finally awakened from her magic-induced sleep. Everyone was pleased to see that she was well, and even the rogue captain went to see her. Jonesy felt her throat constrict at the mere thought of Cervantes, and she strengthened her resolve. It was her goal to rid herself of all romantic thoughts pertaining to him, and she was sure she would reach it within a fortnight. Especially in light of the wager that had been struck between he and Tigerius Solanar.

Jonesy had been appalled when she discovered what was going on between the two men. She heard it described as 'a bit of friendly competition', but in her mind it was all lechery. Most of the women they seduced were girls barely any older than she, if even that. And although Jonesy knew the girls had been with a man before, maybe even several, she still found it distasteful. What was worse, she felt that it disrespected women in general, that they were merely walking pieces of flesh to serve a man's basest of desires. Jonesy couldn't help but wonder what both men thought about her, Aeris, and Jezibel.

Jonesy left the stage area and entered the room that lay behind it. She found Aeris there, dressed in the beautiful gown that had been fashioned for her to wear. It was enhanced since she had last worn it, and if the group was stunned by her appearance before, they would be even more so now. Notwithstanding the paleness of her complexion, Aeris was the epitome of beauty. She was the light that brightened the room, and Jonesy couldn't help but smile in spite of her somber disposition.

Plucking at the beaded neckline of the gown, Aeris turned to Jonesy. "I . . . I don't know about this. Perhaps it's too much. Maybe I should cover . . ."

With a light smile Jonesy swept over to her friend and placed a staying hand on the one that sought to cover Aeris' chest. "The gown is perfect." Jonesy allowed her gaze to sweep over Aeris' pale face. She was concerned for her friend but said nothing. It had been Aeris' choice to perform this night, despite protestations from the group. It was too soon for her to engage in such activity after what she had been through, but Aeris would have no argument. The group needed the money, and she would do her best to see that they get all of what they could before they were forced to move on. Because of the close proximity of the Daemundai, they needed to leave within a day or two. And as a result of her infirmity, precious time had been wasted. Gods knew there was very little of that to spare.

While Jonesy saw to the finishing touches to Aeris' attire, the performance began. Within a few moments she heard Cervantes' voice join those of the other musicians as they played a tragic ballad. The bards were pleased to have him in their ranks, and Jonesy as well. It had been easy for them to become a part of the existing performance, and the dance executed by Magnus and Aeris only added to any notoriety they might have been achieving.

It wasn't long before the time came for Aeris to go out on stage. She cast Jonesy a wan smile as she made her way out. Just as before, Aeris began her dance alone. She moved sinuously to the melody of lyre, and when the cadence began to intensify, Magnus joined her on stage.

Aeris could immediately tell that Magnus was angry with her. She felt it reflected in the tension of his body when they danced . . . sensed it simmering just below the surface of his thoughts. His gaze remained shuttered to her, and his emotions reined closely against him. As a result of their close proximity, she felt his withdrawal keenly. It burned her to the core, and she wished that she had never made the realization she cared so deeply for him. Because then she would not be bothered by the fact that he treated her with the same indifference as he did anyone else. Except, perhaps, for Jonesy. The two had become good friends, and Aeris found herself envious of that.

Aeris and Magnus finished the performance. They were wooden as they completed the finale, having nothing of the fervor of the original dance reflected in their recital. Instead of the fluid pair they had been the first time, they were now aloof and evasive. There was no passion to their performance, and the audience could feel it almost as much as they. The applause was nothing compared to what it had been before, however Aeris could care about nothing but to be out of Magnus' presence.

The lights dimmed, and Aeris tore herself away from him. She swept to the rear of the stage and stepped behind the curtain. She refused to allow the tears to come, unwilling to answer the questions that were sure to come if she were to meet any of her comrades en route to her chamber. She was fortunate that she met no one, for they were occupied with the next performance. Aeris made it to her room without incident, closing the door and locking it behind her when she entered. She thought about allowing the tears to come, but by then they had all gone wherever tears go when they are left unshed.

Aeris stood in the center of the chamber. More than ever, she felt alone. Tiger was not there for a shoulder to cry on, nor was Jonesy available to offer a listening ear. Cervantes was not there to diffuse her enmity, nor was Mateo accessible to distract her with thoughts concerning his training. She was so wrapped up in her thoughts that Aeris almost jumped out of her skin when someone knocked on the door. She put a hand over her mouth to stifle the exclamation that rested at her lips.

"Who is it?" Aeris asked as she moved the hand down to her chest where she could feel her rapidly beating heart.

At first there was only silence, then, "It's me . . . Magnus."

Aeris felt her heart skip a beat. What was he doing there? All she wanted was to be away from him . . . couldn't he see that?

"I'm tired. Go away." She grimaced when she heard the petulant tone of her voice . . . quite similar to that of a whining child.

Once again there was silence followed by, "Please open the door. I want to speak with you."

Aeris shook her head. That was the last thing she wanted . . . to spend another moment in his presence. And it was even worse that they would be alone. She just needed some time to herself . . . to recuperate from the sting of the cold shoulder he had offered ever since she awakened. Not to mention that she was tired. Even though she slept for three days after she cast the spell, she continued to feel the effect it had upon her body. "No. I want to go to bed. We can talk tomorrow." Aeris tried to make her voice sound as conciliatory as possible.

"Open the door, Aeris." His voice had a demanding edge.

Aeris stepped backward, increasing the distance between herself and the door. "Just go away, Magnus. I don't want to see you." She felt a curl of tense anticipation settle low in her belly and her senses became alert. She imagined that she heard a low growl from the other side of the door, a sound of frustration from the man who stood there.

"I see that you are going to make me do this the hard way . . ."

Aeris shook her head once more. No, he wouldn't do it, for the act would be one of a crazy man. Yet, she felt herself oozing with defiance, not in the mood to tread lightly. She was tired of being compliant when all she really wanted to do was give back the harassment she felt she was receiving from him. Her words would surely drive him to do what she thought he might without them. "I dare you to . . ."

Before the words were completely spoken, the door splintered inwards. Aeris barely blinked an eye as Magnus strode through the flying shards of wood, a hand held out before him, palm facing outward. She kept her face expressionless, refusing to let him see that his spell impressed her, especially as it had suppressed much of the noise such destruction ordinarily wrought.

He was upon her in an instant, his hand circling her wrist as she raised her hand to ward him away. "Why did you do it?" He asked the question bluntly and without prelude. His lavender eyes flashed dangerously, and he narrowed them as they focused upon her with unmitigated intensity. He pulled her in close to him, so close she could feel his breath on her face, breath that bore the scent of recently imbibed ale.

Without asking him, Aeris knew what Magnus was talking about. "I don't see the need to explain myself to you. You are neither my father, nor my master. Let me go." She emphasized the latter by pulling at her trapped wrist.

Magnus' gaze darkened perceptively. With a muttered spell and the flick of his hand, the splintered door pulled together and reformed itself into the frame of the entranceway. "You owe me an explanation. You are my responsibility, and have been since the day your brother placed you in my charge. You will tell me why you placed yourself in unnecessary peril . . . including the reason you chose not to inform me of your intentions."

Aeris refused to be diverted by the skill that Magnus possessed with hardly even a fraction of the concentration it would have taken an ordinary sorcerer. "Get out." She felt her eyes flash with the strength of her emotions.

Magnus pressed his lips into a thin line. "I tire of your childishness. You are ever placing yourself and this group at risk. You are a liability and should be treated as such."

Aeris snorted derisively. "So what are you going to do? Hang me from some gallows? Slit my throat perhaps? Or maybe just plunge your dagger into my belly instead and let me die a slow death?"

She hissed the last word, emphasizing it by bringing her face close to his. Magnus' eyes burned with intensity, and his gaze slowly lowered to her lips. Barely a space separated them, and the realization made her think to draw back. Her action came a mere moment after the thought; but by then it was too late.

With a jerk Magnus pulled her into him. Wrapping his other arm around her waist, he brought his lips to hers. His kiss was almost brutal . . . his mouth demanding the passion that lay just beneath her thin exterior. Aeris responded almost instinctively, returning the harsh caress in kind. Her blood hummed through her veins, and her heart beat a staccato rhythm in the chest that pressed so tightly against his. Her thoughts swirled away with the power of the moment, her head reeling as though under the influence of the strongest of ale.

It wasn't but moments later that Magnus' kiss began to temper. He abruptly pulled away, and Aeris suddenly felt bereft. She almost staggered back from the force of his desertion, but looking into his eyes, she saw the struggle reflected there . . . his desire to kiss her warring with that to continue the argument.

"Your brother would hunt me down for all of the days of eternity if I lay but a finger upon you," Magnus said with utmost solemnity.

Like an arrow through the chest, Aeris suddenly felt Magnus' pain. She watched as he walked slowly towards a small table situated against the nearest wall, and then as he ran his fingertips lightly over the surface. She felt him resisting his impulses, straining against his desire to see this confrontation through to an ending more suited to his physical needs.

"You have disrespected me and the relationship we have striven to build, no matter how tenuous they both might be." At first Magnus kept his gaze fixed to the table as he spoke. But then he looked up into her eyes. "You obviously have little care for either, and there comes a time when one must finally let go. What hurts the most is being so close . . ."

Magnus stopped, shook his head, turned, and walked towards the door. At first, Aeris just stood there, momentarily overwhelmed by the sensations that assailed her. What was happening here? Was Magnus leaving? Especially now when the group still needed him? When *she* still needed him?

Aeris continued to watch as he walked towards the door. She swallowed heavily, her heart suddenly sitting in her throat. Magnus was right. She should have let him in on her plan to contact her mother. Perhaps he could have helped her, and then she may not have ended up draining herself so much. Only after awakening and discovering the fact she had been abed for almost three days did she realize the risk to which she had subjected herself. And Magnus felt ultimately responsible because he had once made her brother a promise . . .

What hurt the most was not how close they had come to having found friendship . . . but not knowing what could have ultimately been between them. And now she was watching him walk away.

"Magnus . . . wait." Aeris heard the emotion in those words . . . two words that spoke so many more. She watched as the cimmerean man stopped before the door, his hand poised above the handle. He turned back towards her, his eyes guarded. Yet there was so much more there . . . if she only stopped to gaze beyond the barriers he had erected.

But all Aeris could do was stand there. The heart sitting in her throat had begun to pain her, and she felt her eyes becoming wet with unshed tears. By the gods, she really didn't want him to leave, but she didn't quite know how to go about telling him so.

However, as it turned out, she didn't need to say anything at all. Magnus stepped away from the door, and within moments he was at her side. He tenderly cupped her face in his hands and rubbed his thumb over her lips. He kissed her gently, lovingly. Aeris sighed a breath of contentment, surrounded by the feeling that she had finally found her way to the place where she needed to be.

***

For two days Alasdair, Talemar, and Cedric had traveled west to the city of Gulshaan. The journey was an uneventful one, yet they were tired from the constant pace they kept. Now, on the morning of the third day, they entered the city, thinking only to find Aeris and a good bed for the night. But it was a large city, much larger than any they had ever seen before, save for Grondor. It could take them the larger part of an entire day, if not longer, to find her. This fact did not sit well with Alasdair, for he wanted to see his sister home as soon as possible. Yet, the city was awesome to behold. The entire culture was different from what he was accustomed in central Ansalar . . . from the clothes people wore, to the accent in which they spoke the common tongue. It was difficult not to stop and look at the wares the merchants displayed for sale in front of their shops. They offered a variety of things Alasdair had never seen before, and he hated to simply pass them by. He reassured himself that they would stop on their way out of the city, once his sister was within the safety of his company.

Just as Alasdair predicted, it took them quite a while to discover the whereabouts of one Aeris Timberlyn. Over the course of the day he had discovered quite a bit about her from the local populace, foremost that she was a performer at the Falcon's Crest Inn. This intrigued him, for he had never known his sister to enjoy the spotlight before. Not only that, but he wondered what it was that had driven her to the profession in the first place.

However, it was just as well. It was her reputation as an extraordinary performer that brought him to the doorstep to the inn at which she had made her residence. It was early evening when the three men entered the inn and paused at the lobby. Alasdair raised an eyebrow in appreciation. It was definitely an upscale establishment, one at which patrons would pay top coin to stay. And it was good to know that the place had offered to house Aeris and her company as long as they wished to perform there.

The men began to move towards the common room. However, they were stopped at the entrance by a rather burly gentleman. "How may I assist you?"

"I am looking for someone whom I have discovered is staying here at your establishment," said Alasdair. "Her name is Aeris Timberlyn."

The man shook his head. "I am sorry, but I am not at liberty to disclose the names of the patrons who reside within this facility. However, if you wish, you may stop in a little later this evening and see if you can find her then."

Alasdair nodded. "I will do that. In the meantime, we wish to purchase a room for the night."

The man smiled and beckoned them into the common room. "Right this way. I can procure you some accommodations immediately."

Once the payment had been made, and the keys handed over, the men made their way up the stairs to the appropriate room. It was rather large, and would easily lodge all three of them. Removing travel-stained tunics and trousers, they took turns in the bath they had called up to the room for their use. Then, once the dirt had been washed away, they donned fresh clothing and relaxed in the two beds that dominated the chamber. The accommodation had been a costly one, but Alasdair didn't mind the expense. On the morrow, he would have Aeris and they would be leaving. Content with his thoughts, he drifted into peaceful slumber.

It wasn't much later that Alasdair found himself being shaken into wakefulness by Cedric. His cousin informed him of the time, and glancing out the window, he could see that night had fallen. Alasdair swung himself out of the bed, straightened his appearance, and joined both his cousins as they left the chamber. Making their way down the stairs, they could hear the crowd that had gathered. Alasdair found himself wondering if it was because of the performance, or simply that the place was that reputable.

It took them a few moments, but the men were able to find a table at which they could all be seated. It wasn't long after that the lighting began to dim. The presentation began with the *Ballad of Shinshinasa*. The singer was good . . . exceptionally so. She was young and rather pretty, her brown hair tied back from a face that seemed somehow familiar to Alasdair. However, he couldn't quite think of when or where he may have met her.

Next came a pair of halfen men. Alasdair found himself taken quite aback at first, for he had never heard of many halfen participating in performances such as this. Yet, once Alasdair got past his initial surprise, he found that the brothers were quite hilarious to say the least, telling bawdy tales of adventures that must have come and gone long before. It was easy to tell the men were related, for not only did they look similar in appearance, but they knew one another so well, they could finish one another's thoughts.

The performance continued with a skit enacted by a buxom blonde-haired woman and two men who vied for her attentions. Alasdair raised an eyebrow when he saw that one of those men was his own good friend, Tigerius Solanar. He could see his comrades holding back their mirth despite the laughter of other audience members. By the gods . . . he never thought he would ever behold the type of entertainment that he was now watching.

It was after that the haunting melody began. It was an instrument he couldn't quite place, accompanied by the flute and the lyre. Then the song began. He could tell that the voice belonged to the young woman he heard earlier. When the dancer appeared on stage, the vision took his breath away. She was a flurry of fire and silk, the deep green of her gown contrasting starkly with the crimson of her hair. The curling mass flowed with Aeris as she moved to the cadence of the music, and when it began to increase in tempo, a man joined her on the stage. Alasdair's heart almost stilled in his chest. It was Magnus.

The singer's feminine voice was joined by a masculine one, and their voices matched the intricate movements of the dancers. It was a song of love, loss, and all of those things in between. One could see it all taking place between them . . . from the movement of their bodies to the expressions on their faces. Alasdair could easily tell how the dancers felt about one another when it seemed that they were making love right there on stage.

The audience was enraptured by the performance. The praise was extraordinary, people rising from their seats to applaud the performers. Alasdair had never heard such adulation before, and he felt suddenly humbled. That woman was his sister . . . the younger sister in which he had exhibited so little faith. And now she was commanding crowds of people, simply by executing a dance. How small must he be to have never seen it before, when she had begged and plead with him to trust in her abilities? How daft was he to continue in his blindness, unwilling to see the truth right before his very eyes? It seemed that Asgenar knew her more than he thought.

Alasdair found himself rising with the rest of the audience. Talemar and Cedric followed suit. Each of his comrades seemed similarly affected, and he wondered what thoughts drove them at that moment. He clapped his hands with the rest of them, and when she looked up from her bow, Aeris caught his gaze.

Her eyes locked upon him, widening with incredulity. He saw his name form upon her lips, and then they were pulling up into a smile she made just for him. All of a sudden, Aeris was jumping off the stage, and the audience was parting before her. Within moments she was in his arms, and he was holding her for the first time in so long. Her hair was fragrant with the scent of flowers and her frame seemed so much smaller than he remembered. "You have come for me . . . I can't believe you have finally come for me," she whispered in his ear.

"You must have known that I would," he whispered back. "No matter what, I will always come back for you."

The words suddenly struck a strange cord within Aeris. She felt as though she had heard similar words spoken before, by another man, in another time, at another place. But just as suddenly as it came, the disquiet passed. She took contentment in the arms of her brother, the man who was her best friend in life.

"By the gods, 'Dair, how did you get here?" Aeris asked breathlessly. She couldn't believe it . . . her mother must have received the message she sent!

Alasdair ginned. "I will tell you when we have the time. It appears now that your audience has want of you." He gestured to the crowd around them, everyone wanting to shake her hand, tell her how much they enjoyed her dance, and simply to look at her. Suddenly aware of the people that surrounded them, Aeris turned and began to address everyone. She glanced around in search of Magnus and found him slowly making his way towards her. He smiled at the people he passed, and one of the security personnel employed by the establishment followed closely behind.

By the time Magnus finally reached her, the crowd had begun to thin. He greeted Alasdair warmly, and the two men grasped one another's forearms in the universal gesture of friendship. Aeris turned to her cousins and embraced them both. Cedric seemed happy to see her, and he held her affectionately. However, Talemar was distant. Although he appeared to be pleased to see her, there was an aloofness about him that Aeris had never felt before.

But she didn't have the time to dwell upon it long, for her comrades had emerged from back-stage and were approaching them. A few patrons courteously resigned their tables so that everyone in their party could sit together. Aeris found herself introducing her brother and cousins to those whom they had never before while Tiger enthusiastically welcomed his friends to Gulshaan. She was pleased to see that everyone was open and friendly. Goldare shouted for a serving wench, and within no time they had been fortified with murg and ale.

At first there was talk all around. Cervantes, Jonesy, Tigerius, and the halfen brothers were ecstatic about the show, and knew that the owner of the establishment would pay them well. Many people had come to see their performance, and the inn had benefited from the influx. The owner was a fair man and would pay them accordingly. Now there was another set of performers on stage. They were the bards and other personnel that performed at the inn on a consistent basis. They had been able to enjoy a bit of free time with the advent of Aeris and her companions. However, with the group's departure on the morrow, it would be back to the same routine.

Finally, the talk began to abate. Alasdair looked all around the table. It was hard for him to believe the assortment of personalities . . . the diversity of professions seated there. One man was bald with a myriad of tattoos spread all across his face down into the neckline of his plain tunic. Another bore the stamp of orocish heritage. Alasdair guessed that the other two men might be brigands or corsairs, but he couldn't be sure. As of yet, only their dress set them apart from many of the others. One of the women was the buxom blonde with the lively personality he had noticed on stage, and then there was the other girl . . . the one with the extraordinary voice. Even now she seemed somehow familiar, but he still could not place her in his memory.

He hated to be the harbinger of bad tidings, but Alasdair knew certain subjects had to be broached. There was only one reason why he and his cousins were there, and that was to bring Damaeris home. This moment had been too long in coming, and he didn't want to waste any time. However, he did need to know what events had transpired so as to urge them to brave the open seas. And then, what had kept them there for so long? Alasdair had yet to inform Aeris of the political situation between Elvandahar and Karlisle, the emergence of the dragon-riders, and the potential role that the Daemundai commandeered. As far as he knew, she knew nothing of the death of Asgenar's bride or the destruction of many of the cities in the realms of Selintan and Bekbor by a handful of dragon-riders.

Alasdair spread his hands out on the table and leaned forward. "So, tell us what happened to make you decide to set sail across the Drujasu Sea."

The atmosphere at the table became hushed. He was suddenly the focus of everyone's attention. The casual ambiance became somewhat solemn, and Alasdair began to wonder if he should not have brought it up after all. He knew it needed to be done, but he supposed it could have waited until the morrow, despite the extra time it would have taken.

It was Aeris who broke the silence. He wouldn't realize it until later but, in a way, the others may have been waiting for her to do so. She began with the crystal, and how it had led her to Captain Cervantes, followed by their encounter with the Daemundai. Despite their victory, the knowledge that more of the dark priests were swiftly approaching urged the group to take to the sea. After several days, a storm hit, and they suddenly found their ship foundered on an uncharted island. It took several weeks for them to complete repairs on the ship, and several more to reach the mainland. Once in the port city of Darban, Cervantes' ship stolen by the remaining crew. With all of his coin on board the ship, and everyone else's spent upon rescuing one Jezibel Pyratt from an uncertain fate, the group found themselves destitute. It was then they arrived with the idea that they work for their coin . . . and the work happened to be of the entertainment variety.

Alasdair, Cedric, and Talemar listened to the account with predominant feelings of awe. Aeris, Tiger, and Magnus had experienced quite a bit of hardship since they parted company, and Alasdair couldn't help but feel some measure of respect. Through it all, they had stayed together and persevered over the odds. And in his opinion, they had won.

Once more Alasdair looked around the table, easily saw the strong relationship that existed between the recondian man, Goldare, and the halfen brothers. He could also see the camaraderie that had developed between the man they called Cervantes and his childhood friend, Tigerius. In addition, he saw that Aeris and Magnus had come together as well, in more ways than one. It was the way Aeris looked at the cimmerean man when she thought no one was watching . . . and by the way Magnus casually laid his arm across the back of her chair. Glancing over at Talemar, Alasdair could see the torment reflected in the man's blue eyes. He was glad that his sister was happy, but he hated to see his cousin so downtrodden.

Yet, despite his efforts to remain inconspicuous, Alasdair noticed another man at the table. The faelin's complexion was pale, his hair black, and his eyes so pale a shade of gray, they looked almost silver. If not for the eyes, Alasdair may have taken him for a cimmerean in spite of other differences he noted in the shape of the ears and the cut of his jaw. Or, despite the hair color, a savanlean. Actually, the man was of a descent that Alasdair could not quite determine at all.

However, it wasn't just the man's appearance that was an enigma to Alasdair. It was everything about him. The glimpses he cast in Aeris' direction were not mislaid on Alasdair, and he could not help but wonder what the other man was about. They were not the glances of a man coveting a woman. Rather, they seemed speculative in nature. Oftentimes he seemed almost lost. Regardless, Alasdair was certain the man meant no harm. Inasmuch, he left him to his own devices, whatever they might be.

Aeris began to relax after telling Alasdair her account. It was a long time in the telling, and she was glad to share it with her brother and cousins. She didn't divulge some of the more intricate details, such as the discovery of the metal bird, the emergence of Tigerius' mysterious abilities, or the development of her relationship with Magnus. All of those things were almost superfluous, even intimate in nature. And they didn't lend much significance to the telling of the tale. Except perhaps for the strange metal bird. Now that might be another story . . .

"So, brother . . ." she began, "how does everything fare in the realm of Elvandahar since I have been gone?" She said it in a rather blithe manner, light-hearted and flippant. She didn't expect the grave expressions she received from her brethren, especially the severe tone of voice from Alasdair.

"It's not good. Our relationship with the realm of Karlisle has grown rather tenuous. We seem to be at the brink of war."

Aeris felt her eyes widen with shock. "What? What has happened to cause such a shift in allegiance? Asgenar is to wed the eldest daughter to the king. What says Zerxes of this?" She refrained from glancing in Jonesy's direction, at that moment unwilling to give her friend's identity away, even to her own brother.

Alasdair shook his head. "Elinora was taken by the Daemundai," he said gruffly. "She was killed and then bits and parts of her returned to King Zerxes in an assortment of packages sent by Lord Razlul himself. There will be no union between our realms."

Aeris inhaled swiftly, Alasdair's words harsh even to her own ears. What must Jonesy be thinking now? She couldn't help but chance a look over at her friend. Jonesy's face had become pale and her eyes wide. Jonesy seemed distressed by the news, but not as Aeris thought she should be. Yet, she didn't have the time to mull over it as Alasdair shared the next piece of news with her.

"However, our relationship with Karlisle isn't the only problem we are facing." Alasdair paused and held Aeris' gaze intently. "What may be even more disturbing are the dragon attacks."

Once more Aeris felt her eyes widen, but this time with disbelief. *Dragon attacks? But why?*

"We feel that the degethozak are somehow allied with the Daemundai . . . and they have *human* riders."

Aeris inhaled sharply, suddenly recalling the vision she had when she brought the crystals together. She remembered the dark dragons and their riders . . . the negative aura surrounding them, and the malcontent she felt after the image faded from her mind. Now that vision had become a reality. There was a perversity about it, for it was quite unprecedented for humans to ride astride dragons. Sure, her mother mentioned riding astride Xebrinarth every now and again, but they were bond mates. They loved one another and felt at peace when they flew together. This . . . this was different. These dragons and riders were not sharing special moments with one another. They were using one another's strengths in order to facilitate the downfall of other beings.

"The dragon-riders have been moving up from the southern realms of Selintan and Bekbor. For all we know, they will be reaching Elvandahar within the seven-day," said Cedric.

Aeris could only nod in silence. The news rocked her to the core. Despite the chaotic nature of the degethozak, she never thought she would ever see the day that they would begin an assault on human and faelin kind . . . especially in light of the battle they had fought not only thirty years before. It was together that humans, faelin, degethozak, helzethgryn, and rezwithrys had fought against a common enemy and won. Aeris thought that would have meant something, even to the impetuous degethozak.

"How are Ama and Babu?" Aeris asked in a subdued voice. "I hope they haven't worried needlessly."

Alasdair leaned across the table towards her, capturing her gaze with his own. "Aeris, I have come here to bring you home. That is my only mission in life at this moment."

Aeris took in the intensity of his gaze, felt the tension surrounding his body. She could tell he didn't quite know what to expect from her. Had she really changed that much . . . that her own brother and best friend could no longer tell what she truly wanted? Aeris put a hand over Alasdair's where it sat on the table between them. "Right now, I want nothing more than to return home with you."

Alasdair smiled widely, and Aeris felt her body completely relax. His smile seemed to light up the entire room, reaching into those dark crevices of her soul that nothing had been able to reach since he had left her in Xordrel so long ago. She was ready to go home with him . . . more than ready. And she couldn't imagine leaving there for quite an extensive time.

***

Tholana slowly moved through the streets of Gulshaan. She walked alone, unfettered by the nearly constant companionship of one or another of her varied followers. The goddess had come quickly to the city when she discovered the group would soon be making their way back across the continent. The arrival of the Timberlyn girl's brother had been quite unexpected, forcing Tholana to move more quickly than she would have liked. It put her in foul humor, and her followers knew to stay away.

Tholana took in the activity going on around her. It would soon be dark. These normal people . . . these peasants . . . would soon retire for the evening. The women would see to their children while many of the menfolk went to the taverns to drink, fraternize, and whore around. Such was the way of these people, these puny humans whom she had very little contact. They were like rodents, proliferating at astounding rates. They then slowly lay waste to their own towns and cities with their trash and excrement. It was a wonder that disease wasn't more rampant, for the streets were so filthy, she could barely stand to walk upon them.

Shaking her head, Tholana returned her thoughts to other concerns. She was slowly developing a plan. All this time she had been tracking the group through the eyes of Mateo, for Tholana wished to know the activities and whereabouts of Tallachienan and his companions without the effort of scrying. The endeavor had served her well, and had even resulted in her discovering their preparations to begin traveling back across Ansalar to Aeris' home.

Tholana sighed heavily to herself. As of yet, the Daemundai had not reached the city. No aid could be expected from them this night. However, it wasn't as though she needed it. Those priests were far below par in relation to her own priestesses . . . and maybe even her mages. Of course, the daemon-keeper would never have knowledge of these thoughts. Razlul considered his followers to be rather specialized. Tholana acceded that in some ways they might be, but in her estimation, their knowledge and skills were sorely lacking.

Tholana smiled to herself in the wan light as she shifted her thoughts to Tallachienan. A man approaching at the opposite side of the street leered suggestively at her as he neared. Her smile only widened as he passed, and she widened the swing of her hips seductively. He raised an eyebrow and grinned. She reveled in the attention, no matter where it originated. Yet, her focus quickly redirected itself back to her nemesis. TC still had no inkling as to his true identity. Tholana found this fact to be quite amusing, albeit tempered with a hint of tedium. She didn't bother to consider the possibility of TC's memory never returning to him. He was a god. Such things just didn't happen.

Regardless, she had to decide what she should do now that she was in the city. Already she had begun to formulate a plan, and she had to admit it was a long time in coming. It seemed that years had gone by since Tholana last had Aeris within her grip. She had verbally tormented the young woman, and despite her inability to break the girl down, succeeded in placing a few mind-webs. Tholana then left her to the 'tender' mercies of her comrades. They had thought her to be in league with the enemy, whoever that might be, and they treated her as a traitor.

Now things had changed. No longer was Aeris a potential threat to the group; she was in a position of authority. Whether they realized it or not, it was she whom they followed despite the danger it might entail. It began with Alasdair and Tigerius as they accompanied her upon her mission to find the young Talent, Mateo. It was then perpetuated by Tigerius and TC, followed by Goldare, Vikhail, and Vardec. Soon after, the girl Jonesy had joined their ranks, along with a seafaring rogue and an outcast from the Brotherhood. It was phenomenal how the girl was so much like her mother, for Adrianna had borne a similar effect upon people. It was something about her that drew people in . . . a charisma that made them want to follow in her footsteps. It was a power that few others possessed, and it was even more significant when one of those persons was a god . . . whether he knew it or not.

Now Aeris had the potential to be within her grasp once more. Tholana's hatred of the girl had only grown, and the mere thought of Aeris enslaved within her stronghold brought chills to her spine. Yet, it was more than simply the vanquishing of an old enemy. It was the promise of having Tallachienan at her mercy once again, just as she had all those years ago at his sister's deathbed.

The dark goddess turned and began to make her way back to those who awaited her. There would be no more waiting and no more games. Tholana had to make her move tonight . . .

CHAPTER 19

The Twisted Tankard Tavern was full of people, patrons coming and going at a steady rate. Many would stay for a short while and then move on to the next tavern or inn, hopping from place to place to visit different groups of friends or to experience different forms of entertainment each had to offer. Others would stay at a single establishment the entire evening. Cervantes and the rest of the group had been going back and forth from their inn across the street to the Twisted Tankard. The atmosphere at the tavern was more casual and relaxed, and Cervantes found that he preferred it to the more decorous nature of the inn.

But there was another reason why Cervantes chose to stay at the tavern this evening. His three competitors sat across the room and this was the group's final evening in the city. They had packed up and were prepared to leave Gulshaan on the morrow. With the Daemundai moving ever closer, it was no longer safe for them to stay. Not only had they earned enough gold to buy provisions, with that brought by Aeris' brother, they had more than enough to stock up for their journey to the portal that would take them all back to the western side of the continent.

The arrival of Alasdair, Talemar, and Cedric had put Cervantes in a tailspin. Everything was suddenly changing, and Cervantes had a big decision to make. Either he could stay in Gulshaan to risk being hunted by the Daemundai and eventually killed for the association he had with the crystals and Aeris' group, or he could go with them to Elvandahar and find some semblance of safety with magic-users and warriors of renown. Everyone, including Cervantes, had heard of the legendary Wildrunners, and it was disconcerting to realize that the people with whom he had made his company were direct descendants.

Justifiably, recent events had put Cervantes on edge. Through narrowed eyes he watched his competitors. Just like Cervantes, they also were a part of a larger group. This night, all of them had decided to settle in this tavern to partake in general camaraderie. Taking a cursory count, Cervantes noted at least thirteen or fourteen in their party, and that was including the wives of two of the men.

Unexpectedly, the table before him was reverberating with the impact of several fists followed by shouts of laughter on both sides. Cervantes swung his gaze over to Cortes. His brother was a big man, and as such, his voice happened to be loud. It was joined by the voices of the halfen brothers, Dramid, Jezibel, and Goldare. Half of the patronage in the tavern glanced over to see what was going on at their table, and Cervantes noticed that his competitors looked over as well. He saw one of the men nudge his comrade and both of them grinned.

Cervantes immediately felt himself becoming annoyed. What in the Hells were those two so amused about? And why did Cortes happen to be in possession of the loudest mouth on this side of Ansalar? Cervantes rose from his seat. He suddenly felt stifled and just needed to get some fresh air. Looking over at the adjoining table, Cervantes saw Aeris and Magnus sitting there with Alasdair, Levander, Mateo, Tigerius, and Jonesy. At another nearby table Talemar and Cedric sat apart. It was easy to see that both men seemed somewhat subdued, but Cervantes didn't stop to wonder as to the reason why.

Nudging past the halfen brothers, Cervantes began to make his way to the entrance to the tavern. He had taken several steps when someone bumped against him. It wasn't unusual for a man to be nudged here and there as he made his way through a crowded room at a tavern, but the bump had been a trifle rougher than he expected. Cervantes swung around towards the offender, and much to his aggravation he found it to be the man who had been flirting with Jonesy a couple evenings before. The man's original expression of apology turned into one of insolence. "You better watch where you're going, *friend*." The last word was said with a tone oozing with sarcasm.

Cervantes snorted derisively. "You seem to be the umberhulk in question, so back off, *friend*." Cervantes spat the word back at him. He felt the coiled energy within him begin to swell.

The other man's voice lowered to a growl. "If I were you, I would be careful. You don't know who you're dealing with, and when you find out, you might wish that you hadn't." He then grinned mirthlessly, showing his teeth in a universal gesture of aggression.

Cervantes rose to take the bait. "I assure you, I will have no regrets."

As the two men began to square off, people began to move aside. Within moments Cervantes felt someone at his side. Tiger put a hand on his shoulder and spoke in a light-hearted tone. "Hey Cervantes, let's head back over to the tables. We just got a fresh round of ale and my old childhood friends have a story or two to tell us about their journey here."

Cervantes shrugged Tiger away. The anger within him began to spill forth. His life had taken a radical downturn since the day he met Aeris and her group. Then, when the *Sea Maiden* was stolen, he had been forced to realize that nothing would ever be the same for him again. With the loss of his ship, all of his hopes and dreams had sailed away without him. Now here he was, forced to make decisions he felt he aught not to have to make. Everything was being thrown at him so fast, and he felt he had no control over anything. Until now, he had kept all of his anger and all of his aggression suppressed deep inside. He didn't want to quash it anymore. He wanted a fight, and he didn't care about what any of the consequences might be.

"Hey, you . . ." The members of the other man's party had risen to stand behind their comrade. The speaker gestured towards Tiger . . . a man Cervantes had never seen before this night. "You better keep your friend in line. We don't want any trouble here."

Tigerius frowned. "I assure you, we want no trouble either, but perhaps it would serve you equally as well if you kept your own comrade in his place."

Cervantes exploded. "What in the Hells is wrong with you people? What right do you have to speak about me when I am standing right here?" He pointed to the man standing before him. "This man is a bastard sea-whore and I will be the one to see he is put in his place!" With that said, Cervantes hauled off and bludgeoned the man in the jaw with his fist.

The tavern was suddenly in an uproar. There were people moving in all directions . . . most to the entrance so as to escape the brawl that was to ensue. Others scrambled to join comrades at distant tables, and a few went towards the fight itself. While Aeris, Jonesy, Mateo, and Jezibel moved well out of the way, Magnus, Cortes, and Dramid leaped into the fray with intentions to stop the fight. However, it was soon apparent that such an opportunity had already come and gone. Tiger was already at fisticuffs with a member if the rival party, and the halfen brothers had rushed in with no thoughts towards diffusing the situation.

Circumstances rapidly went from bad to worse. The rival party moved to close around Cervantes, Tiger, Vikhail, and Vardec. Cortes burst through the opposition, his arms flailing. One man went flying into a table, splintering it into two as his body crashed through the center of it. Another man was sent into the nearest wall, his head striking the stone with a sickening thud before he crumpled to the floor.

Passing by the remains of the broken table, Magnus picked up one of the legs from off of the ground. It was a bit on the unwieldy side, but he would make it work. Using the table-leg as a staff, he swung it at the first opponent he reached, a man that had Vikhail in a stranglehold. Magnus hit the man in the leg, sending him immediately to the floor. The man screamed in agony, holding the leg in both his hands. Magnus felt a momentary pang of regret. These people shouldn't be their enemies. It was all a big mistake and now everyone would pay the price for Cervantes' recklessness. Magnus had struck his opponent harder than he meant, and now the man would probably be crippled for the rest of his life. Depending on his profession, that could mean life or death for his family, and Magnus hated being responsible for that.

From her position at the wall near the entrance to the tavern, Aeris watched the brawl with trepidation. People were being seriously wounded even without the use of steel weapons. Jaxom had been hit over the head with a stool as he was engaging another opponent, and he never rose from the blow. Dramid had been thrown over the bar. With a loud crash, his body slammed into plates, bowls, and mugs that were stacked on the other side. Aeris never saw him reappear. She saw Tigerius twist the arm of his opponent savagely behind him, and he released the arm only when the man screamed. It hung unnaturally at his side, unmoving. She swallowed the lump that rose in her throat. What were they doing . . . ?

Out of the corner of her eye, Aeris suddenly noticed activity on near the wall on the other side of the door. It had been propped open to make it easier for people to exit the establishment at the onset of the fight, and she was partially hidden behind it. She saw that two men had entered the tavern and had decided to take advantage of the fact that no one would notice the disappearance of some women. Aeris turned to see Jonesy being struck forcefully upon the head and then slung over the shoulder of one of the men. The other already had Jezibel subdued, and they jauntily walked out the door with their prizes.

Frantically glancing around, Aeris looked to see who might be nearby, someone who could help. It would be foolhardy for her to go after the men alone, despite her skill as a magic-user. She couldn't know what might be out there, waiting for a lone female to exit the chaotic establishment, and she could easily be caught unawares. She saw Talemar close by, momentarily assessing the situation in the tavern. She shouted his name, rushed up to him, took his arm, and began to pull him in the direction of the door.

Levander stood silently by, stoically watching the destruction being wrought before him. The ridiculousness of the situation was not lost on him, and he hated seeing people he had come to respect denigrating themselves like they did now. He stayed out of the fray, unwilling to become entrenched in something he felt to be utter foolishness. Of course he would help them mend from the myriad cuts, bumps, and scrapes they would acquire from the event . . . how could he deny them that? But he would not be involved with the idiocy he currently witnessed.

But then Lev noticed something else going on. Across the room, he saw Aeris pulling Talemar towards the open door of the tavern. Her expression was one of alarm, and he could see that she was saying something to him and gesturing wildly with her other hand. The expression on Talemar's face became equally as concerned as he promptly rushed out of the establishment with her.

Lev frowned. Something was happening, something he should have sensed before. But he had been so wrapped up in his feelings concerning the tavern brawl, he had ignored his perceptions. Chastising himself, Lev began to move in the direction of the door when he felt himself being roughly pushed to the side. It was Goldarc and his opponent, each grappling with the other to achieve the upper hand. Lev lost his balance and he fell, the other two men with him.

As the men landed on top of him, Lev felt something enter his side just above his hip and below his ribs. Nausea suddenly overtook him, and he almost wretched onto the floor so near his face. He struggled to be away from the two men pinning him to the ground, and once he was able to obtain some leverage, he was able to pull himself free.

Lev crawled away from the men, the pain in his side excruciating. Putting his hand there, he felt the hilt of a dagger protruding from his side. Once he felt he was far enough away, he gripped the hilt and began to pull the blade from his side. He clenched his teeth against the agony, but he was able to withstand it until he felt a snap. He slowly brought the broken blade into view, his heart sinking with the realization of what had just occurred. A portion of the dagger remained deep within his side, and he had no way of extracting it.

Shaking his head, Lev quickly got a hold of himself. He still felt the peril to Aeris and Talemar, knew without a shadow of a doubt that terrible danger awaited him beyond the walls of the tavern. Struggling to his feet, Lev staggered out the door and into the cool air of the street outside. It was dark, and only the night lamps were lit. Following his instincts, he turned left, keeping one hand against the buildings as he walked. It wasn't long before he came across the still forms of Jonesy and Jezibel. Kneeling before them, Lev put his fingers to their necks in order to determine whether their hearts still beat in their bodies. Satisfied that both women still lived, he rose and continued onward toward the danger he felt.

It was then that Lev saw a light down the alley way up ahead. He knew it was magic cast by one of the two spell-casters. He increased his pace, hoping he wasn't too late. He sensed power, magnificent power he had felt only once before at another place and another time long ago. Urgency filled him and he moved even faster. When he finally reached the scene, he felt the breath rush out of his lungs. Both Aeris and Talemar hung limply from the arms of two dark-robed priests. A woman stood before them and she turned at his approach. She regarded him only cursorily, taking in the tattoos on his face and the baldness of his head. A flash of recognition passed over her face, but she then gestured towards the women standing around her. "Kill him," she drawled.

Levander slowly came into consciousness to find himself lying in a cold, dark alleyway. Grabbing hold of some protruding stones from a nearby wall, he pulled himself up to his feet, and then began stumbling through the dark streets back to the tavern. He kept one hand gripped against his side and he could feel the warm stickiness of his blood seeping through the fabric of his tunic. His other arm hung loosely at his side. He could hardly move it, and he wascertain that it was broken. Lifting his shoulder, he wearily tried to wipe away the blood that wanted to flow into his eye, and his entire body shook with the effort it took. He knew that it was the wound in his side that was stripping him of energy, and it had been the same when he faced the dark priestesses. He simply couldn't muster the strength to fight them, and it was degrading for him to know how little it took for them to take him down and declare him deceased.

But they were sloppy. They left him for dead, and their queen didn't even bother to check and see if their assumptions were correct. Or perhaps Tholana simply didn't care. He meant nothing to her, a simple member of the Brotherhood, and a dishonored one at that. Now the Queen of Darkness was taking his companions to her dread stronghold. He cringed at the thought, for he had heard the stories. Many times, the cimmereans were worse to their prisoners than were the Kronshue.

It seemed like forever before Lev found himself standing outside the tavern. The door was closed and locked, testimony to the amount of time he must have spent unconscious and then making it back to the establishment. He pushed himself off the wall and careened towards the Falcon's Crest Inn across the street. With any luck, at least some of his comrades resided within. He was sure that many of them were out looking for himself, Aeris and Talemar, and hopefully they had already found Jezibel and Jonesy.

Reaching the door, Lev slumped wearily against it. His breath misted in the air before him. He was tired . . . so tired. All he wanted was to lie down and rest. But he had a mission. Talemar he did not know, but Lev owed Aeris at least that much.

Suddenly the door swung open. Lev fell into the entrance, landing heavily on his sore side. He groaned with the impact and his world went black for a moment. He knew that the wound was killing him, but he still had that mission. He felt hands on him and then a man shouting for some help. He felt himself being lifted, carried, and then deposited gently onto a cushioned surface. A face swam before him, a masculine one. His eyes were a brilliant shade of green . . .

Magnus entered the room to find Cedric hovering above Lev. Rushing to the bedside, he looked into the terribly beaten face of the bald man that had become his comrade. He leaned over and placed his lips near Lev's ear, hoping that the man would hear him. "Lev . . . please tell me . . . where is Aeris?"

Magnus saw the man struggle to remain conscious. Grasping Lev's bloody hand, he asked the question again. He hated to keep Lev conscious any longer, but he knew the man had information as to the whereabouts of Aeris. And if Levander happened to slip into a sleep from which he would never awaken, Magnus would be faced with the possibility of never seeing her again.

Then Lev spoke, his voice a mere whisper in the silence of the chamber. "It was the Dark Queen . . . she . . . she . . ." Lev struggled for a moment and then continued. "She took them both."

It was all Magnus needed to hear. The Dark Queen, Tholana. He had encountered her once before, and since then, he had made efforts to learn more about her. He knew, without a shadow of a doubt, that it was only a matter of time before both Aeris and Talemar met their demise in her wretched stronghold in the Underdark.

Magnus rose from the bed and glanced down at Lev. The poor man had already slipped away into his slumber. As soon as Magnus had all of his provisions in order, he would be leaving Gulshaan in pursuit of Aeris and Talemar. He was certain that Alasdair, Cedric, and Tigerius would be in accompaniment.

***

Jaxom awoke to a sense of intense foreboding. He felt it even before he opened his eyes. Events came rushing back to him: the arrival of Aeris' brother and cousins, the tavern brawl, and then . . .

Jaxom inhaled sharply and then sat upright on the bed. His head swam for a moment, and putting his hand there, he felt it had been wrapped in a cloth. Yet, he had not the inclination to think much about it, for something was seriously amiss. He felt an emptiness that he had never experienced before, a hollowness that seemed vague and unnatural. His thoughts went immediately to Damaeris, and within moments he realized why he felt as he did.

Jaxom swung his legs out of the bed, stood, and then almost fell to the floor. Damn, that hit on his head must have been a hard one for him to struggle even just to stand. But he didn't care. All he could think about was the faelin girl he had denied for so long.

For a moment Jaxom struggled to regain control over his body, his anger quickly escalating. Damn this puny humanoid form! He was forced to keep it with his proximity to the others, but he found himself tiring of the charade. In this form he was nothing, but in his real form . . . in his *dragon* form he was all of the things he needed to be.

Suddenly enraged, Jaxom pulled back his hand, made a fist, and slammed it into the wall. The stone broke with the impact, along with the bones of the hand. He screamed with pent-up frustration. He hated his impotency and even more the guilt he felt. He should never have kept her from him. Like a proper bond-mate, he should have taken her within his protection and removed her from the danger she faced here . . . taken her to Shayamalan where she could discover the truth of her destiny. But he had been selfish. He had considered himself above her . . . above all of those dragons who had gone before and bonded with a faelin. And now he was alone, and for all he knew, he would never feel her near him again.

Jaxom ran his hands through the darkness of his hair. With age it would turn silver. He hated the thought, for he had always been one to believe he would spend the majority of his life in his true form. But for months now he had been in faelin form. He had escaped his father and the continent of Shayamalan to make his own way for himself. All he had found was the girl who was meant to be his bond-mate . . . the thing that urged him to be back upon Shayamalan more than would anything else.

Jaxom hissed with the motion and then cradled the broken hand to his chest. He shook his head with the absurdity of his situation. His realizations had come too late, and he was now powerless to regain control of his life. Not to mention, he had just broken his right hand. Most likely, he could have used it sometime in the near future.

Jaxom uncurled the fingers of his abused hand. The pain was agonizing, but he proceeded with the torture anyways. He deserved no less. Ever since their experience together on the island with the metal bird, Aeris had been waiting for him to come to her. He had known that, but refused to acknowledge the connection between them. He knew that his avoidance hurt her, but he didn't care. All that mattered was his idiotic pride. And now here he was . . .

Jaxom was no fool. He knew of the threat to dragon-kind . . . that the broken Pact of Bakharas was only the beginning of a renewed struggle with daemons. Not only that, but recent events told him that the degethozak had betrayed their own kind, working for those who were in association with the Daemundai. The degethozak had always been at odds with the helzthryn and the rezwithrys, but he didn't realize it would ever go this far.

Jaxom looked up to the ceiling. He clenched both his hands, resisting the terrible pain in his wounded hand and rising above it. It is what he should have done long ago when his heart first yearned for Damaeris, when his eyes set upon her for the very first time. Once, Jaxom felt he had known many things. Now all he knew was that he had to somehow find the woman who was destined to be his companion in life. He then needed to bond with her and bring her with him to Shayamalan to complete his training. It was his destiny . . . and hers.

Jaxom inhaled deeply and then screamed once more. He projected his voice as far as it could go, much farther than any humanoid man. Within it could be heard the voice of a dragon yearning for the strength of his true form, the presence of his bond-mate, and the means to be free. The inn shook with the power of his call, the people within wondering what was befalling them. But then it stopped just as suddenly as it had come. The inn and the surrounding streets were quiet. For now, Jaxomdrehl would be still. But only for now.

***

20 Saliren CY633

Sabian swiftly led his Daemundai out of the city of Gulshaan. They had arrived there much too late . . . the daemon-walker and his group left the city two days before. The reality of it rankled him. He must have passed them en route to the city, for his informants told him they were to be traveling north into the Larramis Forest. *Damn.* He knew what his master would think. Once again, Sabian Makonnen had proven his incompetency.

Since the skirmish at the docks in Yortec, Sabian had nothing in his mind but Tigerius Solanar. For several weeks Sabian had awaited news from Lord Razlul, and when finally it came, Sabian and his priests were instructed to travel into the realm of Karlisle. There, at the far western side of the Selmist Forest where the trees met the feet of the Bryton Hills, they would find access to an arcane mechanism that would provide transport to other places upon Shandahar. The system was comprised of a set of brackets, a mirror, and a spell-book. Sabian was quite familiar with the place, for he had visited it many years ago when he traveled with the Wildrunners. And he knew what he would find when he reached the cavern that housed the teleportation portal.

The mechanism would be in shambles. As far as Sabian knew, no one had made repairs after it's destruction all those years ago. Sabian regretted what he had done, especially when the young Dinim Coabra was able to make the mechanism work with only the spell-book and the portal brackets as a concentrator. Hells, even back then the man was strong enough, and skilled enough, to teleport a group of people with only an incantation and a single spell concentrator.

That was thirty years ago. Since then, Sabian had developed his own power. It would be relatively easy for him to make the mechanism work, even without the specialization of the Dimensionalist. Inasmuch, the Daemundai made the trek to the western edge of the Selmist. Once there, Sabian took them through the portal to another one situated within the forested region of the Tanze Peninsula. It was located only a three days' walk to the city of Gulshaan. The group would also be moving towards that location, and Razlul imagined that they would be meeting there at the same time.

However, something happened to make the group depart the city rather precipitously. He imagined it had much to do with the very entity who had given the Mehta his information in the first place. Lady Tholana had recently visited Gulshaan. As far as he could tell, she had been in and out of the city within only a day. At that point, the group had proceeded after her. And now Sabian was stuck trailing behind. Within the next day or so, he would be contacted by his master. He would then need to give the Mehta all the details of his failure. But until then, at least Sabian would have the opportunity to catch up to them. Perhaps then he would be spared Razlul's wrath.

***

The water was icy cold, just another unpleasant element about the circumstances in which he found himself. Talemar's thoughts tumbled about haphazardly, screaming against the cruelty he suffered . . . the interminable pain of his body and mind. And now he struggled just to breathe. The sacs in his chest burned for air, and just when his mental awareness began to slip, the hand that held his head under the water pulled it back out. The force the man used to pull him back was so strong, Talemar was flung to the ground. He lay there on his back, taking great gulps of air and sputtering against the water that still trickled down his face and into his eyes, nose, and mouth. Once again, the voice of his father filtered into his foggy mind, a voice he had come to despise.

"This is what they will do to you, Talemar. They will break you: mind, body, and spirit until you are no longer yourself, but another person entirely. You must cease your struggles, acquiesce to them completely. The more you fight against them, the harder it will be for you. They will torment you in ways you never imagined . . . with devices that will haunt your dreams for years to follow. The cimmereans will humiliate you and bring you to your knees. They will make you lick their soiled feet and make you beg to do it again."

The voice desisted and Talemar rolled over onto his side. The water he retched splashed his face as it fell onto the stone floor. The spasms were agonizing and his body involuntarily curved around itself. Suddenly there was a sharp kick to his ribs and then another. It wasn't until he was supine again that the abuse subsided. His tormentor put a booted foot over his throat . . . pressing . . . pressing. Talemar ceased all movement. Only the corner of his eye twitched, and he hoped that the man couldn't see it. His father's face came into view to join that of the man standing over him. Dinim spoke again, a hardness pervading his expression. "Then they will kill you."

His mind snapped back to reality as he gasped for air. Then his head was plunged once more down into the water of the murky river. Using calming techniques he learned during his sessions with his father, Talemar sought to relax himself. He would be able to withstand the air deprivation for a longer period of time, and maybe he would live through the experience.

A sudden kick to his gut sent Talemar into a renewed struggle. He pulled at the bonds that kept his hands tied behind his back, thoughts of clawing the faces of his abductors flitting through his mind. They brought him little satisfaction, for they only held him under the water longer. When they finally brought him up again, he barely had enough in him to take the air into his drowning lungs. The men threw him to the rocky ground, and the impact sent water from the sacs up and out his mouth. He sputtered and coughed as they then drug him back up. "Effin wemic!" spat his keeper. The young acolyte pulled savagely at the chain fastened at the collar around his neck. "You'll pay for those thoughts!"

The men half dragged, half carried him through the side tunnel and back to the larger chamber where they had erected the main encampment. The acolyte then handed his chain off to another priestess, one who was of superior rank. He slowly glanced up to find her grinning malevolently, her lavender eyes flashing in warning. Talemar hurriedly looked away, but it was too late.

The whip struck him before he could brace himself for the attack. It slashed viciously across his chest, cutting through whatever fabric still remaining there and deep into his flesh. It electrified him where it touched, sending a buzzing sensation throughout his body all the way to the tips of his fingers and toes. It struck him again and he screamed when the tip of it sliced through the lobe of his left ear.

Two men gripped him from behind to keep him standing as the priestess continued to beat Talemar with the whip. His body bucked with each lash, and he could feel the flesh being stripped from his chest and sides. Warm blood flowed freely from his ear and down his neck to join that which oozed from the multitudes of half-cauterized lacerations. It wasn't long before his consciousness began to flicker. After days of beatings and food deprivation, he was weak. He chastised himself for that weakness, knowing that Dinim had trained him to be stronger.

Once again he was lying on the cold stone floor, his body bruised and broken. It hurt just to move his fingers. His father's gravelly voice whispered in his ear. "Whatever you do, don't look the women in the eyes. It will be held as a sign of disrespect and defiance. It will tell them that you are unbroken and in need of more beating. They will deliver it brutally and without mercy."

Talemar felt himself being lifted off the floor by his ankles, the sound of the pulley creaking from somewhere across the room. The rope became almost unbearably tight as his weight bore down upon it. Disoriented, he shook involuntarily as the last of his body was suspended, and he began to swing. He vomited whatever stomach contents he had retained from his earlier beatings and remained as still as he could until the terrible nausea passed. He rose until his face was equal to that of his tormentors and then they left him there to dangle alone in the damp darkness.

Talemar awakened, and after orienting himself, realized that it was the middle of the night. All around he could hear the sounds of people sleeping, and then the occasional muffled cry from somewhere nearby. He could only wonder if it was Damaeris he heard. He could only imagine what they might be doing to her . . . what atrocities that they had visited upon her within the time she and Talemar had spent as Tholana's captives. He had only seen her twice . . . once before they entered the tunnels, and the other only a few days later. And after only that short amount of time, she looked the worse for wear.

The realization of what had already been done to her rocked Talemar to the center of his being. Aeris was so sore she could barely walk. She was covered in nothing more than a translucent swath of cloth that barely concealed her most private places. His captors had noticed the focus of his attention. Before he was brought to his knees, Talemar saw that she was sickly pale and that deep hollows had taken up residence beneath her eyes. His heart went out to her, and he wished that he had been more cautious when they left the tavern that night.

The company had reached the catacombs faster than he ever would have imagined. Left to natural means, it would have taken them thrice the amount of time to get so far. However, with a goddess amongst them, even a *fallen* one, they were privy to certain advantages. Once out of the city, Tholana had shifted herself and several others of her escort into sepia spiders. Only vaguely did Talemar remember the shift, but it was something to behold. Such creatures were known to be strong and fast, able to move quickly across most terrains with a load twice their body weight.

Wrapped in silken cocoons, Talemar and Aeris were quickly carried across the landscape. Talemar recalled very little of that part of the journey, for they had been placed in some type of stasis whilst they remained within the confines of the cocoons. However, once at the entrance to the tunnels, Talemar and Aeris were released from their prisons. Once awakening from his magic-induced sleep, he had to tear himself free of the sticky strands of the cocoon, and even now he could still feel some of the residue.

Right as they entered the catacombs, Talemar noticed that the small retinue had been met by another group of Tholana's followers. It took Talemar a while to realize that Tholana had to have spent the better part of her strength and endurance in order to shift that many people, and then to travel so quickly and so far without stopping even to have food or drink. The addition of several more priestesses to the company offered more protection to the weakened goddess. He imagined that there were many individuals who wouldn't hesitate to jump at the chance to capture and subdue someone such as the Queen of the Underdark.

Had they still been above, he would see that the third moon was risen, and that the first was ending her descent upon the dark horizon. Talemar wondered if Alasdair and Cedric had any idea what had happened to him and Aeris. He knew that it was doubtful, but he needed the hope to survive in this wretched place. His father had trained him for this eventuality, hoping that his son would retain at least some of the knowledge he would need in order to endure what was to come. As of yet, Talemar had fallen very short.

The moment he awakened after the abduction, Talemar could feel the band that circled his neck. At first it was simply a thing that chafed, one of the many physical annoyances he would be forced to endure. But it wasn't long before he learned of its other properties, in particular the one that conveyed many of his thoughts to his abductors. Already it had nearly killed him, and he wondered why his father had not mentioned it during his training.

Oh yes. His training . . . the part of his life where his own father kept him hidden within the bowels of the Medubrokan Academy and tortured him within but a breath of his life. Dinim claimed that it could save him one day, that the cimmereans might somehow find Talemar within their grasp. And perhaps he would live to tell the tale. Always afterward he resented his father for what he had done. Talemar bore the scars to remember what he had endured, both outward and inward. It was one of the things that ultimately kept him from pursuing Aeris years ago, when he may have had a chance with her. But that time had come and gone, just like so many other times in his life.

But Talemar knew he had to rise above the past . . . knew that he needed to live. Despite her love for another, he needed to live for Aeris. Dinim had taught his son more than just how to survive food and water deprivation, how to keep his sanity through the beatings and the rape, and how to endure the mental torment that would be inflicted. He had taught Talemar how to map out his surroundings without opening an eye, and how to notice minute changes in his physical environment. With these skills he would endeavor to remain physically intact, to retain his mental faculties, and to one day escape Tholana's stronghold. And he would take Aeris Timberlyn with him.

***

Aeris slowly awakened. At first all she felt was pain. It covered her body, all those parts she could identify and then some others she didn't realize she had. It was a struggle to open her eyes, the crust around the lids seeking to keep them sealed shut. She attempted to lift a hand to wipe it away only to realize that she couldn't move it far enough.

Surging to mental wakefulness, she realized that her entire body was bound. Chains attached to cuffs around her wrists and ankles secured her to a stalagmite that rose from among the cushions and pillows that surrounded her. Tied at her back was a diaphanous cloth that barely covered the area between the tops of her breasts to the tops of her thighs. Her flesh was covered with cuts and bruises and she felt a stickiness between her legs. Parting them, Aeris could smell the blood and she knew she had been raped. The fact was validated by the ache she felt inside . . . like she had been traumatized deep within.

For a long time she lay there. She struggled against her bonds, pulled at her wrists until she thought she might break the bones. She cried, but no tears came . . . testimony to water deprivation. Aeris began to remember only snatches of what had happened . . . her capture by Tholana, the almost nonexistent journey to the cavern system, and then her subsequent torture by several of the priestesses making up the bulk of the retinue. They had done terrible things to her, unimaginable things that made her writhe in agony. She would be surprised if she ever had children, and she felt regret. She would have loved to bear children.

Finally they came. The women entered the room and when they found that she was awake, they converged upon her like scavengers to a piece of rotting flesh. They enjoyed their treatment of her . . . like she was nothing but a set of bones with skin and a hole. They bickered over her, each one wondering how much harm could come to the captive without Tholana becoming angered. Her face they left without a scratch, for Tholana liked to preserve the beauty of her playthings. The women loved to hear her scream, and when Aeris came to that realization, she quickly stopped making any sounds at all. It was easy for her to submit . . . the pain was lessened when she simply lay still. After a while they grew bored of her and left.

Aeris lay there, defeated. Her groggy mind told her that she had been there before, that she always seemed to make the same realizations every night, but that by the time she awakened the next day, she had forgotten what had happened before. It was an intricate spell, one devised by the goddess herself . . . for Tholana was a master not only with scrying, but mind-spells as well.

The mind spells . . . it was through Mateo that she had been tracking the group. And it was also through him that she must have influenced events. Aeris didn't really know what those events may have been, but she knew without a shadow of a doubt that it was the truth. And now, thinking of the group, she wondered if any of them knew to where she might have disappeared and if they might come for her. She knew that Alasdair, Cedric, Tigerius, Magnus, and Jonesy would surely come . . . but of the others she wasn't quite so sure. She liked to think that Cervantes would come. With him would be Cortes and Jezibel. And perhaps Goldare and the halfen brothers would come as well.

Aeris held on to those thoughts of rescue and fought against the web-like spell Tholana had placed in her mind. The strands were many and varied, each one sticking to the other in a complex design that could be devised only by a master with such things. But Aeris was determined that her hope would see her through to the end . . . whatever that might be.

CHAPTER 20

The group moved east through the narrow strip of land that connected the Tanze Peninsula with the rest of the mainland. Named the Isthmus of Larramis, the swath was only a few zacrol in width, barely a day's ride on the horses. However, the length was much more than that . . . at least two or three days of riding. Jonesy wondered how Magnus knew where to go, for she did not recall hearing that anyone knew the precise location of their destination.

Several days ago, the group left the city of Gulshaan. Jonesy could see that Magnus was loathe to leave Levander behind, but he had very little choice. The bald man was seriously wounded, and if they moved him, Lev might die. Magnus bade Mateo stay with him, for it was the least that Magnus could offer. Lev would at least have a familiar face to see when he finally awakened. Not to mention that their destination was not a place Magnus wished to bring the boy. He had told everyone of the danger they faced against an enemy such as Tholana, but none was willing to back down. Everyone wanted to rescue Aeris and Talemar from their captors, despite the risks. Jonesy was taken slightly aback by their decision. She hadn't expected such loyalty, and she felt honored to have them as her comrades. It was more than she could have ever asked for, and she knew that Magnus felt the same.

Despite protestations from Magnus, Alasdair and Cedric decided the group's initial destination. Deep within the Larramis Forest two days' unbroken ride out of Gulshaan, the place comprised something Jonesy had never seen before, an object of arcane significance that she knew she may never see again. It was a teleportation portal . . . a means to travel to a distant location without actually having to walk or ride there. Alasdair had hoped that, by actually going there and looking through the tome that resided within the portal chamber, Magnus may be able to divine where he needed to travel next in order to reach Aeris. Unfortunately, no such thing occurred.

Yet, knowing that their families needed to be informed of the present course of events, Cedric used the portal to take him to a place he called Krathil-lon. Once there, the plan was for him to simply hand a message over to one of the druids living there, instruct him as to the recipient of such message, and then immediately use the portal to return to the group. It didn't take long for Cedric to complete this task, and by then Magnus had determined that he needed to be the one to make most, if not all, of the decisions regarding the group's activities.

It was then that Magnus took over leadership of the group. It was only natural that he do so, for it was only he that knew where they needed to go, and only he that seemed to have any information about the opponent that they were up against. Magnus conceded that he did not know how he knew where he should go, or how he knew about Tholana. He informed everyone that they could waste time figuring out how he knew these things, or they could simply have a little bit of faith and follow him. The group unanimously chose the latter. Cervantes sulked about it for a day or two, but it seemed he was becoming accustomed to the situation.

Jonesy would never forget the fight that took place after Magnus realized the peril that Aeris and Talemar faced at the hands of Tholana. The day after the fateful night of the tavern brawl, Magnus approached the rest of the group and informed them of the situation. Alasdair, Cedric, and Tigerius stood behind him, and Jonesy was the first to step forward and offer whatever aid she could to the cause. Next was Cervantes. The expression that crossed Magnus' face was monstrous to say the least, and he directed all of his anger and animosity at the captain.

"No." Magnus spoke that single word slowly and succinctly. "Your services are not wanted."

Cervantes frowned. "How dare you? I will offer my aid wherever I damn well please."

Magnus smiled venomously. "I think not, my dear captain. You have caused quite enough trouble."

Cervantes stalked across the room to stand in front of Magnus. "You pile of lloryk dung . . . what are you tryin' to say?" he sputtered.

Refusing to back down, Magnus narrowed his eyes and moved in even closer. "If it weren't for you and your fool pride, we would still have Aeris and her cousin within our ranks, as well as the comrade who now lies at the Gates of Halthor."

Cervantes narrowed his own eyes. He was silent for a moment as he regarded Magnus, his expression one of angry determination. "If it weren't for you and your own thoughtlessness, Aeris would not have been so anxious to be rid of you." Cervantes paused to allow the impact of his words to sink in. "Yeah, I know about how you betrayed her . . . tied her up like some animal and forced her to keep you in her company. It's a small wonder how she has dealt with you this long."

"Damn you, Cervantes!" Magnus' voice was thunderous. "That has nothing to do with what happened last night and you know it! If you had kept your fists to yourself, none of this would have taken place."

"And how do you know that . . . stupid mage? You think you are the best animal keeper, then? I guess you should know. You've done it before . . ."

Magnus and Cervantes surged towards one another, fists flying. Each man barely had a chance to touch the other before they were pulled away by their comrades. Tiger held Magnus while Cortes hung on to Cervantes.

"Magnus," said Alasdair into his ear, "you can't stop him from coming with us. And think about it, we might need him when we face the enemy that has taken our bretheren."

Magnus ceased struggling at the sound of the other man's voice. An expression of resignation passed over his face, and he pulled away from Tiger's grip. "Fine. But I don't have to like it."

And now here they were. Cervantes had insisted to Jezibel that she stay in Gulshaan with Lev and Mateo, promising that they would return once Talemar and Aeris were back within their ranks. Alasdair left them a pouch of gold, more than enough to see them well through the season and into the next if they were thrifty. Jonesy found that, despite Jezzie's close association with Cervantes, she was loathe to leave her only female companion behind. However, she knew it was for the best. Jezibel was no warrior . . . she would have a difficult time leading the life Jonesy had endured the past few months.

Jonesy stared ahead of her. So much had happened since she left her father's stronghold in the kingdom of Karlisle. She had been ready to part with the group when they were going to be taking the portal system back to Elvandahar, and had shared her reasons with Aeris the evening that Alasdair arrived . . . the evening before Aeris and Talemar were abducted.

Aeris came to her room after many of the others had retired for the night. Jezibel had not yet returned, and Aeris took the opportunity to approach Jonesy. Her expression was one of hurt, mingled with that of perplexity. "Jonesy, what haven't you told me?"

Jonesy regarded her friend intently from across the room. She knew it was time to tell Aeris her entire story. She had divulged bits and pieces of it over the past months, but never the ultimate reason why she had left Karlisle.

Jonesy shook her head and looked down to the floor. "I know I should have told you more, but I just couldn't." She felt her lower lip begin to tremble and she wrapped her arms almost protectively around her middle. "I've just been so scared . . ."

Within moments Jonesy felt Aeris' arms around her, felt the warmth and security of her embrace, and heard the hushed reassurances of her gentle voice. Jonesy told Aeris about the sickness that had befallen her father and the cruelty of her brother. By then, her sister had already been abducted, and they had just learned of the perpetrator. While the king made orders to ready his armies to march against Lord Razlul, his son involved himself in other activities . . .

Jonesy made her way quickly through the streets, eager to be home. She didn't like walking them alone at night, despite the presence of the night watch that patrolled the areas surrounding the palace. She had an uneasy feeling this eve, felt it the moment she left the Margolis residence. And it didn't help matters any that her sister had been abducted by a daemonic madman from the place that should have been able to offer her the most protection.

Jonesy knew she shouldn't be out, but she was quite good at eluding the persons responsible for her well-being, in particular her hand-maids and body-guards. They would surely have told the king of her misdeeds, but she had no real fear of any consequences. The king was consumed with the loss of his eldest daughter. Yet, even before Elinora's abduction, Joneselia had begun to slip through the cracks . . . much as a result of the king's mental deterioration. Despite the reason, it hurt her to realize she had become nothing but an afterthought to the man who had once bounced her on his knee.

Jonesy turned the corner and rushed through the alleyway. It was darker here, and she felt her skin begin to prickle. It was only a moment later that she heard a noise, and she stopped in her tracks. She felt her heart skip a beat, and she held her breath, afraid that somehow it would be heard. She pressed herself against the nearest wall and waited, hoping that she wouldn't hear anything . . . ascribe it all to her over-active imagination and continue on her way.

However, she should have known that she wouldn't be so lucky. Jonesy heard the noise again, and it sounded like it was coming from the adjoining alleyway just ahead. After another pause, she heard the noise again, this time accompanied by the sounds of a scuffle. Regardless of her fear, Jonesy wondered what was going on, and her legs began to move her along of their own volition.

The sounds of a struggle became louder as she approached the adjoining alley. She heard masculine laughter and sound of tearing cloth. She heard a woman cry out, and then the subsequent sounds of someone being struck by a closed fist. In spite of the increased risk, Jonesy crept closer to the turn in the alleyway. Then, once she reached it, she chanced a look around the corner. The scene she witnessed burned itself into her mind.

By the wan light cast by the closest street lamp, Jonesy saw a girl lying upon the cobbled ground. Her face was covered in blood and her eyes barely open. Her layered skirt was pulled up to her hips, and her underpants torn away. A man straddled himself overtop her, grunting with the exertion to achieve his base pleasure. Three more men stood and watched, each with a leer of anticipation on his face. Another man stood in the shadows, his hands working at the laces of his trousers.

Jonesy stifled a gasp and pulled herself back out of sight. She put a hand over her mouth to keep herself from making any noise, and she closed her eyes tightly shut. By the gods, what should she do? There were four men, and only one of her. She quickly came to the realization there was nothing *she could do. They would easily overpower her within moments, and her fate would most likely match that of the young woman on the ground.*

Crouched within the shadows behind the wall, Jonesy heard the piteous moans of the girl as another man took his place between her legs. She couldn't keep herself from peering from around the corner, watching with disbelief as each of the men took his turn with her. Once, when the girl attempted to lift herself from the cobbles, the man riding her struck her so hard, Jonesy could hear the sound of her skull striking the ground when she fell.

At last the men were finished. In horror, Jonesy watched as four of the men picked the girl up from the ground and proceeded to beat her. They then threw her broken body once more down to the ground and kicked her with their booted feet. When they finally stopped, they all stood around her. It was then that the fifth man re-emerged from the shadows on the far side of the alley. It was the one man whom Jonesy had not yet seen, the first man to have raped the young woman who now lay dying on the street.

Jonesy watched her brother step forward to join the men circling the woman. He then unsheathed his dagger. In one swift motion, Rigel knelt and plunged the weapon deep into the girl's chest. He then wiped the blade clean with the fabric of her skirt, rose, and sheathed the dagger at his hip. Then, without speaking, the men left.

Jonesy remained positioned behind the wall for several moments after the men were gone. She wiped away the tears she had shed, and slowly walked towards the broken body. She knew that the girl was dead . . . who could have survived a beating such as that one, not to mention the killing blow of the dagger? Jonesy knelt beside the girl, pressed a hand over the open wound left by the dagger, and cried. It was a shame that she had to die, especially in such a shameful fashion. In a way, Jonesy mourned for all women who fell at the hands of the men who should be protecting them, and she despised her brother more than she ever had before.

It took a while for Jonesy to make a realization. Her eyes widened as she noticed that the blood from the girl's wound flowed freely between her fingers. Leaning close, she could almost feel the faintest bit of a stirring with the breaths that were taken. It was then that Jonesy had hope that the girl lived, and that maybe her life could be saved.

Darting from the alley, Jonesy ran to the only place where she thought she could take the dying girl. The apothecary was run by an aging man who had once been a healing priest of some renown. Pounding upon his door, Jonesy roused the man from a peaceful slumber and brought him to the girl lying in the alleyway. Between the both of them, they dragged the girl back to the apothecary and into the residence above the store.

"Her name is Mikayla." Running her hand along the chain at her neck, Jonesy pulled the pendant free from the neckline of her tunic. It was simple in its design, yet unique. It held a rare beauty, one that was enhanced by the sparkling silver and onyx swirled stone set in the center. "She gave me this so that I would always remember that I saved her life. But to be truthful, I did nothing more than what any other caring person would have done."

Aeris lay a hand gently upon her cheek. "But it wasn't any other person, Jonesy. It was you. To Mikayla, you were something special."

Jonesy nodded, keeping her face lowered. "But it gave me away." She took a trembling breath and glanced up to see the confused frown on Aeris' face. "Rigel remembered seeing the pendant around Mikayla's neck, remembered it because he had seen none like it ever before."

Jonesy heard Aeris' swift intake of breath. She would never forget the horror of that night . . . . the night before she left Karlisle.

Jonesy pressed her back against the cold stone of the tunnel wall. She turned her face away from the man standing before her, felt the rank stench of his breath against her neck. Her mind kept telling her to run, but her body simply wouldn't obey. Her legs were like massive boulders holding her to her current position, trapping her like any cage would have. Despite her growing fear, she strove to keep herself under control.

He put one hand on the wall on each side of her head and leaned in close. Jonesy fought to keep her breathing normal and her heart from beating out of her chest. She closed her eyes to the sight of him and thought that, if she wished it hard enough, he would disappear into the surrounding darkness. "Your brother says that I can have you. I've been waiting a long time for this moment."

Jonesy said nothing, somehow knowing that Luxor spoke the truth. Rigel always had a way of demeaning her, even as a young girl. And now that she approached maturity, she could see how that denigration could take a more twisted path. Sex had become a passion for him, and she imagined that he would love to see her writhing beneath the men with which he had close association. By the gods, what she wouldn't give to have Elinora there with her now.

"I have the feeling that you will have the sweetest taste of any woman I have ever had the pleasure of taking." Despite her closed eyes, she could sense that he smiled. "Rigel said you wouldn't grow up very pretty, but Hells was he wrong. I suppose his sentiments are for the best. What man wants to hunger for his own sister?"

Jonesy inhaled sharply. Truth be told, she wouldn't put it past Rigel to eventually have her for himself. The thought shook her to the core of her being, and only then did she find the impetus to struggle. She thrust herself from the tunnel wall and into Luxor, hoping to catch him by surprise. He grunted and fell back, allowing her to stoop beneath the arm alongside of her. She began to run, and just as she thought she may have been free of him, she felt an impact from behind.

Jonesy staggered to the floor. Luxor reached down and grabbed her by the waist, hauling her back up to face him. She steeled herself for a show of violence, very aware of how Rigel and his men tended to handle their victims. Hells, she had seen it first hand only several evenings before when they had left a girl to die in the streets of Ishkar.

Yet, the assault never came. Instead she heard the voice of her brother from behind them. "I see you thought to give Luxor a bit of a struggle." Rigel chuckled. "Very good, little sister. I never thought you had it in you."

Jonesy went still in Luxor's grip. She hated Rigel's voice, categorized it with those things she considered most vile. She allowed her gaze to seek him out, and when she turned her head, she found him standing several feet away. Alongside him stood the other men of his company.

It was then that Time suddenly seemed to slow down. Jonesy renewed her struggle against Luxor, knowing that her welfare depended upon her being free of him. She watched as her brother leaned against the tunnel wall and curved his lips up into a malicious grin. He then made the gesture for his friend to continue.

Jonesy felt herself swung around and slammed into the stone wall. The impact knocked the breath out of her. As she gasped for air, she felt the fabric of her blouse being torn away to expose her chest. She pushed ineffectually at her assailant, felt his hands at her backside and his mouth at her breasts. Her legs buckled and Luxor followed her down to the floor, pulling up her skirt and inserting a hand between her legs. Jonesy inhaled sharply at the intrusion. She turned her head away from him, unwilling to look at Luxor's face. Instead her gaze came to rest upon her brother.

With an intense look of concentration, Rigel suddenly drew himself away from the wall. He strode over to Jonesy and Luxor, laying a staying hand upon his friend's shoulder. The man reluctantly ceased his activity, pulled away and adjusted the waist of his trousers. Rigel knelt next to her on the ground, put a hand to her chest, and brought the pendant into view. It was the gift given to her by Mikayla, a gesture of friendship and appreciation for what Jonesy had done for her. Rigel's gaze hardened upon the object and then shifted to Jonesy's face.

"Where did you get this?" Rigel's expression was shuttered, but she could hear the tension in his voice.

"I . . . I bought it from a street vendor just the other day," she stuttered.

Rigel must have sensed the hesitancy in her demeanor, saw the falsehood reflected in her eyes. His other hand closed around her throat, and he began to squeeze. Jonesy struggled for breath, clawed ineffectually at the vise-like grip. He leaned over her, bringing his face close to hers. "Where . . . did . . . you . . . get . . . this . . ."

He spoke the words slowly and succinctly, and his blue eyes bore into hers. As Jonesy fought for her next breath, Time seemed to slow once more. Her vision began to fade away at the periphery, and she noticed how Rigel's eyes seemed so barren . . . so devoid of emotion. They were soul-less eyes, ones that she might see belonging to something other than human.

The grip began to ease from around her neck, yet Rigel kept his hand there as he awaited her reply. With vivid clarity, she knew it was useless to continue with her lie. Instinctively, he knew that she knew about the girl in the alleyway. At this rate he would kill her via suffocation, but what would he do when she came out with the truth? "A . . . a girl gave it to me."

Rigel was taken aback by her sudden candor. For a moment there was stillness. He then released her throat, grabbed the tatters of her blouse, and pulled her upper body up from the ground. "What girl?" he growled, some of his brown hair falling over his forehead to cover one eye.

Jonesy swallowed convulsively, wrapping her arms protectively over her breasts. "She was lying, beaten, in the side-streets."

"Was she dead?" he asked in a harsh tone, absently sweeping the errant hair out of his face.

Jonesy paused, thought about telling him another lie. However, she chose against it. She was obviously not very good at that game, especially with Rigel. She slowly shook her head.

Rigel stared hard into her eyes. He was scrutinizing her, wondering exactly how much she knew. She could imagine his thoughts at that moment . . . if he could hear what people were thinking, he would be listening in to her mind.

"Where is the girl now?"

His voice had calmed, and it had an almost predatory quality. Jonesy didn't need to consider lying, for she had no idea of the girl's whereabouts since she left the sanctuary of the apothecarian's residence.

Jonesy shook her head. "I don't know."

Suddenly releasing her blouse, Rigel rose from his crouched position. She could sense the tension emanating from him; saw it in the rigidity of his back and shoulders. Silence reigned in the tunnel as he paced. Jonesy slowly picked herself up from the floor, bringing the remains of her blouse around to cover her exposed chest.

He then swung back around towards her. She could see the indecision on his face and it scared her. Should he kill her? What would be the repercussions of that action? The other men looked to him, ready to do his bidding. His desires had become their laws, and they had very little fear of consequences. Such was the advantage of espousing the future heir to a kingdom.

Aeris wiped away Jonesy's tears as she cried, and with them many of her fears. But it wasn't until her friend was gone that Jonesy realized the power of her own will. Jonesy didn't even remember how she had escaped Rigel. She supposed he had allowed her to leave simply so he could ponder what he should do with her. Now she knew that her brother searched for her, and one day she would be forced to face him. Jonesy shivered at the thought, goose-pimples rising on her flesh. She hoped that day was a bit farther into the future, at a time when she had enough strength within her to fend him away. Now she was weak . . . but she was learning. With her companions beside her, she would be strong. Then she would be able to persevere . . .

***

Talemar knew when she entered the chamber. He inhaled deeply and then out, feeling the magnitude of the power that approached. He knew that she would come eventually . . . it was only a matter of time. Tholana always saw to her pets, no matter how insignificant they might be.

Talemar awakened to find himself lying upon a bed. His head pounded and his body ached in every place imaginable. His father sat nearby, watching him struggle at the loose bonds at his wrists. At least his ankles were free, and he could stretch muscles that were sore and misused.

"There is one thing that will set you apart from other men. The priestesses will feel the flow of energy towards you, a natural response of the environment to a Talent. They will respect that power, and thus have respect for you as a wielder of that magic. You will be given consideration above most other men, but it also means that you will have to watch yourself even more. Not only will the women will be waiting to find a reason to punish you, but the men will be trying to find a way to betray you. Never engage in any form of communication with them, and if possible, avoid them entirely."

Through pain bleary eyes, Talemar looked over at the man sitting not far away. It wasn't the first time he thought that Dinim was a lunatic. What man in his right mind would subject his own son to this type of treatment? Who would give torment to another so easily, and then sit and make small talk? Talemar still had the metallic taste of blood in his mouth, testimony to the brutality of his treatment earlier that morning.

"Then Tholana will come to you. She will be the most divine thing you have ever seen. She is different from the others, will demand that you look at her without an averted gaze. You must obey her without hesitation, for she is an impatient creature. She will coerce you into letting your guard down, seduce you, and then pleasure you to heights you have never known before. Don't even bother to resist, for the action will be one of futility. She is demanding and easy to anger. Yet, she is also gentle, boundlessly sensual, and so sexually charged you will feel her the moment she enters the room."

Talemar felt the breath still in his chest. He could feel her behind him, her radiance so intense he could feel the heat of it upon his back. His body had already responded to her presence, and without wanting to, he would be ready for her. He slowly turned to face her, mindful to keep his eyes downcast. If he had been clothed, he would have tried to hide his body's reaction to her presence. But as it was, his manhood stood erect before him, despite abuse from the evening before. He kept his eyes averted, but he could see the way her gaze perused his body as she neared.

Tholana stopped about two arm lengths before him. She regarded him intently for a moment. He could only imagine what she was thinking. He reeked of dried sex, the excrescence of the previous evenings' orgy still clinging to him, both male and female. And then there was the blood that had dried around the numerous small wounds he had sustained since last he had bathed. Talemar tried to remember when that may have been. Was it yesterday before the orgy . . . or perhaps the day before? He could not recall, for time had ceased to carry meaning, the days melding into one another.

"I see my priestesses have used you well," she remarked in a casual tone.

Talemar said nothing, heeding his father's warning not to speak to Lady Tholana without first having her permission. Once more she stepped forward, closing the distance between them, and then grabbed his hair and pulled his head back until his eyes settled onto a point just past her face. "You are a fine specimen, Talemar Coabra. My priestesses were correct in their assessment of you." She paused for only a moment before she continued. "Raise your eyes to me, mage. I like my men to look upon me."

Talemar obliged, slowly settling his gaze onto her face. The goddess was exquisite in every detail, from her long black hair to the voluptuous curves of her breasts, hips and thighs. She wore nothing but a gem encrusted diaphanous cloth, leaving nothing to the imagination.

Tholana continued to watch Talemar, and when he couldn't keep the expression of appreciation from his face she smiled. She curved one hand around the nape of his neck, and with the other she began to pleasure him. It wasn't long before he was spent. She then stepped away from him, shuddering slightly with the effort it had taken her to resist participation. She kept in mind that the meeting had only been a test of his functionality, for not one of her priestesses had seen him achieve satisfaction throughout any of the orgies in which he had been a part.

Once out of the chamber, Tholana gestured to the nearest acolyte. "Prepare him to receive me later this evening. I want him bathed and oiled."

Tholana left the woman to her task and made her way down the corridor to the chamber that housed a thermal pool. The naturally occurring spring was situated deep within the vast cavern in which her citadel rested. The heat from the pool warmed the air around it, making the chamber the ideal place for bathing. Once within the chamber, Tholana stripped away what little cloth covered her. Then, stepping into the pool, her thoughts focused upon her prisoner. A curl of anticipation tightened deep within her belly. It was more than mere curiosity that had driven her to bring Talemar to satisfaction.

Tholana sank deep into the waters until only her eyes and the top of her head were visible upon the surface. For the most part, she never regretted having no living children. Many, many centuries ago, in another Cycle, she had birthed a male child. The conception had been unanticipated, and angry that she had borne a lowly son, she abandoned him to the elements. No one ever knew, and she kept the secret to herself. Several decades later, Tholana birthed yet another male child. She left him to die in the same place she had left the first. She only vaguely remembered her gaze settling briefly upon the tiny bones of her first son as she lay the second next to them. She felt no remorse, only disparagement borne by the fact that she had mothered only male children.

Recently, things had suddenly changed. She realized that a part of her had always been waiting . . . hoping that one day she would bear Tallachienan's children, be they sons or daughters. That time never came. And now, after having lived so long, Tholana was childless. Since *the Fall*, she had begun to slowly accept the reality of her own mortality. No fool, she began to recognize the benefit of having those to whom one could leave knowledge and skills . . . a means by which one could live on through those to whom a familial attachment existed. A legacy.

Tholana waded slowly throughout the heated pool. The waters sensually caressed her as she moved, relaxing the muscles of her now mortal body. Deep within, she could feel that she was fertile, that if she so chose, she could conceive a child. Those feelings translated to her outside, where she felt an urgent need to be with a man, to have his seed come within her. And she had decided that man should be the one currently residing just down the corridor.

It had been difficult to refrain from enjoying a climax with Talemar, but Tholana still had ample opportunity. She could wait until the time was just right. The conception would be carefully planned, and she was certain of the outcome. This time, she was certain that the child would be female. And she would have power. Talent derived from her sire, coupled with abilities garnered from her mother, would be a boon to any child. Tholana would be there to nurture that power . . .

***

From the shadows at the far side of the chamber, Razlul watched the goddess at play. Amongst varied pillows and furs piled all around, he remained hidden upon the bed situated far enough away that he would remain undetected. He preferred it that way, content to simply watch the romping from a distance. The women were having far too much fun with their plaything to realize his presence. Yet, even without the diversion, he doubted that many of them would have detected him anyway.

Not for the first time, Razlul considered the alliance in which he had found himself. It had been an effortless one to forge, for he and Tholana had come together once or twice before *the fall*. Several moon cycles ago, when his chief mage informed him of the daemon-walker in the midst of those he followed with the dragon crystal, Razlul was astounded by the discovery. Without a doubt, the young man was the offspring of a creature he had been attempting to find for decades: Triath Solanar.

Almost thirty years ago, Triath and his mate had 'disappeared' after their last fateful meeting. Even then, Tianna must have been pregnant with her child, for the young daemon-walker was of the appropriate age. However, the thrill of the discovery was subdued by the fact that the group had escaped the clutches of his Daemundai and set sail into the Biske Bay. Razlul was angry with Sabian for losing this unexpected prize, and if the man had been physically there before him, the Mehta would quite probably have killed him.

Yet, Sabian was fortunate, for he was able to impart some very useful information concerning the group. One of the members had been 'stamped' with the signature of another magic-user. Through that person, the spellcaster was able to keep track of the group. The signature was familiar to Sabian, for he had encountered it once before during his early arcane training. It belonged to that of the goddess Tholana, Queen of the Underdark.

Razlul suddenly had a renewed interest in a woman he had met on only brief occasions in the past. Even then he had known her to be powerful, but now she had something he did not . . . access to a group of people in which he now had a vested interest. An alliance with one such as she could secure him the prize he so much desired, not to mention the benefit of her company, which he had always before found pleasing.

Now, as he watched the scene before him, Razlul found that his lustful side had come to the fore. The young woman that the priestesses used was one of those from the group they followed, a friend of the daemon-walker whom he wished to soon have within his grasp. Indeed, he had been perturbed to discover that Tholana and her priestesses made a move upon the group before his own priests had made it to the city. He initially believed that the capture of this woman and her comrade had hastened the groups' departure from the city. Several days later, when he was able to regain contact with Tholana, he discovered that the group was planning to depart the city the next day regardless of any action of hers. She told him it was the reason for her impromptu decision to make her move upon the group that evening as opposed to waiting until the next evening when the Daemundai had a chance to reach the city.

Of course, his priests did not reach the city the next night. It was two evenings after Tholana's ambush that Sabian finally reached Gulshaan. Razlul grudgingly conceded that just as much of the fault lay with him as it did his chief mage. The Mehta had been under the impression that Sabian was closer to the Selmist portal than he actually was. And Sabian had not realized exactly how much time it would take them to reach Gulshaan from the Larramis portal.

Razlul stared at the captive girl. She was quite stunning, with wild crimson hair and an ethereal beauty that that would enrapture any man . . . no matter his lineage or his power. She cried out when Tholana bit her breast, and only moments later she fell into a heap at the goddess' feet. Her complexion had become deathly pale, and for a moment he wondered if she still lived.

It was then that Tholana's gaze sought him out among the shadows within which he lingered. Razlul could see the lust burning within the lavender depths of her eyes, and he felt an answering call within himself. Dismissing her priestesses to their own chambers, Tholana slowly ambled over to the bed upon which he reclined. Once there, she climbed onto it. On all fours, she crawled over and then sunk into the pillows beside him. She disappeared beneath the furs, and the sensations that began to grip him were intense. Such was the way of Tholana, and it wasn't long before she finished him.

Razlul was a very powerful being . . . something created at an arcane apex. He was human, yet not wholly so, for he had been infused with the essence of a daemon not more than three and a half decades before. He would never forget that day . . . the day he truly came alive. Before the infusion he had been a simpering boy barely into adolescence. His body was weak, subject to all the aches and illnesses that assailed it on a common day. The sorcerer Gaknar had taken him from his home, having chosen Razlul to be the recipient of Tharizdune's spirit. However, something went wrong.

The Wildrunners came. They disrupted the spell, and the process could not be completed. Tharizdune had been forced to leave the host body to return to the Hell from which he had come . . . but not before he was able to infuse it with a part of his essence. Thus, Razlul had been reborn. No longer was he merely a boy subject to the weakness of his frail human body. He had become something more, something beyond what the world had seen before.

Except for Triath Solanar.

For several days now, Razlul had resided within Tholana's citadel. Soon it would be time for him to leave. He resisted the inevitable, but he knew better than to wait overly long. Despite all his strength and power, Razlul had a weakness. He didn't quite know how to explain it, nor did he understand why he was afflicted. All he knew was that every fortnight he had to become submerged within Hell's *Fire* in order to rejuvenate his body.

Razlul considered his situation with calm disdain. If it were at all possible, he would simply carry the *Fire* with him. He had actually tried it on several occasions. Every time he was met with failure. The flames simply could not be sustained outside of the pit in which they were housed. Razlul had tried to discover a way to exist without the fiery bath. There was a time he became so weak, he was unable to move from his chamber. His priests had to carry him to the *Fire* and lay him within it. He stayed there for almost two days before he finally had the strength to finally leave the flames.

Now, lying there within the plush confines of Tholana's bed, Razlul could feel the tell-tale signs his body exhibited when it needed to receive the regenerative qualities bestowed by the *Fire*. He found himself vastly perturbed because he knew the group was slowly making their way closer to Tholana's stronghold in search of their comrades. He had wanted to be there when they arrived, but it appeared as though that would not be a probability. It would take him a few days to reach his own fortress, despite the aid of the portal system he had discovered when he first came across the place where he knew he wanted to make his permanent residence. It had been quite a boon to realize that the device could take him to a place only two day's walk to the cavern system that led to Tholana's stronghold. It didn't take him long to discover the quickest route through the catacombs, and the natural inhabitants of the place promptly learned to leave him alone.

Razlul turned towards his bed-mate, already starting to become aroused only moments after his previous climax. Such was what he had become after his infusion with the daemon's essence, a sexual insatiability that could scarcely be quenched. He had found his match only in the woman before him, a woman whose desires were equal to his own. To him, it was a measure of his strength . . . his perseverance over the weakness that threatened him every fortnight. However, with this imperfection always hanging over him, Razlul had continued to try and discover some way that he would eventually be able to overcome it. It didn't take him long to realize that Triath might be a part of the answer he was looking for.

With yet another reason to have Triath within his control, Razlul increased his efforts have access to the only other daemon hybrid he knew existed upon Shandahar. Furthermore, as far as he knew, Triath did not suffer the encumbrance Razlul was forced to endure. This reality rankled Razlul, for it made him feel somewhat degraded. Why should he be forced to withstand this weakness when another man, one who wanted nothing to do with his daemon side, have no such affliction? Yet, he supposed this reality could act in his benefit. Razlul would be able to take Triath and discover what it was about the man that made it so he did not have to bathe in the *Fire*. Once he knew what that thing was, Razlul could attempt to apply that same quality to himself.

But now there was a new development. There was a son. The boy was a boon novelty . . . something quite unprecedented. Now that Razlul knew that it was possible for a human female to give birth to a daemon hybrid, he would be able to study the intricacies of the daemon/human fusion. He would begin by discovering all he could about Triath's offspring, and then Razlul would attempt to create some of his own. Despite his many partners, he had yet to impregnate any of them. He found this slightly disconcerting, and he wondered about his ability to sire children. However, he thrust those concerns aside when he reminded himself he had yet to make any deliberate attempts. He would concern himself about it later when, or if, he failed in his endeavors.

Just the smell of Tholana's desire for him made Razlul's arousal complete. He tossed her down onto the pillows and straddled her hips. She was willing and eager to have him, and it wasn't long before he was enjoying another climax. He would spend the rest of the day at the stronghold, but that evening he would make his departure. He would not divulge the reason for his leave-taking, although it would be difficult for she knew his desire to have Tigerius within his grip.

It was unfortunate that Razlul would be forced to rely upon Sabian for the boy's detainment, yet he saw no other way. From here on out, Razlul would only begin to lose his strength. As soon as he was able, he would make his way to Sabian and take the boy into his own custody. Razlul could hardly wait to see the day.

CHAPTER 21

Tholana walked slowly around her. Aeris stared straight ahead, refusing to watch the almost predatory movement of the goddess. Only when the woman moved within her plane of view did Aeris note the smile plying about the corners of her mouth. Experience told Aeris that it meant trouble, and she felt a twinge of apprehension settle deep in her belly. Aeris could only wonder what the goddess meant to do with her next, for it was common knowledge that Tholana had become tired of her already. The woman required a steady stream of new partners in her bedchamber, and Aeris had served her well enough for the last several days. However, she could only feel a modicum of relief, for she had felt the cruelty of Tholana enough times to know that the woman had other plans for her prize captive. Aeris had been bathed thoroughly and then given a shimmering gossamer robe and a silken golden cord to tie around her waist. Her curling red hair had been artfully pinned, and thick ropes of it fell gracefully over her pale shoulders.

Finally the dark goddess stopped before Aeris and stepped in close. Lavender eyes set within an ethereally beautiful face bore into her scornfully. The tops of Tholana's breasts bulged out the top of a camisole made of soft leather and jeweled lace, and around her neck was an ebony band glittering with the darkest of sapphires. Once more her red lips curved into a smile, a malicious smirk that told Aeris she was about to learn something about the plans Tholana had for her.

With a fingertip, Tholana traced the contours of Aeris' jaw, and then trailed it down the curve of her neck to the bone that started at her chest. It then continued to the mound of her breast, where it finally stopped at a spot just above the nipple. Aeris fought to remain still as Tholana circled the painful wound with her fingernail. "I must say, you tasted delicious my dear," Tholana drawled.

Aeris said nothing and continued to stare past Tholana. The lesion throbbed with the close proximity of Tholana's touch. It was an injury the goddess herself had bestowed upon her only a few evenings before. Excited by the intensity of the orgy, Tholana had bitten into the softness of Aeris' breast, her elongated canines cutting easily through soft flesh. Tholana then lapped at the blood, her poisonous saliva entering the wound. Aeris was sick and delirious for the two days that followed, and it took her another two days abed in order to begin a full recovery.

Tholana lifted the offending finger. "The feel of your blood in my mouth was intoxicating to say the least." Then she paused for a moment. "But that is not why we are here today."

Tholana paused again and took a step back. "We are here for two reasons, actually. The first is to be an *enlightenment* session." Tholana's grin widened when she spoke the emphasized word. "I know many things that you do not. That, my dear, puts you at a grave disadvantage. Especially since it concerns your lover. What has he been calling himself? Oh yes . . . *Magnus.* Where in the Hells he came up with such a name, I have no idea."

Tholana chuckled when she saw the involuntary flutter of confusion pass over Aeris' face. "I know more about Magnus than you will ever realize, including the truth of his identity."

Aeris finally brought her gaze to focus upon Tholana's face. Her thoughts buzzed with uncertainty, but it was quelled when she saw the authenticity of Tholana's words reflected in her eyes. Aeris waited. She could feel that what Tholana would tell her next was momentous, and she steeled herself.

Tholana raised an eyebrow. "Do you want to know who he *really* is? It might surprise you, especially since you have met him before." Tholana chuckled again. "I can't believe you didn't recognize him when you met him again. Oh yes . . . he must have placed a spell upon you. No one could forget the face of Master Tallachienan Chroalthone, could she?"

Tholana stopped speaking to allow the significance of her words to seep in. Aeris felt the color drain from her already pale face, and she felt her heart almost stop in her chest. Something seemed to happen then . . . and she felt the strange sensation of something crumbling away in her mind. Aeris brought her hands up to her head, and suddenly the memories came flooding back . . .

Tallachienan gestured to the well. "Do you know what this is?"

Aeris regarded him oddly. "It's a well. One obtains water from it."

TC shook his head. "Not this well. I created it to be the mechanism that can teleport one to anywhere on Shandahar one wishes to be."

Aeris nodded, saying nothing. She was confused as to the reason why she was there. Pylar had been unable to answer any of her questions, telling her only that TC wanted her to prepare for travel. She was to bring everything that she would take as though she were to be going on a long journey.

TC took one of her hands and held it within his own. "Aeris, it has been five weeks since you first came here. You are completely healed, and have been ready to return home for several days now. I have brought you here today so that you may do so."

Aeris' frown deepened and she knew that her hurt shone through her eyes. "Are you telling me that I am no longer welcome here?"

TC pitched his voice into a soothing tone. "Your parents are probably worried about you by now. They have heard nothing from you in almost . . ."

Aeris shut herself away from his words. He was telling her to leave. She couldn't believe what she was hearing. Up until now he had said nothing of her leaving, and even seemed happy to have her there. She was such a fool. She had given herself to him, and now that he was tired of her, he thought that he would send her back home.

Aeris removed her hand from his grip. She stared into the empty space before her, her gaze unfocused. "I can't believe this. I can't believe you are telling me to leave." Yet, she could believe it. He was a god, and she only a mortal. She should have expected it.

"Aeris, you are taking this the wrong way." He spoke with a mild rebuke in his voice. "But I am right when I tell you that you don't belong here. You have your entire life ahead of you. One day, I would have you return to me. When you wish it, I will come for you."

Aeris shook her head and refocused her eyes. She penetrated him with her dark gaze, and when she spoke her voice was caustic. "Come for me . . . you make it sound like you will come to find me like I am a thing that you had once lost." Her voice began to rise in pitch, her anger fueling her to continue. "Oh yes. I remember the wemic pup I once had. I must go and find her now, bring her back to be my pet again. Yes, when you remember, please come for me. It will be no problem for me to wait a few hundred years for you to decide that enough time has passed and that I have lived my life to its fullest."

"Damaeris, stop." His voice rang throughout the chamber. "It won't be like that. You could never be an afterthought to me." He put his hands on her shoulders for emphasis. "I will come for you."

Aeris shook her head, her eyes bright with unshed tears. She inhaled deeply, seeking to take control of her emotions. "I don't believe you," she whispered.

Aeris turned away in an effort to hide her emotions. He put his hand beneath her chin and moved her head to face him once more. She kept her eyes averted, refusing to look at him. But TC would not be deterred. He pulled her into his arms and lowered his head to kiss her. Understanding his intent, Aeris pushed him away and pulled herself from him.

"No. You no longer have that right. You are not my husband, and I owe you nothing." Aeris paused and then continued. "You are right. It is time for me to go home. I am ready." Aeris seated herself upon the lip of the well.

Shaking his head, TC knelt beside her. He took her hand and slid a ring over her middle finger. Pulling her hand free, she saw the ring and simply gave him a small smile. Before she could say anything, TC spoke. "I promise I will come for you, Aeris. Never take the ring from your finger. It will protect you and help me find you wherever you might be."

Aeris looked into his eyes. "I should have left that morning. I should never have stayed. But I believed in you, believed in what I felt happening between us. I never thought that you would betray that. I was such a fool. Please return me home, Tallachienan."

Suddenly, TC grabbed her around the waist with one arm and took her jaw in his other hand. When he kissed her, Aeris felt her body tremble. He always had that effect upon her, but she refused to be disarmed by him. His teeth bruised her lips until she almost groaned, but before he could truly hurt her, he released her mouth. His eyes had become dark, and turbulence reflected there. He continued to keep her close as he spoke, "This promise I have made to you, I swear to keep until it has been fulfilled."

Aeris only vaguely understood what was happening, but it sounded like the words one would speak in conjunction with a spell. His voice was full of suppressed emotion, and she could feel the trembling of his arms as they held her. "All you have to do is think of where you want to go. The well will take you there," he said.

Aeris felt the familiar burning ache in her throat as she fought to contain her emotions. She closed her eyes, and in her mind she saw the silver forest that was her home. Elvandahar. Once more, TC tilted her face up to his. She cracked her eyelids to find herself looking into dark pools of lavender. Then he was kissing her again, his lips softly claiming hers in a sweet caress. "I love you." She heard the words as she began to fall, words she had never heard him speak before. Then her mind was whirling away . . .

Breathing heavily, Aeris opened her eyes to find herself standing before Tholana. She shook her head, not wanting to believe the truth she found lying within her own memories. "No, Magnus doesn't remember who he is . . ." Aeris allowed her voice to trail off as the absurdity of the thought struck her forcibly. Of course, Magnus knew who he was. What man could forget that he was one of the most powerful magic-users on Shandahar?

Then, like a massive wave, the feelings of betrayal struck her. Tallachienan had used a spell against her so that she would neither remember him nor his citadel Then he came to her in the guise of Magnus, a man she now knew never really existed. She remembered first meeting Magnus . . . recalled the feelings she had started to have for him. She resisted those feelings, somehow knowing she had loved another and that she must wait for him. Now she knew that man was Tallachienan.

Aeris felt her eyes burn with unshed tears. She swallowed the heavy lump in her throat as she returned her gaze to the goddess before her. Tholana regarded her intently, and Aeris felt a chill creep up her spine. The smile still rested about her lips, but it didn't reach the woman's coldly calculating gaze. Tholana then stepped towards her once more, bringing up a hand to touch Aeris' hair. Her eyes glittered sinisterly. "Honestly, I don't know what he sees in you."

Aeris remained still as Tholana swept her hand into the mass and gripped a handful of the crimson locks. The goddess stepped in close to Aeris, pressing herself sinuously against her. She pulled Acris' head back by the hair and brought her lips to Aeris' neck. She touched her tongue to the pulse just beneath her jaw and then pulled the soft flesh into her mouth and sucked.

Aeris winced but remained still. Tholana ran her other hand over the curves of Aeris' body and rested it over her breast. Aeris resigned herself to what she knew would come next . . . another painful sexual encounter with the goddess that left her bleeding and sore for at least the entirety of another day.

All of a sudden, Aeris felt a change in Tholana's demeanor. She took her mouth from Aeris' neck and turned to the people who had entered the chamber. Four priestesses flanked a man clothed entirely in black leather trimmed with crimson velvet. Aeris took in the situation, for it was virtually unheard of for a man to walk as an equal with his female counterparts in cimmerean society. This man must hold a very high rank, and Aeris wondered what he must have done to achieve his status. His eyes strayed to her for a moment as he approached, and Aeris felt another chill pass through her.

"Ah, Ranaghar. I see you have arrived a bit earlier than I expected," said Tholana.

Ranaghar bowed graciously before her. "I apologize, my Queen. But I found myself eager to accept the gift you have chosen to bestow upon me."

Ranaghar maintained his bowed position until Tholana put a hand to his shoulder. He rose slowly, keeping his eyes fixed at a position below her face. Tholana smiled. "I am pleased at your fervor." Tholana then tapped the side of his face with her fingertips in the cimmerean gesture that a man may look into the eyes his female superiors.

Ranaghar immediately focused his gaze onto Tholana's face. The goddess began to move, walking away from Aeris to circle Ranaghar and the priestesses. "You have been an excellent tool for me, Ranaghar. You know that I reward my most favored followers . . . those that are unsurpassed in their expertise . . . those that are the most devout in their faith of me. I like to motivate my cohorts . . . please them in many of the ways they have pleased me."

Ranaghar nodded. "Yes, my Queen. I have often heard of your generosity. I am gratified to know that you have chosen me to accept such a reward from you."

Tholana continued as she made her way back towards Aeris. "You once told me that you favored the prisoner that I took a few weeks past. I could easily see that you felt lust for her. I have chosen to present her to you as a gift. You may use her as you please, and from my experience, you will do it well."

Tholana stopped beside her. Aeris felt some relief, for she would no longer be subjected to the horrific nightly orgies she had been forced to endure. But she couldn't help but wonder if she would now be subject to anything less, for this man seemed no less cold and callous than his similarly stationed female companions.

Ranaghar smiled. "My Lady, I am greatly pleased by your offering. Your gift is more than I could have ever hoped for. Please, tell me what I can do next to serve you."

Tholana returned the smile. "Patience, Ranaghar. Patience. That is one quality that you must learn to perfect. Nonetheless, your exuberance is noted." Tholana gripped Aeris' upper arm and pulled her to stand before the darkly clad man. He turned his gaze to her, and she felt a sensation of foreboding sweep through. The weight of his stare was disquieting, and she had the sudden urge to flee.

Aeris felt her faith suddenly crumble. She had hoped that Magnus, her brother, and the rest of her comrades would come for her. Of that, she now had no doubt. TC would never allow Tholana to get away with this infraction against him. It didn't matter who or what Aeris was . . . for him it would be merely a matter of pride. The realization of her circumstances was devastating, and a numbness slowly crept over her. As always, she had become a pawn in a game played by those with the greatest power. One of those players was Tallachienan Chroalthone. Of her own volition, Aeris stepped towards the man who had become a part of her destiny. She wouldn't embrace Fate, but at least she could learn to accept it.

***

Pylarith steeled himself for the inevitable attack. The flames struck him, scorching his crimson hide. He foundered momentarily, but then regained his flight momentum. He was lucky . . . his wing had not suffered the fire, and his scales would eventually grow back.

The emergence of the renegade dragons had been a precipitous one. He and Xebrin had been patrolling the eastern side of the Denegal River for several days, and they saw no evidence of recent draconic intrusion. The degethozak hit them fast and hard, their human riders wielding cross-bows whose bolts liked to tear through the vulnerable membranes of a dragon's wings with relative ease. It was the oddest thing to see the men perched on the backs of the dark dragons, similar to the way a parasite might its host.

The six dragon-riders circled the two helzethryn. They had focused the brunt of their assault upon Pylar, the older and more experienced of them. Yet, Xebrinarth already sported the labors of their battle, his reddish gold hide raked by dragon-claw. Pylar bore similar wounds, and he wondered how long they would be able to hold out before the enemy overtook them. He tried to reach the apostate degethozak via mind-speak, hoping to garner the reason for their attacks, but they had blocked their minds to communication. Only after several attempts did Pylar realize the futility of the endeavor. He despaired not knowing what truth they may have divulged if he had simply been able to ask.

The dragon-riders began to move in for another engagement. The six degethozak rapidly beat their wings in succession, swiftly moving to higher ground. Pylar immediately recognized their advantage, as well as the danger that he and Xebrin now faced. *Xebrin, back up! Put as much distance between us as you can!*

As the two helzethryn struggled to reverse their forward motion, their adversaries swept in for the attack. The smaller degethozak dove towards their bright counterparts. Once gaining momentum, they pulled their wings close to their bodies so as to streamline, decreasing any time the helzethryn may have to formulate an effective response to counter them.

Xebrinarth held himself in position. The first of the degethozak came at them with their claws, banking suddenly and swinging their hind legs forward. Having recovered from his last breath attack, Xebrin inhaled deeply and subsequently released his flame. It engulfed one dragon and his rider, and Xebrin nimbly swept aside as the pair careened past. He then followed them down. The pair crashed onto the ground near the river-bank, and Xebrin was instantly upon them. The flame had struck them directly, scorching the rider to near death and the entire right side of the dragon. The rider hung limply from the saddle, the leg strap the only thing keeping him tethered to his dragon.

Upon landing, the dragon was already becoming delirious from the agony of his wounds. Xebrin leaped upon him with alacrity, tearing into the throat of his enemy. Within moments the black dragon was dead, and his rider had succumbed to the same fate only moments before.

Once his task was complete, Xebrin immediately looked to the sky. Pylar was there, locked with another dragon. It seemed that his friend had borne a similar idea to his own, for Xebrin could see the extensive scorching upon the hide of the dark green dragon. Yet, Pylar had not been so fortunate to have caught the rider in his inferno, and the dragon was a bit larger than the one Xebrin had just taken. Not to mention, Pylar was soon to suffer an assault from the rear by another dragon and his rider.

Xebrinarth leaped into the air, shouting to his friend in mind-speak to warn him of the danger. But it was too late. The second dragon grabbed onto Pylar from behind, the degethozak's wicked claws scoring the deep crimson hide. Pylar roared with the pain, but kept his focus upon the enemy in front of him. However, even with the weight of the smaller green dragon on his back, Pylar was able to bring a rear leg forward to dig his claws into the belly of his darker opponent.

Everything suddenly began to happen very quickly. As the smaller green dragon detached himself from Pylar's back, the original two combatants slithered around one another in a sinuous, deathly embrace. The two continued to beat at the air for a moment, and then began their descent.

As the pair plummeted to the ground, Xebrinarth slammed himself into the smaller green dragon. He raked his front claws along the side of his adversary, leaving deep bloody gouges. In retaliation, the green swung his head around and bit into the flesh of Xebrin's shoulder. Xebrinarth shuddered with the pain, but refocused his attention on the rider. The man hung precipitously in the saddle, and upon seeing him dangling there, Xebrin reacted instinctively. With lightning quickness, he struck out at the rider, closing his jaws around the soft fleshy body. He pulled the man easily out of the saddle and then whipped his head savagely about. He heard the pop of breaking bones, and once the man was limp, Xebrinarth cast the man away from him.

For only a moment the two dragons watched the body fall. Then they were a flurry of motion, curving themselves around one another in an embrace similar to the one Pylar shared with the other green. They brutally raked at one another with their claws, each one hoping to gain purchase over the other. And just like the pair before, they began to fall, each heedless to his predicament as they tried to best one another.

It was a shock when Xebrinarth felt his body hit the water. The dragons separated with the impact and swam towards the surface. Xebrinarth thanked the Fates that watched over him, for he could have just as easily felt his body hitting ground instead of the waters of the Denegal. And that was when he remembered Pylarith.

Xebrin broke the surface just as did his enemy. The two dragons eyed one another warily and then began to tread to the shore. Once out of the river, the two continued to watch one another, each calculating the severity of the wounds he had delivered to the other. Then, in an almost mutual understanding, the two dragons parted ways. Xebrin was just as certain as his green opponent that they just might die in their attempt to best the other. The sacrifice suddenly wasn't worth it.

Xebrinarth finally stumbled away from the river. He reached out with his mind, hoping to find the signature of his friend. In the near distance he could sense Pylar, but the signal was weak. He made his way towards it, continuing to stagger along, all the while knowing that the other degethozak and their riders were most likely circling overhead. Xebrin entered the shelter of the trees, and it was then that he saw the bodies of Pylar and his dark opponent.

Upon initial inspection, both dragons appeared to be dead. Yet, Xebrinarth knew better, for if Pylar had died, he would have sensed nothing from the other dragon. Only a dragon who consciously broadcast could send out a signature.

When Pylar reached the body of his friend, he saw the mortal wounds, saw the acid that ate away the flesh of Pylar's face. Concentrating upon his second stomach, Xebrin vomited the water he had swallowed during his fall into the river, spraying it liberally over Pylar's scarred face. Once he was certain the acid could do no more harm, he allowed his body to slump next to that of his friend. He then slipped into oblivion.

***

Magnus screamed in agony. By the gods, it burned. *It burned.* The pain was excruciating, and he grasped at his face, felt around for the eyeball he was certain no longer existed. By the gods, something had attacked them in the night despite the heavy watch they posted as they journeyed towards Tholana's lair. Besides Alasdair and Cedric, Goldare and the halfen brothers were the most trustworthy. Magnus could always count on them not to fall asleep. He paired them with other members of the group so they could keep them on their toes.

"Magnus . . . Magnus stop."

He vaguely heard Jonsey's voice. He wanted to tell her to help him . . . to take away the agonizing pain. There was something on his face, something terrible searing away the skin of his face. His eye was gone. It had to be, for he could no longer see from the orb that once resided there.

"Magnus, you are dreaming." He felt his body being shaken. "Wake up."

What the Hells was wrong with her? Didn't Jonesy see the thing on the face? Ballocks, it was eating away his flesh . . . had already taken his eye. Was she blind . . . blinded by the same thing that now took his own sight?

From the other side of the encampment, Jaxom watched as Magnus writhed upon his bed-roll. The man was delusional, dreaming that something was burning his face when nothing was there. Jaxom narrowed his eyes in contemplation. This was out of the ordinary, especially for someone like Magnus. The faelin man was customarily stoic, relying virtually on no one but himself. He was always the outsider, never making the effort to include himself in any activity being performed by another member of the group. Magnus was a loner, an outcast much like himself. And now Jaxom suddenly found himself wondering why.

Truth be told, Jaxom had considered delving into Magnus' mind once before. However, he was never able to bring himself to do it. Something had told him that somehow Magnus would know, and that he would then divine the truth of Jaxom's identity. But now Magnus was incapacitated. It would be the perfect opportunity to delve into the man's mind . . . figure out all of those things that Jaxom always wondered about him.

Without thinking about it any further, Jaxom began to concentrate. It was easy to focus, for the object of his examination was bright and clear. Magnus' turmoil made him an easy target for mind-search, and Jaxom felt no compunction upon entry.

Jaxom instantly found himself beset by an influx of images. There were so many, he could make no sense of them, each one overlapping the others to create an intricate weave. Jaxom had seen no other mind like it, and he suddenly became afraid that he could become lost. No mortal man should be able to have so many memories and retain his sanity. Jaxom had been in minds before, but none had ever been even close to this one. It was so full; it seemed that the lives of several men had been packed into the mind of a single individual.

Jaxom slowly brought himself to reach out towards one of the images. It was easy to grasp, for it was in association with the turmoil that Magnus now faced. As he touched it, Jaxom immediately felt a strangeness about it, a sensation he had never experienced before during a mind-search. At first there was a disconnectedness about the image, but upon Jaxom's intrusion, it was suddenly thrown into sharp relief.

Magnus screamed. Jaxom recoiled with the sudden shift of energy surrounding the image . . . suddenly finding himself caught up in a maelstrom of memories as they realigned themselves into another lattice-work design. He shrank away at the sound of Magnus' tormented cry, and he felt himself beset by remorse. By the gods, what had he done?

Magnus gripped the sides of his head and screamed with agony. He struggled against the pain and the burgeoning insight being abruptly revealed to him. He reeled with the impact, the discovery of his identity rocking him to the core. There was Pylarith, his dragon bond-mate who lay close to death . . . and Damaeris, the woman he loved more than life itself. Tallachienan waited as the remaining pieces of his life fell into place, and then he sensed the presence of an intruder in his mind.

Tallachienan slammed up his mental barriers. Within moments the sensation was gone. He ordinarily would have followed the mental aura of the intruder, but too much was happening too fast. He still struggled with the recent breakthrough, and the agonizing pain of his revelation was only now beginning to recede. He slowly opened his eyes to find Jonesy crouched before him, anxiety written upon her pretty face. Around her stood the other members of his company. Hells, how would he ever tell them of his true identity? How would they react to the stunning realization that a god resided amongst them? How would *he* have reacted in a similar situation? And how would Aeris react when she saw him? Surely his nemesis had divulged to her the truth of his identity already.

Damnation. Tholana was the last person with whom he would want Aeris to be in contact. Tallachienan had a long, convoluted history with that woman. She was the most ruthless individual he had ever known, and it was his grave misfortune in life to be the sole object of her desire.

The sudden realization behind the capture hit him hard. Tholana had only taken Aeris to get at him. Sure, Tholana bore a strong hatred of Aeris' mother, but it would take more than mere hate for the goddess to go so far out of her way to take a mortal girl with above-average Talent. Somehow, Tholana knew what Aeris meant to him, and she wanted to make him suffer by taking his most valuable commodity. She would break Aeris down to nothing, and then throw her remains at him when he reached her fortress.

Tallachienan gripped the shoulder of Jonesy's blouse. "We have to go now. Aeris is in grave danger."

TC watched the color drain out of the girl's face, and noticed the muscles in Alasdair's jaw tighten. The man subsequently stepped away from the group, made his way over to his bedding, and began to pack it up. Cedric followed suit, and then Cervantes and Tigerius. It wasn't long before the fire was out and the campsite abandoned. In the middle of the night the group traveled to Tholana's stronghold. TC could only hope they weren't too late.

***

Adrianna had finally ceased behaving as though she belonged in an institution for the mentally deranged. Her only daughter had been abducted by cimmerean priestesses, and that was enough to drive any mother to near insanity. Yet strangely, it was the other catastrophes taking place at the same time that drove her out of the madness that was beginning to consume her.

Adrianna could scarcely recall how Fate cruelly twisted her relatively simple life into the the demented reality it had become. One son had gone in search of the missing daughter, and the other son to war with the realm of Karlisle. Her husband left to determine the whereabouts of Triath and Tianna Solanar, friends who had suddenly ceased answering their messages. There was also speculation as to the whereabouts of the son, Tigerius, but Adria dimly recalled that he traveled in the company of her missing daughter.

Standing out on the balcony of her alcove, Adrianna only vaguely took in the scene around her. Surrounding her own alcove was a series of others that made up a pod. Most pods consisted of individuals who were related by blood. Since leaving the sanctuary of his parent's home, Alasdair had his own alcove nearby. Adria's sister, Sheridana, had one just above, and Sheri's son one right next to it. Many of Sirion's cousins also made residence there, and if Anya had been alive, she would have lived there as well.

Sighing heavily, Adrianna stepped back into the darkness of the alcove. It had been difficult for Sirion since their fight against Aasarak. So many years had gone by, but the hardship remained in the forms of Tholana and the new authority amongst the Daemundai, Razlul Daemonkeeper. With his sister dead, all Sirion had was his mother, Lilandria, the woman he had taken as his wife, and their children.

Yet, things had not been easy for Adrianna either. Sheridana's daughter, Fitanni, had died only a few years before. Sheri and Cedric were devastated by the loss, and Adria also felt it keenly. Sirion couldn't help but feel somewhat responsible. As her primary mentor, he should have better prepared Fitanni for the adversity she would encounter in the world outside Elvandahar. He had known her personality type . . . one who was not content to simply stay home and allow events to happen to her, but one who thrived from the impact she could have upon those events . . .

Walking across the room, Adrianna put a hand to her shoulder and rubbed it. *Damn, it hurt.* The pain quickly became excruciating, and she almost cried out with the intensity of it. She put her back to the wall and simply withstood the searing agony. In her mind, she began to sense a disturbance, and with sudden clarity she realized that it was Xebrinarth.

Adrianna reached out to her bond-mate. She felt when his body hit the water, the coolness of it enveloping him and acting to soothe the wounded shoulder. She sensed when he surfaced . . . felt the wariness towards his enemy, followed by worry for his friend. She felt Xebrin's relief when Pylar was found, and then the efforts of his body to help him as best he could. Adria subsequently vomited. Feeling faint, she put a hand to her forehead and slid to the floor. Then there was only darkness.

***

Farenze and the remaining dragonriders flew southeast along the Denegal River. Since the battle, his mind was trapped in a fog. The course of events had not unfolded the way he initially planned, and failure weighed heavily upon him. Looking back, there were things that could have been done differently, things that may have spared the lives of Ramzexis, Frojelnix, and their riders. He should never have agreed to the insanity his comrades insisted upon . . . that whoever met the enemy first should have him for themselves.

Only Alvastrix and his rider Kithanjun had realized the folly of that plan right away, and when Ramzexis and Pelor met the larger of the two helzethryn, they were quick to attack the dragon at the rear. Frojelnix and Borgis had not been so fortunate. Farenze realized that almost nothing could have been done to save them, for they were burned by the second helzethryn's flame the moment they were within range. Yet, he blamed himself anyway. Farenze cursed his stupidity . . . for not only had the riders underestimated their opponents, they had also overrated the caliber of their own skills.

Now the degethozak and their riders flew away from their opponents, leaving them grounded at least a day's ride away. Farenze hated himself for their cowardice, for if they had simply hunted the downed helzethryn where they had fallen among the trees, they may have been able to kill the enemy and be done with it. However, the fact remained that two dragons and their riders were already gone. He missed his companions keenly, and he sensed that Sifrozelnik felt the same. He remembered a time when he couldn't wait until they met their first draconic opponents. He now realized how much more the degethozak and their riders needed to learn before they met them again.

Nevertheless, despite their loss, the remaining dragons and their riders were unwilling to deviate from their path. In that regard, Farenze refused to let his master down. Once more, they would attempt to cross the river and enter the realm of Elvandahar. There they would begin their swath of destruction anew. And this time, they would have no opposition.

***

Aeris sat bolt upright on the bed. Outside the chamber door she could hear movement, and apprehension sliced through her like a dagger. Once bringing her here to his chamber suite, he had promised that he would return to have her within the seven-day. She didn't know where he had gone, nor did she care. All that mattered now was that, true to his word, the mage Ranaghar had come to claim his prize.

Fear seized Aeris as she pressed herself deep into the pillows surrounding her. She had only just begun to heal from the 'tender' ministrations of Tholana's priestesses and, now it would all be for nothing. Her belly clenched spasmodically, and she swallowed at the dryness of her mouth. She sucked at her lower lip and winced as her teeth unintentionally bit down. The metallic zing of blood spread over the tip of her tongue. It would not be the last she would taste of it this night.

Aeris startled as the chamber door was flung open. Ranaghar strode purposefully into the room, his lavender gaze searching and finding her buried within the bed-cushions. He slammed the door shut, his hungry eyes locking onto her. He smiled without mirth, unfastening the cloak from his shoulders as he continued towards the bed, flinging the garment over a chair as he passed. These past few days, he had been craving to have her . . . she could see it reflected in his eyes and in the determination of his advance. Once more, her belly spasmed and she fought against the reflux that sought to pool into the back of her throat. Her body shrank away from him when he sprawled himself next to her on the bed, and noticing her reaction, Ranaghar's gaze hardened.

Aeris screamed when he roughly gripped her arms, his hands burning into her like searing brands. She didn't mean to . . . it just happened, her fear manifesting itself within her voice. Immediately she began to struggle, still screaming, and he struck her . . . once . . . and then twice. When she didn't stop he struck her again, first with an open hand, and then with his fist, the force of his knuckles breaking open the skin around her mouth, nose, and eyes. He pummeled her until she had little voice left, and then tore what little cloth she wore away from her body. Aeris jerked and writhed as he brutally rode her, the grunting of his exertion filling her consciousness. The pain ripped through her body, partially healed wounds tearing open under the violent onslaught. Tears ran down her temples and into her hair to wet the pillows beneath. She began to swim in and out of awareness, and she yearned for the oblivion that lurked just out of reach.

When he was done, Ranaghar left her. Aeris lay, sprawled, on the blood dampened bed, her limbs bent awkwardly and her face turned so that one cheek touched the softness of a nearby pillow. The whole experience had lasted no more than several moments, and within that time, the mage had not uttered a single word.

For a while she concentrated solely on breathing, and only when Aeris realized the cold creeping upon her naked body did she consider moving. She gradually stirred one arm, and then the other, bringing both down to rest gently over her belly. She then slowly brought her legs together, the muscles protesting at the abuse. She carefully turned onto her side and brought her knees up to her chest, fighting the nausea that threatened to overwhelm her. The tears sprang anew and trickled down her battered face to seep into the cushions. Something thick and sticky flowed out one nostril, and the blood melded into the salty dampness beneath her face. Her body began to tremor involuntarily. She struggled to control the shaking, for it caused her to feel the pains of her body even more. But it would not be stopped, and she shook until she pulled the covers all around, wrapping herself into thick cocoon.

Aeris simply lay there, the hopelessness of her situation creeping upon her like a thief in the dark. Then it swept over her in a wave, momentarily stealing her breath away. Desolation reigned, and her mind became numb. Her past seemed to fade away, and all that remained was the misery of her present.

CHAPTER 22

For what seemed like forever, the group made their way east and slightly south through the Pelgrith Hills of the realm of Feldame, Tallachienan leading them with unwavering certainty that no one questioned. He now knew it was because of the ring he gave Aeris that fateful day he took her memory and sent her home to Elvandahar. With every fiber of his being he wished he could take back that moment, undo the harm he inflicted when he made the rash decision to keep her away from him. And despite knowing the extent of Tholana's cruelty, he could not help but hope that Aeris lived and that she might still be whole.

TC swept an errant lock of black hair back from his face, feeling the cusp at his ear as he tucked the hair away. Now he knew why Tholana had been unable to divine his precise whereabouts. The cusp was an object of his own devising, the one thing he wore most consistently. It kept his enemies at bay, giving him a chance to remain ahead of them for a time until they devised another means of tracking him. TC had yet to learn of Tholana's alternative method of discovering his whereabouts. But now it didn't matter. They would not rest unless it was of absolute necessity, everyone knowing that every moment Aeris and Talemar were in the clutches of the cimmereans, the more dire their circumstances became.

After leaving the isthmus, the group made towards the hills. They stopped in a small town in order to stock up on supplies, and since no one was familiar with the land through which they would be traversing, they had the foresight to procure a detailed map and extra supplies. With the slow travel time they made, TC knew they would be fortunate to make their food supply last long enough for them to reach their destination. Keeping track of their location on the map, he could clearly see that they were not heading into human inhabited territory. Inasmuch, there would be no village, town, or city at which to obtain more supplies. This realization worried him, but he said nothing of it to anyone else . . . only his thoughts that they should be conservative with their food, just in case. No one questioned him, even Cervantes, and of that he was grateful.

Since their first day in the hills, the journey had been a slow one. He knew it was irrational, but it seemed that everything was against them. The weather was cold, and it rained virtually every day since they entered Feldame. He knew it could have been worse, for if they had been much further north, it would probably be sleet and snow they would be forced to endure. However, it was bad enough, for the rains often came down in torrents, soaking the ground they walked upon. Already, two of the horses had foundered upon the treacherous rock-laden terrain. They couldn't be ridden, and instead they were used simply as pack animals.

Several days later, Tallachienan began to feel they were close. He could feel the pull of the Underdark slightly tugging at his peripheral senses. He bade the group to halt and slid down from the downtrodden animal he rode. He then told them to set up camp, and that it would be their last evening above ground for quite some while. Once again, no one questioned him. Perhaps it was an aura about him that commandeered their faith, or perhaps it was simply that they had nothing else in which to believe. Either way served TC well, and he would not ponder it too intently.

It wasn't long before TC found the entrance to the catacombs. Situated within a small cave, a single dark tunnel led downward . . . deep into the bowels of the world. He thought to go back to tell the others that they should continue. However, he refrained, knowing that everyone would need all of the strength they could muster for the struggle ahead. Alasdair found TC standing there, staring into the darkness. The other man said nothing, merely turning and making his way back to the nearby encampment. There was something about Alasdair, a wisdom that seemed to have come to him during the time that had elapsed since TC saw him last. He couldn't help but wonder if Alasdair somehow knew the truth about him.

Early the next morning, the group moved into the tunnel, leaving the horses behind. Jonesy, Tigerius, and Dramid carried the torches and interspersed themselves throughout the group. TC and Alasdair took the lead, while Goldare and the halfen brothers brought up the rear. Jonesy followed just behind the leaders, Dramid walked in the center with Cervantes, Cedric, and Cortes . . . and then Tiger and Jaxom near the back. It didn't take long for every vestige of light to recede, and all that was left was the eerie blackness. In a moment of panic, Jonesy paused to wonder what would happen should their torchlight blow out. She imagined the blackness pushing against her . . . and then the things lurking within coming for her . . .

Down, down, down they walked. It wasn't long before the main passageway bifurcated, and multitudes of side tunnels began to appear. The ambient temperature became cooler, and everyone began to don heavier trousers, tunics, and cloaks. They rationed their food sparingly, for they didn't know how long they would be within the catacombs. Magnus continued to lead them without faltering. They continued to rest only when necessary, and only for short periods. Before long, most everyone had begun to lose sense of Time, for the sun and the moons were no longer visible above to tell them. Besides Magnus, only Vikhail and Vardec seemed to keep their perception of it's passage. Jonesy wasn't surprised, for she knew that the halfen people traditionally kept their homes in the hills and mountains. They were quite accustomed to the darkness

The group passed tunnel after tunnel as they moved deeper into the cave system. The place was a virtual maze; Jonesy would have lost her sense of direction long ago, even if she had chalked the walls. She was uncertain that the effort would have been a worthwhile endeavor, not only because she would have lost track of the markings, but because of the strangely luminous moss that seemed to pervade the place. It wasn't until a certain depth had been reached that the stuff grew in clusters large enough to be noticeable. Now it lit their way as they walked, and the group had even decided to do away with the torches. The greenish light given off by the moss was enough for them to see comfortably enough.

It seemed like they walked for a very long time. Fatigue began to set in, and food rations became smaller and farther between. Only water was plentiful, for they passed several streams as they made their way through the massive cavern system. And it wasn't just any water. It was the epitome of purity . . . crisp and clean. Tiger splashed it on his face and ran fingers through his brown hair. Despite the chill, he washed it when they last stopped for a rest, tired of feeling the oiliness of it beneath his fingertips whenever he touched it. He noticed that Jonesy gave in several stops earlier, but most of the others had yet to bother. Everyone was in great need of a washing, including himself. But at least his hair was clean.

Tigerius looked around at the rest of the group. It was easy to see that they were tired, the effects of fatigue etching itself upon the face of every individual. Only Magnus seemed immune, possessing an energy that could not be wholly explained. Honestly, Tiger thought that the man need to never stop, and did so only for the sake of the others. Narrowing his eyes, Tiger contemplated Magnus more closely. He had changed since they left the city, albeit discreetly. There was an element to the man that simply didn't exist before . . . or perhaps a quality that had always been there, but simply hidden away. Tiger couldn't pinpoint precisely when the change had taken place, only that it had happened sometime during their journey to find Aeris and Talemar.

Tiger inhaled sharply at the thought of his friends. *Damn*, it was hard to not have Aeris traveling right there alongside him. They had shared company for so many months, it felt strange to be going along without her. And even though there were so many things about himself he had not divulged to her, Tiger always knew he had the option to do so, should he need it. In a way, he regretted not sharing at least one of his qualities with her, a quality that would now have been a boon. Maybe, just maybe, they would have been able to perfect the mental connection between them, and he would now be able to commune with her, at least on a basic level.

Tigerius shook his head. He supposed he could berate himself for the rest of eternity, but it would change nothing. Despite his best efforts, he could make no connection with Aeris. Pondering it closely, he thought that it might have much to do with the receptiveness of her mind. Something about that day at the docks had opened her mind wide to him. It took him a while, but he eventually figured it out. It was fear. Because she had been afraid for him, she had called out to him with her mind. Without knowing it, she had broadcast to him and he had received her call. All it took was emotion at its most instinctual level . . .

Yet, even despite his newfound theory, Tiger still could not divine a connection between his mind and that of his friend. His dreams had only become more troubled than usual, focusing primarily upon Aeris. He assumed it was the stress he felt upon his inability to find a connection with her. Nevertheless, the dreams were terrible ones. Her suffering seemed so real, and upon awakening, he hated himself all the more for his failure.

Tiger splashed his face with another handful of water and continued to shake his head. There was even more to what was happening to him. Ever since they entered the Underdark, Tiger had sensed a change within himself. He felt strangely vitalized, and his senses had become more pronounced. Not only was he able to see clearly within the darkness of the tunnels, his hearing had become more keen, his smell more acute, and his tactility more discriminating. No longer were the walls of the cavern simply rough . . . he could distinguish between the different rock types as they progressed downwards. He could hear the sound of rushing water from several tunnels away, and could see the intricate glowing jenorchith where they dangled from the ceilings.

"They are worms," said Magnus. "They eat the insects that harvest the pollens from the mosses that cover the walls. Something about the mosses lure the insects to them, but once they are consumed by the nearby worms, the jenorchiths begin to glow with the same quality as the mosses."

It was a strange dynamic, but the members of the group accepted it easily. Tigerius was heartened by this reaction, and he hoped they would be equally as receptive when the truth of his own unusual abilities became known. Tiger was no fool, he knew that it would happen sooner or later. He could only hope that it would be at a time when his comrades knew him more thoroughly as a man that could be trusted.

Tiger stood and was about to turn away from the water when he heard something. It was an odd clicking noise accompanied by what sounded like a soft scuffling. He drew his brows together into a frown of concentration. He had never before heard anything quite like it. He slowly turned, suddenly feeling like he was being watched. The hairs on his arms slowly began to rise and he began to get the vague sense that peril was near.

Tigerius gazed intently into the darkness surrounding the areas of glowing moss. It didn't take him long to realize what was there, and it was at that moment he heard Magnus' voice nearby. "I need everyone to stop what they are doing. Keep still and remain calm."

His voice was steady and composed, but it was easy to hear the warning. Magnus pitched it so that everyone could hear without bringing too much attention to himself. Yet, the things upon the walls scuttled closer, the clicking noises becoming faster and more pronounced. As they moved, Tiger could discern more of the frightening details, and by the time Cortes broke and made a lunge for the one closest to him, many of the mosaic spiders had crept into the sphere of visual perception induced by the fluorescent mosses.

Once, long ago, Tiger had read about such spiders in a book he heisted from the Medubrokan Academy. It was often that he visited Elvandahar, and more often than he wished, his visit consisted of time spent at the sorcerer's school. Inevitably, there were times when boredom overtook him, and he was forced to engage in activities he would never otherwise have taken part. He had found the book simply lying there, a manual consisting of the varied creatures one might find in the deepest jungles or the darkest caverns. Tiger took the book from the academy and never returned it; to this day it still rested upon the only bookshelf in his room back at home in Sangrilak.

However, Tiger had read that book from cover to cover. The mosaic spider was one of the creatures he always found the most intriguing. It was huge, with legs consisting of bony plates with sharp, raised edges that could cut into a person like a sword blade. The body was sleek, bearing a pattern reminiscent of mosaic one might find tiled upon a floor or wall in an upscale home or establishment. The creature could leap horizontally as far as four farlo and almost as high. The poison was particularly devastating, eating away the flesh surrounding the bite until nothing remained but the bone.

Tiger could scarcely blame Cortes for making the first move. As the only member of the group that close to the cavern walls, it was easy to see how afraid he had become by the close proximity of a spider of that proportion. Cortes swung his fauchard at the nearest spider. The curved blade glanced off of the bony plates the creature employed in it's defense. The spider then leaped away from the wall and onto Cortes.

There was a series of shouts and curses as the remaining spiders converged upon the rest of the group. The men fell under the weight of the massive arachnids and struggled to get the upper hand. Most had no recourse to their customary weapons and were forced to grapple at their belts and boots for daggers. Only Cedric had borne the good sense to keep his swords strapped to his person, yet was unable to access the blades where they rested beneath him, sheathed criss-cross against his back. Using all his strength, the blade-singer kept the dripping maw at arm's length.

Tiger heard Jonesy scream just as his back hit the nearest wall. Somehow, none of the spiders had pinpointed him for attack. Overcome with fear and helplessness, he watched for a moment as his friends struggled for their lives. Then, just as he unsheathed his dagger and began to rush to the aid of Jonesy, a streak of popping energy swept passed him. It struck the spider assaulting Jonesy, causing it just enough harm for it to release its victim in order to turn towards its attacker. As Tiger stopped mid-stride, he happened to notice that the same phenomenon had taken place all around the cavern chamber. All of the spiders had turned away from their prey in order to focus upon the enemy at hand. That enemy was Magnus.

Every set of eyes in the chamber was situated onto the spell-caster at the far end, both humanoid and arachnid. Tiger didn't know how Magnus did it, but the man had somehow smitten every spider in the area. Now he prepared to cast another spell, his hands moving in the intricate array of one who was about to let loose his magical arsenal, whatever form it might be. This time it was electricity. The thick bolt first hit the spider hovering near Jonesy, and then sprung from that creature to the next . . . and then the next, and the next until all of the creatures were connected in a sizzling chain of electrical power. Their bodies convulsed unnaturally, and only when the acrid scent of burning flesh filled the room did Magnus release the spiders from his spell. Each and every one crumpled in it's place, dead before it hit the floor.

For quite some while silence reigned. Only the sound of the water from the spring could be heard beyond that silence . . . a silence arising not only from an experience that could have meant the deaths of everyone in the room, but also one of incredulity and awe. Yet, it seemed only Tiger had seen the full extent of the power Magnus harnessed, power he used with barely the blink of an eye. The man had become something more than what he seemed, and Tigerius couldn't help but feel not only mystification, but some measure of uneasiness as well. *Who in the Hells was this man . . . ?*

***

Aeris silently waited in the darkness of the chamber. She smelled of scented oils and the soap used for her bath, a commodity she had the luxury of experiencing every day. Her hair was allowed to remain free of the plait within which she once kept it, falling in ringlets over her shoulders and down her back and chest. Her pale lips were painted and her eyes outlined with kohl. She appeared quiet the harlot, and according to many, she acted as one.

Gazing intently before her, Aeris toyed with the ring that circled her finger. It was the one Tallachienan had given her before he sent her back to Elvandahar, the one he said would lead him to her. Somehow, Tholana had allowed her to keep it, not realizing the power it held. Or perhaps she recognized it but simply didn't care. It was her intention to bring TC to her. Why not make it easy for him to divine her through the power of the ring?

It wasn't much longer before Ranaghar entered the chamber. She had long ago ceased to resist him, simply allowing him physical access to her whenever he chose. She was always readily available to him, for she was rarely allowed outside the chamber. In all regards she was a prisoner within these narrow walls, a caged bird made to sing only at the whimsy of her master.

Yet, Aeris found she had strength still within her. She had power over Ranaghar, for he desired her among all other women. She sometimes found the strength to defy him outside the physical power he had over her, defiance that often resulted in rougher treatment. However, it never came close to the abuse she suffered that first night, and it wasn't long before she knew the reason. His dominion over her would be complete once his seed took hold within her womb. He never spoke the words directly to her, but she knew. *She knew.* For that she hated him even more.

So, Aeris spent most of her days in seclusion. Tholana never came to her, nor her priestesses. She kept her sanity by thinking about her family in Elvandahar and the companions left behind in whatever city they were in when she and Talemar were abducted. She tried not to think about her poor cousin because she could only imagine his death at the hands of these people. They would hate Talemar for his half-blood status, despite his Talent. Yet, Aeris had heard nothing about his demise. It was easy to listen to and understand the conversations of the acolytes when they came to check up on her when Ranaghar wasn't there. They were stupid creatures, not realizing that she understood the complexities of the cimmerean language very well indeed.

But, Aeris could only spend so much time in contemplation of the present. Invariably, her mind began to slip into the past. It was simpler this way, for it contained much less of the physical and mental torment she faced. Not to mention, her childhood past carried many more favorable memories than did the more recent. She remembered adventurous forays into the forest, forbidden excursions through the ancient alcoves of the fortress, and training at the Medubrokan Academy. It was a culmination of these experiences that made her who she was today, and she was sorry to realize she was much below par.

Damaeris always knew that most of the other students at the academy hated her. It had always been that way, since the first moment she became Master Dinim's apprentice. Except for one student, only the most gifted were given into his tutelage. Besides herself, Talemar was the youngest to acquire the status indicative of apprenticeship under Master Dinim. However, as Dinim felt it to be a conflict of interest, Master Adrianna took the boy instead.

Yet, even before Aeris was an apprentice, she had made her second home behind the walls of the academy. Unlike her mother and father, Aeris didn't mind the stone all around . . . never felt stifled by the walls, nor too tightly enclosed. In fact, many times she preferred the security they promised. She knew it was a quality she shared with her eldest brother, Asgenar. However, she never quite found it within her to care, despite their opposition on most other issues.

Nevertheless, Aeris' peculiarities never seemed to be a deterrent for one Raissa Morcallion. Perhaps it was because the girl had her own share of unusual qualities. It was out of the ordinary for a full-blood hinterlean faelin to exhibit Talent, and even more so that the person be a primary Talent. Raissa was such an individual. Even before she knew why, it set her apart from her people; and when she met Aeris, she felt as though she had met a kindred spirit. And Aeris had felt much the same about Raissa.

But now Raissa was dead. Many times as of late, Aeris wished that she were as well. It was a cruel twist of fate that TC's journeyman happened upon the scene and kept her just barely alive until he made it back with her to the citadel. And it was even more cruel that she was brought back from the brink of death. She hated to think what her family may have felt had she died at that time and in that place. However, she was sure it was nothing less than what they would feel when they eventually discovered her fate within Tholana's stronghold. At least her death would have been of the more honorable variety had she been allowed it at the poison of the behiraz. But now, when she eventually met her demise, it would be sullied by what she had become . . . nothing more than a cimmerean whore.

***

Pylar stood stoically before Adrianna, his head lowered. He could sense her anger . . . it cascaded off of her in waves to infuse the space surrounding her. He supposed that she had every right to feel that way, especially given the circumstances. He also supposed that, in part, he deserved what he knew was coming to him. He stood there in faelin form, but even if he had been in dragon form, the result would have been the same. It didn't matter how large he could be . . . the wrath of Adrianna Darnesse Timberlyn was even larger.

"Pylar, how could you keep this from me?"

Startled, he looked up into the darkness of her eyes. Usually they were pools of deep brown warmth, and any man . . . or dragon . . . could become easily lost in them. Now they reflected nothing more than the anger she felt. Yet, it was tempered by hurt, an emotion that had, until now, remained concealed from him somehow. Adrianna had always been able to hide such things from him, and he could never figure out why.

Pylar shook his head. He didn't quite know what to say. He knew it was wrong for him to have held back information, especially when it concerned her children. He could claim that it was loyalty to his bond-mate that made him stay quiet, but he couldn't be entirely certain of the truth of that conjecture. They all knew that Tallachienan had made wrong decisions before, especially when it concerned matters of the heart. Based upon that knowledge alone, Pylar should have made Adria privy to everything he knew right from the moment he reached Elvandahar after *the fall.*

Yet, he had refrained from doing so. In all honesty, Pylar felt that it was because he knew the turmoil it would cause his good friend. Unfortunately, he didn't bother to think beyond the immediacy of the moment, not realizing that one day the truth would be there to haunt them.

"Adria . . ." His voice cracked for a moment, and he cursed the frail faelin form. "I didn't intend to be deceptive. I didn't know how to tell you that Aeris had been to the citadel. She was in trouble . . . close to death. TC found someone who could save her. He kept her alive long enough for her to have the aid she needed. She recovered well, but something happened between them. TC did not want to admit his feelings for Aeris, and he chose to thrust her away from him. He wiped clear her memory of her stay at the citadel, and then he sent your daughter home."

Pylar stopped for a moment and then continued in a lower voice. "And then he *fell* and I didn't know what to do . . . where to turn. I was afraid I would never feel him again." He almost whispered the last. "Once I was here, I didn't want to cause any more upheaval than I had already. Adria, I am so sorry."

Adrianna watched her friend as he spoke. She could hear the sincerity in his voice, feel that the efforts he had made were genuine. She felt her eyes cloud with unshed tears. She was about to turn away when Pylar was suddenly there before her. He embraced her as she cried, and she knew that she was fortunate to have him with her despite his mistakes. Her life would have been so much easier these past several moon cycles if he had simply disclosed to her all he knew. Yet, she could understand why he had chosen to conceal it. Not only did he not want to see her hurt, but he didn't want to betray his bond-mate. Despite what Pylar thought to be the contrary, he still looked out for the best interests of Tallachienan, even if it meant a little bit of hardship.

After awakening from her collapse, she became immediately aware of the trauma suffered by her bond-mate. Adrianna was beside herself. Via mindspeak, she called upon Saranath and Mordrexith. It wasn't long before both dragons were there and they were on their way to Dinim. Then, breaking protocol and an unwritten law, Adrianna and Dinim mounted the dragons backs, and they took wing in the direction of Pylar and Xebrin. Flying hard and fast, it took them only all of a day to reach the fallen dragons, locating their comrades only through the mental signatures they emitted.

It was during the recovery that Adrianna began to make some realizations. With Xebrin putting up very few barriers to keep his thoughts obscure, she was able to obtain information that she would not ordinarily have access. Through those thoughts, she learned that Tallachienan's connection with Pylar had been restored. However, that wasn't the disturbing part. When the connection was reestablished, Pylar was in tight communion with Xebrin, and the other dragon inadvertently transmitted some of his more recent memories. Many of those memories happened to concern TC's last days before *the fall*, as well as those that contained Aeris.

Adrianna was dumbfounded. By the gods, when had Aeris been to visit TC's citadel? Not only that, what was the nature of the relationship between the two people she saw in those memories? And why had Pylar refrained from telling her about it? Initially, she felt little else but anger and betrayal. But now, as she stood within the embrace of Pylar's arms, she could only feel glad that he was healing well from his battle with the renegade degethozak. Despite her disappointment, she loved Pylar, and she would never turn him away. Inasmuch, she knew that he would do the same for her if the need ever arose.

"You are ever my good friend, Pylar," she said in a shaky voice.

Adrianna felt his arms tighten about her. She could sense the power in that grip . . . the passion. And she knew it was all for her. "Thank the gods you are here with me now," he replied.

She knew why he spoke those words. In another time . . . in another life . . . Pylar had come to call her his friend. She had subsequently died in her fight against Aasarak, and he had been forced to live his life until next when the world cycled anew and he would meet her again. For five Cycles he had done just that. But this last Cycle, Adrianna had won her battle against the deathmage, and the curse that made the world cycle over and over again was broken. Adrianna now lived a life she had never been allowed to have ever before. And for that alone he was grateful.

Pylar pulled away and stared into her eyes. "He is going to her now. Adrianna, my bond-mate is going to save your daughter. You have to understand that he would have it no other way."

Adrianna nodded. She knew that Pylar was right. She only hoped that Tallachienan wasn't too late.

***

Cervantes stared disconsolately before him. They were close . . . Magnus had announced it not long before. Somehow, the man had guided them through the maze of catacombs comprising the massive cavern system . . . led them unerringly towards the fortress that he knew was home to the woman who had taken Aeris hostage. It was interesting that Magnus knew exactly in which direction to travel to get to the enemy's lair, and even more interesting that he referred to Aeris and her cousin as 'hostages'. They weren't just prisoners or captives, but hostages . . . prisoners for whom the abductor sought to receive some token or service for their return.

Cervantes allowed his gaze to seek out the man about whom his thoughts had been focused so intently as of late. Actually, it was after their encounter with those giant spiders that he had become ever more introspective and suspicious. Hells, the man had fried the whole lot of them with hardly anything but the flick of his wrist.

Cervantes wasn't precisely sure what happened first. All he knew was that there was a sudden flurry of activity as several spiders suddenly leaped from the cavern walls and onto the members of the group. Cervantes remembered hearing Jonesy scream, and then feeling as though his heart were suddenly stopping in his chest. For a moment he was paralyzed with fear, and then one of the spiders was upon him. Cervantes grappled with the abomination, just barely keeping the dripping maw from his face. It was difficult, for the thing had swath of thick, chitinous material that protected the top of it's body, and the lower portion of it's legs were comprised of sharp hairs that could easily penetrate a man's flesh. But then Magnus had come to their rescue with his thick chain of electrical power that zapped every one of the hideous beasts within the immediate area.

Cervantes shook his head. Hells, it wasn't that he didn't appreciate the aid; it was simply the nature of such aid that had him in knots. Damnation, what kind of man could wield power like that and not be someone whom he shouldn't worry about? His gaze finally came to rest upon the object of his thoughts. The cimmerean man sat apart from the rest of the group. In his hand was a long-knife, and he slowly honed the blade against a hard rock dedicated to the purpose.

Suddenly, a figure walked into Cervantes' line of vision. Refocusing his gaze, he saw that it was Jonesy. Magnus ceased sharpening the blade as she knelt before him. Cervantes felt his eyes narrow. She trusted the man. Cervantes could feel it. He didn't like it, but he knew he simply had to deal with that reality. She obviously didn't have the same reservations about Magnus as he did, and it must be because she hadn't seen the display of power. Not to mention that she must not have thought about the fact that he knew exactly where they were going, supposedly without ever having been there before. *Yeah, right.*

It wasn't long before Jonesy was stepping away from Magnus and walking in Cervantes' direction. The captain found himself rising from his place in order to intercept her, abruptly intent upon her having the advantage of knowing all that he knew about the man she thought of as her friend. He stepped up to Jonesy and stopped her with a hand at her elbow. Her expression was surprised as she looked up at him.

"Oh, Cervantes . . . you startled me for a moment," she said, giving him a lopsided grin.

Cervantes found himself suddenly looking at the curve of her lips, followed by the line of her jaw and the chestnut brown hair she had pulled over one shoulder. Shaking his head slightly to clear those thoughts, he pulled his brows into a frown and led her farther away from Magnus, just in case his faelin ears were to pick up anything that was said. "So, what was that about? What did Magnus say to you?"

Jonesy's expression turned to surprise. "I was just asking him if he had a preference for the evening meal. He told me that he had nothing particular in mind except that he hoped we might have something to satisfy his craving for something sweet. I told him I would try to oblige." Jonesy's mouth began to pull down into a frown as she took in Cervantes' solemn countenance. "Why?"

Sensing that she might become defensive, Cervantes gave a nonchalant shrug of his shoulders. "I was just wondering, that's all. He *has* been acting rather peculiarly as of late, don't you think?"

Jonesy's frown deepened to include her eyebrows, and she stopped to turn towards Cervantes. She skimmed her gaze over him for a moment, forbearing to mention that his own behavior had been a bit erratic as of late. The Captain was not the only one in their group who was feeling strain, and she hated that Cervantes seemed to feel that he had a monopoly on that emotion. He seemed to have conveniently forgotten that it was his actions that had made it easy for Tholana to abduct Aeris. Even though it very well could have happened anyways, Cervantes had recklessly started a tavern brawl that resulted in the injury of many men. One of them had been maimed for life. She doubted that Magnus would ever forgive himself for that.

Jonesy knew that Cervantes couldn't be the only one to blame, especially in light of the extenuating circumstances that lead up to the event, but it wasn't an isolated set of behaviors that he had been exhibiting. Even after the brawl, Cervantes remained somewhat aggressive, belligerent, and uncaring of everything going on around him. The only positive thing he had done was fight for his right to accompany the group on their quest to have Aeris and her cousin freed of their abductors.

"He must be distressed over Aeris' abduction," she said in an almost off-handed fashion. She sought to give Cervantes the benefit of any doubt she had about him, for she felt him to be an inherently good man who had happened upon some hard times. Despite her knowledge of corsairs in general, she respected the Captain greatly, and continued to harbor romantic feelings towards him. Those emotions had only been strengthened when he took the time to teach her the cutlass, and she would always remember him for that.

Cervantes shook his head and brought his face closer to hers conspiratorially. "Joneselia, don't you see it? He knows *exactly* where we should go, not to mention the nature of the woman who has taken our comrades. There is something he is not telling us. How can you trust him?"

Jonesy suddenly found herself struggling to maintain her composure. *How dare he?* How dare this man question the integrity of one of the only members of this party who deserved to have a bit of faith placed in him? Hadn't Magnus proven again and again that he had only the best interests of Aeris and the rest of this group at heart? Magnus could have deserted Aeris after their skirmish with the Daemundai, but he remained by her side as she took to the open sea in order to escape them. Then, after they walked upon the mainland once more, he could have bid her his farewells. Yet, he remained by her side as she struck out across the continent so as to evade her enemies. Now, after Aeris had been taken by one of the most powerful individuals upon Shandahar, Magnus continued to stay with her, no matter what it might cost him. Hells, Jonesy didn't care how Magnus knew where to go in order to find Aeris. She could only call it a blessing from the gods . . . gods who had supposedly *fallen* many moon cycles ago.

"Captain Cervantes, all I see is a man who is jealous of the one who leads this group. I see a man so wrapped up in himself that he sees no one else. I see a man who doesn't really care to have Aeris back, but one who only says the words to make himself look good."

Jonesy's voice rose in pitch. She shouted the words at Cervantes, heedless of what anyone else might hear. Her disappointment ran deep, much more so than she thought it would. Of course, it wasn't just the situation she faced now, but it encompassed other instances as well. It was the degenerate whores game he played with Tigerius, coupled with his initiation of the tavern brawl. Hells, he wanted to kill the dock-master after the realization that the *Sea Maiden* had been stolen. And now he sought to discredit Magnus in the best way available to him . . . through his closest comrades.

Taken aback by her vehemence, Cervantes shook his head. "What do you know?" he sneered. "You are naught but a girl who knows nothing but how to wield a simple bine. And even that is questionable."

"No. Now I know the basics of how to use a cutlass. A foolish corsair once taught me that." Jonesy almost choked on her words, regretting their use even before they left her mouth. She watched the contours of Cervantes face harden, in particular those around his mouth. She had always wondered what it would be like to have those lips upon her neck . . .

Cervantes narrowed his eyes, yet said nothing retaliatory. There was no use . . . if she didn't see it now, then she never would. Regardless, there was something going on that no one else in the group knew about. It was more than just Magnus' use of arcane power, and more than his uncanny knowledge of the catacombs surrounding Tholana's lair. Something had changed in Magnus, something momentous. Cervantes had hoped Jonesy would be able to see it, but she was so entrenched within her own perceptions, she refused to see the possibility of any other.

Jonesy was right . . . he was a fool. He should never have attempted to sway the closest of Magnus' allies. It was rather irrational for Cervantes to assume he could get them to see beyond the veil of Magnus' fabrication. And Jonesy had been his greatest hope. Within her, he had found a boon companion, someone with whom he was beginning to share his innermost self. And now, to have that stripped away from him . . .

Cervantes then turned and simply walked away from her. The expression upon Jonesy's face as he left was disputable. Some would say that it was nothing but blind hostility, but others might claim that it was tempered with fear and hurt. Cervantes didn't know. Nor did he care. All that mattered was that he was now exposed. It would be even more easy for members of the group to lay blame upon him should any misfortune arise. Now, all he could hope was that such adversity did not come about.

***

Aeris stared out the open casement. Sometimes she didn't really know why she bothered, for all she could see was more stone . . . the stone of the vaulted cavern within which Tholana's citadel resided. Yet, it had a beauty to it. The dark rock was blanketed by swaths of moss that glowed eerily green in the darkness. It allowed her to view the contours of the cavern, to see the magnificence of the place. It was the largest she had ever seen, with plateaus hanging from the walls that led into side tunnels, huge stalactites that grew from the ceilings, and even a waterfall that fell at least a zacrol before splashing into the waiting pool below.

Aeris heard the sound of the door being slowly opened. She didn't turn, for more often than not, her visitor was someone she didn't care to see. Most likely, it was one of the young acolytes who had been bidden to come tend to her needs since she would no longer do it for herself. Since her realization of her body's condition, she had ceased to care about such things.

The door closed quietly. At first Aeris heard nothing, but then just barely the sound of naked feet upon stone. Her interest suddenly piqued, she turned away from the casement to look behind her. There, at the open archway to the chamber, stood Talemar.

How he had gotten there, she did not know. Yet, it didn't seem to matter as she slowly stood from her seat and met him halfway across the room. The feel of his arms around her gave Aeris a vague sense of safety she had not known in what seemed like forever. The sound of his soothing voice muffled by the thick waves of her hair eased her heart for at least that moment, and she felt the first calm come over her since their abduction only gods knew how long ago.

Finally, he released her and cupped her face in his hands. "Damaeris, I have been biding my time, waiting to discover your whereabouts so I could come to you," he said softly.

Aeris looked up into his face. It was much more angular than she remembered, the cut of his cheek and jaw much more pronounced. There were hollows beneath his eyes, and the lobe of his left ear appeared to have been cut away. But despite those differences, it was the same beloved face. His eyes were just as blue as ever and his lips had the same curve. Aeris felt the tears come to her eyes, and she didn't resist as she began to cry.

Once again Talemar wrapped his arms around her. He brought Aeris down to the floor with him and then he rocked her within his embrace, shushing her gently. Her body shuddered with the force of her sobs, and just when she began to fear that she might not be able to pull back into herself, she began to quiet.

"How . . . how many moon cycles has it been?"

Talemar sighed. "It's been at least a few fortnights, maybe longer."

She pulled away unsteadily and rose from the floor. She then walked slowly back to the casement and looked out. "How did you do it? How did you get away long enough so as to come here?"

Stepping up behind her, Talemar laid his hands on Aeris' shoulders. She recoiled involuntarily out of habit and then bit her lip in shame. By the gods, it was Talemar there beside her, not Ranaghar . . . not Ranaghar.

"By the eternal flames of the Nine Hells, what have they done to you?"

Aeris heard the strain in his voice, his determination to keep from breaking down. She turned to face him and laid a hand on the side of his face. "Nothing more than they have done to you." She raised herself on tip-toe, brushed her lips against his, and placed her cheek against the other side of his face.

Talemar tightened his hands at her waist and cleared his throat of emotion. "Aeris, I know this has been difficult for you, but you must have faith in me. I *will* get you out of here. I promise."

She inhaled deeply. She wanted so much to believe in him, but she found it exceedingly hard to do so. She had lost hope long ago when she discovered the truth behind Magnus' identity; then even more when Ranaghar began taking her to his bed nightly. And now . . .

Aeris shook her head mutely. There was a part of her that wanted to leave so badly . . . run away from Tholana's citadel and never look back. But for what?

There was nothing for her now. Magnus had never existed, and Tallachienan had already portrayed how little respect he had for her when he took away her memories. Sure, there were her brothers and her parents, but it wouldn't be long before they realized the inevitable truth about her.

Talemar stepped back and took her face in both his hands. "What? What is it, Aeris?"

"Talemar, you must leave this place. Don't worry about me . . ."

His brows drew together into a frown. "Aeris, you can't be serious. You must believe I will find a way . . ."

Aeris shook her head. "Talemar, I am tainted . . . *unclean* . . ."

"Aeris, no . . ."

She overrode his protest. He would tell her that she should forget what had happened to her in the dark citadel so that she could live with herself, perhaps make a future for herself. But she knew better . . .

"Each night he takes me; he spills his seed into me. And before that there was the torment of Tholana and her priestesses." Aeris lowered her voice, almost as though she thought someone would hear. "I have been able to whittle away at some of the web-spells Tholana placed in my mind to keep me from remembering . . . to keep me from using my Talent."

Talemar's expression became haunted. "Then you should find it within you to escape this place! Help me, Aeris. We can do this together," he said emphatically.

Aeris shook her head once more, feeling the tears threatening to fall again. "Talemar, no. It's the reason why I have been able to thwart the mind-webs . . ."

Talemar sighed explosively. "Aeris, it doesn't matter *why*, only that you have been able to . . ."

"Talemar . . ." Aeris spoke his name as she pulled away. She wrapped her arms around her middle, not wanting to say what she must. He would realize the truth of her and he would *know*. " . . . I am with child."

He seemed to age before her, though she knew it was impossible. His eyes reflected his anguish, and she felt ashamed. She should never have told him.

Talemar only hesitated a moment before taking her hands within his. "Aeris, it doesn't matter. The child will grow up in Elvandahar. It need never know the evil of it's father . . ."

Aeris shook her head once more, the tears falling, unchecked, down her cheeks. "But *I* will know. It is an abomination, conceived of violence and pain. It will never know my love. It will grow up and eventually become what I have come to despise the most in this world: the cimmerean race."

"Aeris, it doesn't have to be this way. Your parents and your brothers, they will help you to overcome . . ."

"No. Talemar, save yourself. There is nothing left for me in the world above."

His expression suddenly hardened and he released her hands. "I will not give up on you, Aeris. I will find a way . . ."

"A way for what?" said a voice from the entryway.

Startled, Aeris looked over to find Ranaghar standing there. Talemar had closed his eyes, his jaw tightening almost imperceptibly. *By the gods, how much had he heard?*

"So, you have finally found your way to her. I thought that you might eventually. What kind of spell-caster would you be if you did not?" Ranaghar walked slowly into the room. Talemar still did not turn. He opened his eyes and regarded her with a haunted expression, one she would never forget. She knew his thoughts at that moment, yet he said nothing. They would surely kill him . . .

Ranaghar finally came to stand beside Aeris. "I have heard much about you. They say that you are powerful." Ranaghar passed an insolent perusal over Talemar. "To be quite honest, I don't see what they were talking about."

Talemar fixed his eyes to a position over Ranaghar's shoulder. She could see the strain etched upon his face, and she wondered if Ranaghar saw the same. Aeris suddenly felt Ranaghar's hand circling her upper arm, and by the strength of his grip she knew he was angry.

"So, it seems that my little whore has been busy." Ranaghar cocked his head to the side. "I am sure you have had her before . . . she is quite the treat is she not?" He ran his other hand through the tresses of her unbound hair and grinned wickedly. "It's a shame that you have come, my friend, because now I will have to punish her."

Aeris swallowed convulsively. She could only imagine what the threat might entail. Yet, she wasn't quite as concerned as she might have been. If he treated her roughly enough, perhaps the child would become dislodged and she would lose it. She felt a momentary pang of guilt for the thought, for she was not normally so crass. She had a respect for all life, no matter how small, and this one was no different from any other. Except that it was conceived of the suffering she had endured at the hands of Ranaghar and his Mistress.

Talemar looked directly at Ranaghar for the first time. "No. She has no blame in this. I came here without her knowledge."

Ranaghar's smile widened. "It doesn't matter. She will reap the consequences of your foolishness." His hand moved from her hair down to a breast. He cupped it and began to massage her flesh.

Despite her urge to recoil, Aeris stilled herself under the ministrations of the man she had come to know as her master. She saw the muscles of Talemar's jaw tighten once more, and she could only hope that her cousin would do nothing to make Ranaghar even angrier than he was already. And regardless of the tenuous situation, she was glad of one thing . . . Ranaghar seemed to know nothing of the child she carried.

"Leave her alone. It is I that committed the transgression. Punish me all you want, but leave Aeris alone."

"Now why would I do that? It seems that it would be a greater punishment for you to watch me discipline her than it would for me to find a method to do the same to you." Ranaghar accentuated his message by stepping behind her and bringing his hand from her breast down to the the juncture between her thighs.

Aeris inhaled sharply at the intrusion and felt her nostrils flare in her attempt to remain still. She tried to catch Talemar's gaze, hoping to keep him from the inevitable, but it was to no avail.

"You bastard . . ." Talemar rushed at Ranaghar. The other man simply put up a hand, fingers splayed, and Talemar found himself suddenly brought up short. A force kept him at bay, one borne of sorcery at it's greatest.

Ranaghar's eyes flashed dangerously. "Yes, I can see that you want to watch . . ."

With that, the cimmerean sorcerer pushed Aeris down. Tearing her clothing away, he took her there on the cold stone floor. Talemar remained trapped in his position, unable to do anything but close his eyes . . . giving her at least what little dignity he could.

CHAPTER 23

Jaxom stood stoically by while everyone around him prepared for their entry into Tholana's fortress. Alasdair, Cedric, Goldare, and the halfen brothers donned their studded leather, followed by their weapons of specialty. Cedric sheathed two long-swords crossed at his back, Goldare a single broad-blade, Vikhail a battle-axe, and Vardec a war-hammer. Meanwhile, Cervantes, Cortes, and Dramid affixed to themselves a virtual arsenal, with daggers in each boot-leg and an additional one tucked into sashes or belts around the waist. There were also cutlasses, each at one hip, and cross-bows at the other. Tigerius did much the same, but instead carried a short-sword. Magnus provided Jonesy with the padded leather vest he found at the bottom of Aeris' travel pack and a dagger to tuck into her boot, while Cervantes gave her a makeshift belt upon which hung a sheathed cutlass. It was good to see the men come together to see to the welfare of one of their own and Jaxom thought there might be hope for them yet.

Continuing to watch the group, Jaxom slowly began to slip back through the tunnel, away from the torchlight. He was careful, for he didn't want anyone to realize that he was no longer with them until they were well within Tholana's stronghold. Then they wouldn't even have the chance to think about his disappearance, or even when it was that they saw him last, for they would be busy navigating their way through the citadel, their thoughts focused only upon their immediate survival. Jaxom had remained as inconspicuous as possible during their journey through the catacombs, and he rather hoped that no one even remembered that he traveled with them . . . and with a little *Suggestive* help, it shouldn't be a problem.

As a rezwithrys dragon, Jaxomdrehl had been born with what people would call 'Talent'. As a rezwithrys grew and developed, natural abilities began to emerge, and by the time they reached maturity, they usually had the ability of mild *Suggestion*, including *Fear* that could be instilled when he screamed. Jaxom accepted that he had these abilities, but he did not like using them unless they were direly needed. In all of the time he had spent with the group, this was the first time he had even harbored even the simple *thought* of his skills . . . much less *using* them.

Once far enough away from the group, Jaxom began to work his way around them. It wouldn't be too terribly problematic to find alternative routes that could lead him to the citadel. The only difficulty would be to reach the stronghold before the rest of the group, for he wanted to begin his diversion before they entered. Once he reached the fortress, he knew that he would be tempted to go to Aeris, but he had to restrain himself. Jaxom had to leave the rescuing up to Magnus and the others to do the job he knew he was meant to perform.

Jaxom quickly made his way through the maze of corridors. He relied heavily upon his direction sense, for it could be easy even for one such as him to become lost. It had been quite a feat for Magnus to get the group through the catacombs with relatively little mishap, for not only was it a maze, but the dangers lurking within it were many and varied. Jaxom had sensed those things more than once as they traveled. Somehow the group had avoided them all . . . all but one. And Jaxom vividly recalled what had happened with the mosaic spiders.

Jaxom was relieved when he finally stepped out of the tunnel system to find himself met with the sight of Tholana's citadel. The fortress was huge, the towers and spired turrets rising high into the darkness above. He could sense the danger surrounding the place, denizens of the Underdark that served as guardian minions to the goddess. Jaxom immediately began his transformation into dragon form. Not only did he still feel the necessity to have entry into the fortress before the rest of the group, but also to act as an attractant to those that might harm the group on their way there. The creatures would be able to sense his presence immediately and come to seek him out. The presence of a dragon in his true form was difficult to hide, and it just so happened, Jaxom no longer wished to do so.

The dragon grinned and magnified his aura as he leaped in the direction of the citadel. He felt the rush of impending battle, the singing of the blood through his veins as his body prepared itself. Yes, let them come . . . he would incinerate them with his fiery breath, and then he would scale the western tower. He sensed the presence of Aeris in the opposite direction, but he struck her from his mind. He would be able to do it just this one last time. After this, he would forever be unable to resist her need of him. He could feel the truth of it deep within the core of his being, and just knowing that gave him the strength to do what must be done.

***

Following Tallachienan, the group hurriedly made their way through the darkened halls of Tholana's citadel. He still couldn't believe the set of events that had taken place in order for them to get this far so fast, and it took almost everything within him not to stop and examine the situation more closely. Hells, they didn't have the time to stop . . . the thing that diverted the inhabitants of the citadel would not be able to do so forever. Currently, everyone's attention was upon the creature that had, somehow, entered Tholana's stronghold and begun to wreak havoc in its wake. TC was the only one in the group who knew the type of creature it was, for he had been Bound to one for centuries. It was a dragon.

Once again, the dragon's cry echoed throughout the citadel. It was on the far western side of the stronghold, quite a distance from where they now stood. Yet, despite the space between them, the sound was loud enough to be distinctly heard by every member of the group, and it stopped them in their tracks. Even TC stopped to listen, but as soon as he realized it, he redirected everyone's attention once more, and bade them continue.

Tallachienan continued to follow the pull of the ring. It was a mental beacon that guided him through the corridors without error. The rest of the group faithfully followed him, and he felt heartened by their allegiance. Yet, at the same time he felt more than a small amount of fear. He knew what they potentially faced behind the walls of the citadel, knew that death could find many of them. TC had developed an attachment to these people, and he didn't want to see them harmed. Yet, they followed him knowing the danger they faced. It was their dedication first to Aeris that led them here, and that heartened TC even more.

Tallachienan slowed as they entered the heart of Tholana's citadel. Things had become quiet . . . too quiet. He understood that the priestesses and mages were diverted, but there were others who stood sentinel about the fortress, those who served as protective guardians over those who lived there. TC had seen none of these as they passed, and only now did he feel a vague disquiet.

Suddenly TC stopped. He abruptly put out an arm and slid his body up against the corridor wall. A strange, somewhat familiar, clicking noise could be heard emanating down the adjoining corridor just ahead. The rest of the group subsequently followed suit just as two giant spiders climbed into view. The sound of their combined sixteen legs upon the stone floor made the rapid clicking sound, magnified as the spiders scuttled past the group where they hid within the shadows.

No one made a sound as they passed, everyone transfixed by the sight. They were akin to those the group encountered within the cavern system, yet they had their differences. Their bodies were less streamlined, bulkier in appearance. The legs were longer, extending up past the main body before hitting the knee and coming back down. They were somewhat smaller than their counterparts, and their legs devoid of the sword-like bony ridges. However, they looked like they would be able to jump greater distances, and gods only knew what other attributes with which they might be endowed.

The group remained plastered against the wall for quite some time after the spiders passed. TC was relieved that their presence had not been detected, for arachnids tended to be proficient with such things. The group had been fortunate this time, and he could only hope that their luck would hold out.

But as Fate would have it, the group was close to their destination. They walked through only a few more corridors before they approached a staircase leading upwards. Stopping at the first stair, TC turned to his comrades. Somehow, he knew where the steps led, and he didn't want the entire group following him there. He needed many of them to stay behind, to serve as a blockade to anyone who might try to access the tower behind him. Most likely it was the most commonly used entry, and if the enemy were to infiltrate it, TC could be trapped, for he knew of none of the other paths that could be used to enter the tower.

Tallachienan paused for a moment before speaking. Until now, no one had uttered more than a word or two since entering the stronghold, and everyone had a countenance of utmost seriousness. "It is here that we must part ways. I need the rest of you to stay here to guard the stairwell while I go to find Aeris."

Immediately Alasdair was stepping forward, frowning and shaking his head. "No, we are going with you. Aeris is my sister and their cousin. It is only right that we accompany you."

Tallachienan didn't bother to dispute him. He knew it would be futile, for Alasdair was a forceful man and tended to have his way. Yet, TC remembered a time that Alasdair did not have his way, and his heart suddenly ached. If only Aeris had given in to her brother's demands that day back in Yortec. Perhaps none of this would have happened, and they would all have gone about their lives . . .

But then Magnus would never have known the pleasure of having her love him, and TC might not have subsequently discovered the truth of his identity.

TC nodded to Alasdair and then redirected his attention to Cervantes, Goldare, and the remainder of the group. "This is the stairwell into the easternmost tower. Aeris is somewhere up there. I need the rest of you to stay here to barricade any passage. If Tholana's priestesses come up behind us, we could be trapped. It would be easy for them to take us down."

Goldare and the halfen brothers nodded their assent, followed by Jonesy, Dramid, Cortes, and finally Cervantes. "We won't let anyone through," said Goldare.

TC nodded and then slowly turned to begin his ascent. It was doubtful that the staircase was indeed the only approach to the tower, but the other ways were most likely very inaccessible. In all likelihood they were well hidden, and most people would be unaware of their presence, even those who lived their daily lives within the citadel. Alasdair, Cedric, and Tigerius fell in behind him. Tallachienan was reticent to discover what remained in the tower. He could only imagine some of the atrocities that may have been visited upon Aeris, and he feared what he might find. Would she be scarred or maimed? Would she possibly have lost her mind . . . or perhaps even her soul? Now only time would tell, and the moments were ticking down.

***

The tower was huge. Standing outside of the citadel, one would never have been able to fathom the area taken by the circumference of a single tower, much less that taken by the fortress as a whole. There were several chambers that made up the eastern tower, and the one within which Aeris resided appeared to be the one at the very top.

Tallachienan turned towards his comrades. They had stealthily made their way through the tower, slowly making their way upward. Now he stopped before a chamber door. Beyond it was Aeris. Tallachienan knew they placed themselves at an even greater risk by going inside together. It was the highest point of the tower . . . there was nothing above them but the spire. The only way they could go was down . . . and if they were beset by any of the palace guardians or priestess, they could only pray that there were no others to stand behind.

"This is where they are keeping Aeris. Please, I need you to stand guard out here while I go in to get her," said TC in a quiet voice.

Alasdair nodded. He understood that it was something that Magnus needed to do. He was content to stand guard outside the chamber. Besides, only one of them need go within. He saw the potential for disaster should they ignore guarding the doorway, not to mention that he was afraid of what he might find beyond the door. During their journey through the cave system, Magnus had warned him of the things that might have happened during her captivity, and Alasdair had slept many a sleepless night contemplating those things. In spite of his desire to have his sister back, he was reticent to meet the individual she may have been forced to become.

In more ways than one, faelin were quite different from their human counterparts. Despite the similarities in physical appearance, there were inherent differences in their anatomy, physiology, and mentality. Faelin had a gestation period of close to eleven months as opposed to the nine and a half months of most humans. Faelin children did not age as quickly as human ones, not reaching full maturity until close to twenty-seven years. As such, mentality was often the most striking difference between the species, with most faelin tending towards the academic. Notwithstanding, there was a higher percentage of human children that were illiterate in comparison to faelin ones.

Then there were those who were in between. Children bred from both a faelin and a human parent had a difficult childhood. They neither fit here nor there, too immature for a human upbringing and the opposite for a faelin one. They tended towards the worst of both worlds, having little realization as to the significance of their being . . . for there were no human/halfen hybrids, nor faelin/halfen ones. And there were only some human/faelin children that made it through gestation.

Alasdair shook his head. It was quite possible that the experiences Aeris endured had changed her to the point where it would be difficult for her to fit into normal faelin society. Faelin lived much longer than their human counterparts, and given her youthful age, Aeris was quite impressionable. It was possible that she had been molded into something other than what she had been made to be, and that scared him. In many ways, Aeris was still but a child, and he regretted the decisions he and his parents had made to allow her to leave the sanctuary of Elvandahar at such a tender age.

Nodding to Cedric, Alasdair indicated that they should stand sentinel outside the door leading to the chamber within which Aeris resided. Alasdair watched as Tigerius manipulated his picks into the lock until it opened the door. Then, both Tigerius and Magnus slipped into the chamber. It was a sitting room, a place where a lady might accept her guests. In this case, it was empty. Without making a sound, TC indicated for Tiger to remain there while he went ahead into the main chamber. Tiger nodded and stood with his back to the door, listening for any trouble that might present itself on the other side.

Tallachienan went to the next door and slowly opened it to the adjoining room. Stepping within, he closed it softly behind him. The area was dark, the only light emanating from the fires burning within a couple of wall sconces. Glancing around, he saw a large bed covered with pillows on the far right. At the room's center was a window, and to the left there was a desk and a bureau of shelves upon which rested a variety of books.

Frowning to himself, TC found himself glancing around a second time. It was only then that he noticed movement. A figure sat upon the casement surrounding the window. She was small, so it had been difficult to see her upon initial inspection. But now she moved, bringing one leg up to join the other. If she had noticed the entry of a visitor, she showed no indication.

Slowly, Tallachienan approached the figure in the casement. She wore only enough silk and lace to cover her most private places, clothing that a street whore might wear in the bed-chamber with her latest customer. About her hips pooled a diaphanous swath of shimmering material. With it, she covered her legs. Around her upper arms were elaborately crafted bands that matched the one around her neck. Her hair was pinned decorously away from her beautiful face, the soft crimson curls left to fall down her back. Only when TC stood but a few feet away did he stop. Aeris did not turn towards him . . . and it was easy to see that it was she who sat there.

TC hesitated before speaking. "Damaeris . . ."

The young woman turned to the sound of her name. She regarded him without expression, her gaze coldly taking in his presence. She knew it was he the moment he stepped through the door, yet it meant nothing to her. She had known he would come . . . to Tallachienan it was nothing more than a matter of pride.

TC closed the distance between them, falling to his knees as he reached her. Grasping her hand within his, he bowed his head. "By all that is in me, I am so glad I have finally found you."

Aeris said nothing, and when he finally looked up, her gaze did not waver. She then saw the realization come over him . . . realization that she knew the truth of his identity. Somehow, he must have seen it reflected in her eyes, or perhaps it was simply the fact that she didn't seem to care that he had come for her. Already she was in one of the Hells. She really didn't need to walk into another.

Aeris heard the breath catch in his throat . . . saw the indecision that passed over his face. By the gods, he didn't know what to do . . . for once the great Tallachienan Chroaltone was at a loss as to what action he should take.

"Aeris, it isn't important what has happened to you here, and it isn't important what you think of me. All that matters is that I have come to take you away from this place . . . to take you home."

His gaze was almost beseeching, hoping that she would oblige him and allow him to docilely lead her from the chamber. And much to her chagrin, she found that she didn't even have the strength to care. What fight she had within her was long gone. It was what the cimmereans wanted . . . to break her down into nothing. Now here she was, dispassionately staring into the face of the one who could give her release from her anguish . . . take her away from Ranaghar . . .

But no . . . he would be with her still. She carried a part of him within her womb, a child that made her so sick that she could eat nothing and drink only slightly more. She knew that pregnancy often caused illness such as this, but that irrational part of herself thought that surely the child meant to kill her. It was an abomination, a culmination of the torment she had suffered at the hands of Tholana and then Ranaghar. It was a thing conceived of rape, and she didn't want it. She had hoped to dislodge it during one of her struggles with Ranagahr, but she hadn't been so fortunate, suffering only the other pains his fists and manhood brought to her.

Aeris began to shake her head, to tell him that he needn't bother to take her from the citadel. Her lot in life had been sealed several days ago when her hopes of losing the child had come to a grinding halt. She couldn't bear the thought of the explanations she would have to make . . . to tell everyone how she had been made the whore of a cimmerean mage, to endure him forcing himself upon her and then to carry his wretched offspring. She could only imagine the stares she would get, and then the glances of disdain from other hinterleans in the community once the child was born.

It simply wasn't worth it.

Suddenly there was an explosion. It rocked the very foundation of the tower. Aeris could feel the structure sway with the impact; saw the rocky image outside the window shift slightly with the movement. Tallachienan pulled her up from the casement and without thinking, she allowed him to lead her from the chamber. Once in the sitting room, Aeris saw that the door leading to the outside corridor was open, and there was activity going on outside it. The sounds of battle could be heard, and TC pulled her along behind him as he rushed towards it.

TC stopped at the doorway, putting out his arm to indicate that Aeris should stand back. He then carefully stepped out into the corridor. There he saw Alasdair, Cedric and Tigerius. Before them was a large skeletal serpent. He immediately knew what it was, for he had faced such things before within the centuries he had walked Shandahar. It was a morsvermis . . . death worm. With the skeletal body of a giant snake, the golem had the head of a fanged humanoid skull with constantly whirling milky-white eyes.

TC wasn't surprised to find a construct such as this in Tholana's lair. She had always been affiliated with things such as spiders, snakes, and other potentially dangerous creatures. However, the fact that his comrades had been able to detect its arrival was a feat all in itself, for morsvermis were masters at silent ambush. The men had also been able to overcome the macabre "dance of death". The maneuver was a riveting hypnotic swaying that tended to mesmerize all who viewed it. It was backed by minor magic, for it compelled the viewer to remain entranced by the movement of the golem.

Instead of being surprised by the visit of the morsvermis, Alasdair and Cedric had steeled themselves for an attack. Neither had anticipated the grim dance, yet one of them had thrown an 'explosive' vial, hoping to either deter the golem from it's victims, or to damage it. Most likely, the thrower hoped for both. However, when TC saw the ongoing fight, he saw a morsvermis that was only minimally damaged, snapping viciously at it's newest opponent. Tigerius must have heard the explosion caused by the vial, and immediately went to the aid of his comrades just outside the door.

It was Tigerius who motioned for TC to pass them by. The man shouted and waved his arm. "You two go. We will hold it back so that you can get a head start." He then returned his focus to the skeletal golem, his blade at the ready should it get through the defenses offered by Alasdair and Cedric.

Pulling Aeris from her prison, TC rushed through the short corridor to the main staircase leading from the highest part of the tower. He was relieved to have no resistance, for it would have made everything that much more difficult. Yet, she seemed to be nothing but a vague shadow of what she had once been, and he found himself deeply concerned for her welfare. He had hoped . . . expected that she would have at least been happy that she would be escaping the stronghold. Yet, he had seen no indication of that emotion from her at all.

Once reaching the lower level, they quickly made their way through another hallway. They then went down a staircase that opened up into a much longer corridor. They were within a wider portion of the tower, and despite his propensity for such things, TC found himself struggling to remember which way to take. He knew it was the stress of the moment wreaking havoc on his mind, but it still frustrated him. And it didn't help that he was beginning to realize the damage that had been done to Aeris' mentality during her tenure within Tholana's stronghold. Already it was killing him . . . they had laid their hands not only upon her body, but her mind as well. He could sense it in the very movements she made as she followed him through the corridor, by the color of the ring she wore upon her finger, and the way she refused to look him directly in the eyes. The cimmereans had broken her, and the realization cut him to the core of his being.

Anger suddenly flared within him. Tallachienan would make his nemesis pay for what she had done. Tholana had hoped to get to him while he was vulnerable . . . at a time when he couldn't even remember his own name. But now . . . now that he had his memory returned to him, he would kill her for the damage she had wrought.

***

Cervantes felt his blood turn to ice as he heard them coming closer. He and the rest of the group had ranged themselves within the stairwell, everyone's backs pressed into the stone walls. Glancing across the steps, Cervantes caught Dramid's eye. Fear was reflected there, and despite the cool ambient temperature, Cervantes could see the sweat trickling down his face and onto his neck. Just above him stood Cortes, his crossbow at the ready. As a matter of fact, all three of them had their bows trained upon the area at the bottom of the stairwell, ready to pick off whoever noticed them first.

Below himself and Dramid stood Jonesy and Vardec, respectively. And then below those two were Vikhail and Goldare. The plan was for the archers to use their element of surprise and hit as many of the enemy as they could before the cimmereans began to cast their spells. Then it would be up to the warriors to rush the enemy at the bottom of the stairwell. Cervantes, Dramid, and Cortes would continue to keep the upper ground, and when it was necessary, ditch their bows for the cutlasses they wore at their belts. It was the best strategy Cervantes could come up with, and now they would attempt to execute it.

Two priestesses finally came into view. They walked past the stairwell without noticing the group within it. Everyone remained quiet; hoping beyond hope that all the others would also pass without knowing the group was there. Several more priestesses then came into view, followed by two men. The women continued to, unsuspectingly, pass them by. It was only when the mages walked by that things began to happen.

One man placed his hand upon the arm of his comrade. They spoke in cimmerean, so no one knew what was being said. Yet, Cervantes could only imagine that the man sensed something out of the ordinary. It was then that the second man happened to glance into the stairwell. The expression that crossed his face would have been funny if the circumstances were different. His eyes widened with disbelief, and it was then that a crossbow bolt was suddenly protruding from his chest.

The first mage spun around just as Cortes was releasing his second bolt. Projectiles from Cervantes and Dramid followed, and the mages fell to the floor each with two bolts in the chest. Only a moment later, the priestesses were back at the stairwell. Immediately they began to call upon their goddess-given abilities, and that was when Vikhail and Goldare were rushing them. Still suffering from the element of surprise, the closest priestesses fell to the assault. One was decapitated by Goldare's broadsword while the other was sliced across the midriff by Vikhail's axe. Her mouth gaped open as she tried to hold her guts within her belly. When she fell to her knees, they spilled out onto the floor to join the head of the other priestess. The only sound that came from her was a gurgling moan.

Cortes, Cervantes, and Dramid shot at the remaining priestesses. Cervantes started to see his bolts falling away from the enemy before they could find their target. Dramid was able to hit one priestess, but at the same time the woman had grabbed hold of Goldare. Within moments the man began to scream, and his armor started to glow red from the heat being suffused into it. Vardec rushed to his aid, hitting the woman in the side and sending her against the wall. Goldare then struggled to remove armor that was rapidly burning into his flesh.

Cervantes could smell the scent of scorching flesh even from his position upon the stairs. Breaking formation, he started downward. His intent was to help Goldare with the burning armor, but it was then that the captain noticed that Jonesy had entered the fray. Before her, the girl wielded the cutlass. She sliced ineffectually at the nearest priestess, and the woman grinned and retaliated by casting forth a sprig of flame from her hand. It struck Jonesy in the chest, sending the girl backwards until she reached the first step. Her head struck the stone, rendering her unconscious. Cervantes found himself rushing the rest of the way down. *Damn.* What did she have to go and get herself hurt for?

Kneeling beside her, Cervantes felt at Jonesy's neck to be sure that the pulse of life was still there. He was relieved to find it was, but as he stood, Cervantes found himself confronted by another of the priestesses. Just like the others, she wore a black leather camisole that extended between the legs and buttoned up the back. Her complexion was deathly pale, and her hair colored the darkest black. Her lavender eyes were outlined with khol, and her lips colored crimson. She smiled as she laid her hand upon him, her fingertips only barely touching his face. Meanwhile, he felt along his belt until his cutlass was at his palm. In one fluid motion he unsheathed the weapon and was swinging it up and around towards her.

The priestess quickly sidestepped only to find herself being impaled by another cutlass. She wrapped her hands around the blade where it protruded from her belly, and when Dramid pulled it out she doubled over herself with her hands over the massive wound. She fell onto her side next to Jonesy and a bright pool of blood immediately began to spread outward from her.

It was then that Cervantes began to feel rather strangely. He swayed on his feet and put his hand against the wall to catch himself. He suddenly felt nauseous and a moment later he was dropping his cutlass and turning to vomit behind the stairs. Finally able to collect himself, Cervantes straightened and wiped the sleeve of his shirt across his mouth. Turning back to the melee, he felt his eyes widen with surprise. Giant spiders had begun to enter the scene. Before him was Dramid, valiantly keeping one of the monsters at bay. Jonesy continued to lie at the base of the staircase next to the fallen priestess. Her tunic and trousers were soaked with the other woman's blood. Cervantes took Jonesy under the arms and pulled her behind the staircase . . . past the puddle of vomit and away from the battle scene.

Moments later Cervantes reemerged from the hidden corner. He hated to leave Jonesy there alone, unconscious and vulnerable. Yet, he knew he would hate it even more if he left his comrades to fight the enemy without him. Cervantes continued to feel sickly, but there was nothing he could do about it. He swept a hand over his face to take away some of the sweat he felt beaded there, but before wiping it on his trousers, he happened to look down at it. Strangely, the palm was covered with a haphazard smattering of red spots that seemed to be the beginning of blisters. Shaking his head, Cervantes refocused his attention to the scene. With his fauchard, Cortes had joined Dramid before the giant spider, and the two men were holding their own. Beyond them were two other spiders. Having done away with his armor, Goldare fought against one of the menaces. Cervantes could see the places upon his body where the flesh had been severely burned. Fortunately, there weren't many areas that the armor touched that were not lined with the fabric of his tunic. The cloth had helped protect him from the scorching heat of the metal.

Beyond Goldare, Vikhail and Vardec were fighting the third spider. Off to the side, Cervantes saw three remaining priestesses. They stared vaguely into the space before them, and it seemed almost as though their minds were not there at the scene. It was then that Cervantes made his realization. The priestesses were using their abilities to summon the spiders to the area.

Cervantes immediately sprinted in the direction of the priestesses. The group could ill afford to have another of the monstrosities appear at the scene. He dodged past the individual battles going on between his comrades and the spiders, pausing only as he neared Goldare. It was easy to see that the man would spoon falter, for he was alone in his battle, not to mention seriously wounded by the gruesome burns he had sustained. Cervantes resisted the temptation, knowing that if he did not stop the priestesses, only more spiders would come in the places of these. It would never end until they all lay dead upon the cold stone floor of Tholana's citadel.

Cervantes passed Goldare, and then the halfen brothers. He bore down upon the priestesses, and they only realized his presence until it was too late. With one swing of his cutlass, Cervantes sliced into the nearest one. She screamed in agony, holding the bloody stump of her arm against her side as she crumpled to the floor. The other two sprang into motion, each drawing wickedly curved daggers. Cervantes parried their blows with his cutlass. Yet, when he realized their proficiency, he drew his own dagger to use against them along with his blade.

It wasn't long before Cervantes found himself beginning to tire. He felt seriously ill, and the sweat caused by his exertion coupled with sickness fell into his eyes. He felt himself falter, and the images of the two priestesses swam within his view. *Damn, what is wrong with me?* Once more he faltered, but this time it didn't matter so much. His good friend Dramid was there to counter the attack of the priestesses. For a moment Cervantes stopped to catch his breath. By the gods, as always, Dramid was there to get his back should anything happen.

But then things seemed to spiral out of control. Behind him, Cervantes heard an agonized cry. He spun around to see Goldare lying lifelessly on the floor. The cry had come from Vardec, who was crouched upon the floor next to his friend. Meanwhile, Vikhail cut once more into the spider before them. It finally succumbed, its legs crumpling beneath it as it fell.

Then there was another scream. Cervantes felt his heart stop in his chest, for he would have been able to identify it anywhere. It was Dramid. Cervantes swung back around, saw his friend fall before the last of the priestesses. She straddled his body, plunging her dagger into his chest once, twice, and then three times before Cervantes could tear her away. And then he was savagely pressing his own jagged blade to her vulnerable throat. He sliced swiftly and deeply, felt the sticky warmth of her blood flowing over his hand. He threw her body to the ground, saw it convulse there for a moment as she died. He then went to his friend, knew before he reached Dramid that the man was dead. Cervantes resisted the emotion that threatened to spew forth, fought back the tears that sought access to the outside.

***

The corridor opened up into a chamber. Tallachienan remembered passing through it on their way to Aeris' 'prison', and he knew that they were close to the stairway that would take them back down. The area was quite extensive, with elaborate sconces in the walls and large, glowing floor braziers guarded by gargoyles. On the other side was a set of bronzed doors. TC frowned as he swept into the room. Those doors had been open when he and his comrades initially passed through the area.

Gripping Aeris' hand tighter within his, TC quickly made his way across the chamber. He was careful not to disturb anything, for he did not wish to awaken any unwanted denizens. When a figure stepped out of the shadows, Tallachienan slowed his pace. It was asinine for him to have hoped he would be able to escape the stronghold without encountering the goddess who resided there.

Tholana stopped in the middle of the chamber and crossed her arms at her chest. She wore only enough to cover her breasts and crotch. The rest was only diaphanous material that hung about her waist down to the crook of her knees, a dress similar to the one Aeris wore. Bejeweled bracelets worked their way up her arms and upon her feet were boots made of the most supple of skins, crisscrossed by artful bead-work. Tallachienan slowed his own pace to a halt and pushed Aeris behind him. He could hear the tinkling laughter of the goddess, and it was almost as though the sound of it echoed throughout the chamber.

"So, my dear Tallachienan . . . I see you have finally come for her." Tholana began to walk a sultry dance, her hips swaying to the cadence of a music only she could hear. "I was beginning to wonder why it was taking you so long."

TC said nothing. He watched as she continued to glide towards them. It seemed that her feet barely touched the floor as she moved. She carried herself in the provocative manner he always remembered. Even back in his early years . . . before the cycling of the world, before he became hardened by the power he possessed, before the lives he had taken and the loves he had lost . . . Tholana had been much the temptress.

Keeping Aeris behind him, he kept her hand gripped tightly within his own. He hoped to convey that he was there for her, that he would be her champion and take her away from this place. It was dark within Tholana's fortress, much darker that his own citadel. No matter what Trebexal said, there were much darker places than the place TC called 'home'.

Tholana stopped when she reached Tallachienan and gently placed her hand upon his chest. He didn't move as she swept it up to the curve of his neck and into his hair. She then pressed the length of herself against him. She ran her other hand along his back, down to the curve of his buttocks, around his hips, and then to his groin. She cupped his manhood as she brought her mouth to his. The kiss was deeply passionate, flavored by subtle hints of azimuthal and grenadyne. It was much as he remembered it to be, albeit now unhindered by youth and inexperience.

Despite the temptation, TC made no response. His body reacted to her nearness . . . it was an unintentional response to something so primitively sexual. No man could wholly restrain himself in the proximity of such raw sexuality, and for a mere mortal man there would be no escape. Only Tallachienan's heritage and power kept him from submitting to the woman right then and there.

Several moments later, Tholana withdrew. Her winged ebony brows were pulled into a frown, and her crimson lips a pout. "Tallachienan, you are resisting me." She then began to walk around him. From her place at TC's back, Aeris remembered the goddess' restlessness. The woman could scarcely stand to remain in one position for too long.

TC turned in place, sure to keep his body between herself and Tholana. Aeris kept her peripheral gaze trained upon the goddess, sure that should Tholana touch her that the woman would easily be able to divine her pregnancy. It wasn't something she needed anyone to know, not to mention that Ranaghar himself remained ignorant of her condition.

Tholana's frown deepened. "I thought you would have arrived here sooner, especially considering the fact that you had your silly ring to guide you." She suddenly stopped moving. Aeris saw the hostility in Tholana's gaze and knew that Tallachienan must have seen it as well. "She has been quite the delight . . . so many have told me so. It's a shame that you arrived here much too late."

At that moment, something seemed to happen. It was like a flood-gate had been opened. Tallachienan thrust Aeris from him, and she found herself hitting the nearest wall. The chamber was suddenly filled with a deluge of sound and motion. The two gods leaped at one another, each one preparing to cast their worst.

Aeris felt the crackling of energy, raw power that she had never experienced before. She wondered if she would survive, especially considering her close proximity. It was a dance of fire and ice, a maelstrom of wind, a rumbling of the very foundation of the citadel itself . . . and, of course no small amount of determination. She could feel it when they lost scope . . . nothing mattered anymore but the power and the will to persevere. All she could do was huddle against the wall with nothing but her whore's garb to shield her. Aeris closed her eyes to barely a slit so that all she could really perceive was the sound. Yet, she had hardly the strength to do even that, the child growing within her taking all it could.

Aeris felt the coolness of the stone against her back, the uneven texture of the floor beneath her bare feet, and the heat emanating from the fire burning within the nearest floor brazier. Her consciousness wavered. She heard shouts and curses, the sound of unsuppressed magical energy, and flesh hitting stone. She felt the concussive force of power striking the chamber walls, the subsequent breaking of stone, and a sudden deep rumbling.

Aeris shook her head, seeking to bring herself to some level of mental alertness and to dispel her sudden disquiet. The rumbling stopped, and she opened her eyes to see that neither opponent seemed to have gained the upper hand over the other. She didn't really know how much time had passed, only that it had, indeed, gone by. The fires were lower in the floor braziers, and the chamber seemed to have taken on a darker aspect. Some of the citadel's inhabitants waited upon the sidelines of the battle . . . large scavenger spiders that would make a meal out of anything they could. They knew no fear, and one or two were testimony to that fact, their scorched carcasses already cocooned within the webs of their voracious neighbors.

Tallachienan cast yet another spell. It struck Tholana, only to ricochet away from a body that seemed to be hard as the stone upon which Aeris leaned. The flaming spheres instead careened into the adjacent wall. Once more she felt the rumbling . . . a disturbance that radiated from the tower above them. The goddess let loose her own volley, and TC easily diverted it, allowing it to hit the far wall near the ceiling. The rumbling intensified, and Aeris felt the beating of her heart accelerate. Something was about to happen, and she wasn't sure that she wanted to be there when it did.

Notwithstanding, the battle continued. Neither participant seemed to realize the catastrophe soon to be unleashed. Something had compromised the structural integrity of the eastern tower, and it was swiftly becoming apparent that the consequences of that breach were soon to be realized. Aeris pushed herself away from the wall and began to slowly make her way to the bronzed doors at the other end of the chamber. Despite her negligible circumstances, she would at least try to escape the deathtrap she was certain this place was soon to be. She wasn't quite sure how she would get past the scavenger spiders, but she would cross that hurdle when she reached it.

All of a sudden there was an explosive blast behind her. The force of it knocked her to the floor. Beneath her palms, she could feel the rumbling become ever greater, and Aeris knew that this time there was no escaping it. She scrambled to her feet just as the chamber began to shake. Thick cracks suddenly ran along the walls, floor, and ceiling. From the places where they had fallen, both TC and Tholana began to register expressions of alarm. The floor beneath Aeris suddenly pitched, and she was once more thrown to her knees as a deep crevice formed alongside her. The rumbling had intensified, and it was suddenly all that could be heard. Damn, maybe Tallachienan was wrong. Perhaps she wouldn't escape this place after all.

***

Once more, Talemar heard the scream of a dragon. Glancing around the chamber, he saw that the other men had also paused in their activities. Not more than several moments before, Heldrithia had left in the company of many others in order to ascertain what was happening. By the gods . . . an actual dragon in the citadel. Why in the Hells was it there?

Talemar set aside the broom he was using and, despite the pain, rushed to the entrance. He looked out into the corridor and saw no one. Turning back, he saw the other men watching him, most of them from dull eyes. For so long they had been beaten down by Tholana's priestesses and mages that nothing mattered to them anymore . . . not even the prospect of escape. Many of them had been born into this life of servitude. Yet, there some who still remembered what it was like to have freedom, no matter how little it was. It was these who regarded him with a barely perceptible spark in their eyes.

Since his arrival at the citadel, Talemar had been forced into bondage. His functions were many and varied: during the day he slaved away cleaning the priestesses chambers, and at night he was a plaything to suit the sexual desires of whomever requested his services. Upon one occasion it had been the goddess herself. The experience had been something he knew he would never know again . . . nor was he certain he wanted to.

Regardless, Talemar was nothing more than a slave. He and all the other men were kept under nearly constant surveillance by a team of novice priestesses. It was immediately apparent that they hated their lot in life, for who wanted to stand guard over a bunch of lowlifes such as these? Yet, the priestesses rotated so often, no single one accompanied them more than three or four hours in a given day. In his opinion, their job was more than simple. Not to mention, the constant change in personnel made it even easier for him to get away to see Aeris.

Again Talemar heard the voice of the dragon. It was closer than it was the last time, and it was accompanied by a deep rumbling. Once more he glanced out into the corridor. He saw nothing. Talemar shook his head. He would be damned if he stayed there any longer. Not only could he feel the imminent danger, he knew that it was the best opportunity he would get to escape from the citadel without anyone realizing it for quite some time. By then, it just might be too late.

Talemar didn't bother to look back as he slipped out into the hallway. Without thought, he traveled east towards Aeris' tower. Despite her arguments when last they met, Talemar had every intention of bringing her out of Tholana's stronghold. He didn't care what had happened to her or whose child she carried. All that mattered was that she was free of this place.

Talemar couldn't quite understand why he was still alive after his encounter with the mage he came to know as Ranaghar Sebastoris. That day, after being forced to watch Ranaghar rape Aeris, Talemar was severely beaten and then taken to what the slaves called "the pits". Within the bowels beneath the citadel, he somehow survived his injuries and the lack of any edible food or potable water for at least two days. Then, when he was brought back to the damp chamber he shared with the other slaves, Talemar was given only minimal treatment for his wounds and the customary paltry food rations alloted them upon any given day. He was starving for more sustenance, and it was soon apparent that his wounds were probably septic. As the time passed, they only became more painful. Within another day or two, it was unlikely that he would even want the little food offered to him.

Fueled by determination, Talemar moved swiftly through the passageways. It wasn't long before he began to smell something strange in the air. The rumbling dissonance intensified, and he recognized it as the sound of the dragon as it moved through the corridors. The strange smell became more perceptible and he was dismayed to realize it as the stench of scorched flesh.

Notwithstanding, Talemar continued in the direction he knew would take him to Aeris' tower. For all he knew, there may have been a better way, one that did not involve close proximity to an enraged dragon. However, he didn't have the time to try to figure it out. He began to hear the noises associated with a struggle and startled when he heard the dragon's voice yet again. It was close . . . so close that he knew he would be able to catch a glimpse of the creature if he made only a couple more turns. Slowing his pace, Talemar did just that, and when he turned the final corner, the sight that met his eyes was phenomenal.

It was quite easily the largest dragon Talemar had ever seen. Even within the dim light cast by the few remaining wall sconces, his scales glistened a deep silver. At the top of an elegantly shaped head, there was a bony growth that continued down the expanse of his back. Talemar could only imagine the tail, for the entire dragon could not be seen within the stretch of corridor within which he stood. The massive wings were folded close to the body, for it was impossible for them to unfurl within the close confines of the fortress walls.

Glancing away from the dragon, Talemar watched as Tholana's priestesses and mages sought to keep the creature at bay. So far, it seemed that they had made little progress. Many of them lay upon the floor at the silver dragon's feet. The dragon himself had suffered only minimally from the encounter thus far, sporting only a few lacerations and burns. Talemar felt heartened by this knowledge as he stepped away from the scene. Yet, he couldn't help but wonder why the creature was there in the first place.

Talemar made his way through the corridors behind the one in which the dragon fought. As he passed, he encountered the blackened remains of those who had offered resistance. Due to the numbers he saw there, as well as his memory of the priests and mages still fighting with little headway, he thought that either the dragon was a particularly powerful one, or simply a one who was driven by passion or desperation. Either way, Talemar supposed it didn't really matter. For him, the result was still the same . . . escape without the threat of immediate pursuit.

As quickly as possible, Talemar made his way through the corridors that would take him to Aeris. He didn't really quite recall how he initially discovered her whereabouts, only that he heard her mentioned during the times he conducted his daily activities. He had remained attentive to his exact whereabouts within the citadel upon any given occasion, and receptive to any talk that pertained to either himself or Aeris. Much to his dismay, there was quite a bit of talk about the beautiful hinterlean female that Tholana held prisoner within her personal suite.

Talemar made it his mission in life to discover Aeris' whereabouts and then devise a plan to get them free of Tholana. With knowledge imparted to him by his father, he slowly and painstakingly created a mental map of the citadel. Once he was able to finally determine the general whereabouts of the tower within which Aeris was being kept, he found a way to get there. The excursion almost cost him his life, and Aeris had also paid a hefty price.

Talemar continued through the dark corridors. Some of them were lit with a few sconces set within the walls, others were not. A few times he found himself retiring to the shadows when groups of priestesses and mages walked through on their way to deal with the disturbance in the west wing. He remained quietly still until they passed, and then continued on his way.

Talemar didn't know how long he traversed the corridors. Tholana's citadel was vast, and it took a while to get anywhere. Yet, Talemar knew when he was getting close to the eastern tower for he he had passed the stairwells he knew would take him to the others. Those towers were nothing like the eastern one, for it was the tallest and home to most of the mages that inhabited the stronghold. He felt his jaws tighten at the thought of Ranaghar. Damn that man. Talemar hated him, not only for what he had physically done to Aeris, but mentally as well. Talemar knew that others had played a significant part in her decline, but it was easy to blame the one whose face he could envision in the deep hours of the night. The fact that Aeris was pregnant with the man's child was quite disconcerting, but it was not the debilitating thing it could have been. To him, the baby would be more of a thing created by Aeris, for it was she who would carry the child within her body, nurture it, and despite her thoughts to the contrary . . . love it.

Talemar found himself slowing as he approached his destination. He had left the dragon behind, the powerful voice now a thing of the past. Yet, in the passage ahead, he could hear the unmistakable sounds associated with physical combat. His brows pulled together into a frown as he continued. What in the Hells would be going on that there would be a conflict such as this going on between Tholana's priestesses?

Talemar slowly entered the chamber containing the stairway that would take him to the eastern tower. Before him was a scene depicting the end of a battle between Tholana's priestesses and mages against those individuals whom he had heard Aeris call her friends. The carcasses of three giant spiders graced the floor, along with those who had perished in the conflict. Disconcertingly, not many were left standing to tell the tale.

EPILOGUE

21 Macaren CY634

Tallachienan swiftly made his way back through the tunnels from which they had come. He couldn't just *think* that they weren't being followed by Tholana's followers. He had to *know* . . . Several corridors behind him, the rest of the group struggled to make their way through the catacombs. With them they carried their injured and their dead.

Not long ago, he and Aeris had escaped the eastern tower of Tholana's citadel. As the tower crumbled around them, they made their way through the hallways and stairwells that would lead them to the body of the fortress. Once there, they were met by Cervantes, Cortes, Jonesy, Vikhail, and Vardec . . . the sole survivors of a battle against priestesses and mages dedicated to Tholana. Also there was Talemar, and not much later, Alasdair, Cedric, and Tigerius.

The bodies of Dramid and Goldare were taken from the scene as the group quickly began to make their way out of the citadel. Meanwhile, the voice of the dragon who had precipitously infiltrated the fortress at just the right time continued to get closer. TC had sensed the strain in that voice . . . the pain of his wounds and the weariness of his soul. TC could only wonder why the dragon stayed . . . what his mission may have been in order for him to suffer so heartily.

Tallachienan stopped. Within the catacombs before him he heard nothing. Just as he had thought, Tholana and her minions were not following them. The goddess was too busy nursing her wounds back at her citadel to bother with him and his feeble companions. With a lightened countenance, TC headed back towards the group. They had agreed to rest only for a short time before they started off again. They couldn't take the risk of being caught by staying in one place for too long. Although, if she had wished it, TC knew that Tholana could have had them recaptured long ago.

Talachienan turned and quickly began his journey back to the group. Now he could have them rest. Talemar was becoming increasingly ill from wounds he had sustained whilst a captive within the citadel. Soon after meeting up with the rest of the group, the man had collapsed, and had yet to regain consciousness. Without some type of expert treatment, TC was dubious as to the odds of his survival. Cervantes was also quite sickly . . . the result of some disease that had been given him during their skirmish with Tholana's priestesses. Fortunately, the boils were temporary, and he would be nauseated for only but another day or two. TC would have expected more casualties among Alasdair, Cedric, and Tigerius, but surprisingly, everyone seemed well enough. Most likely, the collapse of the tower had acted in their benefit much as it had for he and Aeris.

It took some time to reach the group. They had already roused and begun to move away from an enemy they thought might not be far behind. Once reaching them, TC was pleased to give everyone the news that all was well, and that no one followed them through the cavern system. For now, Tholana had chosen to let them go. The relief in the air was palpable, and TC felt heartened that he could give them some measure of respite.

Glancing over at Aeris, Tallachienan hoped to see some emotion that might give him an inside as to what she might be feeling. As of yet, he had seen nothing. For the most part, she remained quiet and aloof, saying not much more than a handful of words since their escape. Regardless, he expected that she would soon begin to recover from whatever she might have experienced within the citadel. Of course, without her telling him, he could only imagine her trials. Until then he could only wait.

Tallachienan watched as the group settled down all around him. He could feel the fatigue emanating from each and every one of these persons he had begun to call his friends. In all his many years he had found few of those. Despite his awareness of his true identity, perhaps he could begin to have something he had never been able to sustain before . . .

***

Levander stared intently into the flames. They danced tantalizingly close, but he wasn't worried. The fire was well kept within the shallow pit he made before its creation. The mystery associated with fire had long ago been solved for him, courtesy of his training by the Kronshue. Just beyond it lay his two young companions, wrapped snugly within their cloaks. Just as the innocent were wont to do, they slept heavily. Jezibel and Mateo hadn't enough years of hardship and adversity upon them to do otherwise. He almost envied them for that, only vaguely remembering days when he had been free of the knowledge that weighed upon his soul.

Several fortnights ago, when Magnus led the group out of Gulshaan, Levander had begun taking active part in the augmented rate at which his body healed itself. Instructing Jezibel upon it's use, he started to reap the regenerative benefits bestowed by a device formulated by the Kronshue. It was one of the more benign technological advances the Brotherhood had made, although he couldn't really be sure who or what may have suffered during the development of it.

The device was known as an "injector", for that was it's exact purpose . . . although it could do the opposite as well. Attached to the contrivance was a hollow needle that would be used to puncture the skin and the muscular tissue beneath it. Through it, medicinal potions could be pushed into the body . . . potions that, if merely swallowed, would take much longer to have a restorative effect.

Despite his infirmity, Lev had known when the Daemundai entered the city of Gulshaan. Within the sanctuary of his sickbed, Lev remained cognizant of everything going on around him and the area outside the inn. There was a hush that swept over the populace, news of their arrival spreading like wildfire. Lev wasn't surprised when he heard the whispers of those that came to care for him regularly. Shops were closed early for the day, children were called in off the streets, and many of the taverns became devoid of their customary patronage.

By the time the daemon cult arrived, Lev had been using the injector for almost three days. Jezibel was smart, so it had been easy to instruct her upon the injector's proper usage. The first time had been a bit more difficult, for he had been so weak with fever, he could scarcely stay awake long enough to tell her how to manipulate it enough so as to administer the potion. Yet, she succeeded, and as early as the next morning his fever had begun to break. By eventide, the fever was almost gone, and by the middle of the following day he was getting out of bed and walking to the window.

For several days now, Lev and his young companions had been following in the footsteps of the Daemundai. He had no qualms about leaving Gulshaan behind, for his brother had no use for him. Severus would do what he chose, despite any protestations given by Lev. The young man was so full of anger and resentment, all he cared to do was lash out and leave his mark upon anything within his realm of influence. Lev had hoped to speak reason into Severus, but it had been to no avail.

Lev knew why the Daemundai entered Gulshaan, and as such, they were the perfect means to determine where the group had gone in search of their captive comrades. He couldn't help but berate himself for his paltry performance on the evening of Aeris' abduction, and he could only absolve himself of it by the fact that it was the goddess Tholana he faced, and not just any common spell-caster. Now as they approached her lair, Lev found himself wondering about this repeat operation and if the end result would be the same as the last. The only difference was that he now had two others that depended upon him. They had no others upon which to fall back if something went wrong.

The next morning, Lev and his comrades once more continued their dalliance behind the Daemundai. Lev could only shake his head at the lot of them, for none had even remotely begun to realize they were being followed. Either that, or they simply didn't care. By mid-day they had reached the entrance to a cave. He was not the best spy, but Lev was at least able to discover that it was an expansive cavern system that lay the path to Tholana's stronghold.

An executive decision was made, and the Daemundai set camp outside the cavern. Lev imagined the plan they had in mind. When the group finally emerged from the system, they would be met with the unfortunate surprise of their presence. A fight would ensue, and of course Lev would be 'obligated' to participate. The bald man smiled to himself. It would be interesting to see what might happen then.

GLOSSARY OF TERMS

Alcrostat (al-kro-stat) – the largest city within the realm of Elvandahar - residence of the Sherkari Fortress, home to the King

Alothere (al-o-thayr) – large porcines that are cousins to the wild boar – they live in the forests and steppes of the temperate regions of Shandahar

Andahye (an-duh-high) – mystical city located at the northern edge of the Sheldomar Forest – it is the place where many mages receive their arcane training

Ansalar (an-sal-ar) – one of the three continents of Shandahar – it is the most inhabited

Azmatharcana (az-math-ar-kana) – a mystical tome that delivers many necromantic secrets, including those contained within the Azmathion

Azmathion (az-math-ee-on) – the arcane artifact that gives Aasarak much of his power – it is a geometrical work of art, and one must work the puzzles contained within it in order to divine its secrets

Azmathous (az-math-us) – the most powerful of Aasarak's undead creations – with the power of the Azmathion, they are reborn and are able to retain the skills and abilities they possessed in life

Baalor (bay-loor) – the largest of the greater daemons, their skin is deep red, and massive black horns come out of the sides of their heads – they are one of the most powerful in the Nine Hells

Behiraz (be-heer-az) – a worm of gargantuan proportions, it lives beneath the ground finding it's prey by the vibrations they make upon the surface – swift and deadly, very few survive an encounter

Buffelshmut (buffel-shmut) – a slang term for buttocks

Burbana (bur-ban-uh) – a small ermine-like animal with exquisitely soft fur

Calotebas (kal-o-tee-bas) – a foul-tempered creature that lives near swamps – the taste of their flesh is equally as repugnant as their personality

Cenloryan (sen-lor-yan) – a creature made of the twisted magic of the Kronshue, it has the lower body of a lloryk and the upper torso, arms, and head of a faelin

Chag (chag) – a drink made from the large seeds of the chagatha plant, which grows in the more southern regions of Ansalar

Chamdaroc (sham-dar-ok) – a shrub that grows within Elvandahar and other forested regions of northwestern Shandahar – it has small white flowers that are said to have intoxicating qualities

Cimmerean (sim-ur-ee-an) – one of the sub-races of faelin – also known as 'dark' faelin, they live in vast labyrinths below the surface of the world

Common (com-mun) – the universal language across most of the main continent of Shandahar

Cortubro (cor-too-bro) – a realm situated north of Elvandahar

Corubis (kor-oo-bis) – large canines that have tawny fur with dark dappling – they live in packs headed by an alpha male, but many of them find companionship with faelin, especially hinterlean rangers

Daemundai (day-mun-die) – an organization of those who strive to give daemon-kind influence and power in Shandahar

Daladin (dal-a-din) – a hinterlean house

Degethozak (deg-eth-o-zak) – the smallest and most numerous of the dragon sub-races – at maturity their color ranges from black to varying shades of green with darker backs and feet – their alignment tends towards evil and chaos

Denedrian (den-ed-ree-an) – one of the human sub-races – they are largely nomadic, originating from the western plains and deserts

Dimensionalist (dim-en-shen-al-ist) – a sorcerer who specializes in other-worldly knowledge and travel

Doppleganger (dop-pel-gang-er) – a bipedal being made of magic, it has the ability to shift its shape into any humanoid between four and eight feet tall – it is a master of trickery and disguise that works for the most powerful of sorcerers

Elvandahar (el-van-da-har) – large forested region in the vee of the Terrestra and Denegal Rivers – it is ruled by Hinterlean faelin, and bears the largest population of these people

Ezekul (ez-e-kul) – star-shaped projectile weapon devised by the Kronshue

Farlo (far-low) – the equivalent of several feet

Filopar (fil-o-par) – one of the five domains of Elvandahar

Fistantillus bush (fist-an-til-lus) – a bush that has poisonous thorns that can make a person violently ill for several days

Garbatezu (gar-bat-eh-zoo) – a greater daemon that appears to be a large oroc with the hind legs of a lloryk – they tend to be the most treacherous and intelligent, rallying other daemons to their cause

Golem (goh-lem) – a magically created automaton - usually used as a guardian or sentinel for something of great value

Grang (grang) – slightly shorter than halfen, these small, bony humanoids live primarily on the steppes - they are primitive and voracious, but not very smart, their greed often getting in the way of thieving strategies

Gremlin (grem-lin) – an intermediate daemon that has the ability to scale walls and manipulate metals with supernatural ease – they are often the stolid followers of the baalor and the Garbatezu

Griffon (grif-fon) – large animals that have both feline and avian features – they are friendly and intelligent, and can often be found in the company of druids

Haldorr (hal-door) – one of the worlds of the Seven Heavens – it is the place where dragons reside

Hamzin/Hamza (ham-zin/ham-zuh) – the title given by the King to the one who rules within one of the five domains in Elvandahar

Helzethryn (hel-zeth-rin) – one of the dragon sub-races – at maturity their color ranges from pale gold, to deep bronze, to fiery red – they have the highest propensity towards Bonding with other species

Hestim (hes-tim) – one of the three moons of Shandahar

Himrony (him-ron-ee) – a type of grass that grows abundantly throughout the central Ansalar – the preferred vegetation of larian

Hinterlean (hin-ter-lee-an) – one of the faelin subraces – they live in treetop villages within temperate forests

Humanoid (hue-man-oyd) – any creature that walks upright on two legs (bipedal)

Hybanthis (hie-ban-this) – a vine that has poisonous blue thorns – poison has brain-based   affects that heighten a person's emotional state, making emotions difficult to handle

Imp (imp) – the least of the lesser daemons, these small creatures are the pests of the Nine Hells – they make themselves present whenever there is any type of activity

Karlisle (kar-lyle) – the realm neighboring Elvandahar on the other side of the Denegal River

Kleyshes (klie-shays) – one of the five domains of Elvandahar

Krathil-lon (kruh-thil-lon) – a forested glen located within the southern reaches of the Sartingel Mountains – it is where Father Dremathian and his druidical Order resides

Kronshue, Brotherhood of the (kron-shoo) – a 'technological' society that dominates eastern Ansalar

Kyrrean (kie-reen) – large blond felines with dark brown dappling and oversized paws – they make their existence on the warm temperate plains and borderlands

Larian (layr-ee-an) – with only minor differences, these are smaller cousins to the lloryk – they are able to carry faelin and most humans

Leschera (le-sher-uh) – very gentle, larian-sized, deer-like creatures that grace the temperate woodlands

Lloryk (loor-ik) – large muscular equine-like creatures that are able to carry humans and small orocs – they are omnivorous and beneath the top coat of silky fur, have modified hair shafts that appear similar to scales one would see on a reptile

Lycanthrope (lie-kan-thrope) – one afflicted with the disease of lycanthropy – they are humans, faelin, or hafen that can transform into animals (usually wemic, althothere, or kyrrean) – the disease is spread by the bite, and only those who have no tendencies towards evil can resist it

Lytham powder (lye-tham) – a component used in a spell that creates a noxious vapor

Mane (main) – a lesser daemon – they stand only about 2 ft. tall and have vulture-like features - tend to go wherever there is the opportunity to wreak any kind of havoc or chaos

Mehta (may-tuh) – the title given to the leader of the Daemundai

Meriliam (mer-il-lee-am) – one of the three moons of Shandahar

Merzillith (mir-zil-lith) – otherwise known as a mind flayer, this intermediate daemon is from one of the Nine Hells   it has psionic power, the ability to use the energy of the world in a way that is different than the magic that is used by mages

Migallon Mechanism (mi-gal-on) – a device created by a man bearing the name, it is used as a weapon against seascrag attacks

Mirpur (mir-poor) – one of the five domains of Elvandahar

Monaf (mon-af) – the realm neighboring Torimir on the other side of the Ratik Mountains

Morden (mor-den) – one of the halfen sub-races – they live in deep caverns within the mountains

Murg (murg) – an alcoholic beverage distilled from fermented cane sugar

Necromancer (nek-ro-man-ser) – a sorcerer who focuses upon the darker aspects of magic

Oorg (oorg) – one of the humanoid races of Shandahar, they are even larger than orocs and are often called giants – they often fight with brute strength alone, but are not good with any type of real strategy

Oroc (or-ok) – one of the native races of Shandahar – they are muscular and broad, standing at least six to seven feet tall – faelin are their greatest enemies, and the two races find any excuse to maim and kill one another

Pact of Bakharas (bak-hair-us) – an agreement between daemon and dragon kind that does not allow one or the other too much influence over Shandahar

Papas fruit (pay-pas) – a small pink orb about the size of a nectarine – it grows on the papas tree, which is prevalent throughout the temperate borderlands of Shandahar

Ptarmigan (tar-mig-an) – a squat, grouse-like bird that is often hunted for its flavorful meat

Rathis (rath-is) – the leaves of this plant are known for their pain-relieving capabilities

Recondian (re-con-dee-an) – one of the sub-races of humans – they live in the central region of the continent

Reshik-na (resh-ik-na) – an order of druids that lives within the Elvandaharian domain of Filopar

Rezwithrys (rez-with-ris) – the largest of the dragon sub-races – at maturity their color ranges from silver to steel blue to metallic violet – they have a propensity for magic

Samshin/Samshae (sam-shin/sam-shay) – the son/daughter of the hamzin or hamza

Sangrilak (sang-ri-lak) – city located within the northwestern quadrant of the realm of Torimir – it is the place of Adrianna and Sheridana's birth

Savanlean (sav-an-lee-an) – one of the sub-races of faelin – they live in majestic cities built into mountainsides located in the more northern regions of the continent

Seascrag (see-scrag) – aquatic creatures that stand about 2 ft. tall, with four arms, two legs, and a row of jagged spines that form a line down the back - they are considered a pestilence and inhabit the southern seas

Serenitee (sir-en-i-tee) – one of the worlds of the Seven Heavens

Shagendra (shuh-gen-dra) – the root from this plant can be used to make a person's mind vulnerable to suggestions – also causes general lethargy, dulls the senses, and slows reflexes

Shayamalan (shy-uh-ma-lon) – one of the three continents of Shandahar - it is home to the dragon population that has taken residence since the dissolution of the Pact of Bakharas

Shockwave (shok-wave) – a game that is popular throughout the continent - involves cards, bones, and no small amount of strategy and luck

Steralion (stir-a-lee-an) – one of the three moons of Shandahar

Suresh (sue-resh) – the subconscious pull a dragon feels for the one whom is meant to be his bond-mate

Tabanakh drink (ta-ban-ak) – a drink prepared by the druid elders as a right of initiation for their tyros – it has properties that exaggerate the visions of those who are so Gifted

Talsam (tal-sam) – the root from this plant is ground into a powder from which a pain-relieving tea is made

Tambour (tam-boor) – major port city located in southeastern Karlisle

Terralean (ter-a-lee-an) – one of the faelin sub-races – they inhabit many of the borderlands between the forests and steppes and are the most widespread

Thalden (thal-den) – one of the halfen sub-races – they live within the temperate hills

Thelandiron (thel-an-deer-on) – a region of Shayamalan where many rezwith-rys and helzethryn make their homes

Thritean (thrye-teen) – very large silver felines with black striping and six legs – they live in cold northern forests

Tobey (toe-bee) – a small, goat-like creature – many nomadic peoples breed them for the creamy textured milk they produce

Torimir (tor-eh-meer) – the realm neighboring Elvandahar on the other side of the Terrestra River

Tremidian (tre-mid-ee-an) – one of the human sub-races – they live on the eastern side of the continent

Trolag (trol-ag) – one of the humanoid races of Shandahar, they are tall and stooped, their long, gangly bodies covered with dark brown wiry hair – they have the ability to heal quickly

Umberhulk (um-ber-hulk) – large, stout beasts of burden with thick umber colored skin that is virtually devoid of hair – used to pull carts in the towns and villages and many times even in the caravan trains

Varanghelie Vault (vair-an-gay-lee) – a highly protected storage facility located within Andahye – it is where many people keep their most valuable possessions

Wemic (wee-mik) – in some places better known as wolves, these animals appear to be distant cousins to the corubis – they run in temperate to sub-arctic forests and have never been tamed

Wraith (rayth) – a corpse that has been re-animated – they are mindless, following the commands of their necromantic masters – their bodies are ravaged by the effects of decay and they wield only the simplest of weapons

Wyvern (why-vern) – a large snake-like creature with four stubby legs and a poisonous barbed tip on its long sinuous tail – it lives in shallow caverns in temperate climes

Xordrel (zor-drel) – major port city located in the southeast quadrant of the realm of Torimir

Zacrol (zak-rol) – the equivalent of about a mile

Zivet (ziv-et) – the bolt from a specialized crossbow devised by the Kron-shue